# Spellbound After Midnight

## Jenna Collett

# Contents

# Chapter 1

*The Kingdom of Ever*
*Daniels Curses and Cures*

**M**agic had really screwed me this time.

I stared at the herbs in the bottom of the mortar and pretended not to notice the lime green hair escaping Mrs. Anderson's hood. She withdrew a glass vial from her pocket and slammed it on the counter. I eyed the half-used potion. It was my latest creation, guaranteed to give my customers' hair a shiny new luster. Unfortunately, "guaranteed" might be too strong of a word. I probably should have tested the concoction on my own auburn locks before stocking the shelves.

"I want my money back."

"Now, Mrs. Anderson, you know I can't do that." I tapped the wooden sign propped up on the edge of the counter. "No refunds."

Mrs. Anderson's eye twitched, the little spasm a precursor to the boiling wrath beneath the surface. "Look what you've done!" She whipped off her hood to expose a mass of green curls.

The color was awful, but it was the acidic smell

that made tears sting the corners of my eyes. Pressing my knuckles under my nose, I took shallow breaths.

"Did you follow the directions?"

The wooden sign hit the floor, followed by a basket of tea leaves. When she reached for a crystal jar filled with moonstones, I held up my hands in defeat.

"Okay! You can have a refund." I searched under the counter and counted out the coins, which amounted to the entire day's profit. Mrs. Anderson wasn't my only dissatisfied customer; earlier, I'd cast a siren spell and left a young woman mute. A cup of honey-ginger brew had solved the problem, but I didn't expect a glowing recommendation.

"You're a disgrace, Tessa. Your mother would turn in her grave if she could see what you've done to her magic shop." She snatched the coins from my fingers. "And you call yourself a witch."

Her words stung, but she wasn't wrong. My spells came in fits and spurts, and my potions never turned out right. Admittedly, this was the first time I'd ever dyed a woman's hair green.

"I'm sure it's not permanent. Why don't you try this potion to counteract the effects?" I nudged a different vial across the counter. "On the house."

Mrs. Anderson smiled, her lips straining at the corners. Holding my gaze, she lifted the tube and removed the cork stopper to spill its contents onto the carpet. The rug immediately turned bright pink.

I bit my lip. *Too much mugwort?* I was sure I'd

measured that one correctly.

"If your mother and I hadn't been such good friends, you'd be hearing from my solicitor." Mrs. Anderson flipped the hood over her head and charged toward the door.

"I'm so sorry, I don't know how—"

The bell above the door jangled with her exit, putting an end to my apology.

I groaned and dropped my forehead into my hands. What was I supposed to do now? Peeking between my fingers at the carpet, I watched the pink stain vanish, leaving behind a spot in better condition than before. The potion did work. It just needed a minute.

"Everyone is so impatient," I muttered, grabbing the used vials and dropping them in a basket beneath the counter. Quiet filled the empty shop except for the rhythmic tick of the pendulum. I was running out of time, and the grandfather clock in the corner was gleefully counting down the seconds.

Stacks of bills littered the countertop, the invoices mocking me with their vast sums and creeping deadlines. I sifted through them and paused at the notice that outweighed them all. *Argus.* I never should have borrowed money from his gang. It didn't matter that I'd been desperate and on the verge of selling the magic shop. I'd missed a payment, and Argus didn't *do* missed payments.

Three days ago, I'd arrived home to find one of the lanterns on the gateposts shattered. A note had been nailed to the wood containing a single word stamped in red: *Overdue*. Warning number one. Then, yesterday, Argus had sent one of his thugs to lurk outside my shop. The heavy belt at the thug's waist stowing knives and other ominous tools hadn't escaped my notice. When he caught me looking, he'd pulled a blade from its sheath and inspected the end. Yeah, it was sharp. Warning number two. Something told me I would not like warning number three.

I closed my eyes and tried to cast the blame where it really belonged. This wouldn't have happened if my magic had developed properly. In my family's long line of witches, I was the only one who hadn't mastered the calling. My mother had always believed I was special and would become the most powerful witch in our line. Only, in the years since her death, I'd brought the magic shop to the brink of closure and sent most of my mother's dedicated clients running in the opposite direction. A lump formed in my throat as I thought of her. I was number one, all right. A number one screw-up. If anything, I'd mastered the art of warding people away. Too bad I couldn't bottle that up and sell it—proper warding spells sold for a fortune.

With a heavy sigh, I dismissed the bills and circled the counter. My joints ached from too many hours on my feet, and I stifled a yawn as I padded across the floor. At the window, I pushed aside a tasseled curtain and squinted to see out into the dark yard.

A young woman stood on the walkway leading to the shop. Illuminated by the glow of my one remaining lantern, her long blonde hair cascaded down her shoulders, and she twisted a strand around her finger. She bounced on her heels as if trying to decide whether she was coming or going. With a curt nod, she decided. She was coming.

The woman bounded up the steps and pushed open the door before I pulled myself away from the window. I studied her, trying to remember if I'd sold her any botched potions. At least her hair wasn't green, but if she wanted a refund like the others, she'd be out of luck. Maybe I could offer her store credit? No. Better to cut her off before she asked.

"We're closed."

She hovered in the doorway, letting the cold air in. "Are you the witch?"

My teeth clenched at the obvious question. "Witch, fairy godmother, take your pick. We're still closed."

"I need your help. I realize it's late, but you're the only shop open."

"Except, as I mentioned, I'm not." Crossing both arms over my chest, I hoped she'd take the hint and leave.

The woman ignored my remark and sank to her knees. She rummaged through a bag slung over her shoulder.

"I can pay you."

Apparently, she knew a few magical words of her own. "I'm listening."

The front of the woman's cloak gaped open, revealing a filthy smock covered in ash. It spotted her skin too, leaving a gray smudge along her temple. She was most likely a maid, some unfortunate girl saddled with a miserable employer. She wasn't rich. In fact, she looked dirt-poor. Emphasis on the dirt.

"What's your name?" I asked, warming to the idea of turning a profit.

"Ella Lockwood." Pausing in her search, she stuck out a hand.

"Tessa Daniels." I felt the rough calluses covering her palm as we shook. Workers' hands, the kind used to scrubbing floors and washing laundry.

Ella pulled away and resumed her search. "Here it is." She withdrew a small object and held it up to the light. "The ring was my mother's."

The simple gold ring with an ornate design carved into its surface wouldn't sell for much at the pawnshop, but it might bring in enough to cover my missed payment. I considered the trade, even as guilt warred with self-preservation and the little voice masquerading as my conscience urged me to think twice. The ring was a family heirloom, and I'd sold enough of my mother's belongings to know the toll that took. I'd received temporary funds in exchange for a permanent void. Each item was a piece of her slipping away.

"I can't take it. Sorry." I brushed Ella's hand aside and walked over to the door, cursing my morals with each step. Refusing money to save someone else future heartbreak defied logic. Argus would have no trouble breaking something of mine, though I was sure he wasn't about to break my heart. My knees, most likely.

"Wait! I know it's not much, but I'm desperate. I'll do anything."

*Anything.* The word made me pause. I'd been willing to do anything to save the shop, and look where that had gotten me. This kind of desperation rarely worked out in the victim's favor. Still, I'd do it again, and it wasn't like I was taking advantage of her. I needed money, and she needed a spell. I might not be the best witch—or much of a witch at all—but I had a duty. A family creed. My mother would have helped, no questions asked. She'd have done it for free.

I wasn't that foolish.

"If I accept, what do you want?"

A glimmer of hope flashed across Ella's eager face. "The king is throwing a ball for his son tonight, and I have to be there."

My gaze took a second journey over Ella's rumpled uniform and soot-covered shoes. She wasn't exactly ball material, not by a long shot. I should have guessed though. The prince's ball had been the talk of the kingdom since the invitations went out. Prince Marcus of Ever was searching for a wife and every eligible woman in the kingdom was invited, myself included. The idea of trying to snare a prince to solve my money problems had lasted all of three seconds. While my looks had no trouble attracting a man, my spells and reputation usually put them off before I could secure a proposal. You turn a suitor into a mouse one time, and suddenly, everyone's hesitant to kiss you. Honestly, it was an accident, and I changed him back the second I figured out how.

"You need a gown, don't you?"

"Shoes too, and a carriage."

"Is that all?" I laughed. Potions and creams I had, but Ella needed an illusion spell, the least stable type of magic. If I cast it wrong, the illusion might fade and Ella could wind up in rags on the dance floor —or worse, naked. I cringed. There weren't enough smelling salts in the kingdom to manage that scene, and if anyone found out she'd been to see me? Goodbye, magic shop.

Ella grasped my arm, and her voice took on a pleading note. "Will you help? I have nowhere else to go."

"Fine," I mumbled, regretting the words as soon as they left my mouth. Then again, who was I to dash a young girl's dream of marrying a prince? Joy blossomed on Ella's face and her cheeks flushed a pretty shade of pink. In the right light and minus all the dirt, Ella was quite attractive. Who knew, maybe the spell would work, and she'd land herself the prince? In thanks, they'd shower me with gold, and it would solve all my problems. That kind of optimism was usually reserved for suckers, but at my rate, things needed to turn around.

Ella's eyes sparkled with excitement. "How do we start? I've never seen magic in action before."

The last time I performed an illusion, things had gotten dicey. I considered the fragile jars of potions lining the shelves. We were surrounded by way too much glass to cast a spell indoors. I couldn't afford to trash the shop if something went wrong. The ring was supposed to pay for my debt, not damages.

"Let's go into the back yard. Magic works best in the open air."

Ella nodded. "Makes sense. Magic seems so volatile."

She had no idea.

I opened the back door and ushered her outside. "Stand over there," I instructed, waving her away from the house.

Ella lifted her skirt and waded through the overgrown grass. She stepped into a beam of moonlight, and it washed her features of color, making her appear more ghost than human.

"Here?"

"Perfect. Don't move. I can't stress that enough." I rubbed my hands together and let magic build between my palms. Sparks sizzled in the air near my fingertips, and unease rippled through me. I pushed it aside. It wasn't like I could make Ella's clothes any worse than they already were.

I began to chant.

"Wait!" Ella held up a finger and took a step forward, halting me mid-spell. "I'm sure whatever you have in mind will be beautiful, but I've always dreamed of wearing a gown made of chiffon with silver beading. If it's not too much trouble."

"How about a matching pair of glass slippers while I'm at it?" I deadpanned.

"Can you?" Ella lifted her hand to her lips in wonder.

I blew out a breath, my sarcasm wasted. "Just go back to where you were and don't move."

Rubbing my hands to recapture the flow of magic, I made sure Ella followed my directions then let my eyes drift shut. The wind bracketed my face, swirling around my shoulders and neck. I curled my fingers into fists and flung my arms out, sending a warm gust of air across the yard.

Sparks glittered as Ella spun in a slow circle. Soft layers of chiffon billowed from her waist, and rows of silver beads encrusted the bodice of the gown. They glistened and twinkled like the stars overhead. A pair of translucent slippers adorned her feet.

Ella raised her ankle, taking it all in. "It's the most beautiful gown I've ever seen."

Satisfaction expanded inside my chest, and I crooked my finger, signaling her to join my side. "And now, the carriage."

I pointed to an overgrown pumpkin nestled in the garden. Fists together, I shot them out, launching another draft of warm air. It wafted over the target, and the pumpkin grew larger and larger until it cast a shadow over the yard. I nudged Ella and gave her a smug smile.

The pumpkin exploded.

Chunks of pulp hurtled through the air, landing in wet clumps at our feet. Seeds splattered across the fence like organic shrapnel, and I moaned as stringy goo oozed down the side of the gardening shed. The urge to gag pushed at the back of my throat when the odor of soggy gourd filled my nostrils. Regaining my composure—and my gag reflex—I counted the remaining pumpkins and gave a sheepish shrug.

"Want me to try again?"

A beat of silence passed as Ella picked seeds from her gown. "Now that I think of it, there's a carriage post near here. I'll hire one."

"If you think that's best." I swallowed my pride. It was clear I'd reached my magical limit for the day.

Ella gestured to her gown. "How long will the spell last?"

There was no way to know for sure, but I plastered on a confident smile. "Hours, so go ahead and dance till midnight."

"I'm not going there to dance."

Ella's sharp tone made me frown. I forced the concern away. It wasn't my business if she planned on dancing or pick-pocketing guests. I'd done my part. Well, two-thirds.

"Thank you for this. I should go, or I'll be late." Ella pressed the ring into my hand as payment. Our fingers touched, and a shock erupted at the contact.

A fiery pain spread through my palm. Unfurling my fingers to gaze at the ring, I watched it glow bright orange then cool to its original color. The intense heat had branded my palm with the same engraving etched into the ring.

"Be careful, Ella." I wasn't sure why I said it. The

woman was going to a ball, not the grave, but knowing that didn't ease my concern. Ella smiled softly, the gesture not reaching her eyes. She opened her mouth as if to speak but changed her mind. Instead, she straightened her spine, gave a final nod of thanks, and disappeared through the gate.

I examined the symbols on my palm. It was common for spells to leave a mark. The brand would fade along with the illusion. But as I stood in the frigid night air, a chill that had nothing to do with the cold swept through my body. It intensified, making each breath a sharp pain in my lungs. *A bad omen.* As a witch, I'd had a few, and when one occurred, you didn't push it aside.

I moved toward the gate on wobbly legs, fear urging me to find Ella and bring her back. When I reached the road, however, she was already gone.

# Chapter 2

Wisps of fog covered the ground as I bent and shoveled pumpkin chunks into a bucket at my feet. A headache beat at my temples, and I paused to press the ache away with my fingers. Images from the night before flashed through my mind. I'd handled the green hair incident and the annoyance of Ella's arrival, but everything after that was a blur. The ring, the promise to help...*the spell*. I groaned and glanced at the ravaged pumpkin, evidence of my abysmal magic.

I should be glad the pumpkin exploded in my back yard and not near the palace steps. One witness was better than hundreds. Not to mention, the slippery mess would have incurred fines. Lots of fines, ending most likely in debtors' prison.

Breathing deeply, I sank the shovel into the ground and leaned against the handle. A wave of dizziness caused the remaining chunks lying in the grass to tilt and spin. I massaged the symbols on my palm and let the feeling pass. The mark should have faded already, but the imprint remained on my skin. It worried me. Illusions lasted minutes or hours at most. Like everything else when it came to magic, this was further proof I wasn't normal.

"Yoo-hoo!"

I tensed at the warbled call. My neighbor, Sylvia Trager, stood near the gate, resting her weight on her cane. Maybe if I stayed still, her aging eyesight might fool her into thinking I was a garden statue or a scarecrow—an exhausted, not up for visitors sort of scarecrow. It didn't work. Sylvia motioned toward the pumpkin debacle and wrinkled her nose, setting off a chain reaction of flutters around her lips that looked suspiciously like she was trying not to laugh.

"Rough night, dear? Did you drink your potions again?"

My shoulders slumped. Why hadn't I locked the gate? This amount of humiliation required seclusion.

"No, Sylvia. I didn't drink my potions."

"Ah, must be booze then." She clucked her tongue and shook her wrinkled chin. "You're too young to be addicted to the devil's brew. Though, given your difficulties, I'm not surprised."

Sylvia was a fine one to talk. She frequently slipped the devil's brew into her tea when she thought no one was looking. I bit the inside of my cheek, keeping a sarcastic remark at bay.

"Did you need something?"

The old woman's eyes lit up with the spark of un-shared gossip, which was never a good sign. "I heard the most horrific news at the market this morning. You must join me for breakfast." She stabbed her cane into the dirt and trudged back toward her house. That was my cue to follow.

Since I'd been on my own, Sylvia had taken it upon herself to make sure I stayed well-fed, but her food came with a non-negotiable price: gossip. Endless, soul-sucking gossip. Still, the promise of a free meal remained in charge of my feet even if the prospect of infinite chatter caused my mind to rebel.

I followed her into the house and entered the living room, where a fire crackled in the hearth and ruffled powder-blue curtains let in swaths of muted light. The cream-colored walls hosted long shelves lined with porcelain figurines. They stared at me from their paralyzed positions with fixed smiles that seemed to say, "Get me out of here." The room might appear to be a cozy haven, but looks were deceiving. I made sure to check the thick-woven carpet for signs of Sylvia's cat, Fuzzlebottoms, before taking a hesitant step toward the sofa. The sly animal with the ridiculous name lived to bite my ankles and take swipes at me from under chairs. It was completely unfair. I loved cats. They did not love me. Somewhere, my ancestors were cackling at my inability to befriend the one animal that was supposed to be my familiar.

"Here you are." Sylvia trundled into the room carrying a tray loaded with muffins and a pot of tea. The heavenly scent of baked goods made my stomach growl. Sitting on the sofa, I selected a muffin while Sylvia took her usual seat by the window. I was tasting my first bite, savoring the tart flavor of fresh blueberries, when razor-tipped claws sank into my calf. Stifling a yelp, I jerked my leg. The cat hissed and ducked under the sofa.

"Sylvia, your cat—"

"Isn't she the sweetest thing? Light of my life." Sylvia busied herself with the pot of tea.

The monster's claws found their target again, and pain stabbed through my leg. Magic built in my palms, and before I could stop it, sparks shot from my fingertips, striking the carpet near Fuzzlebottoms' furry tail. The cat screeched and bolted, unharmed, but the magic left a burn in the rug. I moved my foot over the still-smoking hole.

Sylvia missed her cup and spilled tea into the saucer. "Good heavens, child. What has gotten into that cat?"

I stuffed both hands into the folds of my skirt, cutting off any residual magic. "You said you had news?"

"Yes!" Sylvia took a dainty sip and settled deeper into the chair. Her hand shook as she lowered the cup into the saucer. "When I was in the market earlier, everyone was talking about the prince's ball."

"How fascinating." I chewed another mouthful of muffin and prepared for a lengthy list of who wore what and who danced with who. Torture, all in the name of baked goods.

Sylvia dotted her lips with a napkin. "It is fascinating, what with the party ending in murder."

"What?" I coughed, inhaling a blueberry. "Who?"

"Lady Lockwood's stepdaughter, Ella."

"Ella Lockwood?" The muffin turned to dust in my

mouth, and I struggled to swallow. Ella couldn't be dead. There had to be a mistake. "Are you sure?"

"Positive. They found her submerged in the palace fountain. Drowned." She pursed her lips and placed a wrinkled hand over her heart. "According to my sources, the killer staged her body. She had a rose tucked between her fingers. Can you believe it?"

I shifted uncomfortably in my seat. "Do they know who killed her?"

Sylvia leaned back and lifted her teacup to her lips. She took her time, enjoying the fact she had a captive audience. My fingers itched to snatch the cup out of her hand and hurry her along.

"Unfortunately, no. The family is shattered. Her stepmother and stepsister are demanding answers. The poor things. They lost Sir Lockwood last year after a dreadful illness, and now this."

Guilt made the muffin I'd ingested churn in my gut. I thought of the ring Ella had given me as payment. What should I do with it now? Return it to her family, or try to sell it as quickly as possible?

*Return it*, whispered my conscience.

*Sell it*, whispered the witch inside me drowning in debt.

And then, a soft current of air tickled my ear. "Help me," the voice pleaded.

Gooseflesh prickled my arms. "Did you hear that?"

"Hear what, dear?" Sylvia didn't seem fazed at all.

I searched the room, positive the voice was real and alarmingly close. My palm itched around the tender skin where the ring had left its mark. Had the symbols grown darker? Closing my fist, I pushed the unsettling thought away.

Sylvia continued, "Apparently, Ella caused quite a stir. She danced with the prince shortly before midnight. She may have even caught his eye. The royal family is beside themselves after what happened. All talk of the prince's hunt for a wife is on hold, and the king assigned a detective from the Royal Agency to handle the case. Let's see, I believe his name is Detective Chambers. They're questioning everyone Ella came into contact with. Rumors are the detective is especially interested in someone she visited before the ball."

*Me.* A slow breath escaped my lips. The detective was interested in *me.*

"Do the authorities know who she visited?'"

"I'm sure they do. Ah, to be young again. I hear the detective is incredibly handsome and moving up the ranks quickly for his age. Now, there's a prospect." Sylvia jabbed her bony finger in my direction. "You would do well with someone like him. A stable man, respected in the community. I said nothing when you refused to attend the ball, but your magic, it's…" She sipped her tea. "It's just terrible."

"Tell me how you really feel," I muttered.

"What's that, dear?"

I spoke louder, "I don't need a husband. I need a—"

"Miracle," Sylvia finished.

A miracle. For once, we agreed. But a miracle wouldn't appear in the form of a detective on a white horse. The man was more likely to arrest me as an accomplice to murder than make me his wife. No, I had gotten myself into this mess, and I would get myself out of it.

Another wave of guilt speared my insides. I should have sent Ella away. Maybe if I had, she wouldn't have made it to the ball, and she'd still be alive. There had been something off about our encounter. I'd sensed it and ignored my instincts until it was too late. Now, Ella was dead, and a detective —handsome or not—would soon be sniffing around my shop.

"I have to go."

"But you haven't finished your breakfast," Sylvia sputtered. "I still have to tell you about the costumes and the buffet."

"Another time, Sylvia."

The mention of food made my stomach revolt. Ignoring her protests, I scrambled for the door and near-ran back to the shop, my mind racing through the inventory on display and the stock I had hidden. A tight feeling constricted my chest. The law and witches rarely mixed. It didn't help that this particular witch owed a debt to one of the kingdom's most notorious crime syndicates. Borrowing money wasn't illegal, but shady dealings with the leader of a gang? It didn't look good even without a meeting before a murder and a basement full of dodgy potions. If anyone found out about those, I'd have some explaining to do.

Back at the magic shop, I took the porch steps two at a time and fumbled inside my apron for the key.

My fingers ran along the seam, and I groaned as my pinky slipped through a hole in the fabric. The key was missing, lost somewhere between my door and Sylvia's house.

I cursed and peered through the front window, then dropped my head against the glass. A laugh bubbled in my throat as I tried to think of another way inside. An unlocking spell would do the trick. Thankfully, the road leading into town was still empty, not a detective in sight. Whispering the incantation, I lifted my palms toward the lock. A current of magic crackled in the air. It felt controlled, accurate. What a relief.

*Thwack!*

The door's deadbolt slammed into place. *Damn it!* My shoe beat a rhythm against the porch while I considered my dwindling options. A locksmith would take too long, which left me with only the terracotta flowerpot at my feet. Well, when a door is double-locked, open a window...

I hefted the pot into the air and swung it over my shoulder.

"Is there a problem?"

The planter slipped from my fingers and smashed against the wooden beams, sending dirt and clay fragments flying. The glass, much to my dismay, remained unbroken. I pivoted toward the end of the porch, where a man lounged against the railing. His boot-clad feet were crossed at the ankles, and his arms were folded over a broad chest, encased in a charcoal gray well-tailored coat.

Amusement sparked in his gaze as I stared, unable to move, with dirt covering my shoes. He pushed away from the rail and walked closer. No, make that *stalked*. The hint of a smile softened the motion, but he still moved with authority. His eyes commanded attention. Blue, like the deep end of a pond where it's easy to lose your footing and drown. He had short copper-brown hair, and a shadow of coarse stubble covered his chiseled jawline. It gave off a formidable impression, and I found myself mesmerized by the hard planes of his face, strong nose, and firm mouth.

He stopped in front of me. Anticipation hummed through my body as I tilted my head back and held his gaze. Up close, his irises appeared darker, and I sensed the intelligence lurking in their depths. I suddenly had the feeling that anyone drowning in them had probably had their feet kicked out from under them first.

"Did you have to startle me like that? Why were you hiding in the corner?"

"I wasn't hiding. I'm waiting for the owner. Are you the witch?"

I hated that question. It only led to trouble.

"No. I'm not."

His brows arched in surprise, and he gestured toward the door. "If you're not the witch then you must be a thief. You were about to break into this shop. I could have you arrested."

My cheeks warmed in embarrassment. It figured I'd have an officer waiting on my porch. Pulling myself together, I lifted my shoulders in an easy shrug and flashed him a smile.

"You caught me." I held out my hand. "I'm Tessa Daniels, the witch."

He closed his fingers over mine. "Detective Derrick Chambers. It's what I do."

"Catch witches?" I choked.

"If they need catching or have something to hide." He angled his head and pinned me with an inquiring look. "How about it, Miss Daniels? Do you have something to hide?"

# Chapter 3

**H**is question caught me off-guard. Heat transferred between our palms along with a jolt of awareness I saw reflected in his eyes. So, maybe I wasn't the only one who felt off-balance. Keeping my features calm, I stepped back and felt the smallest tug, as if he was reluctant to relinquish my hand. He must have realized his mistake because he let go, flexing his fingers before stuffing them into his coat pocket. It was the only crack in his armor since he'd emerged from the shadows.

"Something to hide?" I laughed to cover my nerves. "Not unless you count the shame of a witch locking herself out of her shop."

"I see." Derrick removed his hand from his pocket and revealed a small brass key. "I found it on the walkway. You must have dropped it."

I frowned. The man had watched me make a fool of myself trying to unlock the shop and hadn't said a word? I plucked the key from his palm and mouthed the curse that sat ready on my tongue. Inserting the key into the lock, I twisted the handle, but the door didn't budge. Cringing, I remembered the deadbolt. It was still engaged from my stupid spell. I ground my teeth together and murmured the incantation. The bolt slid back, and I opened the door with a flourish.

"After you, Detective."

He entered the shop, and his gaze roamed over the shelves and display racks loaded with jars and stoppered bottles. Bundles of herbs hung from the rafters, giving off a pungent, earthy smell. Derrick ducked, narrowly avoiding a cluster of sage, and wandered toward a cabinet full of books, running a finger through the grime and dust on their spines as he bent to read each title. I couldn't tell if his lips flattened from the strange subjects or the dust he rubbed between his fingers, but his slow, silent perusal of my shop made me grind my teeth. He crossed to my workbench next and picked up a jar of orange paste, scrunching his nose in disgust when he sniffed its contents. Out came a small leather journal, and he scrawled a notation.

"Those are on sale." I pointed to the jar he'd moved out of smelling distance.

"That doesn't surprise me." He inspected a sprig of herbs resting on the counter with the tip of his pen. "Do you know why I'm here?"

"The kingdom's introduced a new program whereby police drop in for friendly house calls?"

"No." He gave me a dark look. "I'm here on official business. There's been a murder at the palace."

"A murder?" I feigned ignorance and tucked my nervous fingers behind my back. "That doesn't explain why you're in my shop."

A moment of silence passed before he pulled a chair from the worktable and scraped it across the floor. "Have a seat."

I must have looked like a woman walking toward the gallows as I closed the distance and lowered myself into the chair. The wooden spokes pressed into my back, but I refused to slouch, needing every ounce of confidence I could get. He towered over me, so close I could smell the faint woodsy scent of his cologne. I shifted, taking the spice in deeper. It was similar to something I sold, but whatever he'd purchased was better. Damn him.

Derrick placed an elbow on the workbench and leaned in. The move seemed casual, but the rigid way he held himself made me think otherwise. His voice was smooth and even when he spoke, a rich timbre that set off a flutter in my stomach.

"Last night, at the prince's ball, a young woman named Ella Lockwood was murdered. A witness claims she visited you earlier in the evening. Why?"

The symbols on my palm had grown warm again, so I massaged the spot with my thumb. I didn't know anything about Ella's murder. Maybe it would be best if I distanced myself from the situation before I got involved any deeper. It wasn't as if I could point out her killer or give the detective any worthwhile clues.

I tilted my chin and lied. "I had so many customers yesterday, I'm not sure I remember anyone specific."

Derrick leaned closer. The cuff of his sleeve brushed against my shoulder blade. "I see. It must be difficult to keep track of the steady stream of people coming into your shop." He lifted his gaze and stared pointedly at the empty doorway. A full torturous minute passed while he watched all the nonexistent customers. I squirmed in my seat, pleading for the bell suspended above the door to jingle. It stayed silent. Traitorous instrument.

"The mornings are slow. It picks up." My optimism sounded hollow. I would have given anything for someone to enter the shop, even a green-haired Mrs. Anderson.

"You know what I think?" His tone dropped, breath warming my ear. I held still and barely contained a shiver.

"What, Detective?"

"I think you remember meeting Ella." He straightened and reached across the counter, sliding a worn ledger over the surface. Flipping the booklet open to the marked page, he read the items. I knew what he'd find there, and I burned from humiliation, caught in my lie. He tapped the paper with his index finger. "Your sales record from yesterday has two entries. One in the morning, and one in the afternoon. That's not a lot to remember." He paused, letting his words sink in. "If you'd rather have this conversation in my office while I have my men conduct a thorough search of your shop, it's up to you. Who knows what they'll uncover? A witch must have secrets."

A direct hit. I had plenty of secrets, not to mention an underground crawlspace containing what some might consider a morally gray area of potions. My gaze darted to the hatch in the floor. Derrick caught me in the act and smirked. He took a step toward the hatch, then another. Each thud of his boots sounded like a cell door slamming closed. Witches really weren't suited for prison.

"All right, fine!" I grabbed his sleeve, pulling on the material until he stopped heading for the crawlspace. "Ella was here. It was late, and I tried to turn her away, but she was insistent I help her."

"I'm listening."

Slumping into the chair, I continued. "She offered to trade a family heirloom for a dress and a pair of shoes. I cast an illusion spell. It was an innocent—and legal, I might add—transaction."

Derrick studied my face as if the action alone could unearth the smallest lie. Maybe it could. I felt thoroughly exposed beneath his stare.

"So, you used your magic and sent her off to the ball?"

I inclined my head, imitating his sarcastic demeanor from before. "I'm a witch, Detective. It's what I do."

The corner of his mouth hitched, and a tiny thrill shot through my veins. One point to the witch. He hadn't expected me to throw his words back in his face. My victory dimmed when he made another notation in his book, this one longer. I struggled to contain my curiosity. What was he writing about me? Probably nothing good.

He snapped the journal closed, making it impossible to find out, and eyed me warily. "Mind explaining why you were in your shop last night and not at the ball? The royal family invited every eligible woman in the kingdom. You're the right age, unmarried. It begs the question."

"Not every eligible woman is interested in marrying a prince. Especially not when it's based on a single encounter in the presence of hundreds of competitors. There are better ways to find a wife, Detective."

"Is that so?" His gaze traveled over the shabby carpet, a broken shelf I hadn't gotten around to fixing, and lastly, over my wrinkled gown. I resisted the urge to smooth the fabric. My clothes might not be the latest fashion or ironed, but that didn't make me a leech looking to climb to the top of the social ladder.

"Not even if it could improve your circumstances?" he asked.

His insinuation made my back straighten, and a swell of anger hid the prick of hurt from his demeaning remark. "My circumstances are fine, Detective." They were far from it, but I'd drink my worst potion before I revealed that nugget of truth.

Hearing my indignant tone, Derrick retrieved his notebook. If he made another notation, I swore...

"Did you two discuss anything personal? How would you describe her state of mind?"

Thrown by his change of topic, I stumbled over my answer. Was he purposely trying to confuse me? I gathered my thoughts, thinking back to Ella's demeanor.

"Well, she was desperate after I refused to help her. That's why I reconsidered. She seemed happy when I cast the spell but it only lasted a moment. It felt like she wanted to tell me something but changed her mind. I'd say she was upset when she left, almost resigned. I had a bad feeling."

"A bad feeling?"

"Yes, an omen. As a witch, there are times I feel negative energy on a physical level. There are crystals that amplify emotion. I planned on using one to pinpoint—"

He sighed and pushed away from the counter. Irritation rolled off him in waves. His thumb and forefinger rubbed the bridge of his nose as if a headache beat behind his eyelids.

"That's all for now. If you remember anything else, you can contact me at the agency."

His dismissal stung. I'd gone from character witness to crackpot in seconds. "You think I'm mad, don't you? All of this,"—I waved my hand around the shop—"the spells, the supernatural, you don't believe it's worth your time."

Derrick's mouth flattened into a grim line. "I believe in facts. Evidence. Potions and spells don't catch killers. You dabble in illusion and feed on people's weaknesses."

I pushed out of the chair, my face hot. "That's not fair!"

His eyes darkened in challenge. "Is that so?" He strode across the wooden beams, his boots echoing with each step until he came to a stop at the hatch in the floor. The air crackled with tension. "Prove it. You say you have nothing to hide? Let's see why you're determined to keep me out of your cellar."

My mouth opened and closed in protest. How had our conversation shifted so quickly? Why had I baited him? His beliefs didn't matter. He wasn't the only one in the kingdom who found supernatural abilities to be a waste of time. Over the years, people relied on magic less and less, yet his indifference hurt.

"It's mostly cobwebs and broken furniture."

"Open it, or my men conduct a search."

I swallowed my denial and lifted the hatch. Derrick lit a lantern and disappeared down the steps, leaving me to hover on the landing, biting my thumbnail and praying he wouldn't look too close.

"See? No dead bodies."

My joke fell flat. In the cellar, Derrick bumped into a cabinet and muffled an oath. I chalked that one up to a win and moved down two steps. The light from his lantern illuminated a shelving unit along the wall, and I held my breath as he rifled through the drawers.

*Please, don't find—*

He found them. Vials clinked together as he removed a small box from the bottom drawer. The one with a skull and crossbones burned into the wood. They needed to stop doing that. It was a dead giveaway.

"Those aren't mine. They were in with another order, and I was storing them until they could be properly disposed of." Yeah, that sounded believable.

"Either way, they're coming with me." He slipped the narrow box into his coat and climbed the steps. "You can pay the fines for these at the agency."

"Fines! Be reasonable."

"I am. You're lucky I'm not having you arrested."

I curled my fingers into fists, afraid I might go full witch and turn him into a toad. He'd make a good toad. He had the personality for it.

Not realizing how close he'd come to living the amphibian life, Derrick walked toward the entrance. "I'll be in touch if I have any further questions. Don't leave the kingdom until we've cleared you for travel."

I nodded, still steaming from his interrogation. Sylvia was right. He was handsome, but she'd forgotten to add cold and calculating to her description. Loather of all things magic. Good prospect indeed— I'd rather eat poisoned mushrooms than become his wife. Must remember to cast a blessing spell on whoever that wretched soul turned out to be. She'd need it.

He pulled open the door, and the little bell jingled. How could something so cheery accompany his exit? A gong or a crack of thunder would have been more appropriate.

Left alone, I sank into the chair and retrieved Ella's ring. Exhaustion hung like a weight around my neck. I squeezed my fist, feeling the metal warm against my skin. That poor girl. It wasn't enough to die, she had to have Detective Arrogant assigned to her case too. At least he hadn't discovered my connection to Argus, but now, I had a missed payment and a fine to pay. As wrong as it felt, so soon after Ella's murder, I had to pawn the ring.

"Sorry, Ella," I whispered. "Wherever you are." I shivered and rubbed my arms. In the moments since Derrick's departure, an icy chill had filled the shop. Frost crystallized on the windows, and my breath fogged around my lips. How strange.

I moved to the window, apprehension slowing my steps. The frost was on the inside. Pressing my finger against the glass, I left a warm print in the ice and squinted. There was something else there, faint letters, as if someone had written them before the ice formed. As quickly as it appeared, the chill faded, and the frost melted. But not before I'd made out the words. Speaking them aloud like they came from one of my spells, I couldn't deny the two words held a certain power all of their own.

*Help me.*

# Chapter 4

"Y ou're going to melt it down?"

The pawnshop owner inspected the ring with a small lens. "Yup. It's worth more as scrap metal. I'll give you fifty royal coins for it."

"Fifty?" My stomach sank. That wasn't enough to pay my fines. "It's an antique. Can't you do better?"

He tossed the ring onto the polished counter, where it clattered to a rest near a tray of silver trinkets. "I already told you, it ain't worth it. This here is what I call a sentimental piece." His thick mustache hid his lips when he grinned. "You have my sentiments for how cheap it is."

I narrowed my eyes at his joke and scooped up the ring. Cheap, my foot. It had value, sentimental or not. I couldn't let it go for fifty.

The moment the ring's metal touched the mark on my palm, it became warm. It was a pleasant feeling, something I was growing used to, like wrapping cold fingers around a steaming mug of tea. All the way into town, I'd tried to shake the tacky thought of profiting from Ella's murder. Something strange had happened in my shop yesterday when I'd decided to sell it. Those icy words scrawled on the frosted window, barely visible to the naked eye, had me looking over my shoulder. I must have imagined them. It was probably a manifestation of my guilt, or children playing pranks. The ominous phrase repeated over and over in my mind.

*Help me.*

"I'll keep the ring." Tucking it into my pocket, I reached for the bag at my feet. "Will you take these instead?" The knot inside my chest tightened as I placed a stack of worn books on the counter. They were my mother's, a collection that was slowly dwindling. The leather covers had darkened with age, and the parchment had warped through the years. A faint scent of must clung to the pages. "Seasoning the spells," my mother had called it. Mostly, it just made me sneeze.

The man rubbed the white whiskers on his chin and studied the volumes, running his stubby fingers over the text. "Now, these, I can use. People like to dabble in tonics and they usually have no idea what they're doing. I'll mark up the books, and they won't know the difference."

A ghostly finger ran up my spine. *Ugh.* There were definitely generations of dead family witches cursing my name.

"How much for them?"

"I can do one hundred and twenty." The man picked his teeth with a dirty thumbnail, then returned to inspecting the books. I stifled a groan as he left a smudged fingerprint on the cover.

"I want two hundred."

"One-fifty."

"Two hundred, and I don't place a curse on your establishment."

He blinked in surprise. There was a beat of silence before he audibly swallowed, Adam's apple bobbing in his throat. "Deal."

He counted the coins, then yanked my mother's precious books from view. Another piece of her gone. The only consolation was, I'd made enough to pay my fines. Argus was a different story. A vision of me marching into the agency, slamming my money on Derrick's desk, and smugly walking out flashed through my mind. The image morphed into his eyes, darkening in approval, a slow smile spreading across his lips. A hot flush scalded my neck, and I shook the picture away. Why, for the love of spell books, did I care about his approval or the way he smiled?

He had invaded my shop.

Made my money problems worse.

Messed with my head and my plans.

But he had smelled good.

I clenched my fists. He didn't deserve a single thought, not when I needed to earn a substantial sum before gang members started breaking down my door.

"If you have any more of those books, I'll gladly—" The man stopped mid-sentence, noticing my scowl. "Well, if you change your mind."

Hopefully, it wouldn't come to that. I had one other option but it would mean admitting I'd gotten in over my head and ignored some helpful advice. If I remembered correctly, friends didn't let friends borrow money from gangsters. Too bad I hadn't listened.

Slinging my now empty bag over my shoulder, I left the shop.

I waited until the sun dipped low behind the buildings, casting a deep purple glow across the sky. The streets emptied as the market closed. People headed home for dinner or holed up in taverns to wash down the day with a pint of ale. I cut through a shadowy alley on the outskirts of town and came to the entrance of a small dwelling. Candlelight flickered in the windows of Second Chance Souls, doing its best to stave off the growing darkness.

As if on cue, the front door swung open, and a young woman charged down the flagstone steps into the street, her long satin skirt rustling where it swished around her ankles. She snapped her fingers at a waiting carriage. I might as well have been a lamppost for all the attention she paid me. As her carriage rumbled away, I retraced her steps and entered the shop.

Swaths of colorful fabric hung from the ceiling of a cozy parlor. Pedestal candles shed their light over the intricate woven patterns. A multitude of flames created dancing shadows that undulated on the walls, and in the corner, a bowl of incense burned. The acrid smell filled my nose and made my eyes water.

"Come in, child. The spirits welcome you," a velvety voice crooned from an adjoining room.

A wall of hanging beads separated the two spaces, and I pushed through them, letting my fingertips glide over their polished surface. The beads clinked together before swaying back into place. Seated behind an oval table, an ancient woman bent over a glass sphere. Her long fingers were curled at the knuckles. Stick-straight gray hair hung past her shoulders, framing a face of pale, wrinkled skin.

She lifted her head and squinted through a pair of wire-rimmed spectacles. "Oh, it's you."

My lips flattened in disapproval. "Honestly, Viv, I can't believe you're still pulling this scam. Look at you. That outfit is ridiculous."

Vivian James shrugged and cracked her knuckles. "It's realistic though, isn't it? The wig is a nice touch." She curled her finger around a long gray lock. "Don't stare at me like that. My last appointment had it coming. She was infuriating and refused to work with me, said I didn't look the part. As if my abilities depend on my age." She scoffed. "Apparently, Vivian the Crone sells better than Vivian the twenty-something medium. It's why my grandmother does more business than me."

"I'm sure Winifred would be thrilled to learn you're using her likeness."

Vivian resettled the spectacles on her nose with her index finger. "It's temporary, and my grandmother is out of town on an extended trip. She'll never know."

"Oh, I bet she knows. She probably saw it in one of

her visions. There isn't much you can hide from an oracle."

"Tell me about it. Try growing up with that woman knowing everything you're planning to do before you do it." Vivian pushed out of her chair and stretched her shoulders. "Do me a favor and close up? I'm done for the night."

I headed back through the beads and turned the lock on the door. A sign hung in the window, and I flipped it over while Vivian droned on from the other room.

"You know, this disguise was worth seeing the look on Mrs. Saunders' face when I revealed the location of her dead husband's hidden funds."

"The Saunders' fortune? He must have had thousands stashed away."

"Oh, he did, but it's gone now. When he realized his wife cheated on him with his business partner, he spent it all. Tonight, I had the distinct pleasure of sending his widow on a wild goose chase, courtesy of her husband's ghost. He finally found the peace he needed to cross over knowing all she'll find is a buried box of receipts."

"Savage," I said, making my way back into the room. Vivian's wig rested on a wooden stand while she leaned over a porcelain basin, water dripping down her neck. Gone were the wrinkles, revealing smooth, youthful skin. Glossy raven curls spilled down her shoulders as she scrubbed the age spots from her hands. After wiping her palms with a rag, she stowed her spectacles in a drawer.

The transformation was awe-inspiring. Vivian wasn't afraid to play dirty, even impersonating an old woman to serve the lingering souls who roamed the kingdom. The dead were big business, and she had a near-constant stream of clients. I didn't envy her gift though. I'd take magic over fulfilling a ghost's final wishes any day of the week.

"So, how's the shop?" she asked, resuming her place at the table.

"That's why I'm here." I sunk into an adjacent chair and rested my chin in my hand. "I need a favor."

Vivian's brown eyes narrowed. "What favor?"

The truth sat heavy on my tongue. "I need a tiny loan to pay back a creditor."

"A loan?" A second later, she gasped and slammed her palm on the table, making the glass sphere rattle. "Creditor, my ass. You borrowed money from that loan shark, didn't you? What's his name? Shmargus or something? A total crook."

"It's Argus, and you're right, I shouldn't have taken the money, but I was going to lose the magic shop and have the rest of my mother's things seized as collateral. I had no choice." A lump clogged my throat, making it difficult to swallow. I hung my head. "There are fines too," I mumbled.

"Fines! What for?"

"A royal detective found the box of wisteria spinova powder I hid in the basement. He was less than thrilled about it."

"Why was there a detective in your basement?"

Peeking between the thick strands of my hair, I gave her a sheepish shrug. "I might be involved in a murder investigation."

Vivian's lips opened and closed like a gasping fish. It would have been comical if I didn't already feel so lousy. Finally, she held up her hand.

"Hold on. Not the girl from the ball?"

The pang of guilt was back, laced with a healthy dose of self-loathing. "Her name was Ella Lockwood, and she came to see me before the ball. All she needed was a gown and a pair of shoes. There didn't seem to be any harm, and she was going to pay me." It wasn't worth it to mention the carriage. Something told me exploding pumpkins wouldn't help my cause.

"You used magic, didn't you? An illusion?"

I nodded, unable to meet her eyes.

"Tess, you know what happens when you try to cast illusions!"

"Yeah, apparently, people end up dead."

"That's not funny."

"Trust me, I'm not laughing." I blew out my cheeks. "They've assigned a royal detective to the case. His name's Derrick Chambers, and I can tell you right now, he doesn't like witches. One of my ancestors probably sacrificed his family's goats or something."

Vivian tapped her trim nails against the table. "Well, here's something you don't have to worry about—I haven't felt any new spirits in the last few days. Ella should have already crossed over."

"That's the other reason I'm here." A prickly sensation climbed the back of my neck, and I peered over my shoulder, searching the dark corners of the room. There had been a part of me that hoped Vivian might be able to communicate with Ella. Maybe I could have told her how sorry I was for the way things turned out.

"You can relax. She's not here. If she crossed over, it's too late, I can't summon her. The dead hate to be disturbed. Now, if she approaches us from the other side, that's a different story. But as I said..." Vivian licked her finger then held it up in the air, testing the temperature of the room. "See? Nothing. We're alone."

Disappointment knotted my insides, and I glanced at the symbols on my palm. I had thought maybe there was still a connection, and that was why the mark hadn't faded.

"What are you going to do about Argus?"

"I missed a payment, and I'm worried he'll send his goons after me. I sold a few of my mother's books to cover the fines for the illegal powder, so that's taken care of."

"How much more do you need?" Vivian crossed the room toward a small cabinet. Inside, she retrieved a pouch full of coins, which she pressed into my hand. "Is this enough?"

"It's a start. I'll repay you, I swear."

Vivian snorted. "Says the girl who borrowed from a medium to pay back a gangster. Keep it. That's what friends are for."

I crushed her in a hug, fighting a rush of emotion. Sometimes, it felt like she was all I had, and I hated that my problems became hers. Now, I could pay the fines and put the arrogant, witch-hating detective behind me, then focus on getting Argus off my back.

"You're the best, Viv. You know you are."

"Well, if you plan on listing my superior qualities, I won't stop you. Please, continue. You haven't even mentioned my flawless beauty or svelte figure."

I choked on a laugh and tucked the money into my pocket, light-headed with relief. "Your ego can't handle it."

"Probably not." Vivian clasped my shoulders and gave them a gentle squeeze. "Be careful, Tess. This thing with Argus, and now the detective, it's a mess. You need to ditch both of them as soon as possible."

"I know. That's the plan."

Through the windows, I could see a faint drizzle glistening on the cobblestones in the lantern light. The dark street was deserted, and it was a long walk back to the magic shop. Argus's men were probably roaming the alleys looking for me. I'd grown used to seeing them skulking around in my peripheral vision. Still, I couldn't risk spending any of my newfound wealth on hiring a carriage. Not when I needed every royal penny.

"Viv, you aren't using the wig again tonight, are you?" I asked with a smile.

She wrinkled her brow. "No, why? Do you want it?" Vivian plucked the wig from its holder and watched with a grin as I arranged the head of hair artfully over my own.

"How do I look?" I posed, hunched over, one hand on my hip.

"I think I wore it better, but it should keep anyone from recognizing you."

*Perfect.* Pulling the collar of my cloak up around my neck, I shuffled down the steps and into the night.

# Chapter 5

Wigs were the worst.

Thick strands of hair fell into my eyes, the rest hanging in weighty clumps down my back as I hobbled blindly through the dark alley. Bile rose in my throat when a furry body darted past my feet and scampered into a gaping hole beneath a brick wall. The rancid odor of spoiled fish and salt was a pungent reminder I was near the docks, a playground for rats and larger, more dangerous creatures. Maybe I should have taken the hit and hired a carriage after all.

Someone was close by, I realized, when an icy wind tunneled through the alley, carrying the ashy scent of cigar smoke. I braved a glance over my shoulder and caught the orange flash of embers before they dissipated. The urge to run barreled through me, but I maintained my limping gait. One more step, then two. *Keep it together, Tessa.* I repeated the mantra until my heart slowed and my breath evened. See, nothing to it. Just a leisurely nighttime stroll through the kingdom's unsavory back alleys.

A cat screeched from some hidden hovel. An answering howl sent the animal racing through the narrow passage. The cat had the right idea. I picked up my pace, dropping the limp when I heard the echo of footsteps ricocheting off the walls. My pulse pounded against my throat, while up ahead, a lantern cast a welcoming pool of light. I dove for the beacon of safety. Its glow grew stronger, and I reached out as if I could capture it and bring it closer.

Before I could, rough hands clamped around my forearms and hauled me backward. I clawed at my assailant, nails raking along his skin. His grip tightened, digging blunt fingers into my muscles, the pinpoints shooting pain up my arms. He pressed me into the wall. The coarse brick scraped my back, catching on the fabric of my cloak. My shoes slid on the wet cobblestones. Fingers that reeked of cigar smoke covered my mouth. I screamed anyway, the sound a muffled moan in the back of my throat.

Panic surged inside my body as the man's vile, alcohol-soaked breath filled my nostrils.

"All alone, witch? You shouldn't have missed a payment."

A match scraped against stone. Sulfur scented the air, then the soft glow of a lantern expanded in the space. I squinted from the sudden light and renewed my struggle, managing a well-placed elbow in the man's ribcage. He grunted but didn't let go. My attacker moved to the side, and in his place, another man came into focus.

"Argus," I whispered.

"Caught you." He smiled, and shadows danced beneath the sharp edges of his cheekbones.

Thick ebony hair grazed the tops of his broad shoulders and curled behind his ears. He had youthful, roguish features, but the rigid set of his jaw and apathy lurking in his green eyes spoke of suffering beyond his years.

"Trying to avoid me, witch? You haven't paid me yet. It offends me that you're evading our agreement. I'm a businessman, not an animal." His steely gaze flicked toward the man holding me captive. The corner of his lips hitched. "He's the animal. Try to stay on his good side."

"I'll get your money," I said between clenched teeth.

Argus lifted his shoulders. His leather coat stretched over lean muscle. "Everyone says that."

"I need more time."

He chuckled and looked around like there was a larger audience. "Everyone says that too. So unoriginal." His hand moved toward my neck, and I flinched, expecting his lethal fingers to tighten into a stranglehold. Instead, they rubbed the strands of the wig that had torn loose from my head and gathered in an awkward pile on my shoulder. "Points for the disguise. I don't see that every day. But you weren't wearing it when you visited your friend. Did she give it to you? Did she give you anything else? Money, perhaps? Maybe I should speak to her about your missed payment..."

Anger burned my gut. "Leave her alone. She's not involved in our deal."

Argus pressed his lips together, impatience narrowing his gaze as it traveled down the length of my cloak and honed in on my pockets. "What a pity. I wouldn't mind getting to know the ghost-hunter a little better." His hand dipped into my pocket and withdrew the coins I'd received at the pawnshop along with Vivian's share. He stuffed them into his jacket, then sent me a devilish wink. "I'm not above picking pockets. It reminds me of where I come from. This buys you more time, but now, I want your entire loan paid by the end of the month."

"End of the month? You can't do that!" I twisted in his goon's hold, wincing as pain shot through my arm.

Argus laughed, and disbelief tinged his voice. "Is she serious? Does anybody read the fine print? Witch, I can do whatever I want. You signed a contract."

A shrill whistle pierced the night, and Argus glanced over his shoulder as footsteps started to pound along the alley.

"Someone's coming," the thug muttered, loosening his grip on my wrists.

Pinning me with his gaze, Argus warned, "I want it all by the end of the month."

"I told you, it's not enough time."

"End of the month," he growled, moving past me and vanishing into the shadows.

Alone in the alley, I shrank against the building to make myself invisible. I was tempted to follow Argus, unsure whether I should face the advancing strangers. Better the devil you know...

Light poured into the narrow space, and the footsteps halted.

"Detective? What are you doing here?" I pushed away from the wall and moved into the inviting glow. Fear drained from my body, leaving me hollow and unsteady.

Derrick Chambers stepped in front of his patrolman. His gaze traveled over my disheveled form, lingering for a moment near my jawline. Heat flushed my cheeks as I realized the tangled strands of the wig were stuck to my chin. I tugged the offending piece from my head, leaving my drizzle-damp hair hanging past my shoulders.

As the corner of Derrick's mouth kicked up in amusement, I finger-combed the mess back into place. So much for the disguise. What had worked for Vivian had utterly failed me. Mortified, I considered using magic to create a crater in the ground big enough to swallow me whole. The only saving grace was that behind Derrick's frank enjoyment was a hint of concern. That softening look tightened something in my chest. I needed to squelch the emotion or I might think he cared.

My hands balled into fists. "Were you having me followed?"

"I thought I should, after our discussion yesterday. You seemed like a runner." He eyed the wig, which resembled a ball of snarled yarn rather than a hairpiece. Out came his notebook, and the impulse to rip the pages from his fingers to see what he wrote down raged inside me. But giving in to temptation would only reveal my curiosity.

"Stay out of my business, Detective."

He grabbed my arm as I swept past him. Pain exploded in my wrist when his hand clamped over the spot Argus's thug had injured. At the sound of my hoarse cry, his grip gentled, and he snapped his fingers. The man holding the lantern loomed closer.

Derrick eased the sleeve of my cloak up to reveal an ugly welt and traced his thumb over the edges of the darkening bruise. The soothing touch should have calmed my tension. Instead, it ratcheted it higher, making the air thick inside my lungs. All amusement faded from his face, replaced by a rigid determination.

I couldn't deny the flare of pleasure it gave me.

"Did you get a good look at him?" The fury in his tone tightened my throat. It would be so easy to tell him my problems. I almost believed he would solve them. I imagined him bending over my knuckles and pledging to rid the kingdom of anything in my way; a knight in shining armor fantasy that was about as real as my illusions. Derrick had followed me because my shop was one of the last places Ella visited. He didn't trust me, and he wasn't interested in my troubles unless they related to catching a killer.

A strained silence hung in the air while he waited for my answer. His men had backed away, leaving us on the fringes of the dim light. I tugged my arm from his grasp, feeling the loss of his touch more than I should.

"It was too dark." As I lowered my sleeve in a jerky motion, the wig fell, landing with a wet slap against the cobblestones. "They ran off when they heard you coming. I suppose I should thank you for your good timing."

"No thanks necessary. It's what—"

"You do. Yeah, I remember," I grumbled, mimicking our prior exchange.

He bent to retrieve the wig. It looked like a mangy animal in his large hands. What had I been thinking, wearing such a thing?

"I can explain the disguise."

"I think you should."

I fumbled for a suitable story and settled on something resembling the truth. "I went to visit a friend, and as you know, this part of town can be dangerous for a young woman at night. It was a silly idea, but I thought I'd be safer. Respect your elders and all that."

"I see." Except the skepticism that flashed across his face said he really didn't. Not that I could blame him—it was a ridiculous explanation. I half-expected him to put me in cuffs for impersonating an old woman. Was that a crime? Unlikely. But knowing Derrick, there was probably a fine.

"Am I free to go?" I asked.

He hesitated as if he had more to say, then gave a swift nod. "Abrams?" Derrick barked over his shoulder. "Escort Miss Daniels back to her shop."

"I don't need an escort."

He ignored my comment and edged closer, until

the same woodsy scent he wore during our first encounter flooded my senses. Damn him for smelling so good while I definitely smelled like a dank alley.

Bending his head, he spoke near my ear, "I expect to see you in my office to pay your fines this week, Miss Daniels."

He wasn't going to let me forget those. He might have dazzled me with his concern and pleasantly scented cologne, but they were just distractions from the truth. Argus had taken all of my money and upped his deadline, which meant I needed a new plan.

"I'll be there, Detective. I always pay my debts." My confident smile felt plastered-on, and I had no idea how to accomplish what he asked. I retrieved the wig and brushed past him, head high, shoulders straight, wig trailing in the gravel behind me like a dejected tail.

My escort hurried to catch up. I studied the young officer Derrick had assigned. He didn't look like he could take a bribe—not that I had much to bribe him with—but he might provide an angle that would help me deal with the stubborn detective.

*Keep your friends close, and your detectives closer.*

After a few blocks, I offered him my most charming smile. "So...tell me, Abrams, what's it like working for Detective Chambers?"

\*\*\*

A mile later, I had my answer. I'd also learned a valuable lesson: Don't ask questions you won't like the answers to. According to Abrams, Derrick was a paragon of the community. His key qualities were solving crimes, helping old ladies out of carriages, and donating to kingdom charities. The list went on and on. He came from money, his family owned a fancy estate in the country, and he'd risen through the ranks to become the youngest detective the kingdom had ever seen. If Abrams told me the man spent his weekends rescuing kittens out of trees, I'd have keeled over from rolling my eyes too hard.

"Overachiever," I muttered, kicking stones in my path.

"What was that?" Abrams paused in his praise of the famed detective.

"He's achieved so much," I answered, my voice nothing but sugar.

Abrams nodded, and a tangle of curly hair fell across his face. His woolen cap struggled to contain the unruly strands. He unlatched the gate leading to my shop, and his eyebrows drew together when he spotted the busted lamppost.

"Is everything all right?"

"What, the lamppost?" I chuckled. "A delivery cart backed into it. Drivers these days, huh? Anyway, you were telling me about joining the agency...?"

"Yes, well, Detective Chambers took me under his wing. I'm only a rookie officer, but he lets me help with cases. I plan on being a detective one day." Youthful ambition flickered in his eyes, and I felt like a heel for wishing I could knock Derrick off his pedestal.

"That's very admirable, Abrams." I yawned as a wave of exhaustion washed over my body, muscles and joints sore from my encounter with Argus and his henchman. It had been a rotten couple of days. Everything I'd touched had ended in disaster. Ella was dead, my money was gone, and it seemed that by the end of the month, I'd be out on the street. It was as if my failure at magic had bled into every corner of my life. My mother would be *so* proud.

"Thanks for walking me home. It was unnecessary, but I appreciate it all the same."

"It was my pleasure, Miss Daniels. But I disagree, it was necessary. A young woman shouldn't walk alone at night. Not after the murder."

"You're probably right." I hesitated, curious to see if he'd be as free with information about the case as he had been with the detective. "Did you attend the ball? Were you there when they found her?"

Abrams tore off his cap and twisted it in his hands. "Yes. Everyone at the agency was invited." He leaned on the gatepost and lowered his voice. "The clock struck twelve, and not ten minutes later, the courtyard doors burst open. You could hear the screams over the orchestra."

"Who found her?"

"A young couple taking a stroll around the garden. We cordoned off the fountain and waited for Detective Chambers to arrive."

"I thought he was already there."

"Oh, no. He made an appearance to satisfy his superior, but he left early. If you ask me, he's afraid of getting roped into an arranged marriage by association." Abrams laughed softly, his fingers clenching around his cap. "I've never seen a room filled with so many opportunistic social climbers before."

"Isn't it every young woman's dream to marry a prince?"

"It doesn't seem to be yours, Miss Daniels."

"Me?" I scoffed. "Hardly. They look like more trouble than they're worth. Besides, I don't think the royal family would let me practice magic in the great hall."

Abrams flattened his lips to contain a grin. "Detective Chambers was right, you are different."

"Different? I guess a witch has to take any compliment she can get."

"I'd say it's high praise, coming from the detective." Abrams secured the hat on top of his head, then stuffed his hands into his pockets. "I should return to my rounds." With his chin against his chest and his boot scuffing the dirt, he seemed embarrassed, probably realizing he'd spoken out of turn.

"Of course. Have a good night, Abrams."

*What a strange evening.*

Inside my shop, I pushed the door closed and hovered near the threshold. Abrams' unexpected reveal echoed in my mind. Derrick thought I was different, huh? What had I expected? The comment was no "you're a ravishing beauty" or "you have a stunning intellect," but it was something. Better than being called a fraud. I smiled as I trudged toward the kettle, a feat that seemed impossible considering my circumstances.

Water sloshed in the pot as I swung it over the grate in the fireplace. A few pieces of kindling and a couple jabs with the iron poker stoked the dying embers to life. The fire crackled, and the scent of smoke wafted in the air.

I slumped into a chair and waited for the water to boil. It had felt like ages since I'd last slept, but even so, my body hummed with leftover energy. Tomorrow, after a good night's sleep, I'd find a way to come up with the rest of the money, but for now, a cup of tea liberally laced with my mother's famous sleeping powder would help to put the entire night behind me. A witch needed her beauty sleep. Unskilled witches needed twice as much. Unskilled witches hounded by thugs and overachieving detectives, well, they needed to be put into a powder-induced coma.

I prepared the tea from memory, dropping a pinch of powder into my cup. Mint leaves followed. Breathing in the fragrant steam, I took a tentative sip that warmed my insides. Waves of heat from the fireplace soothed my aching muscles and dried my damp hair. The potion took effect, and soon, sleep wove its tendrils around my body. My head lolled to the side.

It was as my eyes were closing that I heard a faint rustling sound, like leaves scattering across the beams. The temperature plunged. I shivered.

Something was wrong.

Struggling to stay awake, I peeked through heavy

eyelids. A figure moved into my line of vision, but it was too late. The sleeping powder dragged me under and shrouded my final thought in a dreamy fog.

***

I woke to darkness.

The grandfather clock chimed, and I pressed my fingers into my eyelids to relieve my blurred vision. It was freezing! With a shudder, I glanced at the fireplace to find the embers still glowing. It shouldn't be this cold. My breath expelled in white puffs made visible by a strip of moonlight.

A strange sensation flowed through my body as I remembered the eerie feeling of being watched before falling asleep. Was someone inside the shop? My heart pounded faster when the clock continued to chime. At the twelfth bell, it stopped.

I held my breath. Nothing moved. A strangled laugh caught in my throat. I was being ridiculous. Then, from behind, a bottle dropped from a shelf and rolled across the wooden beams. I froze, too afraid to look.

"Is someone there?" My voice cracked. Fear grew like vines around my ankles, rooting me to the floor. A burning pain sliced through my palm. The tattooed symbols were glowing.

"Help me," came a soft whisper.

My chest constricted. I turned toward the rasping sound. Unable to blink, I watched a shimmering figure float closer. The woman's hair flowed around her face as if she were underwater. She wore a ball gown studded with silver beading. I knew that gown. I knew that face. I finally blinked, hoping the specter would vanish, and was horrified yet slightly relieved when she didn't.

"Ella? Is that you?"

The woman nodded. Her image wavered as she drifted into the shaft of moonlight, almost becoming one with the bright beam.

Her lips parted, and she whispered again, "I need your help."

# Chapter 6

"**O**pen up!"

Vivian's door vibrated where I pounded my hands against it. Eventually, light appeared at the window, and she arrived rubbing sleep from her eyes. The latch turned with an audible click, and I charged into the parlor, sending Vivian back on her heels.

"What are you doing here? It's after midnight." She tightened the belt on her silk robe and stifled a yawn.

I ignored her question and searched the shadows. Had Ella followed me? My muscles burned, and my side ached from running the entire way into town. I hadn't handled the situation at my shop well. Then again, what was the proper reaction when you came face-to-face with a dead girl? Fainting into a pile on the floor had been a real concern. I might be best friends with a medium, but I'd never actually seen a ghost.

"What are you looking for?"

Pushing through the beaded curtain, I stopped. Vivian bumped into me.

"Not what—who. Over there."

She stilled as her gaze landed on the ghostly woman dressed in a ball gown. "Is that who I think it is?"

"That's Ella Lockwood, the girl I told you about."

"I don't understand. Can you see her?"

A hint of hysteria tinged my voice. "Not only can I see her, she spoke to me. An actual ghost, see-through and everything! This isn't happening. I need to sit down, but she's too close to the chairs."

Vivian pressed a slender hand to her throat. "She can't hurt you. The poor thing is more scared of you than you are her."

"You seriously underestimate the horror of seeing dead people," I whispered. "What do we do? Make her go away."

Vivian rolled her eyes. "Tess, you can't snap your fingers and get rid of a ghost. They have to leave on their own when they're ready. My entire line of work is based around that concept."

"That's why I'm here." I ground my teeth together. "Do the thing you do with your customers."

"It's not that simple." She approached Ella slowly, holding up her hands as if nearing a skittish animal. "Excuse me... Ella, right? You need to walk toward the light. Everything will be okay."

Ella stared blankly at us. Her form was a faint flicker in the dark room. She gestured with her pale hands.

"There isn't any."

Vivian's brow creased. "There's no light?"

Ella shook her head, sending her blonde curls

swirling in the air.

I tapped Vivian on the shoulder. "Is that bad?"

"It's not ideal," she responded under her breath, pulling me aside while Ella drifted over the floorboards, intrigued by a shelf of colored medallions. I watched out of the corner of my eye, afraid to lose sight of her.

"She has unfinished business, doesn't she?" I asked.

"Murder victims usually do. A light won't appear until she's found peace. What I don't understand is, how can you see her? It's rare for someone who isn't a medium. Often, people can sense a spirit, and we attribute that kind of experience to a haunting—but it's unusual for non-mediums to see them, let alone hear them speak."

I opened my palm, revealing the ring's symbols. "This might be why. It's a spell marker. They're supposed to fade when an illusion does, but Ella's was cut short. If she died while under my spell, it could explain why there's a connection between us."

"That makes sense." Vivian bit her lip in thought. "A medium's purpose is to help the dead. Witches help the living. But the lines got blurred, and your magical link wasn't severed with her death. Your connection might be what's keeping her tethered to this side—which means, if you want her gone, you'll have to help her...again."

Another complication. Between Argus, the detective, and now, Ella, I was giving black cats and broken mirrors a run for their money.

"When did she first appear?"

"Midnight, after the final chime."

Vivian nodded. "Time of death. It's when her ghostly form will be strongest. As the night wears on, she'll fade, but she'll reappear once her essence grows strong again."

This was insane. "So, what does she need to cross over?" I asked anxiously. "A chance to say goodbye to her family? A letter to her lover? What?" A frigid chill flowed through my body, and I let out a strangled cry as Ella's haunting face appeared inches from mine.

"I need you to find my killer."

Vivian chuckled. "You asked." Moving away from us, she picked up a tea set and placed it on the séance table. Pulling out the chair next to her, she patted the cushion. "Here, Ella, you can levitate on this one." She poured herself a cup of cold tea and added a spoonful of sugar, leaving mine unsweetened before nudging it across the table.

A witch, a medium, and a ghost try to solve a murder. It sounded like the beginning of a joke, yet that was what Vivian expected us to do. I took the final chair with a reluctant frown, and Ella's gaze connected with mine. I felt a pang of sympathy. Why had she been killed? Was it a random act, or something more sinister? Knowing the answer wouldn't make the outcome any better. A woman's life had been cut short. Her plans for the future, all her hopes and dreams, stolen by a faceless monster.

Vivian rapped her knuckles on the table, bringing

our gathering to order. "Ella, I know you must be frightened and probably a little confused. My name is Vivian James, and I'm a medium. I work with ghosts who find themselves unable to cross over. We can help you transition to the other side. It won't be easy, but we'll do everything we can to simplify your journey."

Ella rubbed her bare shoulders. She appeared so vulnerable hunched over the table. "I feel strange. It's like waking from a dream and not knowing where you are."

"Tell us everything you remember," Vivian said.

Ella's brow crinkled. "I hardly remember anything. There are holes where memories should go." She paused, arranging her thoughts. "It's odd. I know what I have to do, but I don't know how to do it."

Vivian nodded and moved her chair closer. "That's perfectly normal. A ghost's memory is intertwined with their death. The more horrific, the less they can recall. I've seen ghosts who can't remember their names, and others who can recite what they ate for breakfast when they were ten."

Ella closed her eyes. "I remember flashes, beautiful gowns, dancing..." Her lips trembled as she continued. "A clock tower, fear...so much fear." Her eyes opened, and they were filled with confusion. "How did I die?"

"You drowned," I said in a hushed tone.

"Oh, I don't remember."

"You probably feel disassociated, like your death

happened to someone else. That's normal too. It doesn't mean we can't help," Vivian said.

"That's right," I added, trying to sound reassuring. "The royal family assigned a detective to your case. He seems very..." I paused. What was I supposed to say? I couldn't tell her what I really thought. Besides, my feelings for the man had no bearing on his qualifications. "He seems very capable."

"He does?" Hope colored Ella's voice, making it rise in pitch.

"Mostly." I fumbled for something to add and questioned my sanity. What did I know about solving a murder? I wasn't good at *my* job, let alone someone else's, and yet Ella's circumstances struck a chord with me. She needed my help now more than ever. I couldn't turn my back on her, even if the urge to stick my head in the sand seemed like the safer bet. An odd fascination gripped me: What would happen if I saw this through? I had to admit, I was scared to find out. Everyone always told you to face your problems, but no one ever mentioned what to do if you failed at that too.

"You know, there is one thing I remember." Ella smiled, the action brightening her features, making her appear almost human again.

Vivian latched onto this in excitement. "What is it?"

Ella pointed at me, and dread blossomed in my chest. "Were you able to get all the pumpkin pulp off your lawn?" she asked.

Droplets sputtered onto the tabletop as Vivian

choked on her tea. "Pumpkin pulp?"

Ella's grin widened. "Tessa tried to turn a pumpkin into a carriage, and it exploded. There were seeds and goo everywhere."

It figured that would be her one remaining memory. The only witness to my garden mortification, and even the erasure of death couldn't keep it hidden.

I pursed my lips in irritation. "Yes, well, most of it's still there. I've been busy."

"I see." Vivian fiddled with the sleeves of her robe, but I knew she was trying to restrain a giggle.

"Let's stay focused on the murder, shall we?"

"Whose? Ella's, or the pumpkin's?" Vivian teased.

My eyes narrowed into slits. "Ella's."

Vivian winked and pushed out of her seat. "In that case, there might be a way you can help solve Ella's murder and get the money you need to pay Argus."

"Don't forget my fines."

"I thought you had enough for those." Vivian crossed her arms over her chest.

"I did, but I had a run-in with Argus after I left your shop. Also, fun fact, your wig was useless. It's now ruined and smells like a wet animal."

Vivian tsk'd and glanced at Ella. "That was my favorite wig." She dug into a drawer on the other side of the room and pulled out a scroll. "A royal messenger delivered this today. I'm supposed to hang it in the window." Unfurling it on the table, she placed a candle at each end. Ink-stained calligraphy covered the parchment. I read to the bottom and realized

SPELLBOUND AFTER MIDNIGHT

Vivian's intentions.

"You want me to collect the reward money?"

"Exactly. The royal family is offering a fortune to anyone who helps capture Ella's killer. That person could be you. There's just one part you won't like."

I drummed my fingers on the table. It wasn't a bad idea. The money would solve my problems, and Ella would find the peace she needed to cross over.

"What's the part I won't like?"

"You'll need help from the royal detective."

I slammed my teacup against the table. "Absolutely not!" Dark liquid spilled over the rim, pooling onto the glass. "I have no intention of asking that man for anything. He's smug, thinks he knows everything, and gets a distinct pleasure from ordering me around."

Ella bit the side of her lip. "I thought you said he was capable."

"Capable, my foot. He's—"

"Your only option," Vivian cut in. She checked items off on her fingers. "Let's see, you don't have access to the castle, so you can't visit the crime scene. He's already suspicious of you, so the moment he gets wind you're questioning suspects, he'll be even more suspicious." She wriggled her third finger. "And you have literally no experience solving crime. None."

"Oh, is that all?" I drawled, sliding my fingertip through the puddle of tea. The fragrant liquid bubbled at my touch and evaporated. Ella's eyes widened at the simple spell. "I have a few cards up my sleeve.

Detective Chambers doesn't have magic at his disposal."

Vivian smirked and pointed at my neckline. "Neither do you. Not good magic anyway."

I glanced at the tea stain soaking the front of my dress. Damn. I'd crossed an evaporation spell with a relocation spell. The tips of my ears heated as I brushed uselessly at the wet fabric. So much for proving a point. Professional help might be warranted after all.

"All right. How do I convince Detective Chambers to let me investigate the case? He won't welcome me with open arms and spill his secrets."

Neither woman answered. The clock on the mantel ticked off the uncomfortable seconds. Vivian squirmed in her seat and rubbed the back of her neck. She had nothing.

"Well? This was your brilliant idea, Viv." I slumped in my chair.

Ella broke the silence. "Use me."

"What do you mean?" I asked.

"I may not remember much, but he doesn't have to know that. There's got to be some detail they didn't release to the public. When he realizes you can see my ghost, he'll have to let you help." She drifted into a pool of candlelight, and her gown sparkled, giving off an ethereal glow. The hemline ended at her ankles, where a crystal shoe poked out from underneath. A single shoe.

My gaze snagged on the translucent slipper. I recalled the details Sylvia had mentioned. She'd discussed the fountain, and the rose left between Ella's fingers, but nothing about a missing slipper.

"I have an idea." I pointed to Ella's feet. "You're only wearing one shoe. The other must have come off during your struggle with the killer."

"Do you think that's important?" Ella lifted the hem of her gown and stuck out her bare foot.

"It might be if they didn't find it at the scene. Either way, it's information I can use when I visit the detective."

Vivian looked skeptical.

"What? You said I needed Derrick's help, so why the face?"

"It's just, telling people—especially people in authority—you see ghosts doesn't always go the way you'd expect. He might react poorly and..." Her voice faded, and she bowed her head. I knew that look. I'd seen it before when we were younger and Vivian had learned not everyone appreciated her ghostly calling. It was a lesson that still gave her nightmares.

"He might think I'm crazy?"

Vivian fidgeted with the handle of her teacup, unable to meet my eyes. "He could have you committed. There are worse places than prison."

"It won't come to that." My gut churned. Our entire plan rested on the whims of a man who already found me lacking. There was a high chance I'd be leaving his office in some form of restraint. I didn't like the odds. Not one bit.

# Chapter 7

Sunshine glinted off the arched windows of the Royal Agency. The rays of light did little to improve the grim stone facade and iron gate separating the building from the crowded street.

I stood in front of the bars and pulled my cloak tighter around my body. A chilly wind carried brittle leaves through the air and numbed my exposed fingers while I gathered the courage to go inside.

Ella had vanished before dawn, and I'd remained at Vivian's trying to get a few hours of sleep. Not that it did any good. I'd tossed and turned, plagued with nightmares that dissipated like smoke when I opened my eyes. The plans we'd made in the dark felt flawed in the daylight.

"Good morning, Miss Daniels. Are you here to see Detective Chambers?"

I located the voice, spotting Abrams walking toward the entrance. He rubbed bloodshot eyes, a sign his night shifts were taking a toll. His uniform was wrinkled yet clean, and he tugged the cap from his head, twisting the brim in his hands as he gave a weak smile.

"Yes. I need to speak to him about my fines."

Abrams nodded and leaned closer, lowering his tone. "He's a stickler when it comes to the law, but I'm surprised he came down so hard on you. Others would have turned a blind eye."

"You don't say?" Irritation shot up my spine. What was it about me that made Derrick so prickly? I'd never met anyone who ran as hot and cold as he did. One minute, he was laying on the charm, and the next, he was accusing me of being a charlatan.

Abrams grew serious and furrowed his brow. "About last night... I shouldn't have revealed as much as I did. It's not a good trait for an aspiring detective. I'd appreciate if you didn't let Detective Chambers know. He'll have my head."

A flush colored the tips of his ears, a mixture of embarrassment and the cold. I realized we were both a little intimidated by the man. Lucky for him, I needed every ally I could get, and if keeping secrets from Derrick was our common ground, I'd take it.

"Your secret is safe with me. We wouldn't want to darken his mood any more than it already is."

"No, we wouldn't want that." Abrams chuckled and pushed open the gate, making the iron bars whine in protest. He gestured for me to go first.

I swallowed my nerves and climbed the stone staircase. Inside, a narrow hallway opened into a waiting area. The room teemed with people. Shouts competing for control echoed into the rafters as a pair of angry merchants fought over stolen merchandise. Their fingers jabbed the air, inches from a street urchin's smirking face. The kid polished an apple on his threadbare jacket, then crunched his jagged teeth through the fruit. It was a defiant gesture, one that sent the merchants lunging for the pilfered apple.

Abrams nudged me past the commotion toward a wide desk that served as the entry point to the back offices. A silver-haired woman glanced up from a ledger. Her stern features broke into a grin when she spotted Abrams, and her eyes crinkled around the edges.

"Morning, Estelle." Abrams leaned an elbow on her desk and returned a flirtatious smile. "And how is my favorite gatekeeper today? Keeping the riffraff in line?"

Estelle preened and smoothed a lock of hair that had slipped from her bun. "I do what I can."

I glanced at the alluded riffraff, none of whom were in line.

Abrams feigned ignorance, unconcerned by the chaos. "Is Detective Chambers in his office?"

"He's finishing up a meeting. You can go back and wait."

He flashed her another smile, then ushered me down the hallway. We passed doors on both sides with muffled sounds leaking from beneath the frames. I walked slowly, each step twisting the knot in my stomach. My plan sifted in my mind, becoming less appealing by the second. What if he did have me committed? I ground to a halt, but it was too late. Abrams had stopped and was holding open an office door.

I peered inside, unsurprised by the clean, utilitarian atmosphere. A massive desk sat along one wall, its surface void of personal effects. Instead, papers were stacked and ordered in strict lines, and a tin plate disclosing Derrick's prestigious title had been polished to a glistening sheen. I inspected his bookcase, running my index finger along the shelf as he had done to mine. It came away clean. Not a speck of dust.

"Detective Chambers certainly likes order," I mused, frowning when I noticed the titles had been shelved alphabetically. I'd never sorted anything alphabetically in my life. The stark difference in our personalities was on full display. Maybe it wasn't a good strategy to tell a man who was such a pragmatist that I could see his murder victim's ghost. I might as well put the straitjacket on myself.

Abrams scratched the morning stubble covering his jaw. "He likes things a certain way. Function and discipline are key." He paused, but whatever memory clouded his features vanished at the sound of a scuffle from the hallway. Someone grunted, followed by the dense thud of a fist meeting flesh.

"Wait here." He indicated a chair in front of Derrick's desk.

I obeyed as Abrams slipped from the office, closing the door behind him. The disturbance escalated, and slurred voices echoed in the hall before going quiet.

A minute passed, then two. My gaze darted over the desk, and my hands folded neatly in my lap. The urge to snoop intensified. If we were keeping score, Derrick had snooped through my things first. He might have had the tedious fact of probable cause on his side, but I had a reason too. Curiosity.

I checked the door, making certain it was firmly closed, then scooted closer to the desk. Numerous cases formed the stacked piles—robberies, assaults, and a handful of missing people—but nothing on Ella's investigation. I thumbed through the papers just to be sure.

A door slammed in the hall. The jarring sound made me knock a stack of folders onto the floor. Cursing, I slid to my knees and scooped up the scattered documents. They were out of order, but figuring out Derrick's filing system looked impossible. I arranged them as best I could, then noticed one I'd missed. Pushing his chair aside, I crawled under the desk, stretching my fingers to snag the corner of the file.

"Agh!"

My forehead smacked a blunt object protruding from the desk. I hissed in a breath and reached for the evil contraption, running my fingers along its dull edges. No buttons. No holes. Whatever was inside was self-contained.

I was about to pull away when I felt a small groove where the wood met the desktop. Wrapping my fingers around the narrow chamber, I slid it forward. Something cold and metal dropped into my palm.

A key.

Looked like I wasn't the only one with secrets. I

wriggled out and held up the small bronze key. It had to fit something in his office. My gaze wandered the room.

*If I were a smug detective, where would I hide something important?*

His desk drawers weren't locked, and I didn't see any trunks or strongboxes lying around. Finally settling on what looked like a closet on the other side of the room, I climbed to my feet and held my breath to listen for movement in the hallway. Enough time had passed, and Derrick or Abrams could return at any moment. Still, I had time to put the key back and pretend I'd never discovered it. It was the right thing to do.

I laughed. Who was I kidding? Derrick hadn't wasted a second storming my basement and using what he'd found to leverage fines against me. It was only fair I returned the favor.

With a final glance over my shoulder, I slid the key into the lock and turned it until the tumblers disengaged. The door opened, and I swung it wide on silent hinges, revealing a dark, windowless room. It was impossible to see inside, so I searched Derrick's desk for a candle, finding one near the inkwell.

Balling my fist, I murmured a spell and splayed my fingers, sending a spark of magic over the wick. The flame caught and wavered as I brought the candle toward the entrance of the room. Its light cast a glow over a long table, illuminating a cyclone of papers and case files. The methodical order in the other room didn't transcend into this chamber. It was as if a different person occupied both spaces, one rigorous, the other erratic.

Worn journals were stacked along the edge of the table, their covers coated in a layer of dust. I picked one up and flipped through its musty pages, noting the elegant handwriting inside. Returning it carefully, I lifted the light to examine a row of boxes against the wall. Beside them was a cot with a single pillow. A melted candle and more folders sat on a small table, which I moved closer to, running my hand over a wool blanket. An image of Derrick poring over case files deep into the night flashed through my mind. How many nights had he spent here? Judging by the tangled blanket and well-read files, more than a few.

On the other side of the room was a long board affixed to the wall. Notes were push-pinned into the surface. I held the candle higher and moved down the length, slowing as I reached the end, where a trio of roses hung upside down, suspended by their stems. I brushed my fingers over the dry, brittle petals. The scent had long since dissipated, and all but one had turned brown with age. A slip of paper with a handwritten name had been tacked next to each flower.

The third rose was fresh, its stem a wealth of green thorns. They'd found Ella with a rose tucked between her fingers. I read the names pinned near each stem: *Sophie, Jane,* and *Ella.* My hand trembled, and a bead of wax dripped onto my wrist. I barely felt the burn.

"You can't be in here."

Startled, I dropped the candle. Its flame sputtered as it hit the floor, plunging the room into darkness.

Derrick's large frame loomed in the doorway. I reached for the wall, hoping to orient myself, but I misjudged the distance, and my hip slammed the edge of the table. The stack of journals toppled, sending up a cloud of dust. I sneezed, and my foot rolled over the fallen candle, making me lurch and brace for impact.

Before I could hit the hard floor, hands wrapped around my waist. Derrick adjusted his hold, and I landed against the firm wall of his chest, his palm cupping the back of my head.

"Relax. I've got you."

Easier said than done. The low timbre of his voice sent a shiver snaking through my body. How was I supposed to relax with every inch of him pressed against me? A tingling tickled my nose, but I wasn't quick enough to pull away and sneezed twice in rapid-fire into his shirt. The third sneeze rammed my nose into his sternum. Horrified, I prayed for death.

Derrick's chest rumbled. Was he laughing? This wasn't even remotely funny. I'd almost broken my nose, not to mention my neck, and to make matters worse, I was enjoying the way his fingers sifted through my hair. The gentle pressure felt wonderful against my scalp. Did he realize he was doing it? I was afraid to ask because he might stop.

His arms tightened around me, and he backed us

slowly out of the room. Bright light flooded my vision as his office came into focus. With a tilt of my head, our eyes locked, and for a moment, neither of us moved. All traces of laughter vanished from his face, replaced by an intensity that heated my skin. I'd expected anger, not this breathless tension that hung thick in the air.

He blinked, and the moment evaporated. Derrick's hands loosened around my waist, and his lips formed a grim line. The anger I'd expected had finally appeared.

"That's twice I've caught you breaking into something."

I held up my finger. "To be fair, the first time, I didn't actually break anything. You startled me before I could. So, technically, this is the second time you've startled *me*."

His eyes narrowed, but I stood my ground under his impressive glare. I was starting to think it was mostly for show and beneath his gruff exterior was something else entirely. There was only one way to find out.

"We need to talk, Detective."

"About how I caught you going through my locked evidence room? I could have you arrested."

His threats had no effect. I moved closer, smoothing his shoulders and straightening the lapels of his expensive jacket. His pupils were wide as they followed my bold exploration. I curbed a grin at his comical expression. Apparently, he was used to people cowering beneath his glare, not ruffling his feathers.

"That all sounds very familiar, but no. We need to talk about whether anyone else knows."

He crossed his arms over his chest, putting a muscled barrier between him and my wandering fingers. "Does anyone else know what, Miss Daniels?"

I leaned in and whispered, "About the roses the killer leaves behind. I counted three. Ella wasn't the first victim."

# Chapter 8

"It's not what you think."

"It's not?" I scoffed and held up three fingers. "Three roses. Three dead girls. It's exactly what I think. They all have the same killer, one who leaves a calling card."

Derrick scrubbed a hand through his hair. He looked exhausted. Beneath his tailored jacket, his linen shirt was wrinkled and unbuttoned at the top. It seemed out of character for him, the same way the table in his evidence room overflowed with papers and files, a chaotic distraction to the perfect shell of his outer office. Maybe he wasn't one-sided after all.

He walked around his desk straightening the folders I'd knocked over. "They're just roses, Miss Daniels. A potential lead, nothing more." Reaching underneath, he found where I'd taken the key and held out his hand. "I'd like my key back."

It was still in the door. I moved to retrieve it.

"You don't believe that, or you wouldn't have those flowers tacked up like killer trophies. Who are the other girls? I won't tell anyone. I promise."

A condescending smile curved his lips. He studied me in a way that felt familiar, always searching, waiting for a tell.

"A promise from a witch? Is that any good?"

*Ouch.* His barb hit, leaving its mark on my ego where other scars lived.

"You don't trust witches?"

"Would you trust someone who can spin an illusion with a wave of her hand?"

Resting my knuckles on his desk, I leaned forward and held his gaze. "No, but I wouldn't trust someone so quick to judge either. A cynic who only sees what he wants to see." I ran my finger over his nameplate and spun it around to face him. "Like this man."

The confident smile leached from his face. He moved the nameplate out of my reach.

"Miss Daniels, let's be clear—"

"Call me Tessa. If we're going to work together, there's no need to be formal."

His hand froze mid-air. He might have stopped breathing. Had I shocked him into an early grave? Working with me wasn't that inconceivable.

"Miss Dan—"

"Tessa."

His eyes closed while he gathered his patience. I had time. Pulling a chair closer, I sat down and arranged my skirts, then hooked my ankle around the leg of his desk. I wasn't going anywhere on my own. When he opened his eyes, I blinked up at him, the picture of innocence.

"Miss Daniels, I don't know what you think is happening here, but we're not working together. Settle your fines and go. Forget what you saw in the evidence room, and if you don't, and I hear you shared a single shred of information about the case, I will have you locked up where no amount of magic will set you free. For real this time."

Seriously? What was with this man and his jail-house threats?

"About my fines." I picked a phantom piece of lint from my skirt and flicked it into the air. "I'm short on funds and can't pay them, which is why I'd like to offer you a proposal."

His face was easy to read. He regretted confiscating my potions. Hell, he might even regret visiting my shop altogether. Too bad for him.

"I'm offering to help with Ella's case in exchange for clearing my fines."

"No."

"I think you're being short-sighted because of your dislike for me."

"My dislike for you?" He sank into the chair behind his desk and ran a hand over his face. His exhaustion seemed to increase, as if whatever lurked in his mind weighed heavily on him. "Tessa, that's not..." His voice faded when he realized he'd used my given name. The victory was small, but it was mine.

"See, was that so hard? As I was saying, Derr—" His gaze shot to mine, darkening, daring me to finish that sentence. "I mean, *Detective*. Your dislike for me aside, I have information that can help find Ella's killer, and unless your intent is to continue hanging roses on your evidence board, I suggest you hear me out."

"You have information you didn't divulge during our meeting the other day?" He pinned me to the seat with an accusatory glare.

"It's new information, and I'm not sure I would call what we shared the other day a meeting. It felt more like an interrogation."

"You're observant, I'll give you that." He leaned back in his chair and waved his hand with cool indifference. "All right, Miss Daniels, I'll humor you. What makes you think I'd let you anywhere near this case?"

And we were back to surnames. So much for small victories.

I pushed out of the chair and paced the room. Now that I had his attention, I was reluctant to start. Should I lead with Ella's ghost, or ease into it? I glanced at the door. Maybe I should make a run for it instead. It might be a coward's exit, but it held a certain appeal.

I cleared my throat and smoothed my damp palms over my skirt. "Are you aware that some people can see things others can't?"

"Miss Daniels," he warned.

"Answer the question."

"Do you mean, spirits?"

"Yes."

Derrick rolled his eyes as he rounded the desk. Not the reaction I'd hoped for.

"Time's up."

"What? You won't let me explain?" I scooted to the other end of the room. If I had to make him chase me around the office, I would.

"I'm not interested in ghost stories. If you insist, Abrams will take your statement then escort you home."

I stamped my foot, anger at his curt dismissal running through my veins. "I don't need an escort home. I need you to listen. Just because you don't believe in something doesn't mean it doesn't exist. The world is filled with unexplainable things. If you would only open your eyes, you'd see them. And then, maybe, you'd have a shot at solving this case."

He stalked closer. I backed up, bumping into the bookcase.

"You don't listen, do you? This is a murder case. You may have built your living around tricking people into believing you have some mystical ability, but magic? Ghosts? There's no place for them in this investigation, and there's no place for you."

"You're wrong, Detective." I jabbed my finger into his chest. This had become about so much more than eliminating my fines and claiming a reward. Principles were involved now. My reputation as a witch, and this damned desire to make him see me as something other than a con artist who dabbled in potions. "I can help solve this case because I have a link to the victim. A link no one in your investigation has. You need me."

"Hardly."

My patience spent, I blurted out my reasoning. "Ella's ghost visited me last night, and I can prove it.

"How?" He crowded me against the bookcase, but

I refused to back down until I'd finished.

"She was missing her shoe. A glass slipper. None of the reports have that information. If you didn't find it at the crime scene then the killer must have taken it. Find the slipper, you'll find your killer."

I charged past him, clipping his arm with my shoulder. The man was infuriating. Vivian had been wrong. I didn't need his help to investigate the case; I could solve it on my own, collect the reward, and shove it in his face. He'd take me seriously then. Maybe I'd buy the agency and use his office to grow fungus. Really smelly fungus.

A small part of me, the delusional part, had hoped he might be different, that he would see beyond what everyone else saw: the inept witch unable to rise to her true potential. If I was being honest with myself—which was rare but did happen—I wanted him to see me. Not the witch, just me.

"Tessa, wait." Derrick placed his hand on my shoulder. The warm, solid touch and the pleading note in his voice made me pause, melting some of my anger like wax pooling in the bottom of a candlestick.

But it would take more than that.

My dramatic exit lasted two seconds before I crashed into a human-sized wall. The man steadied me as I craned my neck and stared into a pair of dark brown eyes. He smiled, and I swore, it was the most charming thing I'd ever seen. He had a clean-shaven face that accentuated the square cut of his jawline, and thick, jet-black hair that looked tousled from the wind. I could pay my debt with his coat alone. Dove-gray, it was made of the finest material, trimmed with gold thread on the cuffs and seams.

"Are you all right?" he asked, keeping his hands around my arms.

"Excuse me, Detective." I heard Estelle, the silver-haired receptionist's voice through the haze of the handsome man's smile. "His Royal Highness is here to see you."

*Hold the horses and stay awhile.* Prince Marcus of Ever was touching me—and then, just like that, he wasn't.

Derrick seized my upper arm and tugged me out of the prince's reach. I stumbled against his side, and he pressed his hand to the small of my back to keep me there. The move earned him a side-glare.

"Do you have to spoil everything?" I muttered.

"Yes."

"Careful, Detective. Your dislike for me is showing again."

"I don't dislike you," he snapped. His eyes closed, and he exhaled a long breath, looking like a man who'd reached his breaking point. I *almost* felt bad.

"I'm not interrupting, am I?" the prince asked, quizzical.

"No, Your Highness. Miss Daniels was just leaving." Derrick nudged me, but I dug my heels in. This was my chance. I might not have convinced Derrick, but the prince held a higher rank, and if I convinced him, Derrick would have to accept me.

"Actually, Your Highness," I fumbled through a

half-decent curtsy, "I'm here to offer my services with the Lockwood investigation." I removed a small slip of paper from a satchel at my waist. It read *Daniels Curses and Cures* in ink that sparkled when caught by the light.

The prince accepted the card, and his thumb brushed the inside of my wrist. I frowned, not feeling the same intimate sensation as when Derrick had held me in the evidence room. What a shame. Prince Marcus seemed to actually like me.

He read my name and nodded in recognition. "Ah, you're the witch. Your mother was Amelia Daniels, wasn't she?"

"Yes. Did you know her?"

"No, I didn't have the pleasure, but I remember stories as a child about how she cured the kingdom's plague."

My smile dimmed. Little known fact, and something that never made it into those stories: I started the plague. It was an accident and partly Vivian's fault. She'd dared me to curse a boy who'd been teasing her for seeing ghosts. Unfortunately, the curse was contagious. Things devolved from there.

"My mother was an amazing healer. She saved many lives that day."

"I'm sorry for your loss."

"Thank you, Your Highness."

Derrick's fingers flexed against my back. It almost felt like a caress.

"I didn't realize your mother had passed. I'm sorry."

I murmured, "You don't know much about me, Detective."

"I'm learning."

His words set off a flutter in my stomach. Would he like what he learned about me? And why did it matter so much that he did?

We moved into Derrick's office, and Prince Marcus tapped my card.

"Was this your idea, Detective? It's brilliant. Consulting with a member of the supernatural profession is unorthodox but not unheard of. The sooner we close this case, the better. The kingdom's in a panic, and the Lockwoods deserve justice. I know I'm devastated this happened, and on palace grounds, no less."

"Is it true that you danced with Ella, Your Highness? Do you remember meeting her?" I asked.

Prince Marcus hesitated. "Yes, I do remember her. I danced with a lot of women that night, but there was something special about Ella. I wish there was a way I could have prevented what happened."

I felt the same. It was strange looking back at the choices we made. Could we have changed anything? Impossible to know.

"Tessa—" Prince Marcus paused. "May I call you Tessa?"

"Please do." I shot Derrick a look.

"I believe you might have skills we haven't thought to use. We need to examine this case from every angle."

Derrick shook his head. "It's too dangerous, Your

Highness. Miss Daniels doesn't have any experience."

The prince frowned. "There is an element of risk, but I'm sure if you watch over her, she'll prove to be an asset."

*Hear that, Detective?* An asset. If witches could fly, I'd be in the rafters.

"I'll do my best to help in any way possible. It's an honor to serve you and the kingdom in this manner." I caught the remnants of a scowl on Derrick's face before he cleared the emotion. "Don't worry, Detective. I'll mostly be an observer, you won't know I'm there."

"Impossible," he mumbled.

I shrugged. He wasn't wrong. I'd inserted myself into the case, and I planned on being a prominent fixture. After all, they'd need to know who to thank when we found the killer.

Prince Marcus clasped my hands. "Welcome aboard, Tessa. If there is anything you need, please let me know."

The scowl returned in full force to Derrick's lips. "Your Highness, I apologize for cutting this short, but I have witness interviews to conduct today."

I cleared my throat loud enough to be heard across the room. Derrick clenched his jaw.

"Miss Daniels, I hope you can join me."

Prince Marcus winked and released my hands. "Yes, I won't keep you. I'm on my way to a meeting with the director."

"Well, he has all my notes and can give you an update on where we stand."

"Excellent. Tessa, it was good to meet you." Prince Marcus inclined his head and moved to the door, closing it gently behind him. You could hear a pin drop in his wake.

I let the silence extend, feigning interest in a speck of dirt under my fingernail.

"Since you appealed to the prince and got your way, there are going to be ground rules."

Dirt forgotten, I tensed as Derrick moved closer. "I expected as much."

"Think you can handle it?"

"I can handle any rule you throw at me."

"We'll see. Rule number one, you're not allowed to investigate on your own."

I narrowed my eyes. "You'll tell me everything you know about the case, including the roses and the other girls?"

Derrick nodded.

"Okay. Always stay by your side, got it." When he moved another step closer, I smelled the scent of his skin and the woodsy cologne that made me want to breathe deeper until it filled my lungs.

"Rule number two, keep your ghostly encounters between us. No one else can know."

"My friend Vivian already knows, but she's a medium and can see Ella too."

Derrick sighed and rubbed the bridge of his nose. "Don't you have any normal friends?"

"Define normal."

He ignored my question and stated rule number three. "Trust no one. This is the highest-profile murder investigation in the kingdom. Anyone and everyone is a suspect."

I nudged him playfully in the arm. "I bet you thought I was a suspect at first, didn't you?"

He blinked, his face deadpan. I squirmed and scratched the back of my neck.

"You did, didn't you?"

"I follow my own rules."

"Well, I only have one rule, Detective. When you're with me, you call me Tessa." I snapped my fingers. "And keep an open mind about my abilities. No more calling me a con artist to my face."

"That sounds like two rules."

"It is. I'm adding one."

"Deal." He held out his hand, and I slipped my palm against his. Like the first time, a flare of heat shot up my arm. Derrick was right about one thing: we were playing a dangerous game, one I had little experience in. Unease trickled through me. Between battling wits and trying to ignore a growing flare of attraction, finding the killer might be the easy part.

# Chapter 9

*Five days and countless interviews later...*

**M**y head bobbed into my chest.

"Did you get that, Miss Daniels?"

I jerked my eyes open again and caught the notebook before it slid off my lap. "Ah, yes." Checking my notes, I began hastily, "Let's see... First, you danced with Mr. Raymund. He went to get you a glass of champagne, and then, you danced with Sir Thomas. You stopped for a plate of toasted figs, and last, you spoke to the Drummonds about a new carriage purchase. Was there anything else?"

"No, that was everything. Let me ring for more tea, and I'll tell you about later in the evening." Miss Lancaster strode toward the bell pull.

Unlike me, the woman's grandmother was allowed to give in to temptation and had fallen asleep in her chair. A light snore whistled from her nose, and every once in a while, she mumbled something about the good old days.

I glowered at Derrick. "I know what you're doing."

"What am I doing?" He stretched his legs in front of him and folded his arms over his chest.

"Don't play innocent. You're dragging me around the kingdom trying to bore me off the case with useless interviews. You don't attend half of them and then quiz me on my notes afterward. You're just waiting for me to leave to start doing the real detective work. I'm onto you."

He shrugged. The nerve! My fingers itched to wipe the bland smile off his face. I'd been subjected to nothing but cool disregard from him for days, and it was beginning to grate on me. After the heated looks in our early encounters, his lack of interest made me want to test his patience, get under his skin, affect him in some way.

"Do you honestly think I'd go to such lengths to make you resign?"

"I do."

"And is it working?"

"No, and avoiding me won't help. What are you afraid of, Detective?" My knee brushed the outside of his thigh, and I felt him tense, his bland smile faltering. "Are you worried I may prove useful? That you might enjoy working with me? Maybe you'll decide to keep me."

"You're delusional." His words were strained.

"And you're in denial." I flashed him a smug smile as Miss Lancaster returned to her seat.

"Where was I? Have I told you about my stroll through the garden?"

Clearing the rust from his throat, Derrick turned his attention back to her. "What time would that have been, Miss Lancaster?"

"Early in the evening. I'd say around nine." She clasped her hands in her lap and blinked coquettishly at Derrick. *Oh, for the love of spell books.* If boredom didn't make me want to gouge my eyes out, having to watch another simpering female drool over Derrick would.

I exhaled an irritated breath. "Let's skip ahead. Did you see Ella? The prince? Anything relevant to the case at all, Miss Lancaster?"

This was insane. Nearly a week in, and I had nothing. I wasn't any closer to finding Ella's killer and collecting the reward. I couldn't very well tell Argus I'd need more time because every witness went starry-eyed in the face of the famed detective. We needed to move this along.

"Actually, I believe I did witness something."

My back straightened. I hadn't expected that. Didn't these people realize they were supposed to lead with the relevant details?

A servant arrived with the tea, and I nearly groaned while waiting for it to be poured. Miss Lancaster took a dainty sip and offered Derrick the plate of biscuits. He declined. My stomach growled, but she'd already set them aside.

"You were saying, Miss Lancaster?"

"Yes, while I was strolling through the gardens, one of my ruby hairpins must have come loose. I went out again later to find it, and that's when I saw Ella."

"Did you notice the time?" I asked.

Miss Lancaster reached for a biscuit and chewed

thoughtfully. My mouth watered, and I pressed my hand against my stomach as if it would prevent another embarrassing rumble.

"It was shortly before midnight. I remember because of the clock tower in the courtyard. Ella was sitting alone on a bench, and she kept looking up at it. She appeared to be waiting for someone."

Derrick reached across the table and placed two biscuits on a napkin. He set them down in front of me and returned his attention to the witness.

"Thank you," I murmured. The pleasing scent of shortbread teased my nose, and I nibbled on the rich, buttery cookie, darting a glance at his profile to catch the brief crook of his lips before he schooled his features.

"Did you see anyone else while you were out there?" he asked.

"No, but I did find my hairpin. I went back inside, and it wasn't long after that they found her body. Just think." She shivered. "It could have been me. I'm grateful to you, Detective. I feel safer knowing you're on the case."

*Oh, jeez.* My teeth ground the shortbread into dust. *Here we go again.*

"I appreciate your confidence, Miss Lancaster. If you think of anything else, please don't hesitate to get in touch with the agency. Miss Daniels is at your disposal."

She pouted, and her shoulders deflated. "Yes, of course. You must be very busy."

He stood. I climbed eagerly to my feet too, stuffing

the last of the biscuit into my mouth. I dusted the crumbs from my fingers and tucked my notebook under my arm. Miss Lancaster's grandmother snorted in her sleep, and I had to bite my lip to keep from laughing.

Derrick led me out into the street. The interview had lasted most of the morning, and now, the midday sun warmed the cobblestones. It was one of the final pleasant days of fall. I stretched my aching muscles and turned my face up to the sun.

"Who do you think Ella was waiting for?"

"That's a good question. Why don't you ask her?" He cocked a brow, and I wrinkled my nose at his cynicism.

"It doesn't work that way. Her memory's light on details. She remembers little of the actual night. Flashes mostly. But now that I think of it, she did mention seeing the clock tower. What we need to find out is whether Ella was lured out to the courtyard or if she was a victim of circumstance." A mild breeze lifted the savory aroma of freshly baked meat pies to my nose. "Can we stop for lunch?"

"You just had biscuits." Derrick frowned and checked the time on his pocket watch.

"I hope you're joking. I can't survive on two biscuits alone. Besides, you never take a break to eat. It's concerning." I poked him in the abdomen, finding only rigid muscle. He caught my hand before I could explore further. Not that I would. My imagination was doing a fine job on its own.

"All right. A quick break."

"I'll be quick as a flash. Don't worry, I won't subject you to eating with the town witch any longer than necessary."

He bristled at my tone. "I'm not embarrassed to be seen with you. There's a lot to do and no time for leisure activities."

"Lunch is a leisure activity?" I scoffed and dragged him across the street to a food stall. "I'm more concerned now than before. It's a good thing I'm here, Detective." I pressed my hand against my heart in mock horror. "How have you survived this long without me? Wait until you try these. They'll melt in your mouth. You'll thank me later."

The unimpressed detective rolled his eyes.

I smiled at the vendor. "We'll take two meat pies and two apple fritters, extra icing." While he prepared our food, I cast a sideways glance at Derrick. "We've never discussed my stipend."

"That's because you don't have one."

My lips flattened, and I reached into my pocket. I had six royal coins to my name.

"How much?" I whispered to the vendor.

"Eight."

Well, this wasn't good. "Cancel one of the fritters."

"Do you need money, Tessa?" Derrick studied my reaction, but I remained casual even as my mind wept at the loss of my limited fortune.

"No. This is my treat. A peace offering of sorts." I slid the coins across the counter.

"Are we at war?" He leaned against the stall, a grin playing at the corners of his mouth. It made my pulse jump.

"To the death. A witch doesn't take prisoners."

He accepted a meat pie and tipped it in a salute. "To the death then."

I watched him take his first bite and almost stopped breathing. As pleasure softened Derrick's face, my heart did a somersault. If only someone would look at me the way he looked at savory fillings encased in a flaky crust.

"It's good, isn't it? You're glad we stopped."

"It's fine."

"Fine, huh?" My eyes narrowed as I chewed my own meal. "You're hard to please, Detective, but I'm going to keep trying. To the death." I winked.

Derrick choked, his eyes watering as he cleared his windpipe of a chunk of meat pie he'd inhaled too fast. I struggled to hide my amusement.

"So, what's next on my tour of endless interviews? Is there a friend of a cousin's neighbor we haven't spoken with yet?"

Ignoring my question, he braved another bite of pie, devouring the entire thing in seconds. I handed him the apple fritter next, and he devoured that too. So much for dessert. The man was a workaholic who didn't make time for sustenance. I crushed the part of me that was tempted to offer him the rest of my lunch. *Don't swoon over him like every other fawning female in this kingdom. Have some pride. Fake it, if you have to.*

"Actually, I have an appointment with the Lock-woods to update them on the case." He licked icing off his finger. Apparently, my eyes found the activity fascinating. "Come with me. You can interview the friend of a cousin's neighbor later."

A flicker of excitement hummed through my veins. Finally, something worthwhile.

I turned toward the street to hail a carriage. When Derrick didn't follow, I glanced over my shoulder. He was back at the food stall. I'd created a monster. He exchanged a couple of coins for another fritter, then strolled toward the waiting carriage. Extra icing clung to the apple pastry, just the way I liked it. I licked my lips, craving it so badly. He knew it too. His gaze didn't leave my mouth.

Bringing the fritter up as if to take the first bite, Derrick finally chuckled before changing direction and placing it in my hand instead. His fingers brushed over mine, sending sparks of heat across my skin.

*Do. Not. Swoon.*

"What are you doing?"

"Winning the war."

"With a fritter?"

The rough timbre of his voice echoed in my ear as he helped me into the carriage. "Consider it the path of least resistance."

*Ugh.* Maybe I'd let him live after all.

***

The carriage swayed over the ruts in the road, and I held on to the armrest to keep from pitching forward. Derrick sat across from me, better able to manage the bumpy ride. He eyed my death grip in amused silence.

"We could have taken horses. It would have been faster."

I braced against a jolt that made my teeth slam together. "I don't like to ride. Horses can sense my magic. It spooks them."

"Are you sure it's magic and not poor riding skills? Wouldn't you spook the carriage horses as well?"

My shoulders stiffened. Did he have to investigate all the time? The man wasn't happy until he'd routed every one of my flaws. I sniffed the air and peered out the window.

"If you must know, it's horses that spook me."

"You're scared of the fastest, most reliable form of transportation?"

"I'd rather walk."

He made a sound in the back of his throat. "That's right. I remember. You like to walk alone, at night, through the kingdom's alleys. It's extremely dangerous. You're lucky we found you when we did."

"Thanks for your concern, but I've managed on my own for years, and just because we're working together does not make me your responsibility."

"You are my responsibility, Tessa." He leaned forward in his seat and locked eyes with mine. The depth of his stare made the carriage small. Even flattened against the cushion, I felt overwhelmed by his presence. Spooked, the same way I felt with horses, uncertain what to expect or if I'd get thrown and have the wind knocked out of me.

"Are you about to issue another one of your rules? Let me guess, no walking alone after dark? Well, some people aren't fortunate enough to waste money hiring expensive carriages." I crossed my arms. "This one's on you, by the way. I bought lunch. Don't even think about adding the cost to my fines."

He inclined his head and studied me in silence. "How long have you been on your own?"

I broke his stare to examine a hole in the leather cushion. Leave it to a detective to ask the personal questions.

"Seven years. My mother died when I was fifteen. I lived with Vivian and her grandmother for a while, until I was ready to take over the magic shop. I've been running it ever since." Running it into the ground was more accurate, but I couldn't tell him that. One sob story per carriage ride.

He waited until I returned his gaze, and the look on his face struck me. It wasn't pity, which I expected, but understanding, as if he were piecing together my character and had stumbled across something important. I shifted in the seat, uncomfortable with the vulnerable tug on my insides.

"Enough about me. Before we meet with Ella's family, you should tell me about the other girls. The ones whose names are next to the roses in your evidence room. I've waited long enough. Days, in fact."

Derrick leaned back into the cushion. "What do you want to know?"

"Everything. Start with the woman before Ella."

"Jane Porter?" Derrick hesitated, gathering his

thoughts. "It happened about six months ago. She worked as a barmaid at the Laughing Raven. According to witnesses, she kept to herself and didn't have a close circle of friends. No family I could track down. Her body was found in an alley. She'd been strangled, but what set her apart from similar crimes was the rose between her fingers. The detail of the rose was kept out of the papers, but a barmaid's death, at night, in an alley..." He paused for effect. I rolled my eyes. "Doesn't exactly make the front page. Ella's murder changed that. It was public, almost taunting in nature, and on castle grounds. It's been impossible to keep things quiet."

Familiar frustration tinged his voice. I experienced the same deep-seated defeat when I failed a spell, knowing someone was counting on me, and there was nothing I could do about it.

"No one knows about the missing slipper."

"Except for you."

I shrugged. "Perks of seeing a ghost. Trust me, there aren't many other perks."

Derrick looked skeptical. He wasn't ready to believe my ghost story. Thankfully, Prince Marcus had an open mind to the occult and deemed me... What was that glorious word he'd used? That's right. An asset.

"What about the first victim?"

Derrick scrubbed a hand over his face. Talking about the victims was difficult for him. It was obvious he cared about his cases.

"Her name was Sophie. She was young, just

turned sixteen, when she died three years ago. I was out of the kingdom training for the agency. All the information I have is secondhand."

Our knees brushed as I scooted to the edge of the carriage seat. "What happened to her?"

"Sophie was the daughter of a wealthy merchant. Her family traveled to their country estate every fall to attend festivities at the royal hunting lodge. She went missing during one of the king's deer hunts."

"Hundreds of people must have been in attendance. The king used to invite all the affluent families to attend his fall feast."

"That's right. Villagers scoured the forest for days. There was no sign of her until one of the hunting dogs located her body partially submerged in the marsh. Her hands had been placed over her middle, with a long stem rose tucked between her fingers."

"How did she die?"

Derrick's voice grew hoarse. "Strangulation. There were ligature marks on her neck, mud and scratches on her feet, and defensive wounds on her hands. She fought hard."

I tried to imagine that kind of fear. Those final moments, knowing you couldn't win, yet fighting to the end. It left a cold ball of dread in my chest.

"What do you make of the roses?"

"To be honest, I'm not sure. My guess would be a relationship gone sour, but there's no evidence to support any of the girls had romantic attachments. There was a rumor Sophie might have shown interest in someone, possibly even exchanged letters, but

I wasn't able to substantiate that claim. The murders happened years apart. They knew different people, lived at opposite ends of the social spectrum, and there was an age difference between the two. My superior wasn't convinced the roses linked the two women, and there were times I wasn't sure either. Maybe I wanted them to mean more than they did."

"Until Ella?"

He nodded. "Until Ella. It's too much of a coincidence. There's a link between all of them, we just need to find it."

The carriage rolled to a stop in front of a stately manor nestled between a copse of trees. Tangled vines climbed the walls, spreading like gnarled fingers around the window frames. Overgrown topiaries flanked a circular drive littered with fallen leaves and crumbling brick. Nature was doing its best to reclaim what was once a magnificent property.

Derrick exited the carriage and held out his hand to help me down the step. He spoke with the driver, instructing him to wait, and the carriage pulled off the lane to park. We traveled over the cracked walkway toward the door and used the brass knocker clenched between a bronzed lion's mouth. A servant in black livery answered.

"Detective Chambers to see Mrs. Lockwood and her daughter, please."

The servant ushered us into a small sitting room. Heavy brocade curtains tied back with golden tassels allowed the afternoon sun to spill onto the polished parquet floors. Dark wood paneling lined the walls, emphasizing the richly colored furnishings. The difference between outside and in was startling. Every surface gleamed, and the room smelled like fresh lemons. I remembered my first meeting with Ella and how I'd thought she was a scullery maid, but that made little sense given the state of her home and family lineage.

"Have you interviewed the staff?" I wandered toward the edge of the room to examine a marble chess set.

"Yes, but most won't speak out against their employer for fear of losing their jobs. The Lockwood staff are no different."

"I see." I traced my finger over the beveled edges of a rook and wondered why Ella had been wearing a servant's uniform the night of the ball. Had she stolen it to sneak out of the house, or was there something more there?

"Detective, thank you for coming." A woman wearing a satin mourning gown sailed into the room. Tendrils of silver hair framed her face, slipping from the coil on top of her head where a wispy black veil hung down her back.

"Mrs. Lockwood, sorry for the delay. We came as soon as we could."

Mrs. Lockwood waved her hand. "Nonsense. We're happy you could make time. You remember my daughter, Helen?"

A beautiful young woman with elfin features and porcelain skin stepped from behind her mother and performed a perfect curtsy. Her sleek blonde hair curled in lush waves down her shoulders, in stark contrast to her fitted black gown. She smiled demurely at Derrick and blinked heavily fringed green eyes.

"Detective, it's a pleasure to see you again. Our first meeting was under such horrid circumstances. I hope you'll forgive my actions." A blush infused her cheeks. "You were most kind to comfort me the way you did."

Her sugar-sweet disposition made my teeth ache, and I narrowed a look at Derrick. *Comfort* her? Must be great to be a Detective.

Derrick shook his head. "You're forgiven, Miss Lockwood. Grief makes people act in ways they don't expect."

A sly glint flashed in Helen's eyes before she cast them downward in a display of modesty. "You're too kind, Detective."

I fought and barely won against the urge to roll my eyes and move between them. The flattery followed us wherever we went! I cleared my throat. Derrick pressed his hand against the small of my back, and my irritation melted. At least he hadn't forgotten I existed completely.

"Ladies, let me introduce you to Tessa Daniels. She'll be assisting me in the investigation."

Helen sent me a frosty glare. She wasn't pleased with the competition. Not that I thought of myself as competition; I just didn't like the way she was ogling Derrick. This was a murder investigation, not a matchmaking soiree.

"Miss Daniels, welcome to our home. As you can imagine, it's a difficult time for us. Our poor Ella, we miss her terribly." Mrs. Lockwood dabbed an embroidered handkerchief under her eyes. "How could something like this happen? She didn't even want to attend the ball and insisted on staying home."

"Why do you think she changed her mind?" I asked.

"Who knows? The girl was impulsive, always jumping without looking. Took after her father. I fear that trait made her cross paths with a killer. Are there any leads, Detective?"

"I know how anxious you are for information, but we're still interviewing guests as well as examining the scene. As soon as we have something concrete to share, we will. I want you both to know that Ella's case is the agency's top priority."

"Thank you, Detective."

"Since we're here and Miss Daniels is a late addition to the case, would you mind if we take a walk through Ella's room? A fresh set of eyes can only help."

"Of course. We haven't touched a thing. Please, follow me." Mrs. Lockwood swept from the sitting room and up a large, curved staircase. I trailed behind, scoffing quietly at the way Helen captured Derrick's arm to climb the steps. Spare me the sight of an able-bodied woman needing help up a set of stairs. *It's one foot in front of the other, lady. Even a witch can do it. Look! No hands!* I glared a hole into Derrick's back, hoping he could feel it, but when he probed the spot with his fingers and glanced over a shoulder, I dropped my gaze to feign interest in the decorative handrail.

At the top of the steps, Helen stumbled on the edge of the carpet, forcing Derrick to catch her. She murmured a thank-you, clinging to his forearm like a squirrel around a tree branch. Derrick removed her hands, set her away from him, and continued down the hall. Placing a fist on her hip, she huffed and hurried along.

What a piece of work.

They turned left, disappearing from view, and I lingered to let my temper cool. I needed to focus on the investigation and not on watching Helen flirt with Derrick, which only made me want to stick a needle into a doll of her likeness. Realizing I was lagging behind and didn't know the layout of the house, I hurried around the corner but came to an abrupt stop in the empty hallway. It branched off in multiple directions before a second staircase led to another floor. *Blast.* Which way to Ella's room? I listened, hoping to hear their voices, but the house was eerily quiet.

A door creaked. Faster than I could process, something slipped through the gap.

My breath fogged around my lips as a sudden chill gripped the hall. The last time this happened, Ella had appeared. An instinctual pull drew me closer to the door. Derrick would be annoyed if I went off alone, but I had to go where Ella wanted to take me, and it seemed that was this way. I was going to have to investigate a bit on my own.

So much for rule number one.

# Chapter 10

The door revealed a dark staircase that led to the servants' quarters. At the bottom was another hallway. A musty odor infused the air, and water-stained floorboards peeked out from below the edges of a threadbare carpet. As the temperature plunged further, the symbols on my palm started to glow.

Why had Ella led me here? My palm pulsed with heat, luring me to wrap my fingers around the knob of a partly closed door. Heavy eyelids left me feeling like I'd been drugged. When they closed fully, I saw Ella huddled in front of a stone fireplace, packets of letters at her feet. She pored over them, tears coursing down her cheeks, before moving to a thin mattress and sobbing herself to sleep.

The vision faded. I entered the room, and the chill followed me inside. There was the fireplace where Ella had read the letters. A frayed mattress rested on a bed frame in the corner, and a small nightstand had been pushed against the wall. I knelt by the grate, noticing a footprint in a thin layer of soot, and sifted through the charred pile of ash. A few pieces of paper hadn't burned all the way through, so I pulled them from the ruin, edges crumbling in my hands, but I was able to make out some of the words.

*Dear Miss Lockwood,*

*I regret to inform you that we've done all we can to determine the cause of your father's illness. We recommend that you make him comfortable in his final days.*

There were only a few visible sentences on the second letter.

*My Dearest Ella,*

*How your father has missed you. I know these last few months have been difficult, but give them a chance. You'll grow to love each other as I have grown to love your stepmother, Olivia. Treat them well while I'm away.*

Whatever else the letter contained was now lost. Ella likely had a rough transition into her new family. Having her father die so soon after he re-married must have been devastating. I knew how easy it was to feel alone even when surrounded by other people.

Seeing the room with fresh eyes, I imagined Ella sleeping on the mattress, isolated from the rest of her family. Why was Olivia showing Derrick to a room that wasn't hers?

I placed the charred remains on the stone hearth and walked toward the nightstand. The drawer held a worn novel and a fresh apron. Between the fabric folds was a bronze padlock and a key. I frowned, holding the weight of it in my hand. The bedroom door had a metal latch three-quarters of the way up.

Was Ella barring her room at night? And if so, from whom?

An odd bundle protruded from under the thin comforter on the bed, resembling a wad of clothes. Maybe it was more of Ella's letters? I reached toward the mound.

"What are you doing down here?" Derrick's voice boomed from the doorway, making me jump. The thud of his boots echoed on the floor at the same time a loud hiss filled the room. I knew instantly what had made that sound. *Of all the rotten luck.*

A cat.

The blanket fell away, and sharp claws sank into my outstretched hand. I yelped, spinning away from the attacking beast. Derrick wasn't so lucky. The black cat leaped from the bed, mewling and hissing as it darted between his legs. He tried to get out of its way but lost his balance and crashed into me. We fell, tangled together, landing hard against the mattress. He caught himself with his hands, our faces inches apart.

"We need to stop meeting like this, Detective." My gaze was drawn to his mouth, and a rush of heat spread through my body. His lips moved, and it seemed to take ages for the sound to reach my ears.

"What did I tell you about rule number one?" He caught me staring, so I flicked my gaze back up to his. Derrick's eyes darkened, tension coiling through his arms. More heat pooled through my limbs. I licked my dry lips and shifted beneath him. The movement evoked a low groan in the back of his throat.

My breath caught. I wanted nothing more than to hear that sound again.

"You'd better write down the rules if you expect me to remember them all."

"Rule number one." His voice dipped an octave deeper, sending a shiver through my spine. "It's dangerous to investigate alone."

"You're right, I could have been killed by the cat. So *dangerous.*"

He lifted his weight, and I instantly regretted my sarcastic response.

Reaching for my hand, Derrick examined the scratch. A tiny rivulet of blood seeped from the edges. I sucked in a breath as he ran a feather-light touch along the broken skin.

"Cats hate me. I know that goes against logic. They're supposed to be a witch's best friend, but every one I encounter wants to dig its claws into me. You should see my neighbor's cat. I've tried everything. Leaving it fish, scratching behind his ear. I even tried casting a spell. That only made him mad. His eternal goal is to hiss at my grave."

Derrick sat up, taking me with him. "I'll have him arrested."

I bit my cheek to contain a laugh. "You better be serious. It may be him or me one day. Don't make me promises you don't intend to keep."

A beat of silence passed. His gaze mimicked what mine had done, dropping to my lips. The air seemed to thin, and my lungs burned when his hand brushed against my waist. Barely conscious of my actions, I leaned closer, my eyes drifting closed.

Immediately, Derrick pulled back, his expression switching to a mask of indifference. I nearly punched the mattress until I saw the tic in his jaw, signaling he wasn't as unaffected as he tried to be.

"I never make promises. Rule number four."

The whiplash of his emotions washed over me, and I crossed the room, taking a deep breath to calm my pounding heart.

"Well, while you were upstairs following around Mrs. Lockwood and her clingy daughter, I stumbled across something."

The bed creaked as Derrick rose to his feet. His tone was all business again.

"What did you find?"

I pointed to the fireplace and the remnants of Ella's letters. "Whatever they showed you upstairs, I wouldn't believe it. I think this was Ella's room, and I don't think she was happy here. She might have even been afraid."

***

Olivia Lockwood toyed with the sleeve of her mourning gown. "It's true, Ella wasn't happy before her death. Her father contracted an illness after he returned from his last trip. It was a long and debilitating ailment that eventually claimed his life. We consulted with specialists, hoping to find a cure, but we were unsuccessful. After Maxwell's death, we tried to help Ella cope, but she completely shut down and refused to sleep in the main part of the house."

I studied Ella's stepmother from my seat near the window. Her red-rimmed eyes shimmered with unshed tears. Helen sat beside her mother's elbow on the plush sofa, and Derrick remained standing, notebook in hand.

"Do you know anything about the padlock I found in her drawer? Was there a reason she might need it?" I asked.

Olivia wrinkled her brow. "I didn't realize she had one. This is a safe neighborhood, and we've never had any trouble with the staff. I can only assume the lock was already in the room before she started using it."

Derrick tapped his pen against the page. "After Sir Lockwood's death, how was the relationship between the three of you?"

"Strained at best. It's ironic now that I think about it, but I assumed the prince's ball would bring us together." Olivia smiled wistfully. "It was something to look forward to after so many months of sickness and mourning. But Ella refused to go.

"Did either of you speak with her at the ball?"

"No." Olivia pressed a handkerchief to her trembling lips. "We didn't know she was there until we saw her dancing with the prince. We lost her in the crowd, and a short while later, she was found in the courtyard. It was chaos, everyone terrified, pointing fingers. We were as shocked as anyone."

Derrick closed his notebook and placed it in his jacket pocket. "Thank you for your time, ladies. If we have any other questions, we'll be in touch."

Mrs. Lockwood inclined her head as I passed by the sofa, but Helen wouldn't meet my gaze. There was something about her that seemed off. A memory of shaking Ella's hand made me pause.

"That's a lovely emerald ring, Helen. May I see it?"

Helen pressed her lips together and lifted her hand, extending her fingers. I bent closer to touch her palm, faking interest in the ring. Her skin was smooth and callous-free, a stark difference from Ella's hardworking hands. Turning her palm up, I noticed a two-inch gash starting at the base of her thumb and running to her wrist.

"That looks painful. How did you get it?"

Helen laughed and tried to tug her hand from my grasp. "I'm such a ninny. I was pruning flowers in the garden without wearing gloves, and the shears slipped."

Olivia patted her daughter's knee. "Helen has a green thumb. There's a small garden shed around back. You can go see it, if you'd like?"

Helen smirked and indicated the scratch where the Lockwood cat had sunk its claws. "That's a nasty gash you have yourself, Miss Daniels. You should put something on it, or it might fester. Infections can be deadly."

The way Helen eyed my wound spoke volumes. If it was up to her, I'd lose the hand.

Derrick thanked them again and led me out of the house. He stood in the drive shaking his head.

"What was that about?"

"Did you see the injury on her hand? It's suspicious, isn't it? And her skin was smooth. Ella's wasn't. I thought Ella was a maid, not the daughter of a wealthy family. You should have seen the rags she had on. It doesn't add up." I chewed on the edge of my thumbnail.

Derrick crossed his arms and gave me an odd look.

"What? Why are you staring at me like I have two heads?"

"It's surprising."

"What is?"

"You." He took my good hand and walked off the path toward the side of the house. An overgrown trail of tangled vines and branches made it difficult to go any further, but from where we stood, I could see the roof of a small garden shed.

Derrick gestured down the path. "Go on, this is your lead. I'll let you have the honor of investigating it."

He had to be kidding. I took a cautious step back, and my foot sank into a pile of dry leaves.

"What's the matter? Where's the intrepid witch determined to dive in and solve the case? I thought you wanted those fines removed?"

He was baiting me, the wretch. I eyed the untamed foliage on the neglected path. It couldn't hurt me. There probably weren't any snakes in the overgrown grass. I swallowed. There better not be snakes.

"You know, it's not wise to taunt a witch." I stomped past him, taking a face full of vines in the process. Spitting out a brittle leaf, I jerked an arm to untangle the vines pulling my hair.

Derrick chuckled under his breath. I considered letting a branch snap back into his face but chose the high ground. For once.

The path ended at the entrance to a squat, narrow building. All I needed to find was a single rose bush, and I could shove the clue in his face. Honestly, why people thought being a detective was so hard was beyond me—I'd been doing it for less than a week and already had a prime suspect. Imagining Helen behind bars, unable to bat her lashes at Derrick, played no part. Witch's truth.

I peered through the window pane, cupping my hands on either side of my head to block the light. Inside, chrysanthemums bloomed and ferns sprouted from ceramic pots. A pair of pruning shears rested on the table, but besides containers of potting soil and a watering can, there wasn't much else. There wasn't any evidence of a rosebush, and none were planted in the adjacent garden. Deflated, I slumped against the wall.

"Find any murder weapons? Should I have Helen arrested for not watering the plants enough?"

I scowled. "Rule number three. Everyone and anyone is a suspect. You said so yourself, and that includes irritatingly perfect stepsisters."

"So, you do remember the rules." He plucked a stray leaf from my hair. It was a casual gesture but it felt familiar, almost intimate.

"Just the one."

"You did well back there. I should tell you, my men searched the garden shed days ago, and we noted Helen's injury during her interview the night of the murder. But you asked the right questions."

"Were you testing me?"

"Would it make you happy if you passed?"

"It would."

Derrick tried to hide a smile. "Either way, thanks to your weird connection with a ghost, you discovered Ella slept in another wing of the house. The angle with her father is something I still have to delve into."

"We." I poked him in the chest. "Something *we* have to delve into."

"All right, we." He caught my hand and rubbed a thumb over the dark symbols. "I'm not saying I will start trusting in all of your mumbo jumbo—"

"I think you mean magic, Detective."

"Sure, magic." He examined the symbols, tracing their outline. "How does your link with Ella work?"

"I'm not sure. This is the first time something like this has happened. The mark on my palm should have faded when the illusion did, but since she died while under my spell, we're connected. Before she appeared, I experienced strange occurrences, chilled rooms, voices…"

"You heard voices?"

"Not like that, so forget about carting me off to the asylum, but it is strange how I was able to see her moving through the past."

Derrick looked grim, his features cut from stone.

"They're only visions, right? They can't hurt you?"

"I don't think so. It doesn't seem to be a physical connection."

"If that changes, this partnership is over."

I nudged him in the shoulder. "Is that what this is, Detective? A partnership?"

He was still frowning, but some of the tension drained from his features. "I don't know what this is, but like your connection with Ella, there's a first time for everything."

I didn't bother to deny the pleasure his words gave me. I had a partner. A reluctant one, but given time...

"So, what's next?"

"Nothing. We're done for today." He left me leaning against the garden shed.

I hurried after him, noticing he went in the opposite direction from the way we came. A direction that was vine and foliage-free. My jaw clenched. He would have known this way was easier if he'd had his men search the shed. I had a feeling he was waiting for me to complain, but I would not give him the satisfaction.

He slowed so I could catch up. "I'll be at the magic shop tomorrow afternoon. Be ready by six. We have an interview at the palace."

I nearly tripped over my feet. "Seriously? You're taking me to the castle?" I picked a twig from my skirt and noticed a dark stain near the hemline. "What should I wear?"

"Tessa, we're going to visit a crime scene. Wear whatever." He waved a hand dismissively.

"Excuse me? Wear whatever?"

Derrick sighed. "You look fine."

My mouth dropped open at his lackluster praise. "Fine? Everything is *fine* to you, isn't it? Meat pies, a woman's appearance, they're the same thing. How charming. Hold on while I swoon from your compliments—wait...no. It went away."

He turned so fast, I collided with his chest. Clamping his hands around my forearms and tugging me closer, he dipped his head and spoke low in my ear.

"Trust me, Tessa, you'll know when I'm being charming."

I gave him a mock pout and patted his cheek. "I don't think so, Detective, but good try. Take me home. I need to pick out an outfit."

# Chapter 11

"**N**ice dress." Abrams gave me an encouraging smile from across the carriage.

I surveyed my carefully selected royal blue tunic with its snug waist, custom leather belt, and fur-trimmed sleeves. "Yeah, it's fine, I guess."

"I apologize again for showing up late. I know Detective Chambers was planning on picking you up at six. There was a situation at the agency. He'll meet us at the castle."

Situation, huh? I refused to analyze my disappointment. It didn't matter to me that Derrick had sent his rookie officer in his place, not one bit. Hand on a spell book and strike me down if I'm lying. I coughed and darted a look at the cloudless sky.

The castle came into view, distracting me from further tempting the fates. Nestled among sloping hills and manicured gardens, the palace was the jewel of the kingdom. The setting sun bathed the bleached stone towers and ornate spires in an orange glow. On both sides of the winding drive stood giant topiaries sculpted into spirals. Lantern posts were spaced between them, already lit, illuminating the cobblestones.

We came to a halt in front of a grand staircase. It was easy to imagine the night of the ball, with carriages lined up around the bend and guests in their finest attire ascending the marble steps. If I closed my eyes, I could almost hear the strains of the kingdom's orchestra seeping through the ballroom windows, smell the savory delights, the fruity wine, and the expensive perfumes wafting through the air.

"This is the ballroom entrance. It's closest to the courtyard." Abrams gestured for me to follow him down a long hallway lined with gold-framed paintings and elaborate wall sconces. My shoes clicked over the polished marble, the sound echoing into the vaulted ceiling.

"The crime scene has been guarded around the clock since the night of the murder. We collected evidence, but the royal family wanted the area preserved. You'll be doing a final walk-through before Detective Chambers releases the scene."

We came to a set of doors that opened into the courtyard. Abrams stopped to talk to a guard, while I stepped onto the stone path that led away from the castle. An eerie silence descended. It felt like hallowed ground. My shoes sank into the thick grass as I weaved through the rose bushes and marble statues. Even the fountain in the distance remained silent, its waters tranquil and unmoving.

I walked toward the fountain. It was much larger than I'd expected, more of a circular wading pool. In the center was a tiered statue where streams trickled and poured into the basin. The water was dark, maybe three to four feet deep, surrounded by a stone barrier. I noticed a single rose petal floating on the surface and watched it ebb and flow almost in a trance.

When my fingers brushed over the stone boundary, I felt a jolt through my hand. The symbols on my palm pulsated, and a familiar wave of dizziness crashed through me. *Not again.* Around me, the courtyard faded. I squinted against the gloom. What was happening?

With murky water covering my face and body, the only light came from the ripple of the moon penetrating the water's surface. A weight pressed on my shoulders. Powerful hands held me under as air bubbles escaped my lips, replaced by the tang of icy water. I watched the bubbles rise, helpless to follow.

*Can't breathe...It hurts.*

My lungs burned like a fire inside my chest. Frantic, I splayed my fingers along the silty bottom, looking for leverage. Pebbles scrapped my palms, and weeds slithered against my skin. The last breath in my body withered away. I struggled beneath the firm grip, choking, desperate to reach the surface.

Panic surged. I inhaled water instead of air. The thrashing stilled along with my movements. My eyes were open to the pale moonlight that grew darker and darker. The weight was gone, but I remained at the bottom, looking up.

Forever.

"No!"

I fell to my knees in the grass, gulping in rapid bursts of air. The courtyard came back into focus as I tried to calm my pounding heart, its rhythmic thump echoing in my ears. What a horrible vision. It had felt so real. The pain in my palm faded, and I braced myself against the fountain to stand. Had I just witnessed Ella's final moments? Abrams was still talking to the guard, oblivious to my turmoil. I sat on the stone wall and closed my eyes, taking in deep, soothing breaths of air. This symbol vision thing was starting to get ridiculous. Vivian had never mentioned experiencing a ghost's memories.

A rustling jolted my eyes open. It was coming from a tall hedge that lined the courtyard. A stick cracked under a boot—someone was positioned on the other side. I inched closer and bent to look through a small opening in the hedge, finding a pair of ink-colored eyes staring back. The man had an angular face and a sharp nose, a curl of sandy brown hair covering his left brow. He watched me for an airless moment, then lifted a gloved finger to his lips.

"I'll find you," he rasped before vanishing from the opening.

I ran the length of the hedge and rounded the corner. The man was gone. Trees and shrubs formed a dense cover, and the fading light created pockets of darkness, a perfect setting to hide his escape. Searching the foliage for any sign of movement, his words echoed in my ears.

*I'll find you.*

Not the most comforting phrase from a stranger loitering around a crime scene.

"Tessa?" The deep, flinty sound of my name broke through my thoughts. I almost ducked behind the hedge. Derrick didn't sound pleased, and he'd be less so if he caught me wandering on my own for the second time. Damn him and his stupid rules.

He called my name again, and this time, I heard the hint of alarm. I remembered the look of concern in his eyes when he'd asked about my visions. That look had unnerved me in ways I didn't want to identify. I'd have to tread lightly. Telling him about my vivid death hallucinations and a suspicious man's threat to "find" me was bound to get me sidelined and thrown back on boring interview duty.

"I'm over here," I shouted, stepping from behind the hedge.

Derrick strode across the courtyard, his features morphing between anger and relief, as erratic as a child plucking petals. *He loves me, he loves me not...* Unfortunately, he ended on not, halting with a deep frown.

"Were you looking for me, Detective?" I injected extra sweetness into my tone.

He didn't buy it. In fact, it only made him grouchier. His arms crossed like steel bands across his chest, and I dropped the act fast to point to the hedge.

"There was a man peeking through the branches. I tried to get a closer look, but he disappeared."

"What was he wearing?" Derrick's hard gaze left

mine and searched the grounds.

"It was difficult to tell. I could only see a portion of his face. He appeared to be late twenties, early thirties. And fast. He didn't want to be followed. It was probably a servant who ran off when I caught him snooping." A rush of guilt tightened my insides. I knew I shouldn't keep the strange man's words a secret, but there was too much at stake, and I couldn't risk telling Derrick the truth.

He gave up his search. "It's possible. The king ordered the crime scene off-limits. I'm sure curiosity is rampant. Come with me, there's a witness I want you to meet." He ushered me past the fountain and down the stone walkway.

"Has the fountain been dredged?" I asked, remembering Ella's desperate thrashing beneath the surface.

"It has. There was nothing of consequence, though we did find a thin strip of leather in the grass. It could be unrelated. There's no telling how long it's been there, but we've collected it as evidence along with the wine stem."

"Wine stem?"

He steered me around a marble bench, where I noticed the faint glitter of glass shards. A few more were scattered across the tile, and one glinted beneath a giant rose bush.

"We found the wine stem here." Derrick pointed to the base of the bench. "It had shattered on the walkway, but a portion remained intact."

I nodded, my attention focused on the rose bush.

"The roses aren't the same. The ones in your office are a different strain from the ones planted here."

"Good catch. You're right, the rose wasn't cut here. The palace plants a breed of tea rose, but the roses left by the killer appear to be an unknown strain. We haven't located the source."

We kept moving, approaching an older gentleman wearing a scarlet jacket and charcoal gray pants. Gold buttons the size of coins gleamed down the front of his coat. He bent at the waist in a curt bow, revealing a balding spot on top of his head.

"Tessa, this is Bradford, the King's steward. He encountered Miss Lockwood shortly before midnight."

"That's correct, Detective." Bradford smoothed a puff of white hair near his ear. "Miss Lockwood was acting strange, swaying a bit, and I saw her stumble. She was alone, carrying a glass of wine, so I attempted to offer assistance. Many of our guests had too much to drink that evening. She declined and said she needed some fresh air."

So, she'd had a little too much to drink. I frowned in thought as the man went on.

"I helped her through the crowd, but she stumbled again and spilled her wine on my jacket. She was so embarrassed, she ran off before I could tell her it was all right. I lost sight of her in the crowd. A short time later, she was found in the fountain." He paused, and a somber look hardened his features. "I was in charge of selecting the two vintages we served at the ball since my skills as a sommelier are unrivaled. In the rush of the moment, it didn't seem important, but given the tragic nature of Miss Lockwood's demise, I should tell you that when she spilled the wine on my jacket, it smelled off. Looking back, I believe it had been altered in some way."

Had Ella been poisoned? My mind raced with the implications. It could explain her disorientation and also suggested the killer had premeditated the act.

"There's been so much upheaval in the palace, I didn't recall the discrepancy with the wine until yesterday, and unfortunately, my jacket has been cleaned." Bradford hung his head as if he had single-handedly lost the case.

"What about the wine stem?" I asked Derrick. "You said you collected it as evidence?"

"We did, but it was broken. There wasn't any wine left for a sample."

"Not to the naked eye, no, but to a witch?"

Shadows played over his handsome features when Derrick lifted a brow. I grinned, suddenly feeling a rush of excitement.

"Fetch the wine stem, Detective. It's time I showed you just how much my *mumbo jumbo*, as you call it, is worth."

# Chapter 12

"We're here," Derrick murmured.

I shifted deeper into the cushioned seat. "Five more minutes." My eyes felt grainy and heavy-lidded as I peeked beneath my lashes. I must've fallen asleep while waiting at the agency. The last thing I remembered was him running inside to collect the wine stem.

A sliver of moonlight poured through the window, splashing across his shoulders and the white sleeves of his shirt. Wasn't he wearing a jacket before? The weight of it registered in my mind. He'd draped it over me, and I currently had it pulled up to my chin, collar clutched tight in my fists. It smelled pleasant, so I inhaled a deep breath.

Derrick leaned forward, the moonlight revealing his features, and tugged the edge of his jacket over the exposed area on my arm. "I know you're awake."

I let out a slow breath. "Good detective work. What gave me away?"

"Years of training and a finely tuned sense of others."

"So modest and impressive," I drawled. "You can't blame me, you were inside the agency for a long time."

"My superior wanted an update. I filled him in on Bradford's account and mentioned we're looking into the possibility Ella was poisoned. I came back to get you, but you'd already fallen asleep."

Maybe he did have a finely tuned sense of others. I felt completely drained. The coat sagged as I straightened in the seat. I offered it to him, but he gave a subtle shake of his head.

"Keep it. It's cold." He opened the door, and a blast of night air confirmed the frigid temperature. I wrapped his coat tighter around my body and followed him out of the carriage.

Inside the magic shop, I lit the lamp wicks, and the flames glowed over worn books and clay pots. Placing one of the lamps on the workbench, I swept aside sprigs of herbs and dried leaves, careful not to scatter them on the floor. The chill from outside had made its way indoors, so Derrick coaxed a fire to life. Soon, the burning logs snapped and cracked in waves of heat.

He held his palms over the flames and rubbed his fingers together, a small shiver shaking his shoulders. I glanced at his discarded coat and felt a twinge in my chest. He'd been cold on the ride over and hadn't said a word.

"You can put the wine stem on the table. I need to collect a few things before we get started." I slipped away before he could respond, hoping the unheated air from the supply room would clear my head.

As usual, I was overreacting, latching onto acts

of kindness and making them more than they were. So what if Derrick had given me his coat? It was the gentlemanly thing to do, the bedrock of chivalry, and I'd already established he was an overachiever. It didn't make me special. Still, his gestures went to my head like champagne bubbles and made my stomach fizz. Better not to get addicted. Too much champagne made a person ill.

In the storeroom, I surveyed the shelves. The floor-to-ceiling nook was a shabby shrine to my mother. I'd tried to keep her organizational system, remembering she'd spent hours cataloging the powders and liquids and recording their uses in thick ledgers at her feet. But over the years, my special brand of chaos had seeped in around the edges, and now, the catalog didn't match the inventory.

My fingers grazed wistfully over the vials, searching for one in particular. I ducked beneath a bundle of herbs hanging from the ceiling. The bouquet swayed around my ears, filling my nose with the soothing scent of lavender.

"Where is it?" I whispered, standing on my toes. Dust left filthy smudges on my fingertips, and cobwebs created a wispy barrier to the jars in the back. Plunging my hand through the sticky threads, I prayed its occupant was visiting a neighbor's web and felt around until I grasped a glass container with a raised symbol.

"Gotcha." I hesitated, jar in hand, listening for sounds in the other room. Left to my own devices, I'd discovered secrets in Derrick's office. Was he doing the same now, sifting through my things and making judgments? His attitude during our first meeting still stung, and even though it seemed like he was coming around, I couldn't dismiss the hurt that had burrowed deep inside my chest.

When I reentered, I found him leaning against the workbench, arms casually folded over his chest and sleeves rolled up to his elbows. He looked relaxed, almost in his element. If he had searched, he'd done so quickly and had the wherewithal not to get caught. Smart man.

Derrick watched me cross the room, seeming to capture every nuance of my journey.

"I thought I'd find you snooping in my cupboards the moment I left you alone."

He angled his head, and a lock of dark hair fell over his eye. He had no interest in searching my shop. Whatever secrets he might unearth, he'd discover them by studying me.

"Were you testing me?"

"Perhaps, but I wasn't worried. Witches don't hide dead bodies in their cupboards."

"If I remember correctly, there weren't any in your basement either."

"That's because I only keep them there in emergencies."

He gave a half-smile at my answer. There was something in his tone, a hint of mischief that made those champagne bubbles fizz in my stomach again. The candlelight flickered over his features, and I admired the hard lines of his jaw, the way his lips moved, and the low rumble of his voice.

What was wrong with me?

Dropping my gaze to my feet, I mentally cursed. It wasn't every day—or any day at all—that a tall, dark, and handsome detective occupied my shop, but this was no excuse to go all swoony. Derrick's fondness for doling out fines was partly responsible for the mess I was in, and here I was letting myself be charmed by him. Maybe some things were inevitable.

Yeah, right. The only thing inevitable was my debt coming due at the end of the month.

I placed the jar onto the table and pulled out the stopper. A spoonful of powder went into a clay pot, followed by a cup of herb-laced tonic and a sprinkle of black salt. The liquid bubbled and frothed, emitting a fragrant steam.

Derrick read the label on the jar. "Rosenphyn? I've never heard of it."

"Be careful with that." I plugged the stopper into the container and moved it out of reach. "Rosenphyn is used to detect poison. It's a little secret of mine. When I was younger, my mother never let me mix my own potions—something about her not wanting me to blow the roof off the shop—so, like any good witch, I went behind her back. It sounds silly, but I wanted to prove to her that I could create something useful."

He was silent for a moment, giving me that look again. The one that made me think he saw through all of my bravado to the vulnerable witch beneath.

"That doesn't sound silly to me."

"Yeah, well, you didn't let me get to the part where I went a few months without eyebrows."

He flattened his lips to keep from smiling, then wrinkled his brow. "Why do you do that?"

"Do what?"

"Make jokes at your own expense whenever you talk about your magic?"

I fidgeted with the spoon handle and dropped my gaze. "It saves someone else from having to make them, I guess."

His inscrutable gaze returned, and I ducked my head, tugging the long strands of my hair to hide my flushed cheeks. There was a clog in my throat. I cleared it away.

"Anyways, the eyebrows grew back, and I eventually figured out the correct combination of ingredients. It works by altering the composition of the toxins. In their altered state, the mixture changes color, which can then be used to determine the type of poison present."

"That's incredible! Was your mother impressed?"

"No, um...at the time, I could only detect one type of poison, not a lethal one either, so it wasn't very impressive. It took much longer to compile and test for other types—years, in fact. She was gone by then."

He nodded, and his hand brushed lightly against my shoulder, hovering there for a second before he closed his fist and dropped it to his side. "Well, I'm impressed. It sounds like something that would be useful to the agency."

"Useful only in the right hands. Meaning witches. Watch this." Placing my palms over the bowl, I channeled my magic and spoke the incantation. The mixture popped and then settled with a slow hiss. It was ready.

"Unfortunately, rosenphyn is a deadly poison all on its own. Ingesting even a small amount can kill, which is why you should stay back. I'd hate to have to explain to your superior why there's a dead detective on my shop floor."

He eyed the potion warily. "I don't know, that sounds an awful lot like an emergency. I'd end up in your basement."

"Only until I can bury you beneath the garden shed." I flashed him an innocent smile.

He wasn't amused. "So, you developed a poison to detect a poison? Is that wise?"

"You tell me, Detective. Don't you often have to think like a killer in order to catch one?"

"That's different."

"How so?"

Derrick's jaw clenched as he struggled to answer. "You have to know what you're doing."

"Exactly. It boils down to experience. What is deadly in the wrong hands can be a solution in another's. But don't worry, you're safe with me. I'm too tired to dig a hole."

His comical expression was worth risking his wrath. I stifled a grin and reached for an ox hair brush, then dipped the bristles into the filmy substance.

He stilled my wrist. "That isn't funny. This is dangerous, and I imagine highly illegal. I could—"

"I know, I know, you could have me arrested. Now, hand me the wine stem."

Derrick scowled as he removed the lid from the wooden box and placed the wine stem on the table. "Be careful with that. I'd hate to have to explain to my superior why there's a dead witch on her shop floor."

"No, you wouldn't."

He lifted my chin with his fingers until our eyes met. "I would."

The certainty in his tone wobbled the brush in my hand. Why did he have to stand so close? I could feel the heat from his touch like a brand.

As if I'd spoken my thoughts out loud, he let go and stepped back. Feeling off-balance, I brushed the bristles over the wine stem, leaving a milky-white stain.

"Now, we wait."

"How long?"

"Patience, Detective."

Derrick cast me a long-suffering look and flipped through a leather-bound volume of moon phase rituals. He moved on to a manual on fortune-telling.

"You certainly have a lot of interesting merchandise. Where do you find things like this?"

"Specialty markets, mostly. The charms and candles are all local. I mix my own potions, but some ingredients I have shipped from overseas. That's where you get the good stuff, but it's more expensive."

He nodded absently, his gaze traveling over a shelf of faceted crystals. Beneath it was a series of spells arranged side-by-side under a pane of glass. His brow quirked as he read the small brass plate affixed to the display.

"Beginner Love Spells: Make Him Yours Before He Sees the Real You. Really, Tessa?"

I leaned my elbow on the case and tapped the glass. "Those are some of my best sellers."

"I bet. Do the love spells work?"

"There haven't been any complaints. Why, are you in the market?" I teased.

He leaned closer to read one of the scrolls. "Let's see, this one looks good. The Lightning Love Spell. Ingredients call for lemon zest, hemlock, a mirror shard, and a scorpion's tail. Mix with a lock of your target's hair, and it will send an enchanted bolt straight into your lover's heart." He squinted at the fine print. "Caution. May cause burning." Throwing back his head, his throaty laughter filled the quiet shop.

I couldn't resist a smile. It was nice. *More than nice.* I'd finally cracked his cool exterior. Who knew what lay further underneath?

When his amusement faded, I placed my hand on his arm. He went still beneath my touch, the heat from his skin warming my palm.

"That's the first time I've heard you laugh. I like it. You should do it more often."

A beat of silence passed while he looked at me, his expression haunted and tinged with a sense of loneliness. It was riveting, and I couldn't turn away from it. Didn't want to.

"In my line of work, there aren't many reasons to laugh."

The room had grown unbearably warm. I closed what little distance remained between us, and his hand moved reflexively to my waist, gaze falling to my mouth. The action alone sent a shiver of anticipation through my body. For the love of spell books, he was handsome.

"How tragic."

His voice was rough. "Do you think so?"

"Very much. You might need me more than you realize."

The air thickened. My lips parted, and his fingers tightened against my hip.

"Maybe I do."

I held in a breath as he dipped to brush his mouth against mine in a tentative kiss. It was unhurried, a lingering taste that left me restless. His fingers smoothed over the back of my neck, drawing me closer, deeper. The scent of his skin, the slide of his lips, and the low rumble in the back of his throat became my only focus when our bodies molded together. He didn't kiss like the straitlaced detective with alphabetical taste; his mouth was pure abandon, leaving my senses in shambles.

The pressure of his lips softened, and Derrick drew back, dragging the pad of his thumb across my bottom lip as he expelled a ragged breath.

"I shouldn't have done that."

"Probably not," I whispered.

"It was unprofessional."

"Highly."

"It won't happen again."

I tilted my head to search his dark gaze, and what I saw there made my breath catch. His eyes told a truth his mouth didn't.

"Liar."

"Tessa—"

Another thought stole my attention. "It's green."

His features clouded with confusion when I moved out of his reach heading for the bookcase. I paused for a moment, regaining my composure before selecting a heavy, dust-covered volume, which I carried back to the workbench.

"The rosenphyn worked. The paste on the wine stem turned green."

Derrick stood behind me, so close I struggled to keep from leaning against him. The need was tantalizing, but I feigned interest in turning the pages of the book. His arm brushed my side as he leaned closer, breath caressing my neck and making my nerve endings tingle.

*Oops, I went too far. Back a page.*

Finally, I found the correct section. If it had been any further, I would have dumped the book at my feet and tried testing his vow to not kiss me again. Who needed professionalism?

Derrick read the title next to my finger. "The poison is belladonna root."

"That makes sense. It says in cases of poisoning, symptoms include blurred vision, loss of balance, and confusion. In larger doses, it can cause delirium, slurred speech, and even result in death. The steward said Ella was disoriented. The killer could have poisoned her to weaken her defenses."

"There were hundreds of people at the ball. The killer would have needed to overpower her without drawing attention."

"So, he poisoned her wine and either lured her out to the courtyard or waited until she stumbled out there on her own."

"I agree. What else does it say?"

I skipped to the next paragraph. "Belladonna root is often used in wine to mask its bitter taste and unpleasant odor. That's probably why Bradford could smell it. Ella might not have noticed, but someone experienced with wines would have recognized the difference. If she hadn't spilled her wine, we might have never known it was poisoned."

"It's possible, but without the spell, it wouldn't have mattered. Nice work, Tessa."

A flare of pleasure bloomed in my chest at his praise. "Thank you, Detective. There's a little bit more. It says in the right doses, belladonna root can be used as an aphrodisiac, increasing desire and stimulating..." I trailed off, my cheeks flaming. When I turned my head, our eyes met, and again, our lips were inches apart. My earlier accusation hung between us: *Liar.*

Derrick slipped the book from my fingers and placed it on the table without breaking my gaze. "I think that's enough reading for tonight."

"I think you're right."

He cleared his throat. "Get some sleep. Tomorrow, we'll go to the apothecary and make a list of anyone who grows or sells belladonna plants."

"Sounds like a plan. Goodnight, Detective."

He retrieved his coat and paused at the door. "Goodnight, Tessa."

The soft murmur stayed with me long after he'd slipped through the entrance and into the dark.

# Chapter 13

Sleep was impossible.

The clock on the mantel read 11:50 p.m. as I tossed my legs over the edge of the bed. How was I supposed to sleep when every time I closed my eyes, I imagined him kissing me against a display of spells? At this rate, I'd be out of sleeping powder by the end of the week, or overdose and wind up in a thirty-year coma. At least then, I wouldn't have to worry about Argus or solving a murder. Who knew sleep could fix such a wide array of problems?

I groaned and fell back against the mattress. *Focus on the case. Count suspects or something.* According to Derrick's "everyone's a suspect" rule, there were more suspects than sheep. I'd be asleep in no time.

Or not.

Lighting a candle, I sat and watched the clock march its way toward midnight. When the bell chimed, a chill froze the breath in front of my face. In the corner of the room, a glow began to take shape and grow stronger.

"Welcome back."

Ella floated toward me, the hemline of her ball gown skimming the floorboards. She reached the foot of my bed and twisted the folds of her skirt in her fingers.

"Sorry to wake you. My hauntings aren't exactly at a decent hour."

"It's okay, I can't sleep. It's actually nice to have the company. This place can get kind of quiet. You'd think by now, I'd be used to living alone, but I miss having others around."

"I know what you mean. I used to feel lonely when my father was away on business. When he told me he was getting married, and I'd be getting a new stepsister, I was so excited. Many of my memories are gone, but I know that even after they arrived, I still felt alone."

She drifted closer to the nightstand and fluttered her fingers through the candle flame. The light didn't waver, but she held her hand in it, staring at the orange blaze.

"Does anyone miss me?"

The question caught me off-guard and made me think about our legacies. My mother had left behind numerous people she'd helped over the years, but besides Vivian, would anyone miss me? I wasn't so sure. A few customers were likely planning to dance on my grave for ruining their lives with one of my spells.

"Of course people miss you. I know it's difficult to believe, but your stepmother seemed genuinely upset." It was strange commiserating with a ghost. "I think family can be a blessing and a curse. Even loving relationships can have cracks. Those cracks stay with us and make it difficult to relate to other people."

She resumed playing with the candle. "Something tells me you're speaking from experience."

"Guilty. My mother loved me, but she couldn't hide her disappointment in my abilities. The harder I tried, the bigger I failed. Now that she's gone, I can't bear to see that look on other people's faces."

"Is that why you don't want the detective to get too close?"

"He'll only be disappointed."

"I don't know." She smiled softly. "Here you are, trying to solve a murder case to help a ghost. We'd never even met before I came to your shop. I'm a perfect stranger. Disappointments don't help strangers."

"My motives aren't squeaky-clean. The reward does have something to do with it."

Ella shrugged. "No one expects you to work for free."

"I'm a regular saint then." I sighed. Taking a deep dive into my stunted emotional growth wasn't going to catch a killer or pay the bills, it would only lead to breaking out the elderberry wine and drowning my sorrows. The last thing I needed was to get drunk. "Actually, there is something I need to ask you about."

"What's that?"

"We learned something about your case. It appears you might have been poisoned."

"Poisoned?" Ella's eyes widened. "Are you sure?"

Her fingers brushed her temple as if it could help her remember.

"Yes, I'm positive. We found traces of belladonna in your wineglass. It can make you confused and delusional. It would have weakened your defenses. Have you ever heard of that plant before?"

"No, never." She floated closer, her fingers curling into fists. "I must have been helpless."

Her struggle with the killer flashed in my mind, and I went numb. No wonder death helped you forget. Seeing it through her eyes had been more than enough. Actually experiencing that kind of overwhelming fear? I shuddered.

"You fought back as best you could. Tomorrow, Derrick and I are going to search for the source of the poison. We're going to find the person who did this to you."

"I know you will. I trust you." Ella drifted toward the door. "Try to sleep. You don't need me haunting you all night. If you don't mind, I'll hang around your shop for a while. Don't worry, I can't touch anything."

I laughed. "Remind me to lay out some spells for you next time. It will give you something to read."

"Do you have any love spells? Those are my favorite."

My eyes squeezed shut. I had almost put the kiss out of my mind.

"Yeah, I have a few. They're my best sellers."

\*\*\*

Dawn broke through the curtains. It was too early to get up given my night had involved discovering poisons, alluring detectives, and conversations with ghosts, but I rubbed my bleary eyes and unwound my legs from the blankets, reaching for the thick robe that hung next to my bed. Cocooned inside the heavy fabric, I considered going back to sleep—but my eyes popped wide open when a horse neighed in the yard.

*Impossible.*

I scooted off the bed and peered through the window, blinking at the sight of the royal agency's carriage parked on the gravel road. Apparently, when Derrick had said morning, he meant first thing. Like, before breakfast, and before normal people got out of bed.

At a knock on the door, I whimpered in protest.

"Tessa?"

Darting in front of the mirror, I massaged the bags under my eyes and examined the pillow creases imprinted on my pale cheeks. Running a brush through my hair only made static fuzz the ends.

"Tessa, open up."

"I'm coming. Give me a second." As the door shook from another round of knocking, I pinched color into my cheeks and tightened my robe. It would have to do—there wasn't time for a beautification spell. Not that I trusted myself with one. They tended to have the opposite effect.

I hurried down the steps and opened the door, my gaze narrowing on the ill-timed intruder. "You're early. Witches need their beauty sleep."

Derrick's gaze traveled from my unruly hair all the way down to my bare feet in a slow but thorough perusal. His mouth hitched.

"We don't have that much time."

My lip curled in a grumpy snarl. "Did you expect a bright-eyed and bushy-tailed witch, ready to conquer the day and hunt killers? You don't pay me enough."

"I'm not paying you at all."

"That's a conversation for later." I waved him into the shop, then headed for the stairs. "Wait down here. Make tea or something."

"Tea?" He gaped as if no one had ever asked him to perform such a menial task.

"Yes, tea. Leaves are in the cupboard by the window. Water's at the pump, and I know you can start a fire. I'm going to change."

He began to protest, but I shot him a grim look that he buckled beneath. Or maybe it had more to do with my wild hair than any sense of authority.

At the top of the stairs, my stomach rumbled, and I shouted, "Make toast too. There's bread in the pantry."

He grumbled something unintelligible, and I relished the image of the gruff detective making me breakfast. Early morning visitors weren't so bad after all. Especially the freshly shaved kind, who wore perfectly tailored clothes that accentuated their broad chest and arms, all before daybreak, no spells needed.

I lingered in front of my wardrobe until the kettle whistle blew, then pulled a hunter-green tunic dress over my shoulders. A leather strap cinched my waist. My hair took more time, refusing to stay in a simple braid to keep the thick strands out of my face. I frowned in the full-length mirror. I felt plain. It was a foolish thought that had me questioning its origin. A witch didn't impress with her clothes, she impressed with her spells. Too bad I was zero for two.

Needing a little something extra, I rifled through my mother's jewelry box. She had collected odd but compelling pieces. Her favorite pendant rested at the bottom, strung on a metal chain. It was the size of a large coin and shaped into an oval with an inlaid cat's eye stone. I hooked the chain around my neck, pleased with how the pendant complimented the dress. Some of my plainness slipped away.

Derrick pinned me with a pensive stare from his place near my workbench as I descended the creaky stairs. There wasn't a smirk on his face as his gaze traveled over my body, as if to confirm there was nothing plain about me.

"I couldn't find any jam." He ran a hand through his hair in a sheepish confession. His collar was unbuttoned, his hair still wet at the ends. He looked nothing like the arrogant detective who had visited my shop the morning of Ella's murder.

My stomach clenched under the weight of his gaze. I wondered if he saw the same witch?

"Jam's in the pantry. It's right next to the bread."

"Right." He winced.

"I hope you're better at finding killers than locating breakfast items."

He shrugged and took a sip from his mug. "I have a cook. She makes my meals."

"Must be nice. It seems you've done all right for yourself. The tea's hot, and the bread is sliced evenly. I'll let it slide...this time." Reaching for the plate, I ripped off a hunk of bread.

Derrick watched me chew. "Now I know where you keep the jam, I'll get it right next time."

*Next time.*

His words caused the bread to catch in the back of my throat. I coughed to loosen it, feeling heat climb my neck. Would there be a next time? And why did the thought make me want to get up even earlier and greet him with something other than a surly attitude and tangled hair? I downed my tea, letting the hot liquid burn the roof of my mouth.

"Let's get a move on, Detective." I collected his mug before he could finish, swiping it out of his hand. He didn't argue but gave me a strange look, which I ignored.

I ignored him in the carriage too.

We parked in front of the apothecary. A light frost painted curlicues on the paned windows, and I shivered beneath the thick fabric of my cloak. Snow flurries tangled in my hair and stuck to my eyelashes, each flake melting on contact. The air tasted of the first bite of winter. I rubbed my numb fingers together and blew into the palms of my hands.

Derrick stood beside me, his gaze on the hanging

sign. It swayed in the wind, whining on a rusty hinge. A bustling crowd surged around us, their heads low against the bracing chill.

"Ever been to the apothecary?" I asked, shuffling closer to Derrick to avoid being trampled by a merchant hauling a large sack over his shoulder.

Noticing my near miss, Derrick guided me in front of him. The crowd funneled on either side of us, keeping me out trampling range.

"No, I prefer being treated by a medical professional."

"You mean, Old Sawbones McAllister? I guess you don't enjoy living." I shuddered. The so-called "Doctor" considered leeches to be a medical advancement.

Derrick nudged me toward the entrance. "I enjoy living just fine."

The iron handle felt icy against my palm. Caught in the warm confines between Derrick and the door, I paused, reluctant to go inside.

"You know, there's a lot to be said about natural remedies. I bet you didn't know that ginger root can relieve cold symptoms, and peppermint leaves help with indigestion. In fact..." I trailed off when I noticed Derrick's eyes glazing over and elbowed him under the ribcage. "You're not listening."

Catching my hand, he trapped it between his own and frowned as he rubbed the warmth back into my fingers. "I'm paying attention." Tilting his head, he cast a wary look into the street.

I pretended to straighten his coat and glanced

over his shoulder. A burly man with a turned-up collar lurked in the shadows of a shop canopy. Another man, lanky and grizzled, hovered near a wall of flyers.

"Do you know those men?" he asked.

Apprehension knotted my stomach. I did know them. More importantly, they knew me. Argus's goons were getting sloppy—unless they wanted me to see them, which was certainly possible. I ignored their less-than-subtle intimidation. He had given me until the end of the month to pay my debt, so they'd leave me alone until then. The bigger problem was keeping Derrick from making the connection between me and the unsavory thugs.

"No. I've never seen them before." The lie burned in my throat. I knew it made things more complicated, but I couldn't tell him the truth. Our partnership was rocky at best, and any hint I might have an ulterior motive would get me thrown off the case. After my talk with Ella, I couldn't jeopardize her trust. It was better this way. I could handle Argus on my own.

Derrick's lips thinned. He stared me down, searching for the lie, but I was seamless.

Plastering a smile on my face, I pushed open the door. Waves of heat instantly thawed my bones, and I breathed in the sulfurous smell mixed with invasive pungent herbs. A weaker constitution would have run screaming. Derrick nearly did. He covered his nose with his coat sleeve.

"Come here." I laughed and pulled him toward

a bowl of a waxy substance. "Hold still." I dabbed some onto a fingertip and lifted it near his nose. "It's lemon balm, to mask the smell. It's also very calming."

He relaxed under the pleasant scent, breathing normally again. "And you wonder why I avoid places like this."

"Can I help you?" A woman emerged from the back room and rounded the counter. Her gray apron covered a long purple gown with wide sleeves.

"Yes, you can. I'm Detective Chambers from the royal agency, and this is my assistant, Miss Daniels. We're looking for information regarding a specific herb and the names of anyone who supplies it."

The woman hesitated, eyeing us cautiously. An uncomfortable silence filled the room.

Derrick cleared his throat. "We'll need a list of—"

"You have a beautiful shop," I interrupted, admiring a display of glass jars. "I hear you have the largest selection of aromatic oils in the kingdom. I dabble myself, but I haven't mastered the extraction process. Do you prefer the steam method?"

The woman gave me an encouraging smile. "I do prefer the steam method, it enhances the oils. I didn't realize you practiced perfumery."

I nodded and leaned in conspiratorially, gesturing toward Derrick with my chin. "A little, but this one doesn't appreciate my hobby. He calls it frivolous."

She huffed. "Men never appreciate the skill." The woman extended her hand. "Please, call me Ada."

Derrick rolled his eyes at my performance. I ignored him. If I'd let him keep going, we'd have gotten nowhere. Merchants didn't give up their own.

"Thank you, Ada. You see, we're here with a bit of a problem, and since you're the reigning authority on medicinal herbs, we came directly to you."

Ada preened, smoothing the ebony locks of hair tucked behind her ears. "Whatever you need."

I motioned for Derrick to continue, sending him a wink for good measure.

"As I was saying, we need a list of anyone who supplies belladonna root."

Ada bit her lip. "I don't stock that here, and I can't think of any reputable shop that does."

"What about non-reputable ones?" Derrick asked.

Ada grew silent. She looked around the empty shop as if the jars had ears, then inched closer, her voice barely a whisper.

"There is one I know of, but you didn't hear it from me."

We waited, eager for her answer, but she backed away when the bell above the shop jingled.

"Welcome!"

An old lady bustled inside, complaining about her aching joints, and Ada led her to a shelf along the wall to select a cream. "I'll be right back," she said to the customer before making her way to the adjoining room.

Derrick groaned as another couple entered the shop. "She'll never talk to us like this."

"Should we come back?"

"If we leave, she might change her mind about

talking altogether."

"Then, what do we do?" I bounced nervously on my heels.

Ada reappeared and nodded toward the customers, then brushed past me, slipping a folded piece of paper into my hand. Without stopping, she continued on, ushering the customers to a large table filled with canisters.

"Let's go." I showed Derrick the paper concealed in my palm.

Back on the street, he led me down a quiet alley that shielded us from public view.

"What does it say?"

I unfolded the note. "It says, Flamelock Den."

"Where's that?" Derrick frowned, taking the note from my hands.

"You asked for the non-reputable shops," I pointed out. "Flamelock Den isn't really a shop, more of a hole in the wall. It's part of what we in the biz like to call—"

"The black market," Derrick cut me off and lifted an accusing brow.

"Very good." I tucked my arm through his and peered into his scowling face. "I'm afraid they don't let members of the royal agency wander around there. You'll need someone who can get you in, and that, Detective, is why you're lucky to have me."

# Chapter 14

"I can't believe you talked me into this. Explain to me again why you're forcing me to wear tweed?" Derrick grumbled as he tossed his charcoal vest and black woolen coat over the wooden dressing screen. His dress shirt followed, and I smothered a grin along with the wicked thought of him standing behind there without a shirt.

Handing the snidely referenced coat around the screen, I replied, "Because you wouldn't let me change your clothes with a spell. I believe your exact words were, Tessa, you don't have a good history with illusions."

"You don't."

"How kind of you to remind me. Either way, it doesn't matter. You needed to change. It's called going undercover, I'm sure you've heard of it."

"Oh, I've heard of it, but for someone who has yet to explain how she knows so much about the black market, you're enjoying my discomfort a little too much."

"Discomfort?" I selected a matching tweed flat cap from a rack. "I hardly think changing your outfit falls under *discomfort*. You'll draw too much attention if you walk around wearing expensive wool and a starched collar, and I doubt you own anything of lower quality."

The screen rattled where Derrick bumped into it. He muffled a curse, and I bit the side of my cheek to keep from laughing. Cursing again, this time, he poked his head around the screen.

"Something's wrong with this shirt. It's itchy." He pulled the fabric away from his skin and scratched furiously at his side, eyes narrowing at the guilty press of my lips. "You did this, didn't you? Some sort of spell?"

"Of course not. I'd never use my magic for evil. Besides, I don't have a good history with spells. Now, come here."

He stalked from behind the screen, frown firmly in place. I stood on my toes to place the cap on his head, admiring the way the linen clung to his muscular frame. Derrick fidgeted, unable to get comfortable, and scratched the back of his neck where the shirt collar met his skin.

Maybe I shouldn't have cast the spell, but I couldn't resist. His lack of confidence in my magic was irritating, so I'd made his shirt irritating. Seemed like a fair trade.

"Hold still," I muttered, sliding my knuckles down the back of his neck and over his shoulders.

He tensed at my touch but instantly relaxed as the irritation spell faded. "I knew it." He caught my hand. "You're a vengeful witch." His thumb stroked the center of my palm, and I felt the contact all the way down to my toes. "Now, tell me the truth."

"Tweed suits you." I tugged my hand from his and straightened the lapels on the jacket. I had to admit, he was even more handsome in the casual coat, with his shirt unbuttoned at the neckline and cap at a slight angle. In his formal suit, he looked remote and formidable, but dressed like he was now? The opposite. He looked approachable.

Derrick stared at me. "That's one truth, but not the one I was hoping for."

"Oh, I thought you were fishing for compliments." I patted his chest, then turned, only for him to catch my wrist and pull me back.

"Tessa, regardless of your attempts to inflict painful spells on me, I need to know how deep your association goes with illegal activity. Is there anything I should be worried about? or anyone?" He let the question hang in the air.

The truth was on the tip of my tongue. *I'm indebted to an underground kingpin and occasionally purchase illicit ingredients for my spells.* But I shook my head.

"Most of what I know is secondhand, and as far as the market, I've only been one time." *That you know of.*

He released my wrist, taking me at my word. The small act of trust made me wince and rub the twinge in my chest. I needed to stop lying, but then I'd look at Derrick and feel the fragile thread of our partnership tighten and nearly snap.

I hated lies. Hated that I had to hide the real me when I was getting glimpses of the real Derrick. He wouldn't understand, wasn't the type. His look of disappointment was what I feared the most, and that fear was growing stronger after each encounter, so now, the mere thought of it salted my old wounds. He needed me to be more. Ella needed me to be more too, and with my familial line of dead, judgmental witches as my witness, I'd try to be.

Even if I had to fake it.

The merchant approached and cleared his throat. "Shall I add the items to your account, Detective?" When he wrote the purchases in a ledger and calculated the cost, I choked at the sum. For casual attire, it was insanely expensive.

"Yes, and add these too." Derrick retrieved a pair of dove-gray leather gloves from a shelf. He guessed the size and handed them to me. "And before you say anything, I won't add the cost to your fines."

"I can still do magic with these on," I teased. "Your shirts aren't safe."

The hint of a smile played around his lips. "I don't doubt that. Wear them anyway. Your fingers are always cold."

I breathed through the tightness in my throat and acted like the gift hadn't annihilated my defenses. He'd noticed how cold my fingers were, and magic was harder when my hands were freezing. Slipping them on, I let my eyes drift shut. The supple leather felt like heaven against my skin. I'd never owned anything as luxurious.

"You like them?"

I opened my eyes to find Derrick watching me with satisfaction. "Yes, very much. Thank you, they're lovely." A flicker of guilt made me admit, "And I apologize for casting the irritant spell on your shirt. That was childish. Amusing, but childish."

He thanked the merchant, then turned me by the shoulders toward the door, breath brushing against my cheek as he leaned in to whisper, "Apology accepted. But just so you know, I never get mad. I get even."

\*\*\*

"Hurry up, or we'll be late."

I took a shortcut through a dingy alley. The smell of decay hung in the air between the buildings, and if we saw anyone, they scurried out of the way, keeping to themselves. This part of town wasn't exactly savory. Best to not make eye contact if you could help it. The alley emptied into a busy street, and I scanned the crowd.

"Over there. By the lamppost."

Derrick followed my gaze. "That's him? He's a child."

"Don't let him hear you say that. Finn's sensitive about his age. He takes care of his mother, not the other way around. On these streets, that deserves respect."

We approached the young boy leaning against the lamppost. He had flat gray eyes, shaggy brown hair, and a curl to his lips that said bugger off. Finn straightened when he saw us, his expression narrowing on Derrick.

"It's all right, Finn. He's with me."

"You workin' with the agency now, Tess?"

"Just doing them a favor. Did you bring it?"

Finn dug into his pants' pocket and tossed me a medallion. "Three blocks west. The abandoned warehouse."

"Thanks, Finn." I tousled his hair, and he cringed. Kneeling at his side, I slid a bag off my shoulder. "I stopped at the magic shop after I sent for you. This is for your mother's headaches. Make sure she takes it with food, one teaspoon a day in a glass of water." I pulled a jar of yellow powder from the bag, and he nodded solemnly, accepting the responsibility. "And these are for you." I dropped a packet of peppermint candies into his outstretched palm.

Finn unwrapped one of the mints and tucked it into the side of his cheek. He grinned. The boy might not like to be called a child, but he had a child's sweet tooth.

I looked up at Derrick. "Pay the man."

Derrick stifled a smile and handed over ten royal coins. Finn eyed the money but didn't take it.

"What's wrong?"

Finn scratched the back of his neck. "Tessa said not to accept anything less than twenty."

"She did, huh? That sounds like something she'd say." Derrick upped the amount, and Finn pocketed the coins.

I stood and brushed the dirt from my knees. "Next

time, Finn, wait for twenty-five. Now, run home and give that powder to your mother, and when you run out, come by the shop."

Finn nodded and shot Derrick another leery glare. "If you need help with this one, Tess, you know where to find me." He popped a peppermint into his mouth and disappeared into the crowd.

I flipped the medallion and showed it to Derrick. "This will get us inside the market. They don't let you in without one, and even if they did, the market moves around. Finn helps some of the vendors, so he always knows the way."

"He seems protective of you. How did you meet him?"

"His mother is sick, and he can't afford a doctor. He came by the shop one day, and I caught him trying to steal one of my potions. I have a pretty stringent no-stealing policy. After I threatened to turn him into a crow if I ever caught him stealing again, I went to visit his mother. Ever since, I make sure she has the medicinal powder she needs, so he has one less thing to worry about. He's a good kid."

Derrick grinned. "That almost makes me want to forgive you for telling him to hustle more money out of me."

"What can I say? Teach a kid to fish, and he'll catch fish. Teach a kid to negotiate, and people will catch fish for him."

"I don't know whether to laugh or call you a genius."

"Clearly, I'm a genius, Detective."

He tucked a strand of hair behind my ear and let his fingers graze along my jaw. "What you do for Finn matters, Tessa. You have a good heart."

I shrugged. "It's no big deal."

"It is. You're constantly surprising me." His gaze softened, and I flushed, not sure what to do with his approval. All I knew was it did a funny thing to my insides.

We walked the three blocks west and found the abandoned warehouse, its entrance covered with a stained burlap sheet. I ducked beneath it and followed Derrick down one dark hallway, then the next. A couple of men standing guard by another door gave us the once-over, but I showed them the medallion, and they let us through.

The market lay sprawled inside the vast ruins. Bricks and mortar littered the ground along with broken beams. Thick canvas awnings were strung over the wood, creating makeshift stalls, and where the roof had caved in ages ago, midday sun caught dust motes in the air and made them glisten. Exotic animals in gilded cages squawked and pecked as we passed by, one even calling out in a strangled cry, "Give me a cracker, and I'll tell you where the gold's hidden."

Derrick hesitated, but I waved my hand, dismissing the parrot. "It's a scam. He'll say anything for a cracker."

I inhaled the seductive scent of spices smuggled in from foreign kingdoms as we weaved through the thin crowd. Derrick remained close. Too close. His sharp eyes missed nothing as he steered me around a transaction of daggers made with enchanted steel. A young blonde woman wearing a teal scarf over her face tossed an apple into the air, then flipped the dagger, slicing it clean through the crisp fruit.

"Enchanted steel isn't illegal. You don't have to give it such a wide berth." I glanced over my shoulder in awe.

"Maybe not, but it's damn sharp, and I don't need a bloodied witch on my hands."

"Come on, Detective. I'm not foolish enough to walk in between a knife demonstration."

Derrick's grip on my arm tightened, yanking me back as a blade whizzed past my face, nearly clipping off my nose. It sank into a post. The hilt vibrated from the force.

"Sorry! That one got away from me." The blonde woman tossed up her hands before returning her attention to the customer.

"You were saying?" Derrick growled in my ear.

"That could have happened to anyone."

"Unlikely." He maintained a loose hold on my arm as we continued to walk.

Near the back was the stall called Flamelock Den, and I was miffed to find it empty. Merchandise lay strewn across a scarred table, but the merchant was nowhere in sight. Instead, a swarthy man wearing a black tunic and trousers slipped out of the shadows. Derrick tensed, and before I could say anything, the man swept up my hand and leaned over it, brushing his whiskered lips against my knuckles.

"Tessa, my love! My favorite customer."

I squirmed out of his grip and made a slicing motion at my neck. Eyes wide, I spoke between clenched teeth, "Charlie, is it? I can hardly remember since we only met the *one* time."

Understanding was quick to dawn, and Charlie rubbed the beard under his chin. "That's right, it was the one time. You're hard to forget, my love. And who would want to?" His praise was over-the-top and likely dished out to every skirt that walked past, but it caused Derrick to bristle. He made a sound behind me, and I could practically feel his displeasure burning a hole through my cloak. It was distracting. There was no way he believed my story about the market now. Why had I bothered to mislead him?

"Charlie, this is Derrick. He's a Roy—" I stopped, realizing my mistake. We hadn't discussed a suitable cover story, and I'd almost botched it. Horrified, I changed direction. "He's a colleague."

Charlie furrowed his bushy eyebrows. "You mean, he's a warlock?"

A bark of nervous laughter burst from my lips. "No! What I meant was..." My mind emptied, and I grappled for words like a flustered idiot. Why had I said colleague? Anything else would have been better. Acquaintance, a buyer, a friend! I should have said friend.

"He's a fri—"

Derrick's arm snaked around my waist and pulled me firmly against him, cutting off my introduction. "Tessa, don't be embarrassed."

I froze, heart thudding violently in my chest as his head lowered. His breath ruffled my hair, firing every nerve ending. My body seemed to know his intentions before my brain, and I arched my neck as he pressed a possessive kiss against my skin.

"Tell him the truth," he murmured. "I won't be mad." *I never get mad. I get even.*

He wasn't wasting any time exacting his revenge for my spell. The devil actually thought he had the upper hand. And maybe he did, for a moment, as his mouth dropped to my collarbone, warm lips sending a shiver coursing through my body. He was a dead man.

A wicked grin spread across Charlie's face. "No explanation needed." He winked and reached under the counter, glancing covertly in both directions. "It's obvious why you're here. I have just the thing." He placed a vial of blue liquid onto the table. "Since you're a preferred *one-time-only* customer, I'll give you a discount."

All color drained from my face.

Derrick nuzzled my neck and whispered, "What's that?" Unease tinged his voice. It should.

"Take a guess." I turned in his arms and kept up his ruse. "Charlie thinks we want to spice things up." Winding my hands around his neck, I watched Derrick's eyes darken when he made the connection. My fingers lazily mussed the hairs at his nape, and I bit my lip until his gaze dropped to my mouth. "Still interested in getting your revenge this way, *sweetheart?*" His throat worked, and his chest expanded on a sharp inhale. I almost pitied the man.

"Up to you." His voice was deeper than normal. *Affected.* It was such a shame we had to solve a murder.

"Maybe next time." I pouted for Charlie's benefit and disentangled myself from Derrick's body. The things I did for ghosts. "Actually, we're looking for something else."

"I'm nothing if not your servant, my love." Charlie grinned, laying the charm on thick, hoping to make a sale. Derrick sent him a deadly look and hooked his arm around my waist.

*Ugh, men.* I'd reached my limit for flattery and petty jealousy. Apparently, I had one. Who knew? But with Derrick's all-too-quick revenge making my skin tingle, I was suddenly surly. What I needed was a glass of wine and a good spell book. Everyone else could go count frogs.

"One of my potions calls for belladonna root. It's impossible to find, but if anyone knows where I can get it, it's you."

Charlie smirked at my appeal to his vanity. "That's a slightly more dangerous aphrodisiac. Too much, and you wind up dead."

I winked. "Then let's hope I get the dose right. Where can we get some?"

"This time of year, I'd say nowhere. But as it happens, I've heard of someone who deals. The name will cost you, and it's all I got. More phantom than anything else. Tracking it down will be up to you."

Derrick withdrew a sum of money and placed it

on the counter. Charlie made a quick count, then flashed his teeth.

"That's it? I don't take less than fifty."

I coughed, face flaming.

"Oh, really? That sounds familiar." Derrick narrowed his eyes. "Take it or leave it."

"Derrick," I hissed. Now wasn't the time to see who had the bigger...*negotiating skills*.

His arm tightened around me as the ultimatum hung in the charged silence. Charlie rolled his tongue over his teeth, then snorted.

"Fine." He pocketed the coins. "You're looking for Ironhazel. That's all I know."

The name wasn't familiar. "Thanks, Charlie."

"Anytime, my love." He nudged the vial of blue liquid toward me while Derrick wrote the name in his notebook. "My gift to you."

Discreetly, I snapped up the vial. *Never turn away free potions.* It was a witch's creed, also good business sense. We moved away from Charlie's stall.

"Was that necessary?"

Derrick shrugged. "It felt good."

"Well, as long as it felt good." Fisting my hands on my hips, I asked, "Where to next? Want to see a dragon's egg encased in amber? They're that way." I pointed deeper into the market.

"Dragons aren't real. It's probably a painted goose egg they placed in amber so you can't tell the difference."

"Aren't you a killjoy. Even if it's fake, it's still interesting."

"We shouldn't hang around this place longer than needed. It's asking for trouble. We got what we came for. Actually, we got more than we came for. Hand it over."

"Hand what over?" I danced out of his reach as he tried to capture my gloved fist.

"Tessa, I'm warning you." He sidestepped a vendor juggling illuminated marbles and stalked closer.

"But it was a gift! Like the gloves. You can't take away gifts, it's rude."

"Rude? So is lying about how many times you've come here. One time, huh?" He feinted left and went right. I fell for it and stumbled into him, holding my hand in the air as if it didn't make my fist level with his forehead. Lowering in defeat, I unfurled my fingers. The blue vial rested in my palm.

"Fine, take it." Some of my surliness slipped through, and I snapped, "A coldhearted detective like yourself needs it more than I do, anyway."

"Coldhearted?" His features hardened. He snatched the vial and backed us up until my shoulders bumped a wooden post, caging me in with his body. "Is that what you think?"

Um...no. There was nothing cold about the look in his eyes; it left a trail of heat across my skin. I squared my shoulders, trapped between him and the post, and tried to regain the upper hand.

"What was that back there? You shouldn't have pretended we were together in front of Charlie. It wasn't fair."

"Do witches play fair?"

"No, but we're witches. It comes with the name. You're a detective." My fingers curled in the lapels of his tweed jacket, tugging him closer. "You're honorable, reserved." He went motionless beneath my hands, and I pressed myself closer still, molding against him. "A man of virtue." His breath grew harsh as we stared each other down, and I stood on my toes to whisper in his ear, "Don't stoop to my level, Detective."

With sober features, he slipped the vial into his pocket. "Don't underestimate me, Tessa. And stop lying. If you lie to me again, we're through. I mean it." He grazed a knuckle under my chin. "Whatever it is. I can handle it."

# Chapter 15

A few days later, I woke to the sound of pounding on my front door. Shading my eyes from the sun peeking through the curtains, I smiled. Another early wake up call from Derrick? What should I have him make me for breakfast this morning? Did I dare try for a poached egg? Rolling to my feet, I padded to the mirror and checked my appearance. Not terrible.

Instead of a ratty mess, my dark curls had a freshly tousled look. Combing the long strands forward, I hurried to the wardrobe and pulled on a wine-colored dress. The pounding sounded again, and I yelled over my shoulder, "Just a minute."

I flew down the stairs and came to an abrupt halt on the last step. Sylvia Trager peered through the window pane. She rapped her cane against the glass.

"Hurry up, dear. It's freezing out here."

The smile slipped from my face, and I felt a pang of disappointment. What was wrong with me? I'd been acting smitten for days, taking extra time with my appearance, grinning like a fool when we stopped for lunch—a regular occurrence now—and soaking up those moments when I'd catch Derrick watching me with a gaze that made my heart pound. Anyone who knew me would shake their head in pity. Even I would shake my head in pity and then burn some sage to clear the air of secondhand embarrassment.

Sylvia barged inside and smacked me with a rolled newsprint. "You sly girl! After all that nonsense you spouted about not being interested in marriage. No wonder you didn't attend the ball. I want details. And tea. Get me tea."

"Sylvia, what are you talking about?" I swung the kettle over the coals and stoked them back to life.

"I'm talking about the Ever Gazette." She tapped the newspaper with her bony finger.

"That's a gossip rag. More society pages than news. Didn't I tell you to stop reading it?"

She made a shushing sound and waved me away. "There's truth in every rumor, and I want the truth from you about this." The paper crinkled as she flattened it against the table.

Funny, she wasn't the only one demanding my honesty these days. Derrick's ultimatum rang in my ears. Tell the truth, or else.

"The truth about what?"

"The front page! Take a look for yourself."

Apprehension made me approach the paper like it was a snake in the grass. When I got close enough, my stomach dropped. A hand-drawn image of me standing under the eaves of the apothecary shop covered the front page. But I wasn't alone. The moment had seemed innocent at the time, but the way the artist captured it told a different story. Derrick stood in front of me, his hands closed around mine, our heads bent together as if we were sharing an intimate secret. The headline made it worse.

*Agency's Famed Detective Has Fallen Under A Witch's Spell.*

I jabbed the illustration. "It wasn't like that. We were—"

"Canoodling?"

"We were not!" Heat flushed my cheeks. At least, not there. Give us a couple of hours and a stroll through the black market, and then, yeah. Good thing the artist hadn't witnessed that exchange. "Detective Chambers and I are working together to solve Ella Lockwood's murder. This is taken completely out of context!"

Sylvia winked. "His expression says differently, my dear. A man hasn't looked at me that way in ages."

"They drew him like that to sell papers. It's gossip fodder, nothing more."

"Gossip or not, it's a fantastic likeness. You'll get more customers from this. Everyone reads the Gazette."

Which meant everyone would know about my association with Derrick, and it wouldn't take any effort to discover my role in the case. I worried my lip between my teeth. Public curiosity was one thing, but the scrutiny could become a problem. Crossing to the fireplace, I removed the kettle and banked the coals.

"Sorry, Sylvia. I have to go to town. There's no time for tea."

"Are you going to visit your detective?"

"He's not my detective." I retrieved my cloak and ushered Sylvia out the door.

She paused on the landing. "I want to meet the man. Bring him by for a meal. Fuzzlebottoms and I will judge whether you two are a good match."

"No way, Sylvia. You and your cat aren't getting involved."

"But I already promised Fuzzy! You know how much he enjoys the company. His tail gets all fluffy."

*Unbelievable.* This was my life now, catering to a nosy neighbor and her dreaded cat while wading through the quicksand that was my partnership with Derrick. Tack on murder with a side of haunting, and a permanent vacation from the kingdom was starting to sound like a good idea.

"I'll think about it." I guided Sylvia down the walkway and set her in the direction of her house.

"Wonderful! What's his favorite meal?"

"Rosemary chicken and glazed potatoes."

Sylvia narrowed her eyes. "That's your favorite, dear."

"Well, what do you know? It's kismet." There was no way I'd submit Derrick to Sylvia's meddling, but maybe, if I was lucky, I'd get a home-cooked meal out of the lie.

She sniffed the air and made a face before trudging back to her cottage. Derrick would be furious. He hadn't wanted me around to begin with, and now, I was more involved than before. Steeling myself for his lecture, I headed into town.

***

The agency was busier than ever. Publicity from the paper had people standing around the entrance, hoping to catch a glimpse of the famed detective cavorting with the local witch. I ducked down a side street and peered around the corner. So far, no one had spotted me, and I wanted to keep it that way.

Scooting further down the alley and away from the onlookers, I noticed someone break away from the crowd to follow behind. The urge to run vibrated in me. I'd need to go in through the side entrance since the last thing I wanted was to conduct interviews on the street. I scrambled backward and collided into a stack of crates, which crashed to the ground, taking me with them.

The man caught up and hovered over me, offering his hand. I sucked in a breath and rolled, trying to get out from beneath the crates. It was him. The man I'd found hiding in the hedges at the crime scene.

"Stay back!" Adrenaline boiled my magic. I needed to regain some control before I could harness it. "I saw you at the palace." The words slipped bravely from my mouth, an accusation I feared might do more harm than good.

He took a step in my direction, flexing his gloved fingers. His face was all angles and sharp lines with deep-set brown eyes. He was younger than I'd thought, with thin lips pressed into a determined crease.

"Don't come any closer. I'm a witch. I'll turn you into a toad." Probably. Hopefully. My lips trembled. I didn't want to die in an alley, a hundred feet from the royal agency. It wouldn't look good. I could see the headline now: *Famed Detective's Paramour Found Dead Steps From Help. Her Spells Couldn't Save Her. Detective Swears to Never Love Again.* The last part, I added for my own benefit. I would be the dead party after all, so I should be mourned properly and with devotion.

The man's deep voice captured my attention. "I won't hurt you."

"No. I wouldn't advise that, unless you want to eat flies and live the rest of your days in a swamp."

He shook his head, and the hint of a smile curved his mouth. Great. My threats were funny to him.

"I just want to talk."

"You could have made an appointment."

"Will you at least listen to what I have to say? I won't come closer."

I gave him a curt nod and climbed to my feet. "Why were you hiding behind the hedge at the crime scene? And why did you threaten to come find me?"

"It wasn't a threat. I didn't know if I could trust the authorities, but you're not one of them. My story might be safer with you."

"Why can't you trust the authorities?"

A dry laugh escaped his lips. "They work for the royal family. Their loyalty is with the king. Anything that puts the royal family in a bad light may be ignored. I could disappear."

He had a point. "Who are you?"

"My name is Liam Barber. I was one of the servants assigned to the prince the night of the ball."

"I see." I relaxed, and the fear drained from my muscles. "What do you want to talk about?"

"I need your promise that you won't tell anyone you spoke with me." His gaze darted to the end of the alley, where the crowd mingled out of earshot.

"I'll keep your identity a secret. You have my word."

"What about your friend, Detective Chambers? I saw the papers."

"You can trust him." It was strange, but when I said the words, I believed them wholeheartedly. "Tell me what you know, and we'll protect your name."

Liam came within a few feet of me and lowered his voice. "The prince's alibi is fake. Regardless of what anyone told you, at the time of the murder, the prince wasn't in the ballroom."

Shock made me silent for a few seconds while I processed his words. "How do you know?"

"Shortly before midnight, he traded masks with me. He's done it before at masquerade balls. I was the one who danced with Ella. She whispered something to me. She wanted me to meet her alone in the courtyard."

"Did you?"

"Of course not. I stayed in the ballroom, that's why everyone thinks he has an alibi. He returned through a side door after midnight. We traded back. Minutes later, they found her body."

The prince was lying. Where had he gone during the narrow window of Ella's murder? And if he had killed her, what was the motive? Not to mention, the motive for the other two women, one of whom had worked in a tavern and had likely never crossed paths with a prince in her life.

"I have to go. They'll question me if I'm gone too long. I don't know anything else, but I couldn't keep quiet after what happened to that poor girl."

"Thank you for coming forward."

He nodded and backed away, leaving me alone in the alley. I had to tell Derrick. This changed the course of our investigation.

The prince might be our killer.

# Chapter 16

"I'll let him know you're here." Estelle gave me a sympathetic smile as her gaze shifted between me and the newspaper sitting on her desk. After hearing Liam's witness account, I'd almost forgotten about the baseless article. Her look didn't bode well for Derrick's mood. It might be a veiled warning to turn around and high-tail it out of the kingdom. You couldn't kill a witch you couldn't find.

What a mess. First, the cozy picture and headline in the Gazette, and then, my encounter with Liam. I didn't know what to address first. Maybe the new lead would soothe Derrick's ire. It certainly cast the case in a new light—a dangerous one if the prince was somehow involved.

Estelle returned to her desk and gave me a serene smile. It seemed practiced, the kind you give someone who's about to enter a lion's den and you're trying not to make them panic.

"Detective Chambers will see you in his office."

I chewed on my lip, unease making my feet leaden. "How is he?"

She glanced around the waiting room discreetly,

then leaned forward. "Between you and me, dear? Run."

Her words took a second to arrange in my head. Oh, boy. It was worse than I thought. My nerves doubled, but there was also a prick of disappointment. Was it really so bad? I had qualities. Lots of them! Derrick would be lucky to end up with a woman like me. I mean, lucky was pushing it—I did have a mountain of debt, a rundown shop, and my spells were dismal. But beyond all that, I was a total catch. He just needed time to come to that conclusion on his own.

I backed away from the desk. "Tell him I left the kettle on." We could talk later.

"Good one, dear."

Halfway through my escape, his clipped voice echoed through the waiting room. Even the criminals ceased their grumbling.

"Miss Daniels, my office is this way."

*Damn.* The exit was so close. *Should I make a run for it?* Maybe Estelle had the right idea.

Turning, I tried one of her serene smiles, but it wobbled in the face of his grim features. Couldn't he smile a little at his fake paramour? Love could move mountains but apparently not the corners of his lips.

"Detective, you didn't need to come and get me. I know the way to your office."

He lifted a brow. "Apparently not. Follow me." Derrick propelled me into the hallway that was suspiciously empty considering the time of day. He lowered his voice. "I knew you'd chicken out."

"I didn't chicken anything. I left the kettle on at the magic shop. If the place burns down, it's on your head. I'll expect reparations."

His throaty laugh surprised me. Wasn't he furious? I found myself grinning in response.

"You're something else, Tessa."

We paused in front of his office door, and I placed my hand on his sleeve, feeling the warm expanse of skin beneath the fabric.

"About the paper, I was as shocked as you. This wasn't my intention. They made it seem like I was trying to ensnare you in a love spell. It's absurd."

"So, you're not then?" His gaze dropped to my leather gloves—the gift he'd given me. I probably shouldn't have worn them.

I tucked my hands behind my back. "Don't be ridiculous. I don't need a spell for that. You should know, I have my share of suitors."

Something dangerous glinted behind his eyes. "Name one."

Naturally, he'd call my bluff. I fumbled for a name, going all the way back to my childhood to find the only boy brave enough to follow around a budding witch. Too bad I hadn't seen him in years.

"Trevor, the baker's son. He's enamored with me and constantly compliments my stunning beauty and clever intellect."

Silence met my answer. Derrick stilled except for a noticeable tic in his jaw. I grew bold, spurred on by the dark look in his eyes, and inched closer until the hem of my skirt covered his boots. The air seemed to thicken in the narrow hall.

My voice dipped. "There's also the blacksmith's apprentice. I'm very fond of him."

"What's his name?" Derrick growled. The rumble sent a shiver through my body. He was so close, I felt the vibration in his chest.

"Are you jealous, Detective? Does the thought of another man pursuing me drive you mad?

"Don't play games, Tessa. You know what will happen if you lie to me again."

Anger sparked through me. "Is that right? A man wanting me is a lie?"

His lips parted. The hunger emanating from his stare forced me to question the sanity of provoking him. It also encouraged me to go further and find out what lay on the other side of that look.

"No." His answer, when it came, made my stomach flip. "It wouldn't be a lie. It's more possible than you realize." His hands circled my waist, bringing me flush against him.

My heart pounded, and liquid heat flowed through my body. There wasn't anything gentle about the way Derrick gripped my hips. It was like he was staking a claim against my fictional suitors. This wasn't a game—at least, not one I had any shot at winning—but with his mouth hovering near my ear, he made me want to play.

"I better not see either of them around given our current situation."

"It's a blip in the papers." My mouth felt dry as

sand. I wet my lips. "Tomorrow, it will be forgotten."

"You think the public has such a short memory? I certainly don't. It'll take a hell of a lot more than the next day's news to make me forget this."

"We'll have them print a retraction."

"Not a chance. Besides, it's too late for that." Derrick pushed open the door, releasing me at the same time Prince Marcus rose from his chair.

"Tessa, it's a pleasure to see you again. Please, come in. We need to talk."

"Your Highness," I stammered. His presence was a bucket of ice water dousing the simmering heat from the hallway. Liam's warning echoed in my mind. How was I supposed to tell Derrick what I'd learned with Prince Marcus in attendance? It would have to wait.

"Have a seat, Tessa." Derrick rounded his desk and waited for us both to be seated before he took his own. There was a whipcord tension in the set of his shoulders. Either he was still affected by our hallway encounter, or he knew what was coming before I did.

Prince Marcus faced me. "It seems we have a situation on our hands, but I think it's perfect."

"You do?"

"It's the kind of distraction we need. It will take the kingdom's mind off the murder. A relationship between you two will drown out the speculation and keep details of the case off the front page."

I questioned the prince's motives, curious to see if he welcomed the distraction too. This was royal propaganda at its finest. Love and murder went hand-in-hand, and if there was anything more salacious than a crime, it was a scandalous romance between a royal detective and a low-born witch.

"Is this what you want?" I held my breath after asking the question, a secret part of me wanting Derrick to say yes and mean it.

"It's what's best for the case." His hands clenched around the edge of the desk. He was following orders. Whatever he wanted wasn't up for discussion, and it was clear he disapproved. Could I blame him? This went way beyond a simple partnership. Things could get messy.

They already were.

"Well, whatever's best for the case then."

Prince Marcus cleared his throat. "Don't worry, Tessa, it's a temporary arrangement. I understand how this could make your life difficult. You'll be compensated accordingly."

Money. They were going to pay me to be Derrick's love interest? It was too ironic. I should have been thrilled, but the transaction felt dirty. I refused to meet Derrick's stare, even though I felt it like a weight around my neck.

"I could use the money."

"Great. It's settled."

Was it settled? It didn't feel that way. I shifted in my seat, hating this moment.

The prince continued. "We'll test the waters tomorrow evening. The Lockwoods are planning a small memorial dinner to honor Ella, and my father has offered to host. There will be a wreath-laying at the fountain. A few select guests have been invited along with the owner of the Gazette. You'll be expected to speak with him."

A sour taste flooded my mouth, made more bitter by the prince's charming smile. He wore it like a mask, and I longed to delve beneath it to the truth below the surface. The only benefit of tomorrow's ordeal would be the opportunity to observe his demeanor. Derrick and I just had to pretend to be lovers first.

"If you'll excuse me, I have some preparations to make." I rose, giving Prince Marcus a slight curtsy, still unable to meet Derrick's eyes for fear there might be pity in them.

"We'll send a carriage tomorrow at seven."

"Sounds wonderful." I slipped from the room and leaned against the closed door, shutting my eyes at the sting of tears.

What a silly reaction to the ruse we were about to play. I pressed my thumb and index finger into the corner of my eyes and took a shuddering breath. This dinner was for Ella, and I planned on playing my part to perfection. I owed her that much.

If the prince wanted a show, he'd get one.

\*\*\*

"This is a bad idea." Vivian paced my bedroom floor, winding a long strand of hair around her finger. "When's the carriage supposed to arrive?"

"Thirty minutes." I picked through my closet, frustrated by my lack of ball gowns. A long black satin frock caught my attention. I held it up against my body.

Vivian pulled a face. "No. That one makes you look drab."

With a groan, I returned the dress and stepped away from the closet. Vivian resumed her pacing.

"I can't believe they're paying you to pretend to be Derrick's love interest. When I saw the paper, I thought maybe it was true. I was happy for you. Now, I want to clock him in the face." She spun on her heel. "You don't have to do this. It's one thing to offer your help with the case, but this is different. I don't want you to get hurt."

"He can't hurt me," I muttered, rifling through a trunk near the bed. "He'd have to care about me enough to actually do that. Besides, the act makes sense, and it gets me invited to the memorial dinner." I slammed the trunk closed and sat heavily on the lid. "There's something off about Helen, and the prince is suspicious. The whole royal family could be involved, or maybe it was one of the servants. Not to mention, a friend of Ella's. The list is endless, but most of that list will be there tonight."

"And the other victims? How do they fit in?"

"I have no idea, but you can't mention them. You're not supposed to know."

"Technically, neither are you. Things happen, and we don't keep secrets from each other. Especially not a killer-roaming-the-kingdom kind of secret." She shuddered. "What about your lead on Ironhazel? That seems like a more promising avenue than a fancy dinner."

"One of tonight's guests could have paid Ironhazel to poison Ella."

Vivian tapped her foot anxiously against the floor. "I've made a decision. I don't think you should go. You're getting too involved with the case, and it's dangerous. We'll find another way to pay off Argus and help Ella. You're my best friend. I can't in good conscience let you hunt killers anymore."

"Now you sound like Derrick."

"Then he cares enough about you to be worried."

I crossed the room and gripped her hands. "I'll be fine, Viv. This is my shot to get a close look at the suspects. Besides, you're the one telling me I should get out more."

"Yeah, I meant, like, join the Ladies Tea Society or take riding lessons, not solve a murder."

I scoffed. "You know I'm scared of horses, and I hardly think the Ladies Tea Society would accept a witch."

"You know what I mean, and the Tea Society is a bunch of bores who think fashion is a conversation starter. You're better off without them."

"Maybe so, but none of that helps me with my current situation." I snarled and tossed up my hands. "It's official, I have nothing to wear. I'm going to have to use a spell."

"You are?" Vivian cringed. "You know, the satin gown didn't make you look *that* drab."

"It did. I saw the look on your face." I rubbed my hands together, bringing the first sparks of magic to

JENNA COLLETT

life.

"Hold on, what if you accidentally turn us into mice? I can't live on cheese alone."

That made me pause. "I probably won't."

"Comforting. Let me step behind the changing screen before you go full-spell." She scurried for cover. Her faith in me had reached a new low.

Closing my eyes, I took a cleansing breath. How hard could it be? I'd transformed Ella's gown, and while that scenario hadn't worked out exactly in her favor, she had looked good. Behind my eyelids, I imagined an emerald gown with an empire waist, lace gloves that skimmed past my elbows, and a crown of crystal flowers woven through my auburn curls.

I popped one eye open. Nothing yet. What was I doing wrong? I refocused, channeling all of my mental energy. Sensation flowed through my body, starting in my fingers and rushing to my feet. Light shot from my palms.

Vivian screeched and poked her head from behind the screen. "You did it, and nothing is broken!"

"Don't seem so shocked." I gazed into the mirror and smoothed the silken fabric at my waist. The dress molded perfectly to my frame.

"Derrick's eyes are going to pop out of his head when he sees you," Vivian said, walking over to me.

"Let's hope so. It will make our act easier."

Her lips thinned. "You two are playing a risky game. The lines might blur."

The lines had already blurred, starting with the kiss in my shop and fading into oblivion after our trip through the market.

A knock interrupted our conversation.

Vivian squeezed my shoulders. "Looks like Prince Charming has arrived."

I swatted her hands away. "Don't call him that."

"Why? He can't hear us." She gave me a nudge and winked. "Good luck. I want details. *All* the details."

Wiping my slick palms on my gown, I descended the staircase, pausing to do a final dress check before opening the door. Derrick stood in the cool night air, dressed completely in black. His formal jacket was perfectly tailored across his broad shoulders, giving him a dark, roguish appearance. My heart pounded as his gaze traveled agonizingly slow from the top of my head to the tips of my satin heels.

His jaw tightened. "You look..."

At his pause, I filled in the silence. "I believe the word you're looking for is fine. If I remember correctly, you said I always look *fine*."

He stepped over the threshold, lifting a hand to tuck a stray curl behind my ear. As he did so, his finger traced the outer shell of my earlobe.

"Then I'm a fool. You're beautiful."

A smile spread across my lips. "I'll remember you said that, Detective."

"This is a bad idea." He scrubbed a hand through his hair.

"The worst," I whispered.

Vivian appeared out of nowhere, rushing forward with my coat. She draped it over my shoulders, then pushed me. Hard. I stumbled into Derrick, forcing him to steady me as I shot her a furious glare.

"Have fun, kids. Bring me back a killer." She hustled us onto the porch, mouthing, "Be careful," before slamming the door in our faces.

"Who was that?" Derrick asked.

"That was Vivian. She doesn't get out much."

"Ah, the medium." He held out his arm, and I placed my gloved fingers over his sleeve so he could guide me down the steps to a waiting carriage. "Are you ready?" he asked after climbing in behind.

I met his searching gaze through the dimly lit interior. "I think so."

Derrick knocked on the roof of the carriage, and we jolted forward. The wheels clacked over the ground, hitting every bump in the roadway. I sat rigid, trying not to sway into the wall. Minutes passed as we traveled in silence.

"About our plan tonight," Derrick said, breaking the quiet.

"Don't worry, I'll hold up my end."

His voice rumbled in the enclosed space. "We don't have to do this."

"It's what's best for the case. You said so yourself."

He leaned closer, resting his arms on his knees. "Maybe I want what's best for you."

What was best for me? I hardly knew what that was anymore.

"I need the money," I said, turning my head to look out the window.

"Forget the money for a second—"

"I don't have that luxury. I don't live your life. We

need to find Ella's killer so you can get back to yours, and I can get back to mine."

"Is that what you want?"

I let his question go unanswered, stifling my emotions, then redirected the conversation. "The prince wants us to play this part, and I will. But before we do this, I need to tell you that I saw the man from the crime scene yesterday. The one hiding behind the hedge."

Derrick tensed. "What happened?"

I told him about Liam switching masks with the prince and ruining the young royal's alibi. "We can't trust Prince Marcus. It's time to consider he might be involved."

# Chapter 17

"This is what they call a small party?" My gaze roamed over the ballroom.

It seemed half the kingdom had been invited. Helen and Olivia Lockwood were at the head of the receiving line, dressed in black satin and smiling softly at the guests' condolences as they shuffled through.

Derrick offered his arm for us to descend the wide marble staircase. "It's a distraction. A gathering like this so soon after the murder shows the rest of the kingdom there's nothing to fear, and it's an honor to be welcomed by the royal family."

"If you ask me, it's insulting and in poor taste. Ella's dead, and they throw a party? If someone you cared about had been killed, would you be able to stomach this affair?"

The muscles in Derrick's forearm clenched, and he paused on the steps. "If someone I cared about was murdered, I wouldn't stop until I found their killer."

"That's your job, Detective."

"Yes, it's my job. I've made it so." Something lurked in his tone, a painful note that hinted of past hurt. Had he lost someone he loved? It was ridiculous that I envied whatever memory formed his hardened expression.

"Maybe there's more to you than I thought," I said, as we reached the bottom of the stairs and stepped into the receiving line. His arm wrapped around my middle, pulling me against his chest. Our act had already begun. To our left, a trio of guests whispered behind their fans, watching us with gossiping intent.

"What do you mean?" he murmured close to my ear.

"Well, on the outside, you're nothing but rules. Straitlaced, methodical, impassive."

"Coldhearted, if I remember correctly."

"I did say that." Twisting in his hold, I pressed my hand over his heart to feel a rapid rhythm that matched my own. "Here, though, you're a bit lawless. Maybe even ruthless."

The line moved, and he nudged me forward, his head dipping as he whispered, "I can be ruthless when someone threatens something important to me."

"Like one of your cases?"

"Among other things."

"What other things? What's important to you besides justice? Someone you're close to? A girlfriend, perhaps?" He didn't answer and instead turned me to face the front of the line.

Frustration clenched my fists. I'd answered his personal questions that day in the carriage, yet he refused to do the same.

"I'll find out, you know? I'm pretty good at playing detective."

He emitted a wry sound. "I believe you. You knock down every wall someone puts in your path."

"I can be ruthless too, Detective."

"Maybe, but you're not as fearless as you want people to believe." He brushed the hair off my shoulder, and I shivered as his fingers skimmed across my bare skin.

"You don't know that."

"I do. And to answer your question, no. There's no one else."

We reached the front of the line. Olivia Lockwood bent her head and offered us a weak smile.

"Detective Chambers, Miss Daniels, thank you for coming." Her eyes narrowed, and her tone soured. "I saw the papers. I'm happy for both of you."

Derrick took her hand in a comforting gesture. "Whatever you've read, Ella's case has our full attention."

"But not the Gazette's. We're old news." Her lips flattened into a grim line. "Even this gathering isn't really about Ella, is it? It buys our silence, gives closure where there is none, so everyone can return to their lives confident they've paid their respects, while the case grows cold."

"Hush, Mother," Helen hissed, placing a hand on her shoulder. "This isn't the place."

"No, it's not the place, is it? A scene won't help our cause, only finding the killer or maybe another murder."

"Mother!" Helen's face burned red, and she looked around to make sure no one else paid them any attention.

"Is it true, Detective? Were there others? Is my step-daughter dead because you couldn't do your job?"

Regret flashed across Derrick's features. "We're investigating every angle, Mrs. Lockwood."

"It's not enough, Detective." Olivia turned on her heel and plunged through the crowd. Onlookers gaped and whispered in her wake.

Helen winced. "I apologize for my mother, she's overwrought. One of the servants heard a rumor while in the market yesterday. There are so many rumors. If one believes them all, Ella's killer was part-beast. I, for one, trust in your investigation, Detective."

"Thank you, Miss Lockwood. If you'll excuse us, there are others who wish to pay their respects." Derrick moved woodenly out of the line.

I tugged at his sleeve, stumbling back a step when he turned. Anguish lined his features, twisting my heart.

"Olivia doesn't know what she's talking about."

It was hard to breathe around the guilt I saw in his eyes. The same kind of guilt had wrapped around me for years, a failure so deep it effected the way I viewed the world. It had become a part of me, but at that moment, I wanted to take his too. Add it to my own, no matter the weight, because I couldn't stand to see his pain.

Throat tight, I leaned in and whispered, "Ella's murder wasn't your fault. You can't believe that."

"Stay here, Tessa. I should go speak with the king."

"No—wait. I'll go with you."

He shook his head firmly and backed away, the crowd swallowing him up. I resisted the urge to follow, knowing he needed a moment alone. Guests looked my way, and I smiled, feeling my lips strain at the corners. Drifting toward the edge of the room, I watched as Olivia rejoined the receiving line. My chest ached. I pressed the heel of my hand against my collarbone to relieve the pressure. I was right about one thing: Derrick might seem impenetrable on the outside, but inside, he was wracked with guilt over the murders.

It went deeper than that though, I was sure of it. There was fear in his eyes. What if he couldn't stop it from happening again? What if the cases went unsolved? It was humbling to think similar what-if questions plagued my mind. What if I lost everything? What if I ruined my mother's legacy? Derrick and I weren't that different.

I scanned the crowd, standing on my toes to locate him.

"Looking for someone?"

Whirling around, my lips parted in shock to find Argus grinning down at me like a predatory hawk spotting a mouse. His hair had been slicked back, away from his face, and his jaw was clean-shaven. He blended in among the rich guests, dressed in a formal black suit, white shirt, and starched collar.

Only I knew he was a wolf in the henhouse.

"What are you doing here?" I dragged him into an alcove. "Are you following me? You said I have until the end of the month."

Argus tapped his knuckle under my chin, making me snarl. "Witch, not everything is about you. You forget, I'm a man of means."

"Ill-gotten means."

He shrugged. "Gold is gold where these people are concerned. How I came by it makes no difference. Besides, some of my fortune is legit. I'm sure I found a copper in the street once." He winked.

"Why are you here? You can't be seen with me."

Argus gave me a mock pout. "Why? You don't want your illustrious detective to know you associate with a man of my reputation? Will he be disappointed?"

"Yes," I grated.

"Well, we wouldn't want that. I'm escorting my half-sister, Adella Lennox. Even a businessman such as myself has a family, and my family happens to be old money. I don't need to tell you how money opens doors, do I?" He smirked. "Hmm...maybe I do, considering you don't have any."

"And whose fault is that?" My fingers tightened into fists.

He laughed. "Not mine."

"What do you want?"

Argus lounged against the wall, folding his arms over his chest. "You amuse me, witch. It hasn't escaped my notice that you've been helping the detective."

"Not much would escape your notice since you have your men following me."

He tilted his head and cocked a brow. "You noticed?"

"They're not subtle."

"Yeah, well, I don't pay them to be. Let me guess, since you're not helping the detective out of the goodness of your witchy little heart, you must be trying to collect the reward money?"

"That's not your concern."

"It is my concern when you and I are looking for the same person. Ironhazel."

I froze. "I don't know what you're talking about."

"Don't be coy, it doesn't suit you. You're searching for Ironhazel, and I want you to share any information you discover with me."

"Did you trip down the palace steps and hit your head? Why would I do that?"

"Simple. If you don't, I'll let Detective Chambers know about our involvement. What will he do when he learns you're indebted to a gangster and only after the reward money? How about when I tell him you've been working for me this whole time?"

"That's a lie!"

"Only if you make it one."

My palms grew damp, panic making my head spin. "So, this is blackmail? Why are you searching for Ironhazel?"

"That's a personal matter."

"Tell me why."

Argus shook his head. "Decide. Your detective is searching for you as we speak. Want me to wave him over?" He lifted his hand, but I jerked it down. Derrick couldn't find out the truth, not here. I needed more time.

"Fine. Keep your mouth shut and let me work. I'll be in touch." I turned to leave, but Argus pulled me back.

"Say hi to my men when you see them. They'll be watching." His mouth curved into a devious smile, then he brushed past, leaving me standing in the alcove.

"There you are." Derrick found me while I was trying to decide whether I could successfully hide behind a potted fern for the rest of the evening. I gave him a wan smile and peeked over his shoulder to see Argus raise a wineglass in mock salute.

The cad. His existence made my life difficult, and now, he wanted inside information. I steeled my expression, making sure Derrick didn't notice my wandering gaze. As much as being blackmailed by the devil himself grated, there was a silver lining. Argus knew something about Ironhazel, and personal or not, I needed to find out what that was. At the very least, it was an angle; a wispy thread that might lead to the mysterious figure, and possibly, the murderer. I just couldn't tell Derrick about it without revealing the truth. Which meant more secrets. My omissions were starting to eat away at my composure. Every aspect of my life felt like a lie.

"Have you seen the prince?" I asked, rubbing my

fingers over a fern's leafy stem.

"Not yet." His hand closed over mine, and I tensed, still grasping the fern. "Damaging the royal plants is a finable offense."

"You're making that up," I argued, releasing the fern and trying to tug my hand away.

"Maybe, but I won't report you if you tell me what's bothering you."

"Nothing is bother—"

"Tessa." He cocked his head, fixing me with a determined stare. "You fiddle with things when something is on your mind."

"I do not." I tucked my hand behind my back to keep from fiddling with the thin piece of ribbon at my waist. The fact he'd noticed such a small detail made me both delighted and uncomfortable. No one else studied me so closely.

"You do. It's your tell."

I moved away from the fern and feigned ignorance. "I don't know what you mean, Detective, but it's cute that you watch me so intently."

"Someone has to," he muttered, following as I glided back into the thick of the crowd.

We only made it a few feet before an older gentleman pushed his way through the crush of people.

"Detective Chambers, good to see you. May I have a word?" The man peered at us from behind wire-rimmed spectacles, his bulbous nose red against the white whiskers that covered his chin and upper lip.

Derrick grimaced. "John, I don't suppose you can wait to set up a meeting through my office?"

"You never accept my requests." The man held out his hand, focusing his attention on me. "And you must be Tessa Daniels, the witch. I'm John Lincoln, owner of the Ever Gazette. Surely, you can persuade Detective Chambers to give me a moment of his time? In fact, I'd love to speak with you both."

Reluctantly, I accepted his handshake, only for him to lift my fingers to his lips. John's mustache bristled against my knuckles, and I slipped into character, turning on the charm. It was time to act like a besotted fool for the papers.

"Derrick and I would be happy to answer your questions."

John smirked, his squinty eyes narrowing into slits. "You would? Detective Chambers never answers my questions."

"Because case details aren't public, John." Derrick glowered at the way the man lingered over my hand.

"No, I suppose they're not. Gotta ask anyway. Do you have any leads on the Lockwood investigation?"

Derrick smiled blandly, refusing to answer. John didn't seem fazed. He switched gears and fired off another question.

"Rumors are, there might be other murders linked to the case. Is that true?"

I fiddled with the ribbon at my waist, unable to stop the jolt of worry at the probing question. Derrick was right: I had a tell. He noticed and snagged my hand, interlocking his fingers through mine.

"Is the Gazette in the habit of printing rumors? Because I heard the killer might be a werewolf.

Should we look into moon phases and start carrying silver spikes?"

John threw his head back and laughed. "That would help sell papers. Readers love the supernatural, and it turns out, they especially love our local witch." An oily grin spread across his lips, revealing a set of crooked teeth. "Readers want to know how you put the kingdom's most eligible bachelor, second only to the prince, under your spell, and whether they can buy a bottle of it at your shop?"

My insides withered at the jeering note in his voice. This was what I'd agreed to, but it hurt to be cast as the seducer in our situation—especially one that seemed like a bottom feeder, grasping for someone above her station. Derrick had gone rigid beside me, and I sensed he was about to blow the whole act out of the water, regardless of the prince's desire to keep up the charade. Probably out of some misplaced protectiveness.

I slipped into the crook of his arm and flashed John a sly smile. "It's called Charmed Lightning, available in cherry flavor." I winked. "Until supplies last."

Another laugh, this one booming over the surrounding conversation. "I like you, Miss Daniels. Finally, a woman who can keep Detective Chambers on his toes. He's always so grim. If you ever get tired of the lad, I'll happily drink your potion."

"I'll keep that in mind if I ever need to advertise in your paper."

"You do that." He chuckled and wiped the corners

of his eyes. "You're a lucky man, Detective. She has beauty and wit."

"She does. I know how lucky I am." Derrick pulled me tighter against his side. His voice was warm and laced with meaning, a husky sound that made my face flush and a tiny flutter start in my stomach. He was good at this game. Even I was convinced.

John changed topics, holding Derrick hostage with a question about agency policy. I tuned out of the conversation, suddenly longing for a breath of fresh air, anything to douse the rioting emotions inside my chest. Glancing around the room, I caught sight of Argus again. He was speaking in a circle of guests, an elegantly dressed young woman clutching his arm. The resemblance was striking. He really hadn't been lying about escorting his half-sister.

Argus must have felt my gaze because he returned it, lifting a brow. I definitely needed air.

"If you'll excuse me, gentlemen, I'm parched." I hurried away before Derrick could protest, using the crowd for cover. Relief washed over me as I neared the edge of the room. From this angle, I didn't have to look at Argus or feign interest in agency politics with Derrick's arm snug around my waist. The first problem was detestable. The other was becoming almost essential.

Massaging the bridge of my nose, I scoured the ballroom for the missing prince. Where was he? There wouldn't be many opportunities to watch his behavior—in fact, this would probably be the only chance I'd get. I couldn't let Liam's tip go to waste

JENNA COLLETT

since he'd risked his job and possibly his life to bring it to me. With one last glance to check nobody was watching, I inched behind a marble statue to observe the room unseen.

Helen and her mother held court near the winding staircase. Olivia Lockwood appeared drawn and exhausted, but Helen seemed to thrive under the attention. I watched her sip from her wineglass, dabbing her eyes with a handkerchief every so often while regaling her audience with some tale. It looked forced, as if maybe Derrick and I weren't the only ones putting on an act.

"What a tragedy. I can hardly believe it," a woman stage-whispered on the other side of the statue. Her companion made a noise of agreement, and I peered around a marble elbow at the two ladies, hoping to catch snippets of their gossip. Maybe something would turn out to be useful.

"Honestly, he's too good for her. A witch of all things, not even a talented one. I heard she once set a barn on fire with one of her spells. Thankfully, her mother arrived to cast a rain spell, or the whole structure would have been lost. She, rest her soul, was the last of the good ones."

"Have you seen Mrs. Anderson's hair? The underside is still green from using one of the witch's potions. Poor thing can't leave her house for another week."

"I don't know what Detective Chambers sees in her. It's only a matter of time before he comes to his senses and finds someone more suitable."

I shrank behind the statue, horrified the gossip wasn't about the murder but about me. Shame stabbed my chest while the two ladies continued their banter, listing my faults and failed spells, before wandering away from the statue. Tears stung my eyes. I pressed my thumbs at the source.

"You look like you need this." Abrams approached with a glass of wine.

I accepted the offering but didn't drink it. "Let me guess, Derrick asked you to keep an eye on me tonight?"

"Guilty. He gave me the signal when you slipped away and left him at the mercy of John Lincoln." He tsk'd and sipped from his glass, tossing it back until nothing remained. "Not that I blame you. I'm actually grateful. This beats overnight rounds by the docks. I'm supposed to keep a low profile and make sure no one gives you a hard time. Don't tell him I approached you and gave up my cover."

"Seems like you and I are constantly keeping secrets from Derrick. I'll keep yours if you don't tell him about those two ladies. I'm already mortified as it is."

"Deal. Drink your wine, it will make you feel better."

I swirled the red liquid in the glass and scoffed. "I don't know if I'll drink anything ever again, not after what happened to Ella." Abrams' eyes widened, and he stared into his empty glass. I choked on a laugh. "I'm sure your wine was fine. You don't feel dizzy, do you?"

"I don't think so. But if I die, you have to promise to destroy the strongbox under my bed." He grinned, a mischievous light in his eyes.

"More secrets, Abrams? I might have to tell on you after all."

"Not secrets, love letters." He shuddered. "The sappy kind. No man should be caught dead with them. Ruins their mysterious image."

"I see. I'll make sure to take care of them for you."

He tipped his empty glass into mine. "What about you? What's the one thing you want to keep hidden? Your greatest fear?" The playfulness had left his voice, and I bit the side of my lip, not liking the edge in his tone. Even though we had developed a camaraderie, he was one of Derrick's officers. Reveal too much, and all my hard-won secrets could wind up in Derrick's hands before I was ready to explain them myself.

I handed Abrams my full wineglass. "If I think of one, I'll let you know. I'm going to get some fresh air on the terrace. I won't go far."

Abrams nodded, and I slipped past him, out the side door. When I looked over my shoulder, he was still watching me. I felt the track of his gaze until I moved out of view. A shiver worked its way up my spine at the thought he might have seen me talking with Argus. I'd have to be careful. It was easy to forget that I was technically an outsider, and Abrams' loyalty belonged to Derrick.

The terrace was lit with rows of lanterns, and guests mingled near the railing. I made my way to the gravel path leading deeper into the courtyard. The night air was cool but felt wonderful after the stuffiness in the crowded ballroom. My shoes crunched over stones, becoming the only sound as the hushed voices on the terrace faded.

I recognized the path as it wound its way along the side of the castle. The enormous clock tower loomed overhead. In the distance was the fountain where they'd found Ella, the giant stone basin illuminated by flickering lanterns. A man sat on the edge, staring in.

Prince Marcus rolled up the sleeve of his white shirt and plunged his hand into the black water. Strands of hair fell across his eyes, and his lips moved as he muttered to himself. I crept closer, trying to be as soundless as possible.

"Where is the blasted thing?" He swirled his arm through the basin.

At the edge of the fountain, a twig snapped under my shoe, startling us both. Prince Marcus whipped around. His eyes appeared glassy, almost dazed. He didn't recognize me. In one smooth motion, he clamped a hand around my arm and knocked me off-balance. Gravel slid under my heels, and the momentum sent me over the ledge. I cried out, sucking in a final breath before hitting the water. The frigid temperature shocked my body, and I sank below the surface.

# Chapter 18

Panic and pressure built simultaneously as the water closed over my head. My gown tangled around my legs, a restrictive weight, dragging me to the bottom even as I tried to stay calm. The water was only a few feet deep. I just needed to get my bearings.

The prince fisted the fabric of my gown to pull me back up, but when his hold shifted and his fingers dug deep into my forearms, my relief gave way to the realization he was holding me under. I struggled to shake him off, using the bottom for leverage. Lungs on fire, I choked in a mouthful of water—then, suddenly, my head breached the surface, and my next breath was all air.

He dragged me over the fountain ledge to land like a wet bundle in the grass, where I coughed, gulping in air. Leaning over me, the prince tugged soaked strands of hair out of my face.

"Tessa! My God, are you all right? You startled me, and I thought..." His voice faded. "I don't know what I thought, I just reacted. You fought me when I tried to pull you up."

I shivered as the night air pressed against my wet

skin, the shudder wracking my entire body. It had happened so fast. Was he trying to help? A watery cough was finally followed by a clean breath, and I lifted my head to see the worry in his wide, frantic eyes. I must have been confused, susceptible to the vision I'd had of Ella's final moments.

"I'm okay."

"No, you're not." He scrubbed a hand over his face. "After what happened here with Ella…" His throat worked, and he cursed.

My gaze dropped to his left arm, the sleeve rolled up past his elbow. "What were you doing out here? I saw you searching for something in the water."

Prince Marcus exhaled, and his eyes closed. "I was leaning over the fountain, my reflection staring back at me, and then, Ella's face was there beneath the water, the way she looked after they found her body. It spooked me, and I knocked my wineglass into the water. I should have left it, but I was trying to fish it out when you approached." He winced, the moonlight highlighting the movement of his jaw. "What happened to Ella was my fault. I should have been there. I was supposed to be." His voice cracked.

"What do you mean?"

"Shortly before midnight, I switched costumes with a servant. I never danced with her. It's all a lie. My alibi, all of it." He slumped in the grass, defeat etched across his face. "I never wanted any of this. The ball was my father's idea. He's demanding I marry and said if I don't find someone on my own, he'll pick someone for me. Do you know what that's like? To have no control over your life?"

Water dripped from the ends of my hair, skating down my arms. "I do know."

"Yeah, well, I've had enough of his ultimatums."

"Where did you go?"

"Back to my rooms. No one saw me, if that's your next question. They found her floating in the water not long after I'd returned to the ballroom. Every time I close my eyes, I see her face. I feel guilty for not being there, and guilty because her death gave me more time. There's no more talk of marriage." He gave a dry laugh. "Some would say that's a motive, don't you think, Miss Daniels?"

I didn't answer. His confession seemed genuine and matched Liam's story, but it didn't mean it was entirely true. What steps wouldn't we take to regain control over our lives? I'd borrowed money from a gang; it wasn't a stretch to think a prince could commit murder.

"You're dripping wet." Prince Marcus scowled and climbed to his feet. Reaching out a hand, he pulled me up. The action shifted the cuff of his rolled sleeve, and I noticed the raised injury on his bicep.

"Did you hurt yourself?" My mind flashed to Ella's struggle with the killer. Had she injured him while being held under the water?

He absently touched his arm, confusion flickering over his features before he laughed. "No." He lifted his sleeve higher. "It's a Vitalis mark. Your mother gave it to me."

"My mother? I thought you said you'd never met

her."

Prince Marcus shrugged. "I was a baby at the time, I don't think that counts as a meeting."

I stepped closer, wanting a better look at the spot where my mother had cast her spell. It was a strange feeling to see the evidence her magic had left behind.

"I didn't think royals still practiced the tradition of Vitalis marks. They stopped ages ago."

"Because they're barbaric, but try telling that to my father. He's superstitious. The mark is supposed to be a mystical blessing granted to royal sons, but no offense to your mother, it doesn't seem to be working." He pulled his sleeve back down, hiding the scar from view. I shivered again, and Prince Marcus frowned. "You need a change of clothes. Is that what you were wearing?"

No, it definitely wasn't. The spell I'd cast had faded, leaving me in my gray tunic dress. My emerald silk gown and matching slippers had vanished. A small pang throbbed around my heart, bringing home how temporary magic truly was. It was why seeing the mark on the prince's arm affected me so much. He had something of my mother's that wouldn't fade. It couldn't be sold off like her books or the magic shop.

"Let's get you inside before you freeze to death. We'll go in through a side entrance so no one sees." He slipped an arm around my shoulder and led me back to the castle.

We'd only made it a short distance when Derrick

found us. I watched him pick up the pace, my whole body trembling with cold. Concern pinched his features as his gaze slid over my soaked dress.

"What happened?" he shouted, shrugging out of his jacket. Derrick reached for me, pulling me gently from Prince Marcus's hold, and slipped the jacket over my shoulders. I felt instantly warmer.

"She fell into the water. It was my fault, I—"

"It was an accident," I interrupted, as Derrick's hands roamed my body, searching for an injury.

"Were you hurt?" he asked.

"No, just embarrassed and soaked. I'm fine." I captured his hands between my own. "I'm fine," I repeated, my voice barely more than a whisper.

"I'm taking you home."

"What? No." Flattening my lips, I made a subtle motion with my eyes toward the prince, signaling we had more to investigate.

Derrick ignored me completely, giving his head a firm shake. "We're done for tonight. Your Highness, please excuse us." He didn't wait for a response, slipping his arm around my waist and urging me toward the waiting carriages.

I ground my heels into the gravel. "Slow down."

"Not until we're in the carriage. Pick up your feet, or I'll carry you."

"You're being ridiculous. It was an accident. We should—" I yelped when Derrick bent and swept me off the ground. He kept walking, my dress leaving a trail of droplets in the grass. "Aren't you curious about what I learned? I mean—"

"Tessa, not now. You're freezing. You could have been seriously hurt. What if you'd hit your head on the stone? What if..." He tightened his hold around my shivering body. "Ella drowned in that water. You could have died too."

Shame kept me silent. He was right, a life had been lost. It wasn't trivial.

Derrick gave a driver directions to the magic shop and ducked into a carriage, where he placed me on a plush seat then rummaged beneath the footrest for a blanket. Draping it across my lap to keep away the chill, he settled in too and pulled me against his side.

"Come here."

"No." I wriggled away, taking off his coat. It was horribly damaged. "I've already ruined your jacket. I can't—"

"I don't give a damn about my clothes, they're replaceable." His words made me pause, the significance warring with my emotions. Did that make me *irreplaceable?* His tone gave me hope, but that was wishful thinking. No. He didn't mean me specifically. His declaration was a natural response to his oath as a detective. Life was precious, even the life of a laughable witch.

Still, I dropped the coat at my feet and sank into his embrace, pretending he truly meant me.

"Can you do a spell?"

Removing my numb fingers from beneath the blanket, I tried to rub my palms together. Nothing. I was too drained and cold to channel any magic.

"No. I'll have to get dry the old-fashioned way."

He smoothed the damp hair away from my face. "Tell me what happened."

"I went outside for fresh air and found myself retracing Ella's steps. I ended up at the fountain, and that's where I saw Prince Marcus. He had his arm in the water, searching for something, which I found out was just his wineglass. I startled him, and he knocked me off my feet. He probably thought I was the killer, back for another round. I was only underwater for a few seconds before he pulled me out. I'm mortified more than anything, especially since I panicked in four feet of water and actually thought he was trying to hold me under."

"How so?"

"When I tried to get my footing, my gown weighed me down. I thought his hands were on me, pushing. I...I was scared and fought back, but then he dragged me out, and I'm not certain what happened."

"I should have been there. While you were outside nearly drowning, I was fielding useless questions." His voice was deep with self-loathing.

"I didn't almost drown." I placed a hand against his chest. "Besides, I was able to get Prince Marcus to confirm Liam's story about switching masks. He was furious with his father for arranging the ball and for forcing him into a marriage he didn't want."

"That means his alibi is nonexistent."

"True. As far as we know, no one can account for his whereabouts at the time of the murder. He claims he never met Ella. I don't know whether to believe him or not. It's a good thing I fell in the water. It made him open up. Leave it to the witch to break the ice—or, in this case, the surface of the water." I laughed softly, hoping to lighten the mood.

It had the opposite effect.

The laughter died on my lips as Derrick's hand cupped my jaw. His thumb brushed the side of my cheek, and I swallowed, nerves tingling, caught in the silent moment.

"I won't let anything happen to you. I'll keep you safe, I swear it."

His promise made my heart pound. The carriage lantern illuminated his stark features, and I struggled to find the words to answer him.

"Nothing will happen to me, and even if something did, it wouldn't be your fault. I hate what Olivia said to you. You're not responsible for Ella's death because you didn't solve the other murders. I haven't known you for long, but I know you care about your cases and the people in this kingdom. I admire that." I wet my lips as a flush warmed my cheeks. "I admire you. More and more every day."

A string of emotions played across his face, his expression moving from denial to desire in a heartbeat. He pulled me closer to murmur my name, the rough sound quickening my pulse. When his lips found mine, soft and achingly slow, his tongue against the seam of my mouth teased a moan low in my throat. Derrick reacted to the sound like I'd struck him with magic, deepening the kiss.

My heart drummed faster. Need burned a path

through my body. I moved against him, running my hands over the wall of his muscled chest. This was crazy! We were supposed to be acting, and yet none of this felt like an act. Not the longing that coiled low in my belly or the raw urgency he poured into our kiss.

We broke apart, breathing heavily.

"Tessa..." His voice shook as lust darkened his gaze.

"More," I breathed. "Please, more. Almost warm."

He growled, capturing my chin between his fingers and fusing our mouths together. His hands fisted my wet hair, slid down my damp skin, and air caught in my lungs as his knuckles brushed the underside of my breast. They skimmed lower, until his fingers locked around my hips and dragged me onto his lap. With my palms flat against the back of the carriage seat, my head fell on my shoulders at the warmth of his mouth on my collarbone. Derrick tasted my skin, stroking the column of my neck and banishing the cold and any lingering fear.

When his lips found mine again, he cradled my face in his hands. Slowly, he pulled back with a reluctant groan to rest his forehead against mine.

"You admire me, huh?"

"Don't let it go to your head, Detective."

The carriage rumbled over ruts in the road, swaying us closer together. Derrick wrapped his arms around my waist. I was warm all over, shivery but not from the cold, as his earlier words washed through me: *I'll keep you safe.* That kind of vow was addictive to a witch who courted disaster as much as I did. It shook something loose inside me—something I hadn't ever dared hope for.

"Looks like we saved the best of our act for when no one was watching. Mr. Lincoln will be so disappointed."

His mouth brushed over mine again, then trailed slowly along my jaw. "Who's acting? I've wanted to kiss you again for days."

"You have?" My breath hitched at the delicious tracks his fingers made over my skin.

"Yes, every time you force my hand and get your way. You're relentless."

"That doesn't sound like a compliment, Detective."

"Mmm...it doesn't, does it? How about stubborn, headstrong, unshakable?"

"You're not getting any warmer. Sounds like you're out of practice."

"Maybe I am." He smiled, and I melted beneath it until a worry surfaced.

"Aren't you afraid this might be one of my spells? That you'll wake up tomorrow and wonder what hit you?"

Derrick paused and met my eyes. "You forget, I investigated you. You aren't that good at magic."

My laughter filled the carriage. "My secrets are exposed."

"Something tells me I'm only scratching the surface of your secrets."

I wanted to tell him everything right then. He

might understand, and maybe we could work together to handle Argus. But when I opened my mouth to try, he captured it in another lingering kiss.

As much as I wanted honesty, I couldn't do it. Some truths were bigger than attraction; bigger than whatever was building between us. The moment passed, and pretty soon, the carriage was rolling to a stop in front of the magic shop.

Derrick walked me to the door, checking again to make sure I hadn't hit my head or suffered some other injury. It felt nice to be cared for. That luxury always got pushed aside in favor of survival. For the first time in a long time, my struggles didn't feel so overwhelming, and a tiny pinprick of hope blossomed.

I listened to the carriage pull away while breathing in the earthy scent of the magic shop. There was a chill in the room. I half-expected to find Ella hovering in the shadows, but she wasn't there, and I was surprised by the wave of disappointment. I'd become used to her appearing out of thin air, and found myself wishing I had someone to talk to.

The clock inched closer to midnight. After lighting the lamps, I headed upstairs to change out of my damp clothes. Finally dry, I heard the midnight chimes and returned to the shop, pausing on the bottom step. There she was, a silver glow near the back door.

"You're here. I have so much to tell you. I think we're getting closer."

She stood motionless, then lifted a translucent arm toward the door that led to the back yard. It was slightly ajar. Was it open when I arrived home? Was that why it was so cold?

"Someone was here. They left something on your step."

I peered out into the dark and found a box wrapped in red ribbon. Someone had entered my back yard and left the gift while I was away. It felt like a violation rather than an act of kindness.

Bending to lift it, I shook the box. It wasn't heavy, but something shifted inside. Sensing unseen eyes on me, I hurried back and slammed the door shut.

Ella didn't take her gaze off the box. "What's in it?"

With shaking fingers, I untied the ribbon and removed the lid. It landed with a thud on the floor.

A glass slipper rested on a wad of tissue paper. There was a note tucked beneath the heel, which I unfolded and held up to the light for Ella to read aloud over my shoulder. Her voice trembled, catching on the last word.

"If the slipper fits, you're next."

# Chapter 19

"This was on my doorstep last night."

Vivian peered into the box and read the note. She scrunched her nose in distaste.

"If the slipper fits? The killer's taunting you."

I removed the shoe from the box, running my fingers over the smooth glass. Like a crystal spike, the faceted heel glinted in the light. The warning was clear: *I know who you are, I know where you live, and if you continue to hunt me, you'll be next.*

"I told you this case was too dangerous. What are you going to do?" Vivian placed the note on the table.

"The shoe is evidence. I can't hide it. I have to show it to Derrick." I winced, remembering his reaction to finding me after my accident at the fountain. "He won't be happy."

Vivian chuckled and leaned back in her chair. "That's an understatement. You should tell him everything. He needs to know Argus is blackmailing you."

A knot formed in my stomach. "Viv, you know I can't do that. He'll think I'm working for the enemy."

"Aren't you?"

"No! I have zero intention of helping Argus. I just think if I can figure out why he wants information on Ironhazel, it might reveal a clue about Ella's case."

"That's fine, but do you have to go behind Derrick's back to do it? When will you learn that you can't do everything on your own? You have to let other people help you."

"I do let people help."

"You do not. Case in point, rather than coming to me about your shop, you borrowed money from Argus."

I couldn't meet her gaze. "I handled it."

"No, Tess, you didn't handle it. You turned one problem into many. You're basically a magician of catastrophe." She sighed. "Look, it's okay if people see you struggle. No one expects you to be perfect, and what happened with your mother wasn't fair."

"Stop, Viv. I don't want to talk about it."

"You need to talk about it eventually. It's been seven years, and you still see yourself through her eyes. When are you going to quit punishing yourself? She never should have placed such unreasonable demands on you."

"I said, stop!"

Vivian didn't understand. She'd never failed at anything. She'd never had to live within the confines of disappointment. If Derrick learned the truth, he'd see how desperate I'd become. The depths of my failure would be on full display. I was already a laughingstock among my mothers' past clients, and I couldn't stand to be one in his eyes too. The entire kingdom could joke behind my back so long as he wasn't in on the punchline. To make matters worse, I'd already crossed the line by keeping my association with Argus a secret. My quest for the reward, no matter how much I needed it, was enough to taint my motivations.

Vivian placed a hand over mine. "All I ask is that you think about it. Give Derrick the benefit of the doubt. He might surprise you."

\*\*\*

Her words stayed with me as I walked toward the agency. Some of my resolve had crumbled, but I wasn't ready to reveal everything, not until I was sure I could handle the repercussions.

I stood outside Derrick's office gathering the courage to knock. Part of me was nervous to show him the box with the slipper, and the other part couldn't stop replaying our kiss in the carriage. Guess which part won? I smiled as I remembered the feel of his mouth, hot and insistent, against mine, and the way his fingers threaded through my hair, molding my body against his. A perfect fit.

Everything had faded away—all the secrets and lies, the case. Nothing else had mattered for a brief moment.

The door opened while my hand was still hovering in the air. Derrick halted in front of me, a stack of folders tucked under his arm.

"Hi." I cringed at my lame greeting. Couldn't I think of anything better to say?

"Good morning, Tessa."

"Are you headed out?" *Wow. What a scintillating conversation.*

He glanced at the folders and nodded. "I have a meeting with the director to go over the events of last night." The corner of his mouth lifted. "Well, not all the events of last night."

I smiled, and some of my nerves slipped away. "Don't tell me the honorable Detective Chambers is keeping secrets from his superior? I've corrupted you."

He pulled me into his office and shut the door. I backed up against it.

"Corruption is a strong word," he murmured, cupping a hand around my cheek, warm and solid. I was desperate to lean into it. "It's more like I'm trying out your investigative methods."

"Well, I've been called an asset before, but it's nice to see you finally realizing it."

Derrick's thumb traced my bottom lip. "I wouldn't go that far." But the heat in his eyes said otherwise. "What do you have behind your back? You're hiding something."

With a heavy sigh, I showed him the box containing the slipper. Derrick clenched his jaw in silence while he read the note. I placed my hand on his chest to feel the vibration of anger beneath my palm.

"Before you say anything—"

"The killer knows where you live. He's watching you."

"It wouldn't be hard to find out. It's not like there's

an abundance of witches in the kingdom, especially not involved in the investigation and romantically linked to the lead detective."

Derrick scrubbed a hand over his face, concern darkening his features. "We should have kept your association a secret. We shouldn't have flaunted it."

"I don't agree. I think this means we're getting closer, striking a nerve. The killer wouldn't lash out like this otherwise. Why risk it?"

"Because the killer thinks they're in control, that they can manipulate the investigation by issuing threats. If you're right, and we're getting close, a threat like this might make us sloppy."

"But we won't be." I searched his gaze.

"No, we won't. But I don't want you to stay alone at the magic shop anymore."

I didn't relish staying alone either. I might be downplaying the slipper for his benefit, but the gift had me worried, and the shop no longer felt safe. Besides, it wasn't like I had any real customers. After the article in the paper, everyone only wanted a glimpse of the witch who'd enchanted the kingdom's lead detective. That wouldn't have bothered me if it also meant they'd part with their money, but so far, it hadn't worked out that way.

"I can stay with Vivian in town. It's closer to the agency."

"That will work. I'm in meetings all day, but Abrams should be available soon. He can take you back to your shop to get your things. Let him escort you to Vivian's this evening." Derrick gave me an adamant look.

His rules echoed in my head. *No wandering off alone.*

"Fine, I can sort through evidence while I wait. A fresh pair of eyes might help. I just need the key." I held out my hand, not missing the shock in Derrick's eyes.

"What? You mean you aren't going to break in?"

"Not this time, Detective. This time, I'm asking."

He lifted a brow in surprise. "Maybe I'm the one corrupting you?"

I patted his cheek with a wink. "I wouldn't go that far."

After opening the evidence room, I was left alone to sift through the victims' personal items. I started with the folders detailing the circumstances of each murder. There wasn't anything there that Derrick hadn't already mentioned, and I found my attention wandering to the board where he'd tacked up the roses, one for each of the girls.

Why did the killer leave roses? There had to be some significance. I shuffled through the papers to find a list of possible strains. The roses left at the scene were distinctive and unlike the ones found at the palace. Derrick hadn't been able to determine the origin. Could they have been imported? The first killing took place three years ago, which meant searching ship manifests for imported seedlings would be useless. Unfortunately, they hadn't paid attention to the rose at the first crime scene, and the passage of time made everything more difficult.

Putting the list of roses aside for now, I reached for one of the journals, pausing when I caught sight of a familiar object. The notebook Derrick carried around with him poked out from beneath a stack of papers. An image of him making mysterious entries the day we met flashed through my mind. Inside were his first impressions of me and my shop. Impressions that probably weren't kind.

With a glance over my shoulder to make sure I was alone, curiosity made me pick it up, but guilt kept me from opening it. It was one thing to read the thoughts of a dead person, but it was another to pry into the thoughts of the living.

In the end, curiosity topped guilt.

I flipped open the book, searching for the date Derrick first visited my shop. I found it toward the middle and scanned through. As I feared, his thick scrawl covered the page in judgment. He described my shop as untidy and hazardous, making special note of the foul-smelling potions I'd offered him at a discount. I flattened my lips, reading further.

*Miss Daniels displays a lack of respect for authority and is secretive when asked direct questions.*

Okay...not wrong, but also not flattering. I skipped to the next entry, drumming my fingers on the desk in irritation.

*Miss Daniels is evasive and crumbles easily when cornered. She's unlikely to be a suspect in the Lockwood murder, though she does appear to have information re-*

*garding the victim's mental state before her death.*

Not wanting him to find my illegal potions meant I crumbled easily? More like self-preservation. I huffed and flipped the page.

*After meeting with the subject's neighbor, it appears Miss Daniels relies on her magic to support herself, though, according to the neighbor, Miss Daniels' magic is subpar.*

I snapped the book closed and considered taking the candle flame to its pages. Subpar? Sylvia could forget about the friends and family discount I gave her on wrinkle cream. Humiliation made my neck hot. How dare he?

Then again, I had called him Detective Arrogant and considered turning him into a toad. I scratched the back of my neck. Hadn't I also referred to him as cold and calculating? It didn't matter that I hadn't written it down, I meant it at the time. I opened the book again, flipping past the negative entries to the one he'd made when he found me in the alley. This one was different.

*Miss Daniels is resourceful in the face of danger and exhibits street smarts.*

And then, one final entry, dated after we interviewed the Lockwoods.

*Tessa is perceptive and catches onto things quickly. Her questions during interviews are clever and intuitive. She may turn out to be a valuable asset to the Lock-*

*wood investigation.*

An *asset.* Something that felt a lot like pride burned in my chest. There was nothing in the last entries about my failed magic, and it felt good to be judged for skills other than the ones I'd been born with. Derrick had misjudged me in the same way I'd misjudged him. We had both fallen victim to poor first impressions.

"He's a workaholic, isn't he?"

I jumped, dropping Derrick's notebook. Estelle stood over my shoulder, her gray eyes probing, casting a look between the notebook and the piles of information scattered across the desk.

"Sorry to startle you, dear. I wanted to bring you a cup of tea and let you know Abrams is available to take you to your shop whenever you're ready."

I accepted the cup and breathed in the sweet aroma. Steam wafted over the rim.

"Has he always been like this?" I gestured to the cluttered piles. "On the outside, he doesn't give much away."

Estelle clucked her tongue and leaned against the desk. "This case is different. It's personal. It's the one case he hasn't been able to solve. It eats away at him."

"Personal? How do you mean?"

She shrugged. "It's not my story to tell, but I will say that ever since you came along, I've seen a lightness in him that wasn't there before. I even caught him whistling this morning, if you can believe it. You're good for him and good for this case."

I laughed, the sound more scornful than I intended. "I haven't been very good at anything in my life."

Estelle angled her head, considering my statement. "Well, maybe you haven't found the thing you're good at yet. That's the fortunate thing about life, you can always try something new. Just because you aren't good at one thing doesn't mean you'll be bad at another. Not if you find what you're meant to do." She gave me a sly smile and leaned closer. "Or the person you're meant to do it with."

What if she was right? I was caught in a vicious circle, repeating mistakes and doing things the way I'd always done them. It wasn't until I'd stepped out of my comfort zone that I finally felt useful. Maybe the potential my mother had always wanted me to achieve didn't look the way we'd thought it would.

"Thanks, Estelle. You can tell Abrams I'm ready to go. Something tells me, after last night, I'm going to be on research duty for a while. I'll have time to go through everything here."

Estelle's eyes went wide with sympathy at the mountains of paper. "Better you than me, dear."

\*\*\*

Abrams unloaded my bags from the carriage while Vivian stood in the doorway, her hands balled on her hips, counting each bag.

"How long are you planning on staying?"

"The duration of the case, I assume. Be careful with that one, Abrams." I gestured to the oversized bag clinking loudly as he set it down.

Vivian cocked her head. "Is that what I think it is?"

"Of course. Did you think I wouldn't bring it?"

"Will we need that much?"

"It's better to have more than you need, don't you agree?"

"Naturally."

Abrams furrowed his brow, his head bouncing back and forth as he tried to follow our conversation. He hefted the bag over his shoulder.

"What's so important about this one? Is it full of deadly potions?"

I picked up the last of my bags and followed him inside. "No, that's the wine."

He burst out laughing and shook his head. "I hope there's some in here for me. It's been a long week."

Vivian grinned. "There's more than enough. I'll get us all a glass, and we can make an evening of it. I've been dying to try out the new tarot deck my grandmother sent me."

She showed Abrams where to store the bags, then disappeared into the kitchen. The sound of a cork popping could be heard from the séance room where Abrams and I sat around the oval table. He peered warily over his shoulder.

"Is it true that Miss James can see ghosts?"

"Yes, all her life. They can't hurt you though. You're fine." He didn't seem convinced.

A knock sounded on the door, and I rose to answer it, but Abrams held up a hand.

"Let me. It's late, and with last night's threat,

you shouldn't answer it." He pushed through the hanging beads to enter the waiting area. The door opened, and I strained to hear the muffled conversation.

"Where is she?"

Recognizing Derrick's voice, I turned as he entered the room. Abrams remained behind him. It seemed the poor guy wouldn't be getting that glass of wine after all. He was probably stationed on the stoop, standing guard. I'd have to sneak him a glass later.

My eyes locked with Derrick's, and warmth spread through my chest. He looked exhausted, his clothes rumpled after a long day at the agency. There was tension around his eyes, but he relaxed when he saw me. Offering him the chair next to mine, I resisted the impulse to smooth the wrinkles from his jacket. Any excuse to touch him.

"All settled in?" he asked at the same time I asked how his meetings went. Our questions collided, canceling each other's voice out.

I chuckled and answered first, "Yes, all settled. Vivian's playing hostess. Can you stay for a glass of wine? Maybe some dinner? She has a new tarot deck. If you're lucky, she might read your fortune."

"Is she any good?" He removed his jacket and undid the button at his collar. My gaze dropped to the patch of exposed skin, then slowly climbed back up to find him watching me. Awareness flared in his eyes.

"No, she's terrible at it."

"That's too bad. What about you?"

"Are you asking if I can read your future?"

His mouth curved in amusement. "I don't know. You look like you'd be good at that sort of thing."

I scooted closer. "I'm good at lots of things, Detective. Hold out your hand."

He turned his palm up, and I set it in my lap. His skin was rough against mine where I traced the lines of his palm with my fingernail, reveling in the way his breath caught at my touch. With my thumb, I rubbed small circles into the base of his fingers, watching as his eyes grew heavy-lidded with pleasure.

I bent over his hand. "What would you like to know?"

"How long will I live?"

Pretending to examine his lifeline, I bit my cheek to keep from smiling. "Hmm… It seems you'll live long enough to admit how valuable I am to your investigation."

"So, I'll be old and gray."

I pinched his thumb. "What else do you want to know?"

"What's that line tell you?" He pointed to the one running at the top of his palm.

"Ah, that's your love line." I tsk'd. "It's the shortest one I've ever seen. It means you're disagreeable and impatient. I don't know," I hedged, "this doesn't look promising."

"Tessa," he growled, "you're making that up." Twisting my hand, he captured it in his own to drag me closer.

I couldn't keep the smile off my face. It was nice to see him this way. Even nicer to know I'd played a part in wiping the haunted expression from his eyes.

"Don't be mad, Detective. I read it like I see it."

He grinned, seeing through my lie, and I felt my heart stutter as his thumb circled my wrist, sending little frissons of heat up my arm.

"I already told you, I don't get mad, I get even."

*A girl can hope.*

"Read it again. For real, this time."

"All right, hold still."

I ran my finger along his heart line. There was a gap near the start, and my touch lingered there. I knew what it meant, and my voice dropped with sympathy.

"This break means you suffered the loss of a loved one. It was quite significant. You're not over it."

His silence confirmed my fears.

A pang of jealousy throbbed around my heart. It was probably a first love, and knowing him, there was an elaborate shrine to the woman somewhere in his house. It would explain a lot. He'd said there wasn't anyone else, and it was because she was dead. It was hard to compete with a ghost. Not that I was competing. A witch never played second fiddle.

"Is that all? It ends there?" Misery laced his tone, almost as if he'd been hoping for a different answer.

I sighed, peevish, and continued the reading. "No. See this, here?" My finger trailed the length of his palm. "After the break, the line is long and deep.

That's a good sign. It means you'll find your true match. And see this small curve on the end?" He nodded, dark eyes watching me and not the curve on his palm. "It signifies a willingness to sacrifice everything for love. That's pretty noble of you, Detective."

"I suppose. You wouldn't do the same?"

My laugh came out harsh. "Sacrifice everything for love? That sounds like a fairytale, and my life is no fairytale. Prince Charming doesn't end up with the witch, Detective."

"Maybe he should." His fingers intertwined with mine, and he brought my hand to his lips. "Tessa, there's something—"

"Here we are!" Vivian's voice startled me as she entered the room.

I jerked my hand out of Derrick's, feeling silly for getting caught—or maybe it was just fear. Whatever he was about to say had felt important. *Altering.* But I wasn't meant to hear it. If his fortune told me anything, it was that he was destined for great things, not a lousy witch who could barely support herself.

Vivian paused when she saw Derrick, her eyes narrowing at our odd expressions. "I'm going to need another glass." Plunking the tray down on the table, she headed back to the kitchen, only making it a few feet before she froze. Her hands lifted, fingers trembling in the air.

"What is it, Viv?" A sense of foreboding curled my stomach.

"We're not alone."

I glanced at the clock perched on a nearby shelf. It wasn't midnight. It couldn't be Ella.

Vivian confirmed my thoughts. "It's not Ella. It's someone else." Slowly, she angled her head toward Derrick.

He shifted in his chair. "What's happening?"

Vivian's eyes became glassy and her skin drained of color. "Detective Chambers, there's someone here who wishes to speak with you. Her name is Sophie."

# Chapter 20

Derrick stumbled to his feet, tipping his chair and backing away from the table. "Sophie?"

The way he said her name with such devotion mixed with fear made my heart ache. Secrets were buried in that tone—secrets that even death couldn't hide. Vivian heard it too. She glanced my way with the question in her eyes.

"Sophie was the first victim."

"I see. Detective, it's rare for those who have crossed over to reach out from the other side. In these circumstances, it's best if we let them communicate as they wish. If you take your seat, we can get started."

Derrick eyed his fallen chair as if it might bite the moment he reached for it. The sound of it hitting the floor had prompted Abrams to step through the beaded curtain.

"Is everything all right?" he asked, taking in the scene.

We stood around the table, afraid to move as the room plunged in temperature. I shivered, recognizing the same chill that announced Ella's arrival—except this time, I was truly scared.

"It's Sophie," Derrick said, picking up his chair. He lowered himself into the seat.

"Impossible." Abrams' skin turned gray.

Candle flames flickered, bouncing shadows against the wall. The forms circled us like giant monsters waiting for their meal. Our frozen breath hung in the air, while above our heads, a chandelier swayed, creaking on its rusty chain.

"Sit down, Abrams," Derrick instructed. His voice was tight, leashed with an intensity that made my pulse pound.

Vivian lit the wick of a white pedestal candle, then reached for a bundle of sage. She burned the end until a stream of smoke and a strong odor wafted in the air and placed the sage into a clay pot. A line of smoke curled lazily from the rim.

Beside me, Derrick remained seated, his body rigid. I reached for his hand, and he flinched. His resistance stung.

Along the wall, the candles extinguished one by one, plunging the room into darkness. I gripped the edge of the table, hoping it would ground me in the blackout.

Abrams choked out a mangled cry and pushed away.

"Don't move," Vivian said, striking a match. The hint of sulfur reached my nose as she re-lit the candle in the center of the table.

"Stop this!" Abrams snapped. The sharp planes of his face glowed in the candlelight, his lips curling in a sneer. "I won't commune with spirits, it's unnatural. Sophie is dead. Let her be."

"Sit," Derrick ordered.

Abrams bent forward, his fists balled on the table-top. "You aren't seriously entertaining this?"

Derrick held Abrams' horrified stare. Yes, he was entertaining it. The same man who had tried to throw me out of his office for mentioning ghosts now sat with a measure of desperation etched across his face. A stab of regret stuck like a shard in my chest. Estelle had said the case was personal to him. Seeing his reaction, I worried it was more than that. Was Sophie related to the broken line on his palm? He'd never looked so tormented. I longed for his stare of cool indifference instead of this raw insecurity.

"I said, sit down. Do this for me, or leave." A fierce look passed between them.

Abrams blew out a harsh breath. "They're deluding you, Detective, just like the others. I won't be a part of that. I'll wait outside."

A stilted silence followed as Abrams barged through the beaded curtain. Vivian bowed her head, and I watched the beads sway back into place. What did he mean, we were like the others?

Derrick gave nothing away, his attention focused on Vivian. "Continue, please."

"Of course, Detective. Start by placing your hands palms-down on the table." She waited until we'd followed her instructions, then closed her eyes. "Sophie, are you here with us?"

Nothing happened.

"Sophie, please make your presence known."

A rush of air snaked over my skin, the breeze unexplained in the windowless room.

"I can feel her," Vivian whispered. "Sophie, speak to me. Tell us what you've come here to say."

A crystal vase splintered. I shrieked and shielded my eyes. Derrick wrapped his arm around my shoulders, dragging me to him as tiny razors flew through the air. I looked up to find blood welling along his jaw.

"You're bleeding." I tried to stem the flow with my sleeve.

Derrick caught my wrist, his gaze running urgently over my body while he brushed glass from my hair. "I'm fine. Are you hurt?"

"No. Viv, are you—?"

A void passed over Vivian's face, and her mouth went slack. She rocked in her chair before slumping against the table. Strands of dark hair pooled over her limp form.

"Viv!" I squeezed her shoulders in an attempt to rouse her. Sweat coated her skin, dampening the neckline of her gown.

Derrick crouched at her side and pushed back Vivian's hair, searching for a pulse. The instant his fingers touched her neck, her hand clamped around his wrist. She lifted her head off the table and fixed us with a feverish stare. Blood streaked her cheeks in thin rivulets from a piece of glass embedded in her skin.

"Oh, Viv," I moaned.

She crooked her head toward me, still latched onto Derrick's arm. When I bumped the edge of the table, her chin tilted in the other direction, and she studied me like a bird perched on a branch.

It wasn't Vivian.

Fear seized my insides. Her lips moved, speaking in a lilting voice I didn't recognize. It sent a shiver down my spine.

"All the petals are gone, only the thorns remain." She faced Derrick, threading her fingers through his. "I shouldn't have kept secrets from you." Her voice broke on a whimper.

"Sophie?" Derrick tightened his grip. "Is it really you?"

Sophie nodded. Tears streamed down her face, mixing with the blood and turning pink. "I tried to run. Couldn't. I begged. Pleaded. I needed you." Her shoulders trembled, sobs wracking her body.

Derrick's voice cracked with emotion. "I should have been there. I'm sorry." He pulled her against him, smoothing the hair at the back of her head. "Tell me what happened. I'm here now. Who did this to you?"

"All I see are roses. Their petals stain the earth like blood. Their thorns cut to the bone."

"I don't understand. You're not making sense. Sophie, please…"

She stared at me over Derrick's shoulder. The air seemed to vanish, and I couldn't breathe. Something flashed in Sophie's eyes—an understanding. Her lips curved into a soft smile.

"Take care of him for me. He needs you."

I must have nodded because she turned back to Derrick and held a slender finger to her lips. "Shh... Everything is all right now. Follow the roses." Her eyes rolled into the back of her head, and she swayed on her feet.

Derrick gripped Vivian with shaking hands. His shout of denial echoed off the walls. The candles flared, bathing the room in flashes of white light, and Vivian's body shuddered before she slowly regained consciousness. Derrick helped her to a chair, steadying her until she could stay upright.

"What happened?" she groaned, placing a hand at her temple. "Sophie's gone. I can't feel her anymore. Did she say anything?"

With eyes closed, Derrick's face contorted in pain. "I need a minute." He staggered from the room. I wanted to follow but couldn't leave Vivian.

"Go," she said. "I'm all right."

I squeezed her fingers. "I'll be back."

Abrams waited outside, his lanky frame leaning against a lamppost. He watched me travel down the steps, searching the near-empty street for Derrick.

"Happy now?" he asked.

"Where did he go?"

"Around back. Through the gate." He grabbed my arm before I could leave, fingers digging into my skin. "What did she say?"

I tried to shake him off, but his grip tightened.

He shouted again, "What did she say?"

"Let me go. You're hurting me."

Abrams loosened his grip, and I stepped back, rubbing a hand over my wrist. He clenched his fists, bringing his emotions in check.

"Who is Sophie to Derrick?" I asked quietly.

"He didn't tell you? Sophie was Derrick's sister."

His answer stunned me. It made sense now. Derrick's determination to solve the case ran deeper than preventing a murderer from striking again. His anguish at Olivia Lockwood's accusations—even his drive to keep me safe—stemmed from the same well of guilt. He hadn't been able to solve his sister's murder, and each subsequent one reopened the scar.

"I didn't know. I need to talk to him. Can you sit with Vivian? She shouldn't be alone right now."

Abrams nodded reluctantly. "I told you this was a bad idea."

Maybe it was, but it was too late now. Seeing Sophie invade Vivian's body had affected me more than I realized. Her words from beyond the grave tore at my heart, and more than anything, I wanted to comfort Derrick.

I found him standing in the small patch of Vivian's back yard, looking up at the sliver of the moon. He heard me approach but didn't turn around.

"I should have told you. I'm sorry," he said.

"Don't apologize. It's hard to talk about the people we've loved and lost. Even the happy memories are torture." I sat on a stone bench. "Can you tell me about her?"

Derrick sighed and scrubbed a hand through his hair. "Sophie was stubborn and reckless, always getting into trouble, but it was impossible to stay mad at her. Everyone loved her. My parents doted on her, and I was her big brother, the person who was always supposed to look out for her."

Solemn, I nodded my head for him to continue.

"We'd been at the country house for a week, attending the king's feast and annual hunt. The whole village was excited—except for Sophie. She'd been acting strange, sullen. It wasn't like her. I was preoccupied with preparing to leave for training abroad."

"Because you'd been accepted into the agency?"

"That's right. The morning I was supposed to leave, Sophie barely said a word. She always told me everything. Most times, I couldn't get her to stop talking, but that morning, she was closed off. I teased her, thinking I could get a rise out of her, but she became furious. She stormed off, and that was the last time I saw her."

"She wasn't there when you left?"

"No. It wasn't until much later that I found out she'd gone missing that day. The search lasted almost a week before they found her. I wasn't informed until I returned home a month later. By then, my parents were destroyed, and her case was cold."

"I'm so sorry." I rubbed my arms, the night chill settling in my bones.

Derrick sat beside me, drawing me against his chest to share warmth. "You're cold. I should get your coat."

"No—wait." I closed my fist, then splayed my fingers over a small hearth near the bench. Magic sparked and caught fire. The flames grew brighter, snapping as they took hold of the kindling stacked in the grate. "Some spells are easier than others," I explained with a smile, resting my head into the crook of his shoulder.

We sat in silence, the fire keeping us warm. A question burned on my tongue, but I was afraid of the answer.

"Can I ask you something?"

He nodded.

"What did Abrams mean when he said we were like the others?"

It took him so long to answer, I started to think he wouldn't.

"After Sophie's murder, my parents were desperate. There were no leads, no suspects. One day, a witch traveled through the village, and she heard about the murder. She offered to help—for a price. I begged them not to go, but they were willing to try anything. For the first time in months, they had hope. The witch promised to cast a spell that would lead them to the killer. It sounded too good to be true, and it was. My parents paid her a fortune in advance, and when they arrived the next day, the witch was gone."

"Oh, Derrick." I didn't know what to say. I hung my head, tears streaming down my face. It was a miracle he'd opened up and let me near the case after what his family had experienced at the hands of a so-called witch. Their hopes had been shattered by a true charlatan. Was it any wonder he'd accused me of being one when we first met?

"Tessa." He tucked strands of hair behind my ears and tilted my chin up to his. "You're not like that. It took me a while to realize it because I didn't want to go through it again, but in true Tessa form, you battered my defenses."

I hiccuped and swiped at my eyes. "That doesn't sound like a compliment."

"It's the highest compliment."

"I'm sorry I gave you such a hard time. I had no idea."

Wrapping his arms around me again, Derrick pressed a kiss to the top of my head. "How could you? My sister's murder made me realize how important it was for me to excel at the agency. I became a detective so I could solve her case and keep murderers off the streets. But it doesn't make the helplessness go away, the feeling I'm always a step behind, that I can't protect the ones I love. That's always in the back of my mind."

My palm cupped the side of his face, and I turned to look into his eyes, hoping to convey the truth in my words. "You're a good detective, Derrick Chambers."

"You think so?" His voice was a low rumble in my ear.

"I do, and that's my highest compliment."

He smiled, and the tenderness in his eyes made me feel like I was falling off a steep cliff. I realized all the traits I'd found so unappealing were simply his way of doing the best he could for those around him, that he held himself to an impossible standard—and I wanted nothing more than to see him succeed.

"We need to go back to the beginning. What Sophie said about the roses, I think that's the key."

Derrick nodded. "I agree, but no one we've questioned has been able to determine the source."

"Then we haven't been asking the right people. We need to go wider with the information. Someone has to know something."

"The agency doesn't have the manpower to go door-to-door asking about roses. Besides, not everyone likes to be questioned by the authorities. Some people get defensive when asked simple questions."

I smirked. "If you're alluding to me then I know what you mean. But I have an idea. What if we could appeal to a wider audience all at once and frame the question without giving away our intentions?"

"What do you have in mind?"

"We place an ad in the Gazette. Forget trying to find the one person with the answers about the rose. Let's have that person come to us."

# Chapter 21

J ohn Lincoln stretched his legs in front of him and leaned back in his chair. It creaked under his weight, threatening to buckle beneath him.

"Let me get this straight. The agency wants to place an ad in my paper to track down the origin of the rose left at the crime scene?"

"That's right," I said. "Someone out there might have information or know someone who does. The Gazette is the fastest, most direct way to find them. The rose may be the killer's only mistake. It ties him to the murder in a specific way. If we can learn more about it and why it was left at the scene, we'll be a step closer to catching him."

John crossed his arms. "Aren't you taking a risk the killer will see the ad as well?"

Derrick nodded. "It's possible. That's why we want to run another article on the front page, something that will distract attention. The writeup should be critical of the agency and insinuate the killer has the upper hand. He wants attention, so we'll give it to him and let him bask in it while we work a different angle."

"A bait and switch?" John grinned and rubbed a

hand over the whiskers on his chin. "I like it. In addition, the exclusive will sell a ton of papers."

"We thought you'd appreciate that." I placed the glass slipper along with the note in front of John. "This was left on my doorstep following the memorial dinner."

He whistled and reached for the piece of paper. His brow lifted as he read the killer's warning.

"If the slipper fits? What a cocky bastard. I assume this was taken from the scene?" He examined the shoe, turning it over in his hand. "Looks damn uncomfortable if you ask me."

"Beauty is pain, Mr. Lincoln. Hasn't anyone ever told you that?"

He grimaced and slapped a hand over his paunchy stomach. "I'll take your word for it, Miss Daniels."

Derrick handed John a pre-written ad. "This is what we'd like placed near the back of the paper. Inquiries should be forwarded to my office. In the meantime, we'll be running damage control on the evidence leak."

"It's going to be a circus." John shook his head in pity.

"We hope so. A circus draws a crowd. But once we have them packed into the seats, we control what they see and hear."

"Even at the expense of your good name, Detective?"

Tension tightened Derrick's jaw. "My name isn't any good if I don't catch Miss Lockwood's killer."

After learning what the case meant to Derrick, I

couldn't imagine anything he wouldn't try, even if it subjected him to ridicule. He seemed to welcome it, free of the shackles of what people expected and driven only by results.

John tapped his fingers on the desk and eyed the glass slipper. An odd look flashed in his eye.

"You know, there are rumors Miss Lockwood might not be the only victim. Care to address that, Detective?"

"The agency doesn't comment on rumors, John."

"I guess that means you won't confirm the rumors swirling around the two of you? A witch and a detective is an unlikely partnership, especially considering Miss Daniels' background." He flipped through a notebook on his desk. "I hope you don't mind, but my reporters have done some digging."

I clenched the handrails of the chair. Had they discovered my connection to Argus? I'd underestimated what working with the newspaper would mean. My life had become fair game and fodder for the gossip section.

"I can't imagine what you've found, Mr. Lincoln. My past hasn't been that interesting."

John laughed and read from the notebook. "Not according to our sources. They make your life sound very interesting. A comedy of errors, in fact. It's amazing, the people who come out of the woodwork hoping to cash in on someone's reputation. And yours, Miss Daniels..." He winced.

A buzzing sounded in my ears. Derrick spoke, his lips moving, but I couldn't make out the words.

"Take the barn fire on Stratford road about seven years back. The owners claim you were channeling energy for a prosperous harvest and you lit a haystack on fire. Luckily, your mother was there to supervise, or they would have lost everything. She paid them not to press charges."

I shifted uncomfortably in my seat. "That was an accident."

"Maybe so, but what about the time you turned a young man into a mouse when he made an advance on you? We have a source willing to come forward. He alleges it took you three days to change him back. His family put up missing posters. How much did it take to keep them quiet?"

Heat crawled up my neck. It had taken quite a bit. I'd sold a large sum of my mother's books that day, and speculation had followed me for months.

John flipped the page in the notebook. "There are numerous complaints of spells gone wrong." He pushed his glasses up his nose and squinted at the page. "Do you know a Mrs. Anderson? She claims a couple of weeks ago, you turned her hair green then refused to refund her money."

"That's not what happened!"

The notebook snapped closed, and John raised his hand. "Miss Daniels, you're welcome to share your side of the story. It will round out the article. I already have an idea for a headline." He arched his hand through the air. "I'm thinking, *Disgraced Witch Embarrasses Family Name and Endangers Society.* What do you think?"

My whole body went rigid. A sly smile played around John's lips. It was obvious what he was really after: leverage. Apparently, certain men in my life thought they could use me for their own purposes. First, Argus, and now, John Lincoln. I burned with humiliation and a profound helplessness.

Derrick remained quiet, letting the scene play out. I wasn't sure if his silence made me feel better or worse. Either way, I couldn't look at him. My mediocre magic wasn't a secret, but when you put all my destruction together, it painted a vivid picture.

*Worthless witch.*

"What do you want?" I asked through gritted teeth.

John rubbed his hands together and snickered. "I'll run your ad and the article on the slipper for the front page. It's a great idea. But you have to understand, I'm in a tough position. I can't sit on a story like this. I'll need something bigger to replace it." His gaze narrowed. "Confirm whether you're looking at multiple victims, and I'll bury every last salacious account of your shameful past.

I shot out of my chair. "No wa—"

"Fine." Derrick stood and grasped my arm, squeezing gently to keep me quiet. "I'll have a statement sent over. Run the stories and keep Miss Daniels' personal life out of your paper, or you'll deal with me."

John inclined his head, victory stamped across his face. "Pleasure doing business with you, Detective."

Derrick slammed the office door on John's words. It barely made a sound over the commotion in the newsroom, but we walked quickly through the maze of desks and out into the street.

Outside, I shook off Derrick's arm and kept moving, my steps stilted and angry. How dare he jeopardize the case for something so stupid? It was my fault we were even in this situation! If only I'd been better...different. How many times would I go through this before I learned my lesson?

"Tessa, wait." He chased after me, weaving through the thick crowd.

Hot tears gathered under my eyes as shame prickled my skin. A carriage clattered across the street, and I plunged ahead, missing the wheels by inches and making Derrick wait for it to pass. I thought I'd lost him until his hand clamped over my shoulder. Frustration surged through my body, and I whirled.

"Are you crazy? You shouldn't have done that!"

"Do you have a death wish? That carriage almost hit you." His chest rose on an angry breath, and he dragged me off the street and down a side lane where we wouldn't be overheard.

Shaking him loose again, I tried to barrel past, but he blocked my attempt. My throat was so tight it hurt to speak.

"Let me go."

"Not a chance."

I inhaled roughly through my nose, trying to rein in my emotions. It didn't work.

"What is wrong with you? You should have let him print those stories about my past. It doesn't matter what people think about me, they already have a low opinion. Seeing it in print isn't going to change anything."

He reached for me, but I stepped back, certain if he touched me I'd burst into tears.

"Tessa, I swore I wouldn't let anything happen to you, and that includes letting John Lincoln run a smear campaign in your name."

I threw up my hands and laughed, the harsh sound echoing through the narrow alley. "Well, your misplaced protectiveness gave away valuable information. It was my shortcomings that jeopardized this case. You shouldn't have agreed to his ultimatum. I'm not worth it. I never have been."

A look passed over Derrick's face, disbelief morphing into resolve. This time, when he reached for me, he wasn't taking no for an answer. His palm cupped the back of my head, and he hauled me to him, crushing me against his chest. He was warm and solid, and I felt myself crumbling, all of my defenses laid to waste. The rough timbre of his voice sounded in my ear.

"Don't ever say that. You are worth it. I would have given up a lot more if I had to, and even if there was nothing I could do, if they printed those stories, it wouldn't matter to me. Your past doesn't define you. You are so much more than just your spells."

His words reshaped something inside me. They were hard to believe after years of self-doubt, but I wanted to. I wanted to believe them so much it terrified me to my core.

I wiped the tears from my cheeks and took a shuddering breath, my voice watery when I spoke. "I'm sorry I got angry. I couldn't handle it if I ruined this case for you, not after Sophie and everything your family has been through."

He tightened his hold and rested his chin on top of my head. "We've gotten this far because of you. You didn't ruin anything. Admitting there are multiple victims won't jeopardize the case, it might even provide new leads. Using the paper was smart. We just need to stay focused and let your plan work."

"I hate waiting," I grumbled into his shirt.

"Yeah, I know. Patience, Tessa." He rubbed the tension from the back of my neck.

We stood there for a few moments, letting the stress from the last hour pass. My humiliation had simmered down to a manageable level, but mostly, I felt cared-for and instilled with a new sense of hope. More than my spells? No one had ever made the distinction.

Noise from the street leaked into our solitude. Derrick sighed and brushed the hair away from my face.

"I think we need a break. It's been a rough couple of days, don't you agree? We've seen ghosts and dealt with weaselly newspapermen and threatening slippers."

"I went swimming in the palace fountain."

"Don't remind me. I think you mean, you nearly drowned in the palace fountain."

"That's not what happened." I swatted his shoulder, but he caught my hand and pressed his lips against my fingers.

"Let me take you to lunch."

I gasped in mock horror. "Are you seriously suggesting a leisure activity? Are you ill?" My palm covered his forehead. "Maybe you're hearing voices?"

"Neither, so forget about carting me off to the asylum." He winked. "I just happen to enjoy a nice meal of rosemary chicken and glazed potatoes now and then."

"Hey…" I nudged his shoulder. "How did you know that's my favorite meal?"

Derrick shrugged. "Your neighbor told me. Sylvia Trager stopped by my office after she saw the article about us. She said it didn't matter that I was good looking, well-off, or had a prestigious title, she'd whack me with her cane if I treated you poorly."

Leave it to Sylvia to get her point across. I stifled a smile.

"Ah, everything makes sense now. You're scared of a little old lady."

"Yeah, and you're scared of her cat, so I guess we're even."

"That's fair," I chuckled, as he took my hand and walked us back out into the street.

We settled inside the cozy confines of the Spice and Crown restaurant, each placing an order for their roast chicken. I inhaled the delectable scents that wafted out of the kitchen and took a sip of my wine. It was a strange feeling to be seated across the table from Derrick, the same man who, not long ago,

I'd considered cursing. In fact, I was pretty sure I had placed a curse on the woman who would end up falling for such an ogre.

Irony certainly knew where I lived.

All around us, other diners whispered, a few even pointing in our direction. Under normal circumstances, I would have ducked under the tablecloth, but not anymore. *Take a good look, ladies. This witch is trying to do things differently.*

Derrick dipped a slice of crusty bread in a dish of seasoned oil and took a bite. Chewing thoughtfully, he sipped his wine then narrowed his eyes.

"So, tell me, which of your suitors did you turn into a mouse? Was it Trevor, the baker's son, or that other guy, the blacksmith's apprentice?"

So much for not wanting to climb under the tablecloth. "Neither."

He frowned and thumped a finger against his wineglass. "If not them, who? Don't make me open up an investigation."

"That doesn't sound like a good use of agency resources, Detective."

He cleared his throat, and I huffed a breath at his stubborn look.

"Why do you even want to know?"

"It's one less rival I have to worry about."

My cheeks were on fire. "Don't joke like that. People will hear you."

"Tessa—"

"If you really want to talk about rivals, look around. You can't move left or right without some overeager debutante fawning at your feet."

He didn't take his eyes off me even though I was right. Was he blind? If he threw a breadstick, a suitable candidate would probably catch it in her teeth like a devoted puppy. I groaned internally and forced myself to relax my grip on the wineglass before it shattered.

The corner of his mouth lifted, the smile almost wistful. "You never fawn at my feet."

"Disappointed?"

"Not as much as I thought I'd be. You're—"

I held up a hand. "Wait, I know this one. I'm *different*. Abrams told me. Another one of your charming compliments. I'm storing it away along with *fine* so I can swoon later."

His laughter resonated through the room, and at nearby tables, forks clattered against dinnerware. What? Had no one ever heard the man laugh before?

Our food arrived. The heavenly scent made my eyes close in bliss. A comfortable silence followed while we dug in, and I tried to think of something to talk about that didn't involve murder or magic.

Fiddling with the corner of my napkin, I began uneasily, "Um...tell me about your parents. What are they like?"

"Overbearing." Derrick chuckled and sliced a knife through his chicken. "My father ran a shipbuilding company until he retired, and now, he and my mother live in the country, driving my grandfather Edward crazy by keeping him in line. He's a loose cannon and always stirring up trouble. You two are similar. You'll like him."

I choked on a mouthful of wine. Meet his family? They'd run in the opposite direction the moment he introduced a witch. I let his statement pass, feigning interest in the potatoes. After spearing one with my fork, I looked up and met the stare of a burly man seated at a table in the corner, chewing on a hunk of beef. Another bite...chew...stare. It was one of Argus's thugs.

Derrick followed my gaze. "Do you know that man?" he asked.

Denial sat on my tongue, but I hesitated. Vivian had said I needed to trust Derrick and tell him everything. After his reaction to my past failures, maybe she was right. Maybe it was time.

"Actually, I have something I need to tell you. I shouldn't have kept this from you, but I didn't know how—"

There was a commotion at the entrance, and Abrams approached our table. "There you are!" He was out of breath, his chest heaving as if he'd run a distance.

Derrick cast me a sympathetic look. "One moment, Tessa." He turned his attention to Abrams. "What's happened?"

"You're needed at the palace, Detective." He paused to catch his breath. "They've found another body."

# Chapter 22

**B**uzzards circled overhead, their wings black smudges in the cloudy sky. In the distance, an orchard dotted the landscape, and the palace spires rose above the trees. I waded through the tall grass toward a group of officers who stood around the perimeter of the scene. The air was crisp, with a hint of wood smoke and decaying leaves.

"Who found the body?" Derrick asked.

"A couple of servants working in the orchard." Abrams pointed to the three young men waiting with one of the guards. Their faces were drawn and pale, and one held his stomach as if he might lose its contents if he put his arms down.

"Cause of death?"

"It appears to be a stab wound to the chest. No visible murder weapon."

"Has anyone made an identification?"

Abrams consulted his notes. "Yes. The servants recognized him. His name was Liam Barber, also a palace servant."

"Liam Barber?" I froze, remembering the young man's face when he'd confronted me outside the agency. His fear had been palpable, and he'd risked coming forward with information that had raised suspicions about the prince. Guilt crashed through me. Someone had silenced him.

Derrick caught my eye and gave a subtle shake of his head, signaling me to stay quiet. "Are there any other witnesses?" he asked.

"Yes, Detective." Abrams lowered his voice. "Some kitchen staff saw Liam having a confrontation with Prince Marcus yesterday evening. The king has been informed, and as a precaution, he's placed his son under guard. He wants to speak with you as soon as you're finished here."

"I understand. Clear the scene and gather the witnesses at the palace. I'll question them there. Also, arrange for the body to be transferred once we finish examining the area."

Abrams hesitated at Derrick's orders. "I can stay and collect evidence."

"That's not necessary. I have Miss Daniels for that."

Abrams clenched his jaw and shot me a dark look. I remembered our first encounter and the way he'd idolized Derrick. He'd wanted to follow in his footsteps, but I'd charged into the middle, sidelining him in a way he probably hadn't expected. Our interactions had always been friendly, but now, I felt the first indication of his contempt. Part of me wanted to say something to ease the tension, but I remembered the way he'd gripped my arm outside of Vivian's, his anger rising so fast. Maybe it was best if I waited until he left to speak with Derrick.

His lips curled in a sardonic smile. "As you wish, Detective."

He motioned for the guards to follow him and went to speak with the witnesses. I was the only one who noticed his stilted steps and rigid back.

"You shouldn't dismiss him like that, he only wants to help. His outburst at Vivian's was meant to protect you from the big, bad witch and her ghosthunting friend. You shouldn't punish him for it."

Derrick sighed. "I know, but we need to tighten the flow of information. There are only a few people who know Liam approached you. He may have been followed that day. There's already been a threat against you, not to mention the fountain incident with the prince. You said he might have been holding you under."

"I don't know that for sure, and he helped me get out. Don't forget that."

"Doesn't matter. After this, there will be questions, and once the news is released about the additional victims, people will be scared. The fact that the king placed his son under guard means the focus of the investigation will change. It will be up to us to either clear his name or condemn it. It's about to get ugly." Derrick motioned toward the scene. "Are you ready for this? You can stay here while I examine the body."

I swallowed my nerves and exhaled a shaky breath. "No. Liam came to me. I owe it to him to do everything I can to bring his killer to justice."

"All right, here." He handed me his notebook. "You can take notes. If you need a moment, let me know, and we'll stop."

"Quit worrying, I'm fine. Now, get to work. The agency doesn't pay you to hover around me."

"Very funny." Derrick stepped into the clearing, noting the trampled grass. "Looks like the killer dragged the body through here—there are wheel tracks in the mud. He was likely moved to this location in a cart. We'll need to see if we can track it down. Liam wasn't murdered here, there's not enough blood."

I stayed in Derrick's footsteps, careful not to disturb the scene. "Abrams said they didn't find a murder weapon, but it could have been tossed anywhere in this field. The grass is high enough we wouldn't be able to see it."

"Good point. We'll have to set up a grid search. Make note of that."

"There wasn't a rose this time either."

"This was a different sort of killing, reactionary, not part of the original plan. The roses are personal. He selects those victims for a reason." Derrick bent over the body. "No defensive wounds. There doesn't seem to have been a violent struggle."

Making a note, I studied Liam's lifeless form. My knees felt watery, but I held my ground. Blood saturated his shirt near the wound and seeped into the grass. He lay on his back, limbs covered partially in leaves. As acid rose in my throat, I closed my eyes, unable to stare at his lifeless face. Air passed heavily through my lungs in short gasps.

"Tessa, are you okay?" Derrick touched my shoulder, his hand moving up to massage my neck. "I know it's a lot. Maybe we should—"

I forced my eyes open and blinked away the dark spots. "Maybe there aren't any defensive wounds because he was drugged, or maybe it was because he knew the killer. If it was someone he trusted, it's possible he didn't see it coming. Close range, one thrust to the chest, and it was over."

Derrick studied me, respect gleaming in his eyes. "That makes sense. You're good at this. I've seen some of the heartiest officers keel over in the dirt for less."

His praise calmed the rest of my nerves. Estelle might have been right. Maybe I'd finally found something I was good at. Between ghosts, dead bodies, and threatening gifts, I'd certainly developed nerves of steel.

"I have an idea." I dug into the leather satchel at my waist. "I brought supplies. A kit, actually. After we used the potion to determine Ella's poison, I thought about how I could apply that sort of thing to other instances."

Derrick narrowed his eyes. "Are you carrying around rosenphyn? You said it was a deadly substance."

"Relax, Detective, I don't plan on eating it. But maybe we can use it to test Liam's blood? If he was poisoned, it might show up in his bloodstream. Think of the potential! I'm sure, given time, I can develop other potions that can do even more. Magic could become a new investigative tactic. What do you think?"

"I think we should try it, but not in the field. I'll have Liam's shirt preserved as evidence. You can perform your test back at the agency, in a controlled environment, where a rogue gust of wind won't make your deadly powder airborne."

I chewed the corner of my lip. "I see your point. I should pre-mix next time." I made a note in the journal.

"Don't write that down. That's not what I meant."

"Too late. Do you need my help with anything else? I should head to the agency with a sample and perform the test. The sooner we determine if poison was involved, the better. We need to get ahead of this."

Derrick frowned. He looked a little hurt.

"You're not going to question the witnesses with me?"

"I'm sure you can handle it. Besides, you have to speak with the king afterward. Let's meet later. We'll compare notes." I packed away my kit, my mind already racing toward my next task.

*** 

The image of Liam's lifeless body wouldn't leave my mind no matter how hard I tried to push it away. The drive to prove myself useful had become an essential need. In light of his murder, I couldn't sit through hours of idle questioning when my skills were better suited for running tests.

Moving light over the square of fabric from his shirt that I'd placed on the evidence table, I mixed the rosenphyn powder with other ingredients, then cast the spell. The liquid congealed, signaling it was ready to apply. With light strokes, I spread the substance over the stain. The metallic scent of blood filled my nostrils along with the earthy smell wafting from the mixture. Stomach churning, I placed a lavender-infused rag beneath my nose.

I knew I wasn't directly responsible for Liam's death, but it was hard to forget my involvement. Was this the sort of guilt Derrick lived with on a daily basis? The way he controlled his emotions and buried his feelings in order to do his job was admirable. It was one of the things I loved about him, the way he put other people first, protecting them any way he could, even at risk to himself. He could have continued to ignore me when the prince allowed me on the case, and given his history with frauds claiming to be witches, he had every reason to. I might still be sitting in some parlor detailing a guest's every movement at the ball, but instead, he'd opened up, listened to my ideas, and even let me take the lead.

Derrick worried about me too. Usually, people were worried I'd screw up a spell or bring shame to my family name—which, let's be honest, I often did—but they weren't truly worried about me, only what I'd do next. Derrick wanted what was best for me, and I wanted the same for him. He'd faced trauma and lived with the effects every day. He needed someone who could lighten his moods and provide him comfort, and if ever there was a witch for the job...

My hand stilled over the vial of rosenphyn, cork stopper suspended in the air.

Did I love him?

No. I loved things *about* him. That was different. Derrick and I were polar opposites. When the case was settled, we'd go our separate ways.

I slumped in the chair. Returning to the magic shop to sell hair cream and wrinkle tonics made me want to throw up. It wasn't enough. Somewhere along the way, I'd begun to hate the witch who ran a failing shop with no prospects and no plan, who went from one disaster to the next just to stay afloat. That was the girl my mother had shaken her head at in disappointment. This case had changed everything and given me a new sense of purpose. Derrick was proud of my contributions. I had a place here. I'd found something and someone who mattered to me, and I didn't want to let either of them go.

With a groan, I glanced at the bloodstained fabric, hoping it had changed color and could distract me from my revealing thoughts. No such luck, which meant I needed something else to distract me instead. Good thing I was in a room full of evidence.

If Derrick was right, and our investigation had turned toward the prince, we'd need to find a connection between him and all three of the women. Ella's connection was obvious: they'd attended the same ball. He even had a motive. The night by the fountain, he'd admitted his anger over being forced into marriage and the loss of control over his life. Would he kill to regain control? It was possible.

Sophie also had a connection with the prince. She'd been murdered during one of the king's feasts. The prince would have been in attendance. It's possible their paths had crossed. There wasn't an obvious motive, but it was a start.

Jane was the only one who didn't fit. Working as a barmaid, it was unlikely she'd visited the castle, and also unlikely that Prince Marcus had ever visited her establishment. Talk about polar opposites. It meant one of two things: either it wasn't the prince at all, or we hadn't found the right link.

I scooted the chair closer to Derrick's worktable and dug out the box of items taken from Jane's crime scene. There wasn't much. An embroidered coin purse, two hair ribbons, a simple metal chain, and a worn, well-read book of poetry. The tokens of her life were the only witnesses to her crime, but they remained unforgiving in their silence. I thought about the contents in my own pockets and morbidly wondered what would be in them when I died. What story would they tell?

Starting with the book of poetry, I went through it, page by page. The ink was smudged in various places, but there were no notations or clues written inside. I moved on to the coin purse, smiling when I picked it up because it resembled one Vivian had given to me when we were kids. It was the same shape and had the same embroidered pattern. Vivian had found mine on a market stall and thought of me instantly. I'd been trying to sneak spells out of the house, and my mother had started to search my pockets. The coin purse was perfect because it had a hidden compartment.

I opened the purse to find it empty, but sure enough, there was a near-invisible sleeve in the side. Sliding my finger into the pocket, I located a slip of paper. It contained only a handwritten number and a stamped seal.

A chill settled in my stomach. The seal was familiar. I'd stared at it a hundred times, cursing my luck. How was this possible? I glanced at the fabric from Liam's shirt and saw the bloodstain had changed color. Green. Liam had ingested belladonna root, same as Ella.

The slip of paper trembled in my hand. Argus was searching for Ironhazel, and now, I had evidence from one of our victims containing his seal.

Jane had owed Argus money.

I needed to know why.

# Chapter 23

"Are you insane?" Vivian hissed, trailing me down the steps of her shop. She grabbed the sleeve of my cloak and didn't let go. "You're going to visit Argus?"

"I need answers, Viv, and he has them. He knows Jane and happens to be looking for Ironhazel. That's not a coincidence. What if he's the key to unlocking this case?"

She twisted to block my path while still holding onto my sleeve. "Then take Derrick with you. You can't run off to interrogate a criminal by yourself. I forbid it."

"Derrick has been tied up at the palace all afternoon. This is too important. It can't wait."

Vivian scoffed. "You're such a coward. You haven't told Derrick the truth about your debt, and you're afraid of how he'll react, so, instead, you're doing what you always do—which is, trying to solve everything by yourself. Do you think Derrick will be impressed if you come back with information? He'll be furious."

She had a point. Derrick's rules were clear, no investigating alone, and I couldn't deny his protective streak when it came to my safety. He would be furious.

"Look, you're right. I haven't told Derrick about Argus, and he deserves to know, but that's irrelevant to this situation because here's the truth. There is no way Argus is going to answer questions in front of a royal detective. My only chance is to talk to him one-on-one, and even that is a long shot."

Vivian blew out a breath and looked up at the overcast sky. "It's such a bad idea."

"No, a bad idea would be to let this opportunity slip through my fingers. Derrick will never let me speak with Argus once I tell him about my debt, and Argus will never speak with Derrick. I have one shot. Think about Ella. What wouldn't you do for one of your ghosts? You're always charging around, going to abandoned haunted houses. Remember the time you fell through the rotten floor into the basement, and it took us two days to find you?"

She shuddered. "Something was living down there. I landed in its nest, and that's why I'm coming with you to see Argus."

I opened my mouth to protest, but she held up a finger.

"Not a peep. I'm coming with you. If he recruits us into his gang and ships us off to a foreign kingdom to become hardened female assassins, then at least you won't be alone.

I swallowed a laugh. "Honestly, Viv, you have a colorful imagination."

She shrugged. "I think I'd make an excellent female assassin. I have feminine wiles, my aim is decent, and I happen to think I'd look good in the outfit."

"All good points. Except there's one problem."

"What's that?"

"You'll be haunted by all of your kills."

She wrinkled her nose. "That is a problem. The life of an outlaw is tricky. Argus will have to assign me something else."

Clenching my teeth, I pulled her along the street. "He's not assigning us anything. We're just going to talk."

"Sounds like something his last female assassin said before he shipped her off."

I groaned. Vivian adjusted her arm through mine so we were walking side-by-side, two ladies on a stroll to visit a gangster.

"So, how do we find him? Does he have a den of iniquity, or do we commit a crime and he pops up in a puff of smoke like a crooked genie?"

I slanted her a look out of the corner of my eye. "Very funny. Actually, I thought we'd ask them." I pointed across the street at the two thugs leaning against a brick building. "They follow me around enough, they might as well be useful."

The taller of the two ruffians straightened when he caught me looking and nudged his partner. I waved, wiggling my fingers. His partner waved back, which earned him an elbow in his ribs.

"Okay," Vivian muttered under her breath. "I guess we walk up to street hooligans now and ask for directions."

Thug Number One crossed his arms over his burly chest. His tree-trunk legs were spread apart, and he looked like a mountain of muscle encased in a pair of leather boots.

"You lost?" he growled.

"You could say that." I wiped damp palms on my cloak and forced a smile. "I need to talk to your boss. Where can I find him?"

"He finds you, not the other way around."

Vivian pinched my side. "See, it is the genie scenario."

Thug Number Two frowned, the action pulling taut a scar bisecting his cheek. "Genie scenario?"

"Never mind. I need to speak with Argus now. I have the information he's looking for. He won't be happy when he finds out you're standing in the way. He might even—"

"Chop off your fingers, bleach the bones, and use them as writing instruments."

"Vivian, please!"

She cocked her head. "What? Too much?"

Thug Number One hooked his thumbs into his belt and rocked back on his heels. The mountain quaked as a laugh rumbled through his chest.

"All right, let's go. I wouldn't want to lose my fingers. Besides, I think the boss will like this one. Might even give me a raise." He winked at Vivian, and she narrowed her eyes in disgust.

It took us almost an hour to reach our destination. The streets were congested, and we took every connecting alley available. Evening set in, darkening the sky and giving way to a blistering chill. The two thugs led us around the side of a tavern and held open the back door. A pungent tide of cooked meat and stale beer hit me in the face, causing my stomach to roll. Our shoes stuck to the dirty floor, making a suction sound as we traveled through the kitchen and past the door that led to the main part of the tavern.

Thug Number One sauntered down a narrow hallway barely the width of his massive shoulders. He rapped twice on a wooden door, and a panel slid open to reveal a pair of deep-set eyes.

"Is the boss in? I've got the witch and her friend insisting to see him."

The panel slammed shut, and we stood awkwardly in the compact corridor. Vivian hooked her arm through mine, her lips tight. Some of her bravado had slipped now that we were a closed-door's length away from seeing Argus in the flesh. No turning back now. My nerves raced, and a thin river of trepidation flowed through my veins. I was empty-handed except for the slip of paper that contained Jane's seal.

"Let me do the talking," I whispered, squeezing Vivian's arm.

She nodded. "Fine by me, but Argus doesn't scare me."

The door swung open, and we were ushered along another hallway, tighter than the last. Then, after pushing us inside Argus's lair, Thug Number One slammed the door behind us. His boots echoed as they faded down the hallway.

I squinted to see in the dim light. There were no windows, and the lanterns were turned low. We were met with a wave of heat from the fire crackling in the hearth.

"Did you bring my money, witch?"

The voice seemed disembodied, and I spun, trying to locate the sound. Argus leaned against the edge of a giant cabinet filled with crystal decanters. He lifted a glass to his lips, and ice clinked.

"I have until the end of the month."

"So, this is a social visit? What a surprise. If I'd known, I would have laid out snacks. I guess we'll have to make do with bourbon." He swallowed a deep gulp of the amber liquid, then stalked closer, offering a second glass to Vivian. Challenge lurked in his eyes.

She eyed him warily before accepting the drink. Argus crooked his lips to watch her down it. Wiping a lingering drop from the corner of her mouth with a thumb, Vivian swallowed.

"Argus Ward." He held out a hand. "The witch is terrible at introductions."

"Vivian James." She didn't return his handshake, and he closed his fingers with a stony expression.

"You know, your friend doesn't think too much of me. What about you? First impressions?"

Vivian worried her bottom lip. Argus's green gaze dipped to the spot, his knuckles tightening against the glass. She focused her eyes over his shoulder for a long moment, then returned his steady stare.

"I think you're a haunted man."

His arrogance slipped, and an odd look flashed across his face. When he spoke, there was a gruffness in his voice.

"Maybe I am. What should I do about it?"

Vivian glanced over his shoulder a second time and angled her head as if she were communicating with an invisible force. She leaned closer, and Argus went still.

"My consultations aren't free."

His bark of laughter broke the tension, and I exhaled in relief. Tipping his glass at Vivian, Argus rounded a large mahogany desk and settled into a high-backed chair, where he rested his chin in his hand and gestured to the seats in front of him.

"Ladies, please. Where are my manners?"

"First time I've seen any," I muttered, arranging my skirt to take a seat.

Vivian did the same, then reached behind her neck to pull her long, glossy hair over her shoulder. Argus watched, transfixed. When I snapped my fingers to regain his attention, he reluctantly obeyed.

"If you aren't here to deliver my money then I suspect it's because you have information on Ironhazel. Does Detective Do-It-All know you're here? Have you told him about us?"

I ground my teeth together, forcing my irritation down to a manageable level. "I'm here because I need answers, and you're going to give them to me."

He arched a brow. "I'm certainly interested to see

you try."

Reaching into my pocket, I removed the slip of paper that contained Argus's seal and slid it across the desk. I tapped the inked mark.

"Do you recognize this?"

"Of course. You have one with your name on it. In fact, lots of people have them. I'm a busy man. What's your point?"

"My point is, this belonged to Jane Porter, a barmaid murdered in an alley six months ago."

Argus flinched. It was subtle, but it gave him away. He steepled his fingers under his chin.

"Exactly what are you accusing me of, witch?"

"Nothing yet. But I want to know why Jane owed you money, and why you're interested in Ironhazel. Unless you'd rather I hand this paper over to the royal authorities? They might jump to conclusions and think you have a motive for murder. That could be bad for business."

Argus plucked the piece of paper from under my fingers and held it over the candle flame, high enough that it wouldn't burn.

"Too slow." His gaze flicked to Vivian. He hesitated before schooling his features, then lowered the paper into the flame. It caught fire and blackened to ash.

Dipping into my pocket, I pulled out another square with the same seal and Jane's handwritten name. Vivian tossed up her hands and pulled a copy from her pocket as well, waving it in the air.

Argus bared his teeth in a harsh smile. "Nice trick,

witch."

"We can go all night. You'll probably find a copy or two in your henchman's pockets, possibly a few in the pockets of people we passed on our way here. Who knows, I like to leave breadcrumbs. But will you find the real one?" I turned to Vivian, and she shook her head. "Yeah, probably not. Let's skip to the part where you cooperate and tell me what I want to know. We're busy ladies, so get to the point."

Argus stood and refilled his glass. He sipped the bourbon slowly, accompanied by the snap and crack of the fire in the hearth. Finally, he rubbed a hand over his brow and walked toward a shelving unit, from which he retrieved a ledger and returned to his seat.

"Just because I'm answering your questions doesn't mean we're becoming friendly. You still owe me every bloody coin of your agreement."

I nodded, excitement humming through my body. My spell had worked! We had the upper hand for now.

Argus opened the ledger and found the section on Jane. "You're right, Jane did owe me money, but she was also working for me to pay off her debts."

"She worked for you? I thought she served drinks at the Laughing Raven."

"Who do you think owns the Laughing Raven?" He turned to Vivian and winked. "I own quite a few establishments."

She rolled her eyes. "Will murderers never cease?"

"I'm a businessman, love. Take note." He leaned

back in his chair. "Jane was ambitious. She wanted more out of life than slinging ale. She fell on hard times, and I offered her a solution. Men talk when they're drunk, especially to beautiful women."

Vivian grunted, making Argus's smile widen.

"I don't make the rules, and Jane didn't mind. She spied on them and reported back. She was good at her job, maybe too good. I was having a problem with someone who thought they could sell illegal substances in my territory and not pay for the right. I wanted a name, and Jane went after it. She ended up dead in an alley for her trouble."

"So, the person selling in your territory was Iron-hazel?"

"I didn't know that at the time. Jane was killed before she gave me a name, and then, after her death, the seller vanished. Jane's room was trashed. Her things were taken and burned before I got there. All I found was a charred note with the letters *I-R-O-N-H* written on it. I didn't know what it meant, wasn't even sure it was related to her murder, until one of my men reported back about your visit to Flamelock Den. I had a talk with your friend Charlie, and he revealed what he told you."

"Then it's possible Ironhazel was the one who killed Jane?" I asked.

"That's what I want to find out. It may surprise you, but I don't like it when bad things happen to my people. Someone has to pay for Jane's death. The authorities don't care about a barmaid murdered in an alley, but I do."

"That's not true. It's important to me too." I paused, debating whether to ask my next question. "Is there any way Jane might've crossed paths with Prince Marcus?"

Argus chuckled. "In this part of town? No way. She was seen with a young man before her death, but it wasn't the prince, I can promise you that."

"Who was the young man?" Vivian asked.

Argus shrugged. "Not sure. Maybe family or a friend. They appeared fairly close, but she didn't mention him to me, and no one claimed her body after she was found. I paid for her burial expenses through an anonymous donation."

"Derrick said Jane didn't have any family."

"We all come from somewhere. Maybe Jane had a reason for staying away from hers. I know I do." Argus swirled the bourbon in his glass, his eyes darkening.

A loud crash erupted through the tavern, and footsteps raced down the hall. One of Argus's men pounded on the door.

"Boss, get out now! There's a raid. We'll hold them off."

I pushed out of my chair, sending Vivian a panicked look. She scrambled to her feet, and we watched Argus stuff a handful of papers into a bag and pull open his desk drawer. He rifled through its contents, placing more items into the bag, then slung it over his shoulder. He was deadly calm even as shouts from the authorities grew louder. They'd breached the first door.

Terror seized me. If we were caught, we'd be hauled off to prison. But it wasn't the dark, rat-infested cells that made my legs buckle—it was knowing Derrick would find me there before I could tell him the truth.

"What do we do?" I hissed, searching for something to block the door. "Quick, help me with the cabinet."

Argus scowled. "Don't touch my bourbon, witch." He slid a panel in the wall, revealing a dark passage, and waved us forward. "Come on, let's go."

Vivian reacted first, rushing to his side. He looped an arm around her waist.

"That's right, love. Watch your step."

She shook off his arm and dove into the passage.

Argus laughed. "She'll come around. Witch, don't forget to close the panel."

I started to follow but remembered the ledger with Jane's information sitting on his desk. I had to take it with me. A boot slammed into the office door, and I rounded the desk, snatching the ledger, then ran for the passage just as the door splintered open. I shrieked, covering my face from flying debris.

"You, there. Stop!" a man shouted.

It was too late. I slid the panel back into place. At least they wouldn't arrest Vivian.

Numbness washed over me as the authorities streamed into the office. They shouted for me to raise my hands, then one of them ripped my arms behind my back and strung a pair of iron cuffs around my wrists. An officer picked up the ledger I'd gone back for, but I lost sight of him, pushed from behind by a rough set of hands. They loaded us into a wagon enclosed by bars, and I spotted Thug Number One and Two sitting in the back. They inclined their heads when they saw me and shoved the man next to them to make room. The carriage rolled forward, and we were herded away, into the night.

*** 

I waited in the holding cell for an hour, then two. What was taking so long? Everyone else had been transported further into the prison already. Fear rooted me to my chair. Part of me wanted the holding cell door to remain closed, to keep me locked away from the consequences of my actions. I squeezed my eyes shut, fighting against the panic.

Going to see Argus was the right thing to do. I clung to that thought, desperate for it to soothe my frayed nerves. Derrick would understand when I explained why I went there. He'd listen. He always listened, even when I made his life difficult.

Footsteps thudded down the hall and came to a stop behind the cell door. My breath stalled in the back of my throat as the knob turned and the hinges whined. Derrick stood in the threshold, his fingers clamped around a thick folder. I couldn't breathe at the look in his eyes. It was a dark, thundercloud of a look that sucked all air from the room. I'd witnessed disappointment numerous times, but this was something else. *Devastation.*

His gaze pinned me to the seat. I was drowning in

it, choking on the raw anguish. I sucked in an aching breath.

"I'm sorry. I—"

"Save it." Derrick strode toward the table, and the folder landed with a smack against the hard surface. The fear inside my heart expanded, turning my insides to ice. He wasn't going to listen. He stood, chest rising and falling with uneven breaths, his eyes drinking me in. For a fleeting second, they were filled with a mixture of relief and longing so powerful it made my stomach clench.

Then, it disappeared.

"Miss Daniels." My name cracked like a whip. "Start by explaining how long you've been working for a known criminal, and finish by giving me a single reason why I shouldn't throw you in the hole with the rest of his men."

# Chapter 24

I t was hard to speak around the throb in my throat. I closed my eyes to shut out his accusing stare, but I could still see it burning behind my eyelids.

"I know this looks bad."

"Answer the question. How long have you been working for Argus Ward?"

The table creaked with his weight. I opened my eyes to find him braced on his fists, his face an iron mask.

"I don't work for Argus Ward. You're making a mistake."

"Am I?" His lips curled in a sneer. "Then explain why, when I questioned his men, they claimed you've been feeding him information about Ironhazel."

"They're wrong. I'm not feeding him infor—"

"Damn it, Tessa!" He slammed a fist on the table. "I trusted you. Do you have any idea the type of man Argus is? The kind of danger you've put yourself in?" He tore open the folder and spread out its pages.

A series of rugged faces stared back, all of them associates of Argus. Derrick stabbed the top image with his finger. It was the mountain of a man Vivian and I had approached on the street.

"Do you think this is a game? Assault, theft, attempted murder. This criminal is sitting in a cell after tonight's raid. He isn't fit to speak your name, and yet he knows things about you that I don't." A pained expression tightened his features. Derrick exhaled and dropped his chin to his chest. "Tell me, why?"

"I'm trying. Let me explain." I stood and paced the floor, struggling to find the right words. They all sounded inadequate in the face of his anger. "I don't work for Argus. I owe him money. Lots of money." Self-loathing pulsed through my body, a feeling so familiar it felt like coming home. "Are you happy now? I screwed up. I always screw up, don't I? The magic shop was failing, and Argus was a temporary solution that spiraled out of control. I needed to pay him back. I'm sure you of all people know what happens when payments are missed. I was desperate. Ella had been murdered, and then you walked into my shop and charged me with fines! What was I supposed to do? I was sinking. I had to make impossible choices."

Derrick moved around the table and stalked me across the room. I backed up, wary of the severity in his eyes. If I thought my explanation would soothe his ire, I was sorely mistaken. He'd been pushed too far. I wasn't certain he was capable of hearing my side of the story.

"All this time, and you never told me about your

shop. Why? Let me guess, Argus wanted information about the murder, didn't he? And you were already in his back pocket."

"No! I mean, yes, he did approach me at Ella's memorial dinner, but that was the first time. I didn't know he had an interest in the case, I swear it. I never planned on helping him."

"It doesn't matter! A known criminal asked questions about my case, and you kept it a secret because you knew I'd discover your connection to him. You talk about choices? Were you kidnapped and forced to visit Argus tonight, or did you choose to go?"

"I decided." My shoulders bumped the stone wall, preventing me from further retreat.

Derrick took advantage, trapping me in a cage of arms, each one an iron beam on either side of my body. "You chose to hide your involvement with Argus and your knowledge of the men who've been following you. I asked you point-blank if you knew those men, and you lied."

"Because you wouldn't understand."

"You never gave me a chance!"

"A chance?" Adrenaline pounded my ears. I shoved at the immovable wall of his chest. "Why should I? You charged into my magic shop on day one determined to tear me down. You were like everyone else, judgmental to the core. You kicked me out of your office when I told you about Ella. I had to fight tooth and nail to get you to listen, and when you finally started to look at me like I mattered, how was I supposed to tell you what I'd done? You would have thrown me off the case."

The muscles in his shoulders bunched as he pushed off the wall and turned his back to me. A wrenching silence followed.

"That would have ruined all your plans, wouldn't it?"

"My plans?" Dread coiled in my stomach. I felt out of depth, unable to follow his train of thought. Were things so murky between us?

"Why are you here, Tessa?"

"I...I don't understand what you mean."

"Why did you approach me and offer to help with the case?"

"Because I wanted to help Ella."

"No." He turned and wrapped his hand around my wrist, tugging me closer. "The truth."

"It is the truth!" I tilted my head back, confusion knotting my brow. "She visited me as a ghost, and I wanted to make things right."

"So, you offered your services out of the goodness of your heart? How noble."

My jaw clenched. I realized what he was getting at. One final nail in my coffin. Might as well hand him the hammer.

"Fine. You win. I needed the reward money to pay back Argus. What's wrong with that? Everyone doesn't fit into your precise little boxes, Detective. You said my past didn't define me, and yet you've made up your mind about my character, and it's clear you don't believe me."

"Believe you?" His head dipped, voice scraping

against my ear. "You've lied to me from the beginning. Did you think I wouldn't figure out that you used me for information? Maybe you didn't intend to feed it to Argus, but you had other motives." He lifted my chin with his fingers and held me there, our stares dueling. "What I can't understand is why that wasn't enough for you."

My heart pounded beneath his unflinching stare. "What wasn't enough?"

Something snapped behind his eyes. Like watching a dam break loose, the restrained longing he'd held in swept over me, dragging me under.

"This." Derrick angled his head and captured my lips in a punishing kiss.

I swayed backward at the force, but he banded his arm around my waist and lifted me up to sit on the table, then rocked forward, his mouth slanting over mine. Heat fired low in my belly. I locked my ankles around his waist and slid my palms up his chest, feeling the smooth fabric of his shirt and warm skin beneath. My fingers dug into his shoulder blades, drawing him closer.

Turmoil emanated from his body, and I absorbed it, let it sizzle through me like one of my spells gone horribly wrong. His kiss was an act of aggression that quickly turned desperate, both of us fighting without words, trying to explain, asking why.

He made a noise deep in his throat and cradled my head in his hands. The ruthlessness burned away. Our kiss gentled. There was something about the way his anger melted that made me want to sob. It was easy to battle against his fury—I had enough of my own at the impossible situation my life had become, and I could erect a hundred walls, fight fire with fire—but the ease with which he robbed me of that ability made my head spin.

I wanted more. All of him. This was different. It felt diametric, reverent. Derrick grazed his thumbs over my cheeks, breath shaky as his mouth pressed against the curve of my jaw. His tenderness didn't belong in this holding cell where only misery had come before it. My eyes squeezed shut. There had to be a way to make him understand.

"Derrick, wait..."

Emotion thickened his voice. "Was this part of your plan to get information from me? Collect the reward at all costs even if you had to seduce the cold-hearted detective? Maybe you had the Gazette follow us that day by the apothecary?"

"No! I—"

"You know what this case means to me, what it's done to my life. I lie awake at night terrified I'll lose someone else, that I can't trust my instincts. Tessa," he said my name like a plea, and I choked back a sob, "did you have to make me want you?" The pads of his fingers skimmed my neck, and his mouth hovered near my ear. "Make me need you? Make me fall in—?" He stopped, his throat working as air expanded in his lungs.

"How can you ask that?" I cupped his face, horror compressing my heart. "I would *never* hurt you that way. You might not trust me where Argus is concerned, but trust that. Meeting you changed every-thing."

"You're right. Everything has changed." The mask returned, his features impassive, wall firmly back in place. His near-admission echoed in my ears as he removed my hands and backed away.

I remained seated, numb. How had things become so twisted?

Derrick reached for his jacket lying over the back of the chair and withdrew a leather satchel from its pocket. It landed with a heavy thunk against the table.

"What's that?"

"Money. Enough to pay off your debt."

Ice spread through my limbs, and I slid off the table. This wasn't right. The bag mocked me. I hadn't earned the money. This was another example of someone swooping in to clean up my mistakes.

I *hated* it.

"But we haven't caught the killer. The reward is unclaimed."

"It's not the official reward, it's my money." His tone was flat, as if he'd offered me a crust of bread and not a fortune.

My voice shook as a ball of anger wedged against my vocal cords. "I don't want it."

"I don't care. Tessa, it's over." His mouth pressed into a firm line. "I told you what would happen if you lied to me. I meant it. You're off the case. Take the money and be done with it."

I inhaled sharply, a bitter denial on my tongue.

"You don't have the authority to make that decision. The prince—"

"The prince is being held at the castle on suspicion of murder. This is my call." He thrust the satchel into my hands. "Take it. I won't have you indebted to that criminal." His tone lowered, becoming rough. "No matter what happens between us, I need to know you'll be okay."

I scoffed, wishing I could hide behind my own mask of indifference. "You can't have it both ways. We're supposed to be partners! I thought we were more than that. I thought…" Outrage clogged my throat. I was such an idiot. Things weren't different. He'd turned me upside-down with his acceptance and then decided I wasn't worth it after all. "Fine, toss me off the case, but you don't get to throw money at the pitiful witch so you can sleep at night."

"That's not what I mean, and you know it." Derrick's eyes closed as if he were reining in his patience. His jaw tightened. "Tessa, I don't know how to trust you anymore, but I can't lose you either. If something happened to you because of him, I would never forgive myself."

"That's no longer your concern."

"The hell it is!"

My fingers clenched around the bag. I wanted to throw it, smash it against the wall, make it disappear in a puff of smoke. It was absurd. I held the answer to my prayers in my hand, and it felt hollow.

Realization came fast and filled me with certainty. I'd rather lose the shop than fail Ella. I tipped the bag so coins fell from the opening, clinking as they hit the floor. They scattered around my feet, and I shook the bag until it was empty, then crumpled it in my fist.

"Until the killer is caught, the reward is up for grabs. When I find him, I'll be back to collect it. And just so you don't accuse me of withholding information again, the reason I visited Argus was because Jane Porter worked for him. Jane was investigating Ironhazel, and whatever she found got her killed. One of your men picked up a ledger detailing her involvement. You can check with him to see if I'm telling the truth. In the end, it was my association with Argus that provided the clue. He never would have spoken with the agency." I stepped over the coins and walked toward the door.

Derrick grabbed my arm. "Don't do this, Tessa."

"Am I free to go, or are you finally making good on your promise to arrest me?"

The silence that followed had weight to it. It was a crushing force that made my bones ache. His eyes held mine, and I almost crumbled, begged him to take me back. To trust me again. To love me, faults and all.

His gaze fell. "You're free."

Two simple words that pierced my heart. He wasn't just dropping the charges, he was letting me go completely. I squared my shoulders, determined he wouldn't see how much he'd wounded me. A witch never let anyone see her cry.

"Good luck, Detective. Maybe I'll see you at the

finish line." I didn't wait for a response. I didn't even look back.

# Chapter 25

*One week later...*

"How about these?" Vivian held up a set of decorative altar statues.

"Leave them. I'm pretty sure they're cursed." I added another scented pillar candle to a box and closed the lid.

Vivian scrunched her nose and placed the statues into the "stay" pile. She moved on to a shelf of amethyst crystals.

"I can't believe you're packing the shop."

Neither could I, though in some ways, it felt cathartic. Wasn't it always supposed to end this way? I'd spent the week wallowing in my rejection from Derrick while doing my best to track down Ironhazel. Neither venture had been very productive. My only connection to Ironhazel had been thwarted when Charlie went missing after he stiffed a mystical weapons vendor. I guess I would have run too if I had a price on my head, but without him, I didn't have any other leads.

"I don't have much choice. The month is almost up."

"What about the Gazette? Any luck with the ad?"

"Derrick wouldn't tell me if there was. For all I know, he's already found the source of the roses. I mean, obviously, solving the case is the most important outcome, I just wanted to get there first."

"For the reward?" Vivian dumped the entire shelf of crystals into a satchel.

"I don't even know anymore. Sure, I want the money, but it all feels like failure at this point. If I save the shop, then what? I go back to mucking up illusions and selling mediocre potions? I'll end up in the exact same situation as before."

"And you miss him."

Vivian sure knew how to salt a wound. Yeah, I missed Derrick in a way I hadn't thought possible, and it was only an unhealthy dose of pride that kept me from crawling back to the agency. His silence hurt. I hadn't expected him to forgive me, but I thought maybe it wouldn't have been so easy to let me go. Jokes on the witch. He severed ties and didn't look back. I bet he'd thrown a party, had it catered and everything.

My eyes stung, but I blinked away the tears. I couldn't let Vivian see them. Every time I got a little weepy, she threatened to send a ghost to the agency. Apparently, she had the perfect one that wailed like a banshee all hours of the day. He'd never get any work done. It wasn't flattering, but I had considered it.

Derrick had made his choice though, and I'd made mine, and now, we had to live with it. I had a shop to sell and my dreams to crush. There wasn't time for petty revenge. Said no witch ever, which just went to show how far I'd fallen.

Vivian dusted a shelf of spell books and placed them into a box. "You know, I was thinking, with the money you have leftover from selling the shop and paying back Argus, you could purchase the old Derringer cottage."

"It's haunted, Viv."

"So what? You can get it for a steal. I might have already spoken with the ghost to up his haunting activity and scare away potential buyers. The price will come down even further."

"I'm not buying a haunted house." I wiped the candle wax from my hands onto my skirt. "I'm thinking about traveling for a while. Maybe I'll start fresh somewhere else."

"Also known as running away."

"Also known as self-preservation. I can't run into him. What happens the first time I do, and he's with someone else? I'll make a voodoo doll. You know I will."

Vivian smirked. "The poor thing won't know what hit her between the hauntings and the phantom pains. If Derrick has any sense, he'll remain a bachelor."

I gave her a weak smile, and Vivian clapped her hands together.

"See, there's a smile. You're going to be all right. If you insist on traveling, maybe I'll go with you. The Elemental Islands are beautiful this time of year.

It'll be two adventurous women taking the islands by storm. I'll find myself a wealthy land baron, and you'll cast a love spell over a handsome foreigner, and before you know it, Detective No Name will be a thing of the past."

*If only it were that easy.*

I pushed aside the box and stood, stretching my aching muscles. The bell above the door jingled, and I looked over my shoulder at the newcomer.

"Sorry, we're clos—" I paused, recognizing Estelle, the agency's receptionist. She glanced around the shop, her gaze taking in the stacked boxes and packed merchandise.

"Looks like I arrived just in time." Estelle shuffled inside, weaving around the disarray. "I can't stay long, I'm on a lunch break. It will probably be my last one thanks to you. Apparently, lunch is a leisure activity." Her eyes rolled, and she grumbled under her breath.

"Estelle, what are you doing here?"

She waved a dismissive hand. "Someone had to come and talk some sense into you. I don't know how much longer I can keep my job. Mind you, I deal with a waiting room full of ruffians every day, and that's nothing compared to the surly monster Detective Chambers has become. He's unbearable! Officers hide when they see him, and it's your fault."

Vivian cocked her head. "I told you he'd be miserable without you, but you didn't believe me." She turned to Estelle. "This one's miserable too. It's hard to watch."

"Traitor," I hissed.

Vivian shrugged and opened a new box.

Estelle planted her fists on her hips and shot me an accusing glare. "I don't know what happened between the two of you, but something needs to give. I've never seen him like this before. He doesn't sleep, hardly eats, and he has this devastated look on his face every time I open his office door and he realizes it's me and not you. Honestly, my feelings are hurt. I'm worried about him."

The ache in my chest tripled. Had he been having a difficult time? I talked a big game, but I didn't want to see him in pain. It was the last thing I wanted.

"What do you expect me to do?"

"Go talk to him. He needs you, and the dolt has too much pride to admit it."

"I can't do that, Estelle. It's too hard. You don't understand."

Estelle huffed. "I understand perfectly. You're scared. Both of you are. You think it's easier to stay apart, but it's so much worse."

"I'm sorry. I can't go back. It's for the best." The tears returned, and I swiped at them with my fingers. An ugly cry was in my future as soon as I had a minute alone.

"I was afraid you'd say that." Estelle crossed her arms and gave me her best look of motherly disapproval. She nailed it. "I can't make you talk to him, but there is something I can do. I heard you're investigating the case on your own, and by the looks of things, the rumor about you needing the reward money is true. I can give you a tip, something even Derrick doesn't know about. All I can hope for is that you solve the case first and stick around. Maybe, given enough time, the two of you can work out your differences."

I chewed the corner of my lip, my interest piqued. "You have a tip about the case?"

"Yes. Someone came to the agency to speak with Detective Chambers, but he wasn't in. I collected the statement. I haven't shown it to him yet, and I'm giving it to you first."

"If Derrick finds out, he'll fire you."

"Then you and I will both be looking for jobs."

Vivian snapped her fingers. "Tessa and I are going to travel to the Elemental Islands. You could come. There's room for one more. Think of the damage three adventurous ladies could do."

She nodded. "Not a bad idea. But first, follow up on the tip, see where it takes you." She pulled a sheet of paper from her bag and handed it over.

I read the details. "Are you sure about this?"

Estelle pursed her lips and pointed to the door. "If I were you, I'd hurry."

***

The alley was dark, and it grew darker the further I walked. Sunlight tried its best to reach the dirt-packed ground but left only shadows. Oily puddles and debris lined both sides of the brick walls, but I weaved around them, pressing on until I found the right door.

Estelle's tip said a shipment of illegal herbs had been delivered to this location. The neighbors had heard strange noises and smells coming from a room on the third floor. It was only occupied during the night, and during the day remained empty. I glanced at what little sun found its way into the alley. There was time to search before the owner returned. Maybe this was where Ironhazel worked? There could be stores of belladonna root inside.

As I climbed the rickety steps to the third floor, the weathered boards creaked under my feet. If the room wasn't empty, whoever was inside would know I was coming, no way around that.

An earthy, herbal scent grew stronger as I approached the last door on the left of the hall. I paused in front of the portal and put my ear against the wood.

Nothing. It was empty.

I went inside, squinting in the dark. With the shades drawn, there was almost no light. Pushing the door softly until it clicked, I reached into the bag at my hip and closed my fist around two small stones, heating their smooth surface to make a beam of white light appear. Moonstones were a safer, brighter bet than a candle.

When I opened my hand, the glow lit the room. It also lit an advancing figure. Fear constricted my throat a second before they barreled me into the wall, the moonstones landing at my feet. Strong hands clamped my wrists, dragged them over my head, and anchored them to the wall.

"Don't move," a voice commanded.

I couldn't breathe. The force from hitting the wall had knocked all air out of my chest. I wheezed, unable to drag in a breath. While the face in front of me spun, black dots danced in my vision.

"Tessa? Damn it!" The man's grip loosened, and he caught me as I fell forward, lowering me to the floor as his hands cradled my face. "Breathe, Tessa. Come on, just breathe."

Air finally filled my lungs, and I choked out his name. "Derrick? How?"

He ignored my question, hands skimming over my body in search of injuries. "Did I hurt you anywhere else? Answer me."

"I'm trying," I croaked. "Stop. I'm fine."

His search ceased, but he kept pressure on my shoulders when I tried to sit up. "No. Stay still until you catch your breath. I need a minute too. I could have killed you."

"Don't be dramatic, you knocked the wind out of me."

"What are you doing here?" Derrick's voice shook with barely contained anger, though something told me he was angrier at himself. As his fingers ghosted over my jaw, my eyes closed. I missed those hands. He cushioned my head with his thigh.

"I got a tip."

"So did I."

A sneaky feeling coiled in my stomach. "Did Estelle give it to you?"

"Yeah, a witness left a statement."

I groaned. That matchmaking she-devil. She deserved to be fired, and she was definitely no longer invited on our girls' trip.

"She told me the same thing. *Man*, she's devious. She set us up. I'd be shocked if this was even a real tip."

"It wasn't—I already searched. That smell is tea leaves. Perfectly legal tea."

Had anything she said been true? Maybe it was all a lie, and Derrick wasn't suffering in my absence. I was such a fool. A lovesick, pitiful fool.

Then, I focused on his face.

He was miserable. There was a bleakness in his expression that I'd never seen before. The need for sleep was ingrained around his eyes. He might have even lost a few pounds, and he'd had a workaholic won't-stop-for-food attitude before we met. Seeing him like this should have made me feel better, but it only hurt worse. A million times worse.

Unable to resist, I pressed my palm against his cheek. Derrick released a slow breath, as if he'd been holding it all this time and could finally let it go.

"You look tired," I said.

His hand covered mine. "The...*case* is killing me."

"I know. Me too."

"It's the hardest thing I've ever done."

"It's supposed to be hard." A tear slid down my cheek, which he caught with his thumb.

"Not like this. Tessa, some of the things I said to you—"

"I'm going to sell the shop," I cut in, unable to

withstand any mention of our previous fight. Rehashing it wouldn't do any good.

"What? No."

I sat up and cleared the emotion from my throat. "Don't get excited. I'm still trying to beat you, but just in case, I thought you should know."

"I never wanted that. I only wanted..." He didn't finish. "What will you do?"

"Travel. I can't stay here, it's too difficult." I held his gaze. "I should go somewhere where they don't know about my unfortunate spells. Who knows, maybe I'll get a few of them right this time?"

"Don't go."

My lips trembled. "Why?"

"Because people depend on you here."

I laughed. "No, they don't."

"They do. I know they do."

"Name one."

"What about Finn? The kid worships you. Where will he get the medicine for his mother, if you're not here? It's not like you to give up like this."

"I'm not giving up. I'm being practical, something I should have been from the start." I stood and picked up the moonstones. They cast light around the sparse room, and sure enough, shelving units filled with tea canisters lined the walls. "Don't be too hard on Estelle. She was trying to help."

Derrick rose to his feet and stepped closer. His familiar scent filled my senses. How long would I remember it? Would it become a visceral memory every time I smelled anything similar? How cruel.

"Listen up, Detective. If you want to beat me then get some sleep. Eat something. Give me a real challenge, something to remember you by."

"And what about you?"

"You don't have to remember me."

"What if I want to? You have to give me something."

"A spell?" I closed the distance between us.

His hands circled my waist. "No."

"Then how about an illusion?" I wound my fingers around his neck, going up on my toes. My lips found his, and I kissed him slow, thinking maybe it didn't have to end. But that was the thing about illusions. They didn't last.

Derrick let me lead, let me take my time. His mouth was warm against mine, lingering. It wasn't an urgent kiss. Maybe it should have been. It should have been a lot of things, but it was only going to be a memory.

I pulled away and made for the door, taking the light with me.

\*\*\*

My shop looked the same as it did when I'd left it. A mess. Boxes—some full, some waiting—were stacked against the wall. Vivian had made a dent in the display of creams and powders, getting most of them packed away, but she'd left the cabinet of oils for another day. I couldn't look at any of it anymore. It stank of giving up. Vivian was right. I was running away.

I kicked one of the boxes and headed for the stairs. Something shattered beneath my feet.

Looking down, I expected to see a broken bottle, but there was nothing there. Which meant...

My gaze flew to the hatch in the floor. Someone was in my basement.

Slowly, I crept closer, trying to keep my feet from making a sound. I should get a weapon. Why had I packed the crystal spikes first? I had no idea which box they were in now. Maybe fire ant powder? A dash to the face, and any intruders would wish they were dead. At the very least, they'd run screaming, fingers clawing at their skin.

I skirted the hatch and searched the box of powders, finding the jar near the top. Off came the lid, while voices filtered up from the basement. There was more than one of them.

My fingers clenched the jar. Any sane person would run and get help, but they might be gone by the time I got back. The plan: Toss the powder down the hole, and ask questions later.

I flung the trap door open.

"Tessa, is that you? Where do you keep the elderberry wine? All you have is blackberry. You know I can't stand the stuff." Sylvia popped her head into view and gestured with her cane. "It's a disaster down here. I don't know how you find anything."

"Sylvia! Why are you in my basement?"

She rolled her eyes. "The wine, dear. Are you hard of hearing? Where is it?"

"Found it!" A man shouted.

"Who's down there with you?" I set the jar on the floor and clambered down the steps, my shoes crunching over glass and a sticky substance.

"Mind the glass. I dropped a bottle. It's a bit slippery."

"Tessa, my love!" Charlie held up a jug of wine and grinned. "You're just in time. Your neighbor has cooked me the most amazing meal. She's a wonder." He held up the wine bottle. "Does red go with fish?"

"Elderberry wine goes with everything." Sylvia swung her cane, making Charlie do a little side-step.

I shook my head, unable to make sense of the scene. "Charlie, where have you been? I've looked everywhere for you. Last I heard, you were in hiding."

Charlie scrunched his nose. "Never stiff a weapons vendor. When they get mad, they have weapons. I had to close up shop—temporarily, of course. I'm getting back on my feet thanks to this dove." He gestured to Sylvia.

"What?"

Sylvia flattened her lips with impatience. "Charlie heard you were searching for him. I was minding my own business, looking out the window at your magic shop, when I saw him. You weren't home, so I invited him over for breakfast."

"She makes the most wonderful breakfasts," Charlie added.

"He's been staying with me ever since. Fuzzy adores him."

"And I adore Fuzzy."

"Hold on." I ran my hands through my hair, digging my fingers into my scalp. "You've been next door the entire time?"

Charlie shrugged. "I've been meaning to come by, love, but Sylvia has been such a gracious host."

My patience ran out. "Charlie, I've been to the market every day this week. I'm at my wit's end! You're the only person I know who's heard of Ironhazel. Tell me you have new information."

"Of course I do. That's why I came by."

Sylvia grunted. "The fish is getting cold. We should head back."

"Wait!" I blocked the exit, holding up my hands. "You can have all the wine you want, every last drop, but not before you give me the details on Ironhazel."

"You might as well tell her. There's no stopping her when she gets like this. We'll never get to eat," Sylvia said, gathering wine bottles into her arms.

Charlie uncorked the bottle in his hand and took a deep sip straight from the jug. "I know where you can find Ironhazel. What is it, Tuesday?"

"Yeah, Tuesday," Sylvia confirmed.

"There's a ship docking on Thursday with a huge shipment of illegal contraband, and I heard Ironhazel will be there. It might be your only chance to catch him." He slapped his stomach with the palm of his hand. "All right. Now, let's eat."

# Chapter 26

The ship would dock in less than two hours.

I tucked my hair beneath my hood and tightened the belt at my waist. My hands were clammy, muscles aching with tension. Each hour that ticked closer to the rendezvous made it harder to concentrate.

This was the lead I'd been waiting for, but I couldn't shake the hollow feeling in my stomach. All I had to do was lay low and identify Ironhazel. Maybe I'd get lucky and see an opportunity to apprehend him, but the plan was to track him, find out where he was hiding, and take him down there. Catching him would bring us closer to catching Ella's killer and would help bring justice to the other victims.

*Us.*

When would I stop referring to everything with an us attached to it? There was no more us, only me, and maybe Vivian if she'd stop giving me a disappointed scowl every time I opened my mouth. She claimed I was being intentionally stubborn, even using the word pigheaded. Vivian might be the type of friend to follow me into quicksand if that's where

I led her, but she'd grumble the whole way and make sure her last words were, "I told you so."

That was why she didn't know about tonight's caper. Tagging along while I visited with a loan shark was one thing, especially since she'd seemed to charm the scoundrel, but going after a potential killer? No way. I couldn't risk it.

*Ugh*, I was turning into Derrick, the king of safety.

Regret wormed its way into my chest. Our last encounter had been playing on repeat in my mind. The way his hands had felt against my face, the deep, soothing tone of his voice, how there seemed to be so much left unsaid, and how his pain had broken my heart even more than his decision to push me away.

Sometimes, I allowed myself to imagine different outcomes. Funny, how every fictional outcome had us leaving together. *Damn it!* There was that word again. Two sneaky letters that wouldn't leave me alone. Was there such a thing as a selective lobotomy? Is so, sign me up.

I glanced at the time. I'd stalled long enough. My fingers trailed over the small vials of powder I'd attached to my belt. Sure, a witch's weapons were her spells, but just in case, I'd tucked a small sheathed blade into my boot. A pinch of powder and a dose of steel made for one prepared witch.

Vivian's hypnotic voice echoed down the hallway. I paused outside her séance room. Inside, she clung to an older woman's hand, eyes closed, channeling a spirit. Incense burned and candles flickered, though the room was as chilly as an icebox. One of her eyes popped open when I stepped on a loose floorboard, the creak ruining my stealthy getaway.

"Keep your eyes shut, Mrs. Baldwin. The spirit is getting stronger, I just need to light another candle." Vivian slipped out of her chair and pointed a finger. "Don't move." She said the words to me, but Mrs. Baldwin nodded.

Vivian followed me into the waiting room, assuming her scowl of disdain. "Where are you going dressed as a thief in the night?"

"This is your cloak, Viv."

"Yeah, well, I usually wear that one when I'm about to do something stupid. So, good choice."

"I have errands. Don't wait up."

"Errands, huh? Okay, let's pretend I believe that."

"Go back to your client. I know what I'm doing. I'll be back later." I opened the door and hurried down the steps, the night air freezing my breath and creating an icy sheen on the cobblestones.

Vivian stood in the doorway. "Hey, Tess, before you go, want to know the funny thing about you and ghosts?"

I paused on the bottom step and sighed. Apparently, she needed the last word too.

"What's that, Viv?"

She took a breath and waited until I'd turned to face her. "You act the same. They wander around completely invisible, watching other people live their lives. Most of them don't even understand why. They're stuck. Then, one day, if they're lucky, they meet someone who can see them, and suddenly, they're not alone anymore. I think it might be like that in life too. When you find someone who sees you differently than anyone else, Tess, someone who opens your eyes to new possibilities and helps you deal with the baggage in your past, it changes things. What a shame that you're willing to give it all up." She gave me a weak smile. "But, hey, what do I know? I talk to dead people." The door closed as she went back inside.

My hand trembled on the iron railing. A full minute passed before I took a wobbly step into the street. The wind stung my eyes, making them well up. Yes, it was the wind and not an emotional response to Vivian's lecture.

The ghosts were messing with her head. I wasn't invisible. Not literally, but wasn't there a part of me that had always felt unseen, the witch who wished she was better? All my life, I'd lived in my mother's shadow. A shadow that only got bigger after her death.

That didn't make me a ghost.

I kept walking, letting my conviction carry me down the road until even that felt thin and useless. My mind churned. Derrick had set aside his prejudice. He saw my intentions, welcomed my ideas, and treated me like an equal. His accusations in the holding cell had hurt. It made me think he didn't know me as well as I'd thought. Except I didn't believe that. I'd shaken his confidence and let my misconceptions about my worth spoil everything I'd accomplished.

It was ironic how I'd insisted I wanted a partner, then didn't treat him like one. I hadn't trusted him even after he'd asked me to, and it had been my lies, not my failed spells or poor life choices that had driven him away.

Maybe it wasn't too late?

If I wanted to set things right, I'd have to be completely honest. *Ew.* Okay, honest about the big stuff. A white lie here and there never hurt a witch. But that also meant being honest with myself. *Double ew.*

The truth was, I wasn't ready to give up. Not the shop, not the case, and especially not Derrick. Shouldn't I at least try to win him back? What better way to lure a detective than with the clue we'd been searching for? *Damn.* Vivian had the last word and an, "I told you so," coming her way.

A carriage rumbled past. I raised my hand, picking up my pace to chase after it. The driver pulled over, and I climbed inside.

"Where to, Miss?"

"Take me to the Royal Agency. Fast as you can."

Twenty minutes later, I was standing at Derrick's office door. If he threw me out again, I didn't know what I would do, especially since I'd decided I wanted to finish the case together. My knuckles connected with the wood, and I heard his clipped voice call out from behind.

"Enter."

Derrick's head was lowered, his attention buried in a stack of paperwork. He didn't react when I walked into his office.

"Did you bring me the case file?" His heavy sigh made the candle flame waver. "Put it on my desk and head home. It's late."

"Do you always talk to your secretary that way, Detective?"

His hand stilled, a splash of ink welling where the pen stalled. He lifted his head, and the intensity in his gaze made me falter.

"Tessa, what are you doing here? Is everything —?"

"We don't have much time. I know where to find Ironhazel, and I need your help. No, I want your help." My voice cracked, and I had to clear my throat before I could continue. "Detective, can we be partners one more time?"

\*\*\*

The wharf swarmed with sailors unloading cargo. Crates swung over the ship railings and were slowly lowered down to the dock. Shouts and animated conversation filled the air. Derrick had placed officers around the perimeter, so there was no way in and no way out without one of them seeing.

We moved through the crowd in search of the ship Charlie had written down. A crate of fish spilled open in our path, and the floppy monsters stared at us with beady, lifeless eyes. Their smell clogged the air.

I used my sleeve to cover my mouth and pointed to the furthest ship. "Over there. That's the one."

Derrick hesitated, reaching for my arm when I

tried to move past him. "Tessa, wait."

I recognized the indecision on his face. "No. Don't even think about it. I'm going with you. We're partners, remember? That was the deal."

He sighed and gripped my shoulders. "Yes, I remember. Promise me, you'll be careful."

"Always. We should split up."

"I'm not letting you out of my sight."

"You're being unreasonable."

"Tessa..." His hands fisted my cloak, pulling it tight. "Don't push me."

"Fine. We'll stay together, but we need a plan so we can get closer without attracting attention." My foot tapped lightly against the ground while I considered our options.

A group of men stumbled past, bumping into a stack of crates. They laughed and kept on moving, leaving a trail of empty bottles in their wake. I picked one up and handed it to Derrick, then retrieved another for myself.

"Cheers." With a clink of my bottle against his, I swayed into him, wrapping my arm around his waist.

Derrick took the full brunt of my weight, dragging my hood over my head when it slipped free. He chuckled at my drunken act, and the mood lightened. His smile made my heart stutter.

We wandered closer to the ship, weaving unsteadily through the mob of people. Near the gangway, I sank to my knees, peeking beneath the curve of my hood. A man with a ledger directed crates and passengers in different directions. We watched for almost half an hour, heads low, leaning drunkenly against a wooden post.

"Are you sure this is the right place?" Derrick asked.

"Why? Is there somewhere else you need to be?"

"No, nowhere else." The arm he'd wrapped around my waist tightened.

I relaxed into his side, taking comfort in his solid warmth. Stakeouts were my new favorite thing. Next time, I might bring snacks and definitely some real wine. Assuming there would be a next time. Derrick had agreed to this little mission, but it didn't mean we were back together.

"Why did you change your mind? I thought you wanted to win."

Silence stretched between us. I fiddled with the top of my bottle, circling my finger around the rim as I stalled for time. I didn't know how to start.

His hand closed over my fingers. "You always fiddle with things when you're nervous. Stop. Tell me the truth."

"I can't believe you notice that."

"What? Fiddling with things? You do it all the time." He paused, angling his head to rest against mine. "I notice everything you do. You play with my collar when you're trying to get your way, and I pretend I don't like it. You turn your head when you curse. I don't know why you bother, I can hear you loud and clear. And I know you can't see it, but you get this look in your eyes when you're about to cast a spell. It's half-terror and half-hope, and every time, I want the spell to work because I know you're going to flash me one of your smug smiles."

"I do *not* have a smug smile."

"You do, and for some reason, I find it incredibly charming." His voice lowered. "So, tell me why you changed your mind."

The stupid wind was making my eyes sting again. How was I supposed to talk around the lump in my throat? I cleared it away.

"It was this thing Vivian said about ghosts and being invisible. You kind of had to be there. She's probably been waiting her whole life to use ghosts in an analogy, so I have to give her credit." I looked up at his face. "But she had a point."

"And what was that?"

With embarrassment heating my cheeks, I bowed my head. "You see me. No one else does, but you do."

"Tessa..."

"I know. I'm botching it. I said, you had to be there. Of course, you can see me in a literal sense, but —"

Derrick placed his hand over my mouth. I inhaled a sharp breath, my eyes growing wide. He had not just shushed me while I was attempting to bare my soul!

"Tessa, look." He gestured toward the man with the ledger. A hooded figure approached and handed a heavy pouch to the crewman.

"That way," the man muttered, pointing to a pile of crates. The figure turned, and the hood fell back to reveal a familiar face.

*Helen Lockwood.*

What was she doing here?

I met Derrick's equally wide gaze, and he pressed a finger to his lips. With a nod, we climbed to our feet and followed her toward the crates, keeping our distance. Another man cracked the lid with a crowbar. The pungent scent of herbs mixed with the salt in the air.

"Is that all of it? Where's the nightshade?" she asked.

He cracked another lid, revealing jars of dark berries. *Nightshade.* Another name for Belladonna.

Helen was Ironhazel!

My mind raced. This whole time, she'd been hiding in plain sight. I was right to be suspicious of her from the start. My instincts were good—there might be something to Vivian's "I told you so"'s after all. They should make me a detective.

"Have it delivered here." She handed over a slip of paper, and the man nodded then crooked his finger until she leaned closer. Whatever he whispered in her ear made her go rigid. Derrick had turned his back and was tugging on my sleeve for me to turn as well, but I was so busy planning my victory party that when Helen angled her head and looked right at me, I froze.

*Blast!*

She took off at a dead run, using the crowd to mask her escape. Derrick signaled his men, and we began to chase after her, losing sight altogether when she turned a corner. Frustration pumped my legs faster. We couldn't lose her. She'd go to ground, and we'd never find her again.

I rounded the corner into a dark alley and spotted her slipping between a narrow crevice. It was too small for Derrick to fit. He grabbed my arm as I attempted to squeeze through.

"No. We stay together."

"She's getting away! Go around the other side, I'll be okay." I shook off his arm, his fingers grasping then slipping through mine.

"Damn it, Tessa!" The flat of his hand rammed the wall as I navigated through the narrow space.

"Go!"

Grating his teeth in fury, Derrick disappeared from view. His footsteps faded as he ran parallel down another alley.

I caught sight of Helen's blonde hair and ran after her. I needed something to slow her down, or I'd never catch up. Digging deep, I channeled my magic, hoping a burst of energy would take her down or knock something into her path.

My fists shot out, sparks arcing from my fingers. I missed, but the jolt of magic hit a barrel, which exploded, sending a stake of wood into Helen's leg. She shrieked and limped to the end of the alley, then stuttered to a stop. A wall of crates blocked her path. To her right was another alley, but she'd never make it on her injured leg. She turned to face me, lungs heaving on gulps of air. I bent at the waist, a stitch burning my side.

Man, she was fast.

Helen was pulling a knife when I looked up again. Out of options, she advanced. I rubbed my hands together to resurrect magic but nothing happened. Fists clenched, I tried anyway, splaying open my fingers to complete and utter failure.

*Time for plan B.*

I grappled at my waist for the vial of powder. Helen attacked. It slipped from my hand and rolled across the ground as I ducked. Her blade whistled past my face. I dropped to a knee, reaching for the knife in my boot instead. Out of the corner of my eye, I could see Derrick charging from the other direction. He was too far out to stop a second attack, but at least Helen wouldn't get away.

Unable to reach my weapon in time, her knife flashed in the moonlight. I tried to roll and dodge it but only managed to lift my arms and shield my body.

"No!" Derrick's guttural cry ricocheted off the brick building.

The blade sliced through the sleeve of my cloak and bit into skin. I gasped as I reached for the wound. My fingers came away sticky with blood.

Helen backed up, her eyes wild, then thrust the knife again, aiming for my chest.

Magic finally surged from my fingertips, releasing into her. Her body convulsed, and she staggered back. It bought me enough time.

Falling within reach, Derrick tackled her to the ground. The knife skittered across the stones while

Helen shrieked, fighting with her whole body, but his knee pressed firm into her back, forcing her face to the gravel. He wrenched her arms behind her and circled iron cuffs around her wrists.

"It's over, Helen. You're under arrest."

Heaving her to her feet, Derrick passed her off to a waiting officer. More had converged on our location, watching as Helen tried to dislodge the man. She looked arrogant. Her laughter filled the air.

"It's not over. Not even close."

Derrick barked instructions as officers dragged her away. Another burst of her crazed laughter made my skin crawl. She was insane. How could she have poisoned her own stepsister?

I pressed my fingers against my forehead. Pressure built behind my eyelids and it hurt to think. Helen had to be working with someone else, possibly the man Argus had seen with Jane Porter before her death. She would talk. She couldn't hold out forever.

We were so close.

So...lightheaded?

A wave of dizziness caused bile to climb my throat. I reached for the wall to steady myself.

"Uh, Derrick? Something's wrong." Tongue thick in my mouth, I couldn't form the words. They sounded slurred, faraway. I tried again, my sentence worse the second time.

"Tessa, are you all right? Let me see your arm." He broke away from the officers, and I blinked to clear my vision as his features split into two. Four arms, four legs, running now, as I swayed on my feet. The ground rushed to meet me. He caught me before I hit the dirt.

Derrick examined my injury, tearing at my cloak until the wound met fresh air. I hissed in a breath as his fingers probed the laceration.

"It's not deep and barely bleeding. I don't understand what's happening."

Another wave of dizziness hit, buckling my knees. His grip strengthened, keeping me upright. Spots danced in my vision. *Of all the rotten luck.* I struggled to speak. Had to let him know…

"The knife," I mumbled. "She poisoned it. Take me to Vivian."

He was already lifting me up, my feet losing purchase on the ground as he tucked me against his chest. "Bring the knife," he shouted over a shoulder. Smart. We'd need that.

Haze clouded my thoughts. There was something we could do. A spell, maybe? I wasn't very good at spells. I never wanted my life to depend on one—it didn't bode well. My head lolled against his chest. Derrick's footsteps were so loud, pounding in my ear. *No.* His heart. It knocked fast on his ribcage, and I pressed my palm against the spot.

"Shh… I'm trying to sleep."

"You can't sleep right now." He jostled me, making my surroundings spin.

My stomach rolled. I hated Helen with every fiber of my being. Whatever she'd laced the blade with was going to make me toss my dinner at Derrick's feet. Hopefully, by then, death would be swift. You didn't come back from humiliation like that, not when you'd had a huge bowl of Vivian's hearty chicken stew for dinner.

Seconds passed. Minutes? Time was fuzzy. We stopped, and Derrick tossed a terse command at someone above him. Who was he talking to? Horses neighed, and I knew.

"Don't talk to the horses," I groaned. "They can't help."

"I'm not talking to the horses."

Somewhere close by, reins snapped. My hands tangled in his shirt, pulling at the fabric.

"You can't make me ride a horse. I won't forgive you. I'm too dizzy, and you're likely to drop me."

"I would never drop you."

"Can't risk it. I'd rather die by poison than be trampled."

"You're not going to die!"

I blinked, my lids closing far longer than they should. "If you say so."

"I do," he snapped. "Keep your eyes open, Tessa. For once, do as I say."

Derrick's hold tightened as the carriage lurched, arms anchoring me to him, absorbing the worst of the bumps in the road. He smoothed the hair out of my face while I stared up at him, trying to follow his orders. His features were pinched with fear, eyes stormy. People only looked at you that way when you were dying.

"There's four of you," I whispered, as his tormented face morphed into many. I struggled against the weight dragging on my eyelids. "Don't be mad. I can't handle four mad detectives. One's bad enough."

"I'm not mad." His lips found my temple. Stayed there. A sharp breath expanded his chest, and he choked on it, gathering me closer.

"You never get mad. You get even. I remember."

"That's right, I do." His voice was husky against the side of my neck. "You're going to let me get even."

"Maybe. But...just in case...give Vivian my share."

The carriage seats spun like a top. Black vines slithered into the corners of my vision, spreading faster and faster, blocking everything else out.

"Your share of what?"

"The...reward."

It was dark all of a sudden. Pitch-black. Like being underwater, Derrick's frantic cry was a muffled echo in my ears.

*Tessa? Tessa!*

And then, there was light. Brilliant, crisp, and blinding white. The sensation of being lifted high, floating on air, leaving my body...

Dropping fast to oblivion.

I felt nothing at all.

# Chapter 27

"There she is."

Vivian's face swam into sight. Easing my eyes open to take in my surroundings, I realized I was in her guest room, propped up on pillows, wearing one of her sleeveless shifts. My clothes had been discarded in a heap near the foot of the bed, blood and grime staining the garments. They needed to be tossed, or better yet, burned. A roll of bandages lay on the side table along with my reference book on poisons. My memory came back all at once, and I groaned.

"Am I dead?"

"Unfortunately, no." Her lips crooked into a wistful smile. "It's such a shame too. I'd already figured out how I wanted to spend your share of the reward."

I scooted back against the pillow, surprised to find my dizziness gone. Even my stomach felt settled. It was a miracle I'd held on to my dignity. There was only a slight twinge in my arm where Helen had cut me with her knife.

"Were you planning to erect a vast monument in my name?"

Vivian blinked. "No, I was going to buy a horse farm."

"Get out!" I shoved her off the bed with my good arm, and she landed on the carpet, her lips shaking with suppressed laughter.

"Come on, that's funny. Only you would rant about horses when you're delirious."

I squeezed the bridge of my nose. Flashes of mine and Derrick's woozy conversation made me cringe. Had I really accused him of talking to horses? Thankfully, I'd been on my deathbed, and you could say pretty much anything when you were about to die. That was a rule I was sure had been written down somewhere.

Vivian remained on the floor, not bothering to contain her amusement as I scrunched my nose in disgust.

"Is nothing sacred? I can't even enjoy a good old-fashioned near-death experience without mockery?"

"Well, you could have if you'd been near death, which you weren't. After Derrick brought you here, I performed your spell with the enchanted rosenphyn you had leftover from testing Liam's shirt. Turns out, Helen dipped the blade in icafrass sap. It's essentially harmless, meant to disarm rather than kill, which is why it's quick-acting. It made you dizzy. Probably nauseous too."

"Don't remind me. I should have gone easy on your stew before I went hunting for killers. Lesson learned." I folded my arms over my stomach and frowned. "Are you sure I wasn't dying a little bit? It was dicey near the end there."

"No. The poison only induces fainting."

"I fainted?" I kicked the blanket off my legs and sat on the edge of the bed, head in my hands. "How embarrassing. Does Derrick know?"

"Yeah, sorry. If it makes you feel better, he wouldn't leave your side. It was very sweet. But it made keeping your diagnosis from him tricky."

*Great.* I couldn't even die properly. I was just a ranting lunatic who'd been dosed with a hallucinogenic. Even my wound wasn't anything to get excited about.

"Is he still here?"

"Yes, he's been pacing outside since I kicked him out of your room. He did not appreciate that. But it's my house, and I thought you might want to get rid of all this..."—she swung her hand in my general direction—"awkwardness before you see him again. Maybe fix your hair."

"What's wrong with my hair?"

"Nothing, if you're going for the 'I was attacked in an alley and it shows' kind of look."

"Gee, thanks, Viv."

She shrugged and had me turn so she could sit beside me on the bed. The mattress dipped as she reached for a brush on the nightstand, then she pulled the bristles through my tangled waves. We were quiet for a long moment, her fingers soft as she sifted through the strands, arranging them so they'd frame my face.

"There, all better." Her hands stilled. "I'm glad you're okay, Tess. I have enough friends who are ghosts."

I smiled. "I know."

Her fingers found mine, and she squeezed. "Are you ready to see Derrick, or do you want me to tell him to come back tomorrow?"

Nerves fluttered in my stomach. There was no sense in putting it off any longer even though I was scared to see him. What if he made sure I was okay and then just left? Did I have it in me to change his mind? If being somewhat adjacent to death's door hadn't made him realize how much he cared for me, I didn't have a ton of other cards to play.

"I want to see him."

Vivian rose and walked to the door, pulling it open a crack to say, "She's feeling better. You can sit with her if you want."

The door was pushed wide, and Derrick appeared in the entrance. Air left his lungs in a rush when he saw me sitting up in bed.

Vivian patted his shoulder. "It's late. I'm turning in. Goodnight, you two." She nudged him further into the room then closed the door, her footsteps fading down the hall.

Derrick stood unmoving, watching me as if I might vanish into thin air. The strength of his gaze made me restless, and I slid to the edge of the bed, wincing when I put pressure on my injured arm.

He was beside me in an instant. "Go slow. Are you dizzy?"

"No, I'm fine. It'll take more than a knife wound and poison to get rid of me." My smile dimmed beneath his fierce expression. Jeez, where was the joy at my speedy recovery? How about, *You're the bravest, most resilient and stunningly beautiful witch the kingdom has ever seen?* Something! At this point, I'd take a fist bump to the shoulder and a, "Hey, good to see ya."

Derrick sank into a chair beside the bed, where he bent over and dropped his head into his hands. His coat was filthy. A long swath of blood had dried on his sleeve, and droplets dotted the side in a scattered pattern. There was no saving it. Apparently, the coat knew how to die properly.

"I think you need to burn your coat."

He laughed, the sound abrasive, almost brutal. "You're always worried about my clothes. The devil take my coat! Tessa, I thought I was going to lose you." He lifted his head, anguished eyes locking with mine.

I went still, my insides rolling from the intensity. His voice was rough with emotion.

"When you blacked out, I lost it. I've spent my entire career as a detective hardening myself against the things I witness every day, and in a single second, seeing your eyes close like that, it ruined me."

"Derrick—" My throat closed. The pain in his voice stabbed me harder than Helen's knife ever could.

"When I found out you'd hid your association with Argus, I had to let you go. I couldn't trust you. How could I protect you when you were lying to me?

It was too hard."

"I never would have betrayed you or the case for him. Not ever."

"I know that. It was wrong of me to suggest you would. The things I said to you, accused you of, I hate myself for it. I was angry. I felt helpless, and I'm not supposed to be. The people in this kingdom look to me to know what to do. The rules, the routine, the structure—it's the only way I know how to maintain control, and you obliterate each one, over and over." He sighed and scrubbed a hand ruthlessly through his hair. "This isn't the time. I don't want to upset you. You need to rest." He pushed out of his chair and headed for the door.

My mouth dropped open. *Wait, seriously?* He was going to leave after saying all that? His hand was on the doorknob. He really was! Heart in my throat, I sprang from the bed, feet tangling in the blanket so I almost nose-dived into the floor. Thankfully, I caught my balance, a feat I'd taken for granted until a short while ago.

"Wait! Derrick Chambers, don't you dare turn your back on a dying girl."

His head dropped forward. "Tessa, you're not dying. It's a flesh wound."

"You don't know that for sure."

"Actually, I do. I bandaged it myself."

This was not going as I'd hoped. "Humor me then! I did faint. That has to count for something."

"All right." He backed away from the door, lips twitching in the barest twist of a smile. "What do you want to say?"

I exhaled and wiped my sweaty palms against my shirt. His eyes followed the action, lingering for a beat at the hemline, which stopped mid-thigh. There was definitely a draft in here. I'd completely forgotten about my lack of attire, and my skin flushed as I fiddled with the bottom of the shirt.

"Tessa, you're fiddling again. Nervous?"

"No, I—hey, stop noticing that." I clenched my fingers into fists. Everything I wanted to say clogged in my throat. So many things. Apologies, demands, explanations—they all sounded inferior in my head. I wasn't good at this! Asking people to stay, hoping they'd look past all my faults, it was madness.

But I needed to try.

"Um…don't go." There. It was a start. I had this. "You asked me earlier why I changed my mind about finishing the case alone, and it's because I want to finish it with you. I shouldn't have lied to you about Argus and my debt. You deserved the truth. I got scared. I'm used to disappointment, but I couldn't handle disappointing you."

"You wouldn't have disappointed me. Tessa—"

I held up a trembling finger. "It's rude to interrupt a dying girl. I'm not finished."

There was that half-smile again. He nodded, and I took a moment to pace. My heart beat so fast, I figured it was only a matter of time before it decided it had had enough and gave out. Then, I'd really be at death's door.

I shook out my hands and faced him. "Okay, you

want honesty? Here's the truth: I'm a mess. My magic is mediocre at best, I'm broke, and I ruined everything between us with my lies. The thing is, I'm not going to wake up tomorrow and be perfect. I'm going to make mistakes, probably lots of them. Pumpkins will explode. I might even cause another plague." I let out a shuddering breath. "But I love you. And if you'll stay with me, I want to be imperfect with you."

The silence was unbearable. Derrick stared. I couldn't tell if he was going to laugh or put a man-sized hole in the door trying to escape. He might do both.

Sick with fear, I broke the silence. "All right…I'm finished dying now. You can say something."

"Are you sure you're not going to relapse?" He moved closer.

"I don't think so."

"Good." A few feet separated us. Then, nothing at all as his hands framed my face. "I wasn't leaving. Vivian mixed some powder to help you sleep, and I left it in the other room. I was going to get it."

"Oh." *Wonderful. First, I faint, and then, I make a blubbering fool of myself.* "You know, I would have changed my speech a bit if I'd know that. Probably focused more on my many qualities."

His fingers smoothed my cheekbones. "I'm glad you didn't. It was honest."

My breath caught. "Well, that's me—or, at least, the new me. Honest to a fault."

He bent his head, lips claiming mine in a devastating kiss. Relief swamped me and made tears gather under my eyelids. Honesty was my new policy from here on out. The reward was too good. Lies? No way, not me.

"Is that a yes?" I asked, coming up for air. A tiny tremor shook my voice. "You're okay with me, knowing the truth?"

His eyes searched mine. "Tessa, how can you not know how much I love you? I've wanted to tell you multiple times, but you never let me get a word in. There's no one else for me. Explode a hundred pumpkins if you have to, make mistakes. Just make them with me."

"You might regret it."

"Never." He brushed my mouth with another kiss.

"I'll remember you said that, Detective."

"Derrick," he growled.

"Huh?"

"New rule. When we're alone together, you call me Derrick."

I grinned. "Finally, a rule I intend to follow." Going up on my toes, I wound my arms around his neck and dragged his mouth to mine.

Derrick groaned low in his throat, hands circling my waist. Delicious friction exploded my nerve endings as he locked me firmly against the solid planes of his chest. The scent of his skin filled my senses, drugging me faster than any poison. His tongue touched mine when I opened for him, and heat surged in my belly, moving lower.

I matched his groan with one of my own, desire

swirling within my body. He backed us up until my legs bumped the bed, his ruined jacket dropping to the floor when I slid my fingers under the heavy fabric to push it over his shoulders. He was never wearing that one again. I kicked it away. His shirt came next, and the air burned in my lungs as my palms swept the hard ridges of his abdomen.

Dropping an urgent kiss along my jawline, he spoke hoarse in my ear, "Are you sure?"

"Yes. Don't you dare deny a dying girl."

He laughed and nipped the sensitive skin of my neck, teeth skimming my earlobe. "You're not dying."

"I fainted. That has to—"

"It counts for something." Hands at my waist, he lifted me and eased me back onto the mattress. My shift bunched around my hips, and I arched my back so his fingers could skate across my ribcage, light as mist. Pleasure tightened my stomach when his thumb brushed my nipple. He did it again, a slow circle that made sparks tingle at my fingertips. The current raced over my heated skin, transferring to his.

Derrick's breathing stopped, his eyes darkening at the sensation. Okay, so I wasn't bad at *all* magic. A possessive growl vibrated his chest, and he ground his hips into mine, teasing my mouth with a hungry kiss. Need pooled in my veins, thick and sluggish, in total contrast to the bruising pound of my heart. *Merciful spellbooks…He was wicked.* His mouth slanted to take me deeper.

"You're so beautiful," he murmured as he sunk his hands into my hair. His kiss turned achingly tender, breaking my heart and mending it back together.

Acceptance softened my edges, rinsing away years of regret and failed spells.

My shift landed next to Derrick's destroyed jacket. The rest of his clothes followed, the action separating us for too long. *Wretched clothes.* I searched for his mouth, melting when his tongue stroked mine. He entered me in a slow thrust that made the first round of sparks seem like a mere flicker. My fingers splayed over his back, sending little jolts into his skin.

Arms like iron, Derrick's whole body tightened, and he wrapped me in an embrace as he found a breathless rhythm. Pleasure spiraled in my core then broke on a wave. He caught my quick inhale with his mouth, following me over the edge. My name was a reverent rasp from his lips.

*Holy enchanted moonstones...*

Time passed slowly. I snuggled into the crook of his arm, savoring the simple satisfaction of lying next to him. Somehow, minutes burned into an hour, and my eyes grew heavy with sleep.

I was absentmindedly gliding my fingernails over his abdomen when Derrick captured my hand and brought my palm to his mouth. I giggled and tried to tug it away.

"That tickles."

"Yeah? So did your fingernails."

I rolled onto my side and propped my head up on

my hand. "What happens tomorrow, Derrick?"

He smiled. "I really like the new rule."

"It's my current favorite, though I have a new-found appreciation for rule number one—always stay by your side."

"The rule is actually don't investigate alone, but your version is better." He sighed. "Tomorrow, we interview Helen to find out her role in the murder."

"I don't think she was working alone. She may have been partly responsible for Jane and Ella's deaths, but I doubt she knew Sophie."

"Me neither. There's someone else out there, but we'll find him."

"Do you think she'll talk?"

"I don't know. If not to me, maybe she'll talk to her mother. We'll bring Olivia to the agency. We need to question her anyway, find out if she knew what her daughter was up to."

I sank against the pillow. "That whole family has been shattered. What a waste. How do you handle the devastation this job uncovers?"

"It's not easy. I'd say you get used to it, but I don't want that for you. I've been numb for so long. It's no way to live."

I suppressed a grin. "I guess it's a good thing I came along and *obliterated* all that."

He laughed and tucked me closer to his side. "Get some sleep."

"Will you stay?"

"Depends on whether your friend curses me with a spirit if she finds us together in the morning."

My silence made him squirm.

"Tessa, tell me that won't happen."

"Get some sleep." I kissed his cheek and pulled the blanket up to my ears. The weight of his arm draped over my middle mixed with the heat from his body made sleep an easy target.

Derrick nudged my shoulder. One of my eyes snapped open.

"What?"

"I forgot to ask you something."

"Is it important?"

He nodded, nuzzling his forehead against my hair. "I think so."

"Okay, ask."

"Did you really start the plague?"

*Damn.* I shouldn't have mentioned that.

"Yes, and I'll do it again if you tell anyone my secret. You'll be patient zero." I rolled over in a huff, but he dragged me back, anchoring me to his side.

"That's my witch."

# Chapter 28

Vivian did not sic a spirit on him in the morning, but that might have had more to do with Derrick complimenting her baking skills than any affront to finding him with me.

She eyed us over the rim of her teacup. "Can I offer anyone another scone?"

He plucked a cranberry biscuit from the plate and dug in, his eyes half-mast as he devoured the pastry. "This is delicious. The best scones I've ever tasted. You're a wizard in the kitchen."

Vivian preened, smoothing a hand over her glossy locks.

I rolled my eyes. "It's a mix. She buys it from the market. Don't get so excited."

Viv kicked my shin under the table at the same time Derrick bumped my knee. "Hush," he whispered. "I want your friend to like me."

"She likes you fine, and will both of you stop hitting me? I'm still in recovery from my harrowing ordeal."

Now, it was their turn to roll their eyes. I might have milked my less-than-near-death experience for as long as possible. It had lost its effectiveness even with Derrick.

Eh, it was nice while it lasted.

"We should get to the agency so we can question Helen."

Derrick nodded in agreement, brushing the crumbs from his fingers. Vivian cleared away the plates, still giving me the eye for betraying her secret recipe. I smiled anyway. It was nice to share breakfast with Derrick and my best friend. After everything we'd gone through, I relished the quiet moment.

I helped her to finish the dishes while Derrick arranged for a carriage. She nudged me with her hip and flicked water in my face.

"What was that for?" I wiped the droplets away.

"I'm happy for you, Tess, and I'm proud of you. I hope you finally see in yourself what we see."

I stacked the plates in the cupboard and leaned against the counter. "All right, go ahead, I know you're dying to say it. I'm shocked you've waited this long."

Vivian blinked her eyes innocently. "I don't have the slightest idea what you mean. Here I am, congratulating my friend who, against all odds, managed to repair her relationship. It's almost as if she was given sage advice...from a goddess, perhaps?"

"Goddess? Please, try a meddler. You know, one day, our roles will be reversed, and I plan to return the favor twofold."

She snorted. "We'll see."

More water hit my face. "Stop that!"

Viv grinned and pulled me into a hug, then dried her wet hands on the back of my dress. I laughed and did the same.

***

The agency waiting room was quieter than usual. Estelle greeted us from her post as we walked in.

"Good morning, Detective. The director wants to speak with you first thing. He's waiting in his office." Her eyes flashed with interest. "Tessa, it's nice to see you. Does this mean…?"

Derrick nudged me past her desk without an answer. Estelle's chest deflated with a sigh. Still, I caught her eye before we turned down the hall and gave her a wink and a thumbs-up. Relief washed over her features, and she beamed.

"I thought I told you to go easy on her." I elbowed Derrick as we walked to his office.

"I did. She's on probation for a week."

"That's not fair. She was trying to bring us together. It was sweet."

He paused in front of his door. "Regardless of her intentions, she sent you into an unfamiliar building. It was reckless. You could have been hurt."

"Come on, Detective." I smoothed my palms over his shirt and played with his collar. "She sent me into a room full of tea. That's hardly a den of peril."

"I don't care if the room was full of puppies." He caught my fingers. "Stop playing with my collar, you're not getting your way. She stays on probation until the end of the week."

"Fine, be surly about it."

"I will." He pulled me into his office and shut the door, then backed me against the wall. His fingers slid through my hair, tugging the strands until I tilted my head to meet his gaze. "I'm feeling very surly at the moment. You're not following the rules."

I bit the inside of my cheek. "Which rules, Detective?"

"You know which one." He ground his hips into mine, and I sucked in a breath.

"Didn't I tell you to write them down if you want me to remember them, *Detective?*"

"Tessa, I'm warning you, I have five minutes before I need to go and meet the director, and seeing as we're alone, I want to hear you say it. *Now.*"

"You're looking at me the way you looked at the cranberry scones, Derrick. Never thought I'd be jealous of a—"

He cut me off, his mouth capturing mine. "You taste better," he growled.

My stomach flipped, and I leaned into him, letting him press his thumbs against my jaw to hold me in place as he savored my lips. I was going to have a hard time looking at breakfast items from now on. Derrick's mouth dropped to my collarbone.

"If you kiss me every time I say your name, I might end up wearing it out."

"That's my plan." He pressed our foreheads together. "Wait for me here. I'll speak with the director, and then we'll interview Helen."

I teased the hair at the nape of his neck. "Can I sit

behind your desk while I wait?"

He tapped his knuckle under my chin. "Don't push it."

"Yes, Detective."

Derrick eyes narrowed dangerously but dragged himself away to grab a stack of files from his desk. The door closed firmly behind him, and I covered my face with my hands, determined not to let him hear my squeal of happiness. A witch didn't squeal. Ever. But if she did, it would sound a lot like the noise I tried to hide.

Today was a new beginning. It was time to say goodbye to past insecurities. My magic might never be perfect, but it didn't have to be. It was enough.

*I* was enough.

All morning, I'd been thinking of new ways to adapt my spells to better fit the agency's goals. The possibilities were endless. I sat in the chair across from Derrick's desk and searched for his notebook, wanting to jot down a few ideas. It was buried beneath a stack of unopened letters. The top envelope caught my eye, and I picked it up, noticing it had been forwarded by the Ever Gazette. Was this a response to our ad?

Removing the letter, I scanned its contents. My nerve endings tingled to life. The ad had worked! We had a lead on the rose. A man named Theo Beckett wanted to meet with us to discuss the plant's origin. I glanced at the address and wrinkled my brow. It wasn't too far from the palace, but the area was remote.

The office door opened, and I looked up to find Derrick. His features were drawn, and there was tension in every step as he entered the room. He dropped his files onto the desk and sank in his chair. His hand scrubbed roughly over his face.

A moment passed before he slammed a fist onto the desk. "Damn it!"

"What happened?" Dread coiled in my stomach when he didn't answer right away. "Derrick, talk to me."

His eyes met mine. "Helen's dead."

"What? How? She was locked up, under guard."

"Someone didn't search her well enough. They found her in the cell before dawn. There were poisonous berries in her hand." His eyes closed, and he took a harsh breath. "It's over, Tessa. The king spoke with my superior. He's closing the case. They're putting the blame for Ella's death at Helen's feet and walking away."

I shoved out of the chair. "They can't do that! What about the other murders?"

"They're turning a blind eye. Helen's connection to the murder of her stepsister is enough to remove suspicion from the prince. It's the only move the king has, unless he's willing to exile his son if this continues and he's found guilty."

I scoffed and turned on my heel, pacing the floor. "Are we sure Helen killed herself? The whole thing sounds suspect."

"I agree, but there are no witnesses and no proof. Helen was our only lead. Without her, and without the backing from the agency, my hands are tied. I'll be reassigned." Derrick's voice was tight with fury. "Sophie's killer is out there. I thought we were getting closer. I thought—"

"Hey, it's not over." I rounded the desk and took his face in my hands. "We're not giving up. We're going to find Sophie's killer and bring justice to Jane and Ella. I'm not stopping until we do, and neither are you."

"Tessa, it's not that simple. I'd have to go behind the agency's back."

"Okay, let me know when there's a problem."

His mouth hitched. "I'll lose my job."

"Then I'll hire you at the magic shop, and if I have to sell it, we'll peddle potions out of a caravan. Besides, I know you. When you care about something, nothing stands in your way. The same goes for me, so let's do this together. Partners till the end. Always."

He pulled me onto his lap, settling his hands on my hips. "I love you, Tessa."

I wiggled my eyebrows. "You say that now, but you'll love me even more when I show you this." Reaching across the desk, I grabbed the letter from Theo Beckett. "We had a response from the ad in the Gazette. It came in this morning. There's someone who knows where the roses came from, and all we have to do is meet with him. What do you say, Detective? Want to keep hunting killers with me?"

He grinned. "Always."

\*\*\*

Theo Beckett had a limp. He also had white hair that curled around his ears and a bald spot on the top of his head. His gnarled hands were tanned from the sun, and dirt was embedded in his fingernails.

We found him in his vegetable garden, sowing seeds that would survive the winter. He stood and held out a hand.

"What can I do for you, Detective?"

"We're here because you sent a letter to the Gazette about a specific type of rose."

Theo scratched his chin, leaving behind a dirt smudge. "Yeah, that's right. I used to work for the palace, taking care of the grounds. I recognized the drawing from the paper. The flower is an Aster Mauve. It's been years since I've seen one."

"An Aster Mauve? I've never heard of it," I said, making a note.

"They're exceedingly rare and aren't local to this region. What makes them distinctive is their heart-shaped petals and hearty growth cycle. They're known to last through heavy frost and even through part of the winter."

"And when was the last time you saw one?" Derrick asked.

Theo furrowed his brow. "Years ago. There was a young woman who worked for me, tending the palace gardens. She had seedlings shipped from overseas, and we grew them in the palace greenhouse with thoughts of transplanting them on castle grounds."

I looked up from the notebook. "Palace greenhouse? I wasn't aware there was such a thing."

"There isn't anymore. It's been abandoned for years, but it's about half a mile from here. There were rumors back then that the king was having an affair. It wasn't any of my business, but the young woman—Diane was her name—got caught up in the rumor. Then, one day, she vanished. Never saw her again. It wasn't long after that we stopped using the greenhouse. I never did transplant those roses."

Derrick caught my eye. He had the same question I did.

"Do you think Diane had an affair with the king?"

"It's possible. I always wondered what happened to her, but to be honest, there was a lot of turnover in the palace staff back then, so someone leaving wasn't out of the norm." He picked up a pair of gardening gloves and gathered a trowel. "Come with me, I'll take you up to the greenhouse so you can have a look."

We traveled the half-mile, the brush getting thicker as we went. The path winded through a dense forest then opened onto a clearing, where a massive glass building resided, it's vaulted ceiling reaching up into the trees. The greenhouse was decrepit. Cracked windows smeared with years of grime peered back at us. Rusted iron trimmed the glass panes and formed an ornamental design along the roof. It looked ready to collapse if not for the overgrown branches holding it in place. Weeds and tangled vines choked the walls and the inside of the structure.

"Diane loved it here. She'd spend most of her time in the greenhouse. It's a shame to see it this way. It used to be beautiful, full of vibrant flowers."

I rubbed a spot in the dirt with my sleeve to peer through the glass. "What happened to the seedlings?"

"Oddly enough, they vanished too. I never could wrap my head around that one." Theo kicked at a mound of dried grass. "Diane must have taken them with her."

It didn't add up. Clearly, Diane fit into the puzzle somewhere, but we were still missing a piece. The fact she had worked at the palace didn't bode well for the prince. He would have been a child when she was around and likely wouldn't have had anything to do with her disappearance—assuming she had disappeared and didn't leave on her own.

I groaned internally and pressed my fingers into my eyelids. Why did every lead create more questions? At least we'd found the origin of the roses. Now, we needed to find out how Diane was connected to the murders.

"Thank you for your time, Mr. Beckett, and for showing us the greenhouse." I opened my notebook and looked over the entry. "One other thing, do you happen to remember Diane's last name?"

Theo rubbed the bald spot on his head and pursed his lips in thought. "What was it? It's on the tip of my tongue." He tapped his shoe. "That's right, I remember. It was Porter. Diane Porter."

My jaw dropped, and I looked at Derrick. Surprise widened his features.

"Did Diane have any family locally?" he asked.

Theo nodded. "Yes, a sister. I think her name was Jane."

# Chapter 29

"Wow. I leave for a few days to investigate a suspected haunting and come back to this? Helen's dead, and Jane had a sister who grew the type of roses left at the crime scene. You two have been busy." Vivian shook her head and added a splash of bourbon to her tea.

My eyes narrowed as she screwed the cap back on the flask. "Since when do you drink bourbon?"

"Hmm, what?" She tucked it under the table and wrinkled her brow.

"Where did you get it, Viv?"

"I...found it."

"You found it? That's the story you're sticking with?"

She sipped her tea, lifting a manicured brow over the rim. "Yes."

I threw up my hands and turned to Derrick. "And you call me secretive."

"Because you are," he muttered.

"Well, it's super annoying."

"Tell me about it."

Vivian feigned interest in her cuticles until it was

safe, then asked, "Are there any leads on what happened to Diane?"

Derrick leaned back in his chair. "Nothing solid. We spoke with a few servants who were around back then, but they knew as much as Theo. One day, she was there, and the next, she was gone. We're pretty confident Diane was having an affair with the king. The problem is, we learned she may not have been the only one."

Vivian snorted. "Shocking."

I drummed my fingers on the table. "So, let's assume something happened. Maybe she found out about the other women or—"

"Got pregnant," Vivian said. "A child out of wedlock wouldn't have a direct claim to the throne with a legal heir already in place. Diane would essentially be on her own."

"And possibly forced to go to her sister." My mind raced with the new theory. "But if that's the case, what happened to the child? Assuming there was one, how would we prove it without confirmation from the king? It's not like we can walk up to him and ask about his potential love child."

"I'm certainly not doing it," Vivian joked.

We both looked at Derrick. He held up his hands.

"No way. I'm not allowed to investigate as it is. We'd have to find proof before I can present it to my superior. Only then can we consider approaching the royal family."

This was impossible. I dropped my head into my hands and sighed. There had to be a way to determine whether Diane had a child. It was the only thing that made sense and could account for the mysterious man Argus had seen with Jane.

The bell over the front door jingled as someone entered the waiting area. Vivian lifted her shoulders. She didn't have any clients booked for the evening.

We all turned when a woman wearing full black appeared through the beaded curtain.

"Please excuse my interruption, but they told me at the agency I'd find you here." Olivia Lockwood stepped further into the room. Her eyes were red-rimmed, lips trembling. She clutched a handkerchief tightly in her hand; in the other, she held a worn journal.

Derrick stood to offer her his seat, but she declined.

"I won't stay long. I've already given a statement regarding my daughter. I knew she was troubled—it was why I remarried. I'd hoped a fresh start would set her on the right path. I never imagined she'd be involved with..." Olivia paused, bringing the handkerchief to her mouth to cover a sob. "That's not why I'm here. I can't change what my daughter has done, but I refuse to let her be branded a murderer. She didn't kill Ella, I know it in my heart. Someone manipulated her and then killed her to keep her quiet."

She extended the journal. I reached out to take them from her.

"I was going through her things and discovered this in her room. It's in Ella's handwriting. Helen must have found it after the murder and was worried it would reveal her association. Ella knew my daughter was caught in something beyond her control. Even though they weren't close, I think she wanted to help her. I have to believe that. I'm giving you this because I want you to find who did this to my family, and I want them to pay."

"Mrs. Lockwood," I began, while Olivia struggled to regain her composure, "we know there was someone else involved besides Helen. We're going to find out who. I promise that if Helen wasn't responsible for killing Ella, we'll do our best to clear her name."

"That's all I ask." Olivia wiped at the tears in her eyes, then turned to leave.

After the front door had closed softly behind her, I opened the journal and read through the entries, passing it to Derrick when I'd finished. It was as Olivia had said: Ella had known Helen was in over her head and had started to follow her. The symbols on my palm had begun to itch, and that familiar warmth had returned. I glanced at Derrick then Vivian as unease coiled my stomach.

"Ella saw her killer months before the night of the ball. She followed Helen to the Laughing Raven. We need to know what she saw." My palm was on fire. I rubbed at the painful spot, wincing when it only grew hotter.

Vivian grasped my hand and turned it palm-up. The symbols glowed orange, giving off their own light.

"I have an idea. There's just one part you won't like."

"You said the same thing when we started this whole mess."

She angled her head and ran her fingers over the symbols. "Yeah, well, this time, you're really not going to like it."

"What's she talking about?" Derrick asked.

"The link between Ella and Tessa." Vivian led me to a chair and flattened my hand against her séance table. "I've been thinking about it. Why the connection? What does it mean? Whenever the symbols glow, you experience a memory or insight into Ella's life. In her house, she led you to her room and her father's letters. Then, at the fountain, you experienced her final moments. When you read her journal just now, your symbols acted up. What if we could use the journal and your link to Ella to discover what she saw the night she followed Helen?"

"How?" Wariness strained my voice.

"Possession."

So, there was the part I wouldn't like.

"You mean, the crazy thing that happened between you and Sophie? No way. Can't you do it?"

"It won't be the same—the link is stronger between you two. With Sophie, the connection was faint. She was disjointed, unable to stay or speak for long."

"But Ella doesn't have her memories." I grasped at straws, trying to think of reasons it wouldn't work.

"Some of her memories will return once her spirit has taken over. We can bind the journal entry to her spirit and amplify the memory. I think."

"You think?"

Derrick stepped between us. "Tessa, you don't have to do this if you don't want to. We'll find another way."

Vivian made a face and slung her arms across her chest. "This is the way. Why else is there a link between them? We can use it to our advantage. You won't feel anything, if that's what you're worried about. It's like taking a nap."

"With a ghost inside you."

"Temporarily."

I groaned and closed my fist, sick of seeing the glowing symbols. Was this what it had come to? Was I even considering it? My whole body cringed at the idea, but Vivian had a point. If we could use the link to our advantage, we had to try. It was the least I could do for Derrick. Well, not the least. There was nothing small about letting a ghost use you for recreational housing.

Honestly, the things I did for ghosts.

"Fine. I'll do it."

Vivian clapped her hands together and flew across the room to gather her candles and sage bundle. She was enjoying this a little too much.

Derrick sat beside me and brushed his thumb across my palm. "Are you sure?"

"Not really. I'm afraid Vivian doesn't know what she's doing, and I'll end up possessed by an evil spirit and give it corporeal form."

"I can hear you."

"I should hope so, I'm not whispering." I squeezed

Derrick's fingers. "But I want to do this for you. Maybe, in some small way, it will make up for what happened before, with the other witch."

"That wasn't your fault."

"No, but if there's something I can do to bring you and your family peace after Sophie's death then I'll do it."

He pulled me against his chest. "Thank you, Tessa."

I fiddled with the cuff of his sleeve and made a reluctant face. "Just promise me that if I become evil, you won't try to chop off my head. Allow me to live out my maniacal days in the mountains somewhere."

Derrick stifled a smile and staged a sigh. "I can't promise you that. The law has very strict rules on letting evil roam free."

Vivian snickered. I was surrounded by court jesters.

"Fine, then wait until you get my bill."

Laughing, he pressed a kiss to my forehead. "Knowing you, it will be huge."

"It'll bankrupt the agency." I glanced at the clock and shivered. All we had to do now was wait for Ella to appear and convince her to invade my body in a super creepy séance ritual.

Good times.

\*\*\*

"I'll do it." Ella floated closer, nodding her head in excitement. "Will I remember everything?"

Vivian chewed her lip. "Not everything. The link works best when tied to an object. The journal is the catalyst for this memory. You won't remember the day you died."

"I understand. I still want to try."

"You don't want to think about it for a while? Maybe take a couple of days?" I asked, wringing my hands in my lap.

"Tessa, quit stalling." Vivian lit the bundle of sage and held it in the air.

"I'm not stalling." I ground my teeth and tried to calm my nerves. It felt like I was on a runaway cart with no option but to hold on and hope for the best. Derrick was going to have broken fingers by the time this was over. I gripped his hand harder to test his limits, but he didn't even flinch.

"Don't let go," I said.

"I won't."

"I'll know if you do."

"No, she won't." Vivian moved the pedestal candle into the center of the table.

Derrick smoothed a lock of hair out of my face. "I won't let go."

I believed him. Nerves settled, I took a deep breath. This was *fine*. What was a little possession among friends anyway? It would make for a great story. I'd be amazing at parties. Not that I went to parties—but maybe someday.

Vivian instructed me to place my palm with the glowing symbols over the pages in Ella's journal. The instant I did, I felt a jolt and a wave of dizziness.

"Are you ready?" she asked Ella.

Moving to stand behind me, Ella settled a translucent hand on my shoulder. "I'm ready."

That made one of us.

Vivian closed her eyes, and the ritual began. The candles dimmed then flashed the room in white light. Warmth flowed through my limbs, sending me drowsy. I tried to keep my eyes open but they drifted shut, and I went numb, fading into nothing.

***

"Ella? Can you hear me?"

My name sounded faraway, and I struggled against the dark, fighting to bring myself closer. I opened my eyes and blinked to clear my vision.

Vivian sat across from me, her concerned gaze searching mine. *How strange.* My hand was clasped between the detective's, his grip firm and reassuring, but there was a hint of fear in his eyes. I'd caused it.

Without thinking, I tried to pull my hand away, but he tightened his grip.

"Don't," he said.

*That's right, he made a promise.*

I took a deep breath, filling my lungs with sage-scented air. It smelled oddly pleasant. There was a teacup next to my elbow, which I reached for, downing the liquid before I could stop myself. Sugar and raspberries burst on my tongue. I wanted more—it was delicious!

The taste soon soured when a throb in my temple made memories cloud my mind. I winced, and my hand shook. This wasn't real. This wasn't my life. It belonged to someone else. The cup dropped and hit the edge of the table, then crashed to the floor.

"I'm sorry. I didn't mean to."

"Shh, it's okay." Vivian grasped my other hand, slowly moving it to rest on top of the journal. They grew warm beneath my palm. "Relax, Ella. Take a moment and get your bearings. Do you know what we're doing?"

"Yes. I forgot for a second. Waking up was disorienting."

"We need to ask you some questions. Do you think you can handle that?"

I nodded. "You want to know about Helen? About what I saw the night I followed her?"

"We do. Take your time, I know this is difficult. What do you remember?"

A hollow feeling grew in my stomach. It expanded into the rest of my body, leaving me sick and shaky.

"I hoped I'd remember more, but so much is fuzzy."

"Do the best you can."

"When my father got sick, I thought Helen had poisoned him. I padlocked my room at night, terrified she'd poison me next. I started following her, recording her movements—I wanted proof. A few months after he died, she visited someone at a bar called the Laughing Raven. I went there and waited in the back until she arrived, then watched her sell a packet of berries to a man I'd never seen before. Something felt off, Helen seemed scared of him.

They went around back, and I followed, but Helen wasn't there. Another woman was."

"Do you know who she was?" Detective Chambers asked.

"He called her Jane. They were arguing."

"What were they arguing about?"

"The poison. Jane told him to get rid of it. She said his plan was worthless and they'd never accept him. He showed her something on his arm, a raised mark. It wasn't a scar from an injury—it was too defined for that. She slapped him when she saw it. It startled me, and I must have made a sound because they stopped shouting and went inside."

"Can you describe the man for us? Did he have any distinguishing features besides the mark on his arm?" the detective asked.

"He was fairly young, early twenties maybe. He wore a cap and a dark coat. There wasn't anything that stood out. He had a soft voice even when he was angry. It wasn't loud, but it was menacing, if you know what I mean?"

Vivian nodded. "Do you remember anything else about that night?"

"When I got home, I confronted Helen about everything. She denied trying to poison my father. She claimed she'd been trying to save him, but he was too far gone. I wanted to believe her. She had her vices, but in the end, I don't think she was a killer." Murkiness blurred the rest of my thoughts, and a whimper escaped my throat. "That's all I remember. I'm sorry."

"You did really good," Vivian soothed.

"I feel dizzy."

She placed a hand over mine. "I think it's time."

"No!" My gaze darted around the room, panic eliciting harsh gasps. "I'm scared to go back. Please, let me stay a little longer."

"Don't be scared. We can't hold you here or leave the connection open for too long—it's not safe for either of you." Vivian's voice grew quieter. She lifted the sage bundle and struck a match, filling the air with the scented smoke.

A weight settled in my body. The lights dimmed.

"Everything is going to be all right, Ella," Vivian whispered.

I closed my eyes.

***

"Five more minutes," I mumbled, burying my head under my arms.

A thick smell crinkled my nose. Why was there so much smoke? Was the shop on fire? If another one of my spells had started a house fire, my mother would kill me.

"I didn't start the fire, I swear!" My eyes burst open, and I nearly fell out of the chair. Someone caught me around the waist, settling me back in the seat.

"Relax, Tessa. There's no fire," Derrick's voice rumbled in my ear.

I searched the room to be sure. Vivian held up the bundle of sage and waved it around. *Oh, yeah. Not fire, possession.* I shuddered.

"Did it work?"

"It did." Derrick wrapped his arms around me. "You were great."

"She slept through the whole thing," Vivian grumbled. "Honestly, Ella and I did all the hard work. Possessions don't just happen, you know?"

I found Ella standing off to the side. She reached for me, and our fingers grazed before sliding through each other's. The symbols on my palm had stopped glowing now, which made me a little sad. Even though the connection with Ella was uncomfortable, I knew I'd miss it when it went away.

There in the séance room, the three of them filled me in on what had happened, retelling Ella's story until a snippet of information made me interrupt.

"Hold on. Did you say the man had a mark on his arm? Was it a Vitalis mark?"

Both Ella and Vivian looked confused, but Derrick's eyes widened. "Isn't a Vitalis mark what you saw on Prince Marcus? They're given to royals as a blessing, right?"

"Correct, which means we were right to think Diane had a son with the king. The child would have been Jane's nephew." I untangled myself from Derrick's arms, excitement humming through my body. "I know how to find his name."

"How?" Vivian asked.

"The boxes of books we brought over from my shop. My mother kept a ledger of the spells she performed. She cast the Vitalis mark on Prince Marcus when he was a baby and would have cast the second mark if there'd been another child. Even out of wedlock, a son would be a candidate for the mark. He'd be listed in the book." I ran to the storage closet.

It took some time to find it, but I retrieved my mother's ledger. The book was heavy, hardbound, and nearly a hundred pages—thankfully, categorized by date. I flipped through and found the year Prince Marcus was born. His entry was listed with his full name, type of spell, and the date. I kept going, slower, in my search for the next few years. And there it was, an entry for a Vitalis mark dated nearly five years after Prince Marcus was born.

I read the name aloud. "William A. Porter."

We'd found our killer.

# Chapter 30

V ivian packed her pedestal candle and sage bundle into a bag and slung it over her shoulder.

"Are you sure you'll be fine by yourself? You're welcome to come explore the haunted mansion. I'll let you wave the sage around."

I scrunched my nose, still uncomfortable after my spiritual invasion the night before. "As fun as that sounds, I'm good. Derrick sent one of his officers over to keep watch, and I want to wait for him to finish his meeting with the king. If he confirms what we learned, we can start hunting William Porter."

"Suit yourself." She twisted her hair into a bun and tied it back. Loose strands tumbled into her face, and she blew them out of her eyes. Hands on her hips, Vivian studied the items spread out over her séance table. "Tessa, you're going back to the magic shop soon, right? Don't get me wrong, I love having a house guest, and the officers Derrick sends over are kind of cute, but you're turning my séance room into a potion mill."

I sprinkled a dash of sea salt into a clay pot filled with an oozing substance and added a crow's feather. A puff of noxious smoke bloomed, sending Vivian back on her heels.

"Yup, I'm going to need you to vacate the premises immediately."

Covering my nose with my sleeve, I waved away the thick cloud spewing from the pot. "Drat, I think I added too much iron dust. Don't worry, Viv, I'll clean up when I'm finished."

"What are you making?" she asked, pinching her nose.

"Dinner," I deadpanned.

"Very funny."

"Actually, I had an idea for a potion that can prevent someone from telling a lie. Imagine how useful that would be in interrogations. I'm going to surprise Derrick with it if I ever figure out how to make it work."

"Honestly, I think you're already there. I'd reveal my darkest secrets from that smell alone."

"Thanks, Viv. It's a work in progress. Have fun on your haunting."

She snarled and headed for the door. "Open a window before that smell ingrains itself in the walls and the value of my house goes down."

"Will do!" I wiggled my fingers and measured a fresh scoop of iron dust.

The front door clicked shut, and I leaned back in my chair to survey the mess. I'd needed something to distract me while Derrick presented our findings to the king. He'd left early in the morning and had already been gone half the day. I still couldn't believe we had a name. Seeing the look of relief on Ella's face had been humbling. She'd placed her trust in me, and I hadn't failed her.

I couldn't begin to imagine what Derrick was going through. After all these years, to finally learn the name of his sister's killer, it must be eating him alive. He'd decided to wait to notify his family, wanting to be sure before he got their hopes up. I didn't blame him. It would be a crushing blow to come this far and not apprehend the culprit.

The hanging beads swayed together, and I pushed aside the clay pot, doing my best to frantically clear the air. "Did you forget something, Viv?"

"It's just me, Tessa." Abrams stood in the entryway, his hands twisting the brim of his cap. "Shift change. I sent the other officer home."

"Really? Vivian will be disappointed when she gets back. I think she liked him the best."

"How long will she be gone?"

I pursed my lips and started cleaning off the séance table. "Couple hours. Unless the ghost is chatty, then who knows?"

Abrams nodded absently, his gaze wandering the room. "I heard you discovered the name of the killer. I'm impressed."

My hand hovered over the basket of crows' feathers. "I didn't realize Derrick told you."

Abrams chuckled. "Why wouldn't he tell me? I used to help all the time with his cases before you came along. I always knew what was happening at the agency. Every little thing."

Unease made my palms itch. "That's right. He always speaks very highly of you."

"Funny, how he only talks about you now. No hard feelings." Abrams lifted his shoulders in an easy shrug. The move contrasted with his tone. His boots were silent as he approached, crowding me against the table. "How about we have that glass of wine you promised me a while back? It will be our secret. We're so good at keeping secrets. Another won't hurt, will it? Can I share one more with you."

"Actually, I think Vivian finished the last bottle. You know how she—"

"You mean, this one?" Abrams held up the full bottle he found sitting next to a bowl of incense.

The pop of the cork echoed in my ears as he pulled it open and was followed by an odd silence while I waited for him to face me again. He was taking a long time, each second making my dread sharpen.

"Let me get some glasses." I edged around the table.

"No need." Abrams blocked my path to the kitchen, tipping the mouth of the bottle in my direction. "Cheers, Miss Daniels, you did it. You solved the murder. Well done. There's just one problem."

I stepped back and bumped the table, rattling the potion ingredients.

"You're not going to drink? I didn't poison it, if that's what you're worried about." He flashed his teeth. "You know, Helen wouldn't drink either. Can you imagine the look on her face when I unlocked her cell door? She was all alone...no other officers around...kind of like you, right now."

I closed my fingers around a feather. Unbelievable! Why did all of my potions call for feathers? An amethyst spike would be so helpful right now.

"You killed Helen? What about Liam Barber?"

"They needed to be killed. Again, kind of like you, Miss Daniels." He swung the bottle.

My arms came up, taking the force, and pain exploded in my forearm, radiating all the way to my shoulder. Elderberry wine poured from the mouth as he swung the bottle again. This time, I ducked, sliding in the blood-red liquid.

Abrams crushed my ribcage where he snaked an arm around my middle. A rag was clamped over my mouth, and I sucked in a breath of sweet-scented air.

Poison.

Trying to get leverage against the table, I used my feet to push us back. Abrams staggered and adjusted his hold. I drew in another sugary breath, dizziness flooding my vision. My lungs ached from trying to keep the poison from filling them further.

The room dimmed. I breathed again. This time, it was soothing, like drifting away on clouds. Reaching up, I grabbed his arm, the action weak. My fingers slid down his bicep, grazing a raised mark.

"That's right," he rasped in my ear, "William Abrams Porter. Do you find it ironic that your mother blessed the man who's going to kill you?" He laughed. "I do."

Darkness rushed in, and my body went limp as I lost consciousness.

***

The light was fading. I struggled to open my eyes and peered through the domed glass ceiling. Thick vines climbed the walls, reaching toward the sky, their tangled stalks obstructing the last rays of evening sun and casting the circular chamber in shadow. Beneath me, dried leaves and dead plants created a cushion on the stone floor. He'd taken me to the palace greenhouse. The one we'd searched days earlier with Theo. Remote. Isolated. The perfect location for a murder.

I remained still, getting my bearings, but my attention was diverted at the scrape of a chain threading through an iron handle. Abrams was on the other side of the glass, testing the chain on a door. Satisfied, he circled around the edge of the building.

Only one other way out, behind me.

I scrambled to my feet, not surprised to find my hands tied behind my back. The move made me bend at the waist as a wave of dizziness threatened to send me back to the ground. I breathed steadily through my nose and twisted my wrists, trying to regain feeling in my fingers.

"Good! The witch is awake." Abrams stepped through the door that led deeper into the greenhouse. "Don't you like it here? My mother did—at least, that's what they tell me. It was kept a lot nicer back then. Sorry I couldn't find a place that reeked less of abandonment, but that is the theme we're going for." He locked the door behind him and held up a key. "There, now we're settled in."

"Why did you bring me here? You could have killed me back at Vivian's."

He angled his head, sending a curly lock of hair into his eye. "Is that how you wanted to die? On the floor of a shop?" He shrugged. "I thought lying inside a glass house, on a bed of vines, with your hair spread out around you and a rose clutched between your fingers was more romantic."

"You're sick."

"And you're exhausting. We wouldn't be here right now if you'd removed yourself from the case after I left that gift on your back step."

Finally regaining life in my fingers, I curled them into fists and channeled my magic. Heat grew in my palms, but it wasn't hot enough to burn the rope. I needed more time. Had to keep him talking.

"Did you really think a glass slipper and a note was enough to scare me away?"

"Maybe not you, but I thought you might get kicked off the case. Detective Chambers has a protective streak when it comes to you. I figured if I threatened the witch, he'd send you packing. He wouldn't want to risk losing someone else he cared about."

I backed up, shoes crunching over brittle leaves, and refocused my magic. "Why the roses, Abrams? Don't you think you owe me that much?"

"Curious, witch?" He stalked across the chamber and tore at the vines, ripping them away from the wall to uncover a thorny bush with a single bloom.

The crimson Aster Mauve rose was a splash of color among the thorns and dried foliage. Abrams cut the stem with a pocket knife and breathed in the fragrant scent, then set it aside on a stone bench. "It's the last one. How lucky for you. My mother cherished those roses. They represented beauty, vitality, and yet, their thorns drew blood. When you cut a rose it dies, turns brittle. The beauty fades and it loses its power. I thought it seemed fitting to leave them behind. I wanted to show everyone how easy it was to snuff out an existance. A simple snip."

My stomach rolled at his callous explanation. "What happened to Diane? Why the other girls?" The heat burned up my wrists, making my teeth clench, but it was working. Only a little longer.

"My mother died when I was a child, and since I had no viable claim to the throne, my aunt tossed me away. But, I knew I deserved better. I was a king's son, no matter the order of my birth. I grew up obsessed with the brother who had it all. I got hired as a stable hand at the king's hunting lodge to be closer to him, and that's where I met Sophie. Sweet, beautiful Sophie."

My insides clenched at the way he said her name. His eyes unfocused, and a half-smile curved his mouth.

"For a little while, everything was different. I loved her. I wanted her."

"But she didn't want you?"

Abrams snarled and prowled closer. I stumbled backward, tripping on a vine.

"She wanted him. They all do! My brother with the royal title. Luck personified. Sophie had been mine until he showed the barest of interest in her. All of it, our letters, the secret encounters, they meant nothing after a single glance from his direction."

A realization formed, and my mind snagged on a memory. "You still have those letters, don't you? They're the ones you mentioned at the memorial dinner. You joked about hiding them."

He clapped, slow, the sound echoing in the chamber. "Very good, Miss Daniels. You would have made a good detective."

"So, you killed her because she spurned you?"

"I killed her because she laughed at me when I told her I was as good as him."

"She was sixteen!"

His boots pounded across the stone. Another step, then two. Fear constricted my chest. Abrams kept coming even when I tripped, landing hard on my backside. His rangy form towered over me.

"Get up."

"What about Jane? She didn't accept you either, and she was family. Let me guess, you confronted her years later, and she laughed in your face?" Twisting my wrists, I felt the first give in the rope.

"Get up!" he roared, grasping my arm and dragging me upright. His fingers bit into my skin, and he shoved me against the wall, my head cracking against the glass.

Lights danced in my vision.

"My aunt was a fool. I was going to take what should have been mine. With my brother gone, I have a claim to the throne. I joined the agency to gain access to the castle, and I waited for the perfect opportunity. It was the perfect cover. Detective Chambers was searching for his sister's killer, and I'd be the first to know if he came close."

"But Ella ruined everything. She saw you with Helen, and then you spotted her at the ball. She was going to warn the prince."

"Too bad for her, he switched masks." Abrams sneered. "Some things just work out in your favor, don't they? I followed her into the courtyard. The look on her face when I removed my mask was really something." He chuckled and the soft sound sent a shiver of fear up my spine. "I liked you, Miss Daniels, I really did. You were a bit of an underdog, and who doesn't want to root for that? But it's over now. I'll lay low for a while, go dormant until memories fade and I can walk freely among the kingdom again. You won't be around for that, but I can guarantee your murder will make the front page of the Gazette. You'll be as famous as your mother."

His hands came up. I drew in a breath before they closed around my throat. My whole body bucked from the pressure, and I lost focus for a second as terror overwhelmed me. The pain in my lungs grew unbearable.

Abrams' fingers dug deeper. I closed my eyes, and Derrick's face flashed behind my eyelids. I couldn't give up. Losing Sophie's killer this way would break him, and *damn it*, if I wasn't tired of being on the front page of the blasted Gazette!

Magic sizzled across my skin, slicing through the rope. It gave away at the same time as my knees. With the last of my energy, I pushed my hands forward and shot a current into his chest.

Abrams flew back, and I sank to the ground, gulping in ragged gasps of air.

He was up before I'd caught my breath. I struggled to my feet too, channeling another beam of magic. He lurched, and I flung my fists out, launching a stream of sparks that went wide.

Throwing back his head, Abrams laughed. "You missed. Wow, you're a terrible witch."

The sparks engulfed a thick wall of withered vines behind him, catching fire. It spread quickly, racing up the walls, jumping from stalk to stalk. Not ideal! I tilted my head back as the flames burned all the way to the ceiling, smoke becoming thick and dark.

Abrams spun, his mouth widening at the inferno. "Foolish, witch! You'll kill us both!"

*Yeah, I could see that!* This was why I shouldn't use magic indoors. I coughed, covering my mouth, and dropped low to the ground. Above my head, there was a popping sound as the glass began to crack from the heat.

Abrams ran for the door. I couldn't let him reach it first—he'd trap me inside.

Fighting against the smoke stinging my eyes, I focused my magic and splayed my fingers. A flaming vine snaked across the ground, wrapping around his leg. It jerked him down, and I heard the sickening fracture as his head smacked the stone tile. He didn't move. Blood pooled beneath his head.

I skirted around him and lunged for the door. My hands shoved against the handle, but it didn't budge. I slammed it again, panic disorienting me. As a figure appeared on the other side of the glass, my heart stalled.

Derrick's stricken face sharpened into focus. "Tessa!" He wrenched the handle.

"It's locked! Abrams has the key."

I scrambled to his fallen form, Derrick's voice ringing in my ears. My hands shook as I searched Abrams' pockets. Empty! The pool of blood had spread, soaking his shirt. His eyes were wide-open and lifeless.

He was dead.

The key was gone.

Raking my hands through the leaves, I inhaled smoke that burned my throat. Glass shattered, raining down on me. It was too late. I'd never locate it among all the debris. Thick, black smoke clogged the air, making it impossible to see, and even harder to breathe.

Dazed, I made it back to the door. "I can't find it." I sounded so calm I scared myself.

Heat flared at my back, and I covered my mouth to cough into my sleeve before sinking to the floor. When I pressed my forehead against the glass, it was hot.

Derrick kicked the door, his boot leaving dirt on

the surface. He shouted my name, and my lips trembled. I didn't want him to watch me die.

"Go away!" I screamed.

He listened. The pounding stopped. When I looked up, he was gone.

Maybe he was never even there.

Tears streamed down my face, blurring what little vision I had through the smoke. At least Abrams was dead. He couldn't hurt anyone else now. Vivian would get my share of the reward money and she'd start her horse farm or some other nonsense just to spite me. I smiled, then felt my lips flatten. So much for not ending up in the papers again.

The wall shattered.

Strong arms scooped me up and carried me outside. The air cleared, but everything tasted like smoke, and I couldn't drag in a clean breath. Voices shattered the silence, shouting for water. All around me, chaos seethed as people ran to extinguish the fire.

I was placed in the cool grass, where someone knelt over me, calling my name. Fingers gently probed the sore bruises on my neck, and I heard a fierce growl.

"Am I dead this time?" I croaked, rolling onto my side. Each cough made my ribcage throb.

"No," Derrick's voice broke low. He gathered me in his arms, and I felt him shudder. "But not for lack of trying."

"At least I didn't faint."

His lips pressed to my temple. I wound my arms

around his neck, trying to get as close as I could, not satisfied even when I felt his heart pounding against mine.

"I'm getting your coat dirty."

He exhaled a shaky breath. "After today, I'm going to start charging you for them. I think that's the only way to keep you from getting hurt."

I laughed, and it scratched my throat. "You might be onto something. Anything to save a coin."

"I didn't think I'd find you in time." He smoothed the hair out of my face, wiping at the soot on my cheeks.

"How did you find me?"

Derrick's features hardened, and his mouth curled down. "Argus."

"What? I didn't hear you correctly, there's smoke in my ears. Did you say, Argus?"

"Two of Argus's men saw Abrams take you out of the house. They followed you and then reported back. Argus found me at the agency. He demanded I meet him on the street. Told me what happened."

"Wow. I didn't see that coming."

"Neither did I, but he was right. I'd just found out about Abrams. The king confirmed everything, even his son's middle name. I couldn't believe it...all this time. He was right there. When I found out he took you—" Derrick pulled me against him, and I nuzzled my forehead into his neck.

"Abrams told me everything. I'm sorry, Derrick. I'm sorry about Sophie and the others. I'll tell you everything he said. There's evidence, too. Letters."

"Later. Tell me later." His fingers sifted through my hair.

I watched over his shoulder as the greenhouse burned. Officers attempted to douse the flames as smoke billowed into the dark sky. There would be nothing left, the final rose incinerated to ash.

A light appeared, glowing brighter and moving closer. It took form as the temperature plunged and my breath fogged in front of my face.

"Do you feel that?" I whispered. Untangling from Derrick's embrace, I climbed to my feet. "It's Ella. She's here."

Derrick stood and peered into the shady canopy. "I'll have to take your word for it." He rubbed my shoulders and wrapped an arm around my waist to keep me warm.

Ella floated to a stop in front of me, her pale features serene. Peace radiated from her body in waves of light

"Thank you, Tessa, for everything. You might not believe me, but I'm glad I visited your shop the night of the ball. You're a good witch. You might fail a spell or two, but I'm lucky to consider you a friend."

"You too, Ella. I'm sorry—"

"Don't be! I got to wear a beautiful gown and a pair of glass slippers. I even danced with a man I thought was a prince. Not every girl gets to live a fairytale."

My throat felt tight with unshed tears. "Fairytales don't end like this."

Behind Ella, a new white light formed. She turned to look at it, and her face brightened.

"Daddy?"

A man stepped from the beam, holding out his hand. She took it, and her ghostly form flickered.

With a smile, Ella glanced over her shoulder at me. "I have to go. Tell Vivian goodbye for me." She paused. "And you're right, fairytales don't end like this, but maybe this is only the beginning."

Father and daughter disappeared as they stepped into the light.

I took a deep breath and let the tears cascade down my face. The symbols on my palm blinded me with brilliant light and then faded altogether. I closed my fist, almost sad to see them go.

"Is she gone?"

I nodded.

Derrick pressed a kiss against my hair. "Then it's finally over."

No. Ella was right.

It was only the beginning.

# Chapter 31

The bag of coins thumped onto the desk. "Consider me paid in full."

Argus eyed the bag. "You're two days late."

I shrugged and leaned back in my chair. "But who's counting? You knew I was good for it."

He spilled the coins onto the desktop and made a quick count. Satisfied, he tucked them away inside a drawer then reached for a crystal decanter of dark liquid.

"It's not every day the king bestows a royal reward on a commoner, especially a witch. You've made the front page of the Gazette every day this week." He poured two glasses and nudged one toward me.

I swirled the amber shot in the glass and inhaled the thick aroma of bourbon. It was easy to make light of it now, but the past week had been a whirlwind. The prince had been cleared of any involvement in Ella's murder, and we'd closed the cases for both Jane and Sophie. There was something about boxing up their belongings and taking down the roses from the board that brought home the finality of it all.

Derrick had left four days ago to visit his family

and tell them the news. He'd missed my audience with the king and the opulent ceremony where I'd received the reward in front of a crowd of onlookers. Apparently, I wasn't allowed to take the money and run; I had to be feted. Fine by me—the buffet was immense. Vivian's eyes had nearly popped out of her head. I was pretty sure she'd stuffed food in her pockets. I certainly had.

Then, things had settled back to normal. Well…as normal as things could be when you were the most popular witch in the kingdom. So far, I hadn't turned anyone's hair green—or any other color for that matter. There was a small incident with a charmed medallion, but I was able to fix it before things got out of hand. All said, the shop was booming, and my debts were paid.

So, why did I feel so unsettled?

"As much as it pains me, I should thank you for…" I paused and cringed, my mouth unable to form the words. I might be grateful but I still detested the man. One good deed didn't erase a lifetime of corruption.

"Saving your life?" Argus finished.

"Yeah, that."

He smirked. "I can't get paid if my borrower is dead, can I?"

And there it was. I clenched my teeth.

"That would have been so disappointing for you."

"What can I say? It's not good for business."

I lifted my glass in a mock salute. "I think we're done here. No more following me around. Steer clear of my shop. In fact, let's see if we can go the rest of our lives without running into each other again."

Argus clinked his glass against mine. "Fine by me. You can see yourself out."

Finishing off the bourbon, I placed the empty glass on his desk and stalked toward the door. His deep voice followed me down the hall.

"Don't forget to tell the ghost hunter I said hello."

*** 

"He's still not back? It's been almost three weeks." Vivian followed me onto the porch of the magic shop.

I sighed and picked up a hammer, then held the sign to the right of the door, trying to find the perfect spot. "No. I thought he'd be back by now, but it must be difficult for his family. It's good he's spending time with them. How's this?"

Vivian squinted and angled her head. "A little to the left. He didn't ask you to go?"

Making the adjustment, I nailed the sign into the wood. "He did. I said no. It wasn't the right time. His parents don't need an outsider—especially not a witch—intruding on them during such a private family moment."

"Yeah, meeting the parents is hard enough, I suppose."

It was, but that wasn't the only reason I'd said no. Not that I would admit it to anyone, but I'd chickened out. For weeks, we'd had the case to drive us, bring us closer, and now, it was over. What if things were different? We hadn't talked about what would happen next, and with each day that passed, I became a little more nervous, to the point I regretted my decision not to go. When Derrick returned, he'd resume his work at the agency without me, and, well...I'd started a little endeavor of my own, and I wasn't completely sure how he'd react to having direct competition.

Ella had said this was the beginning, and in many ways, it was.

I stepped back to admire the sign. The bronze plate, mounted on a cedar plank, glinted in the sunlight. At the top, a simple gold ring had been welded to the metal surface. It wouldn't have gone for much at the pawnshop, but to me, it was priceless.

Vivian hooked her arm around my shoulder. "I'm proud of you, Tess. The sign looks great."

It really did. *Daniels Curses, Cures, and Crimes.* A little wordy, but it covered everything.

All I had to do now was wait for my first case. Thanks to the articles in the Gazette, I was a household name, finally known as something other than the witch who failed her spells. I might not have turned out exactly the way my mother wanted, but I'd made a name for myself doing something that gave me a purpose.

Vivian sighed and glanced at the early morning sun. "I have to go, or I'll never make it to my grandmother's house and back before dark. I swear, that woman lives deep in the woods just to vex me. What's wrong with living in town? At least then, I wouldn't have to hike through the forest every time I visit."

"Winifred's back from her trip?"

"Yes, and apparently, I'm in heaps of trouble for not watering her ficus. The thing is dead with a capital D. I couldn't even find one close enough to replace it this time of year."

"I'm surprised she put you in charge of it. As an oracle, she might have seen its untimely fate. I can't tell the future and I know you would have killed it, so that's on her."

"I'll be sure to tell her you said that." Vivian went back inside and retrieved her cloak. She swung it over her shoulders and tied the ribbon at her neck, the deep red fabric skimming the tops of her boots and a wide hood draping down her back. She reached for a basket on a side table and slung it over her arm. "I'm taking her a couple bottles of elderberry wine to smooth things over. You know it's her favorite."

My mouth dropped open as a realization formed. "You don't think she saw you were going to kill her plant and used the opportunity as a devious way to get free wine, do you?"

Vivian paused in the doorway, her brow creasing. "Well, I do now." She tsk'd. "Honestly, some days, I wish I had her powers. Imagine what you could do with that kind of knowledge..." She trailed down the steps, waving a hand over her shoulder. "Wish me luck!"

"Watch out for wolves!" I teased, then laughed as

Vivian made a rude gesture and slipped through the gate.

I remained on the porch for a while longer, fawning over my sign. Using my sleeve, I blew a hot breath onto the metal and polished away my fingerprints. Perfect.

The gate creaked as it swung open. I bit the side of my cheek to keep from laughing.

"Did you decide to bring extra wine, Viv?"

There wasn't an answer.

I turned and peered into the yard, but it was empty. Maybe the wind had opened the gate? Climbing down the steps, I examined the latch, and sure enough, it was jammed. I smacked the palm of my hand into the bolt, but it didn't budge. It needed something stronger. I searched the ground for a rock and found one just the right size.

"Is there a problem?"

The rock slipped from my fingers and landed at my feet.

Derrick was leaning against one of the gateposts, his eyes lit with amusement. He'd traded his expensive wool jacket for the tweed we'd purchased in town, and he wore the flat cap at an angle over his dark hair. He was back, and it took everything in me not to launch myself at him.

Until he opened his mouth.

"I'm looking for the owner. Are you the witch?"

I narrowed my eyes at his little game. Did he think this was funny? He'd been gone for three weeks, not a single letter! I'd checked—every day.

My arms crossed over my chest. "No, I'm not."

"That's too bad." His brow wrinkled. "I heard the witch had opened up a side business, and I happen to have a new case. I was looking for a partner, someone who might be an asset to the investigation."

I left the gate ajar and walked back to the magic shop, speaking over my shoulder, "Assets are hard to come by."

"They are." He followed, boots crunching in the gravel.

"Well, Detective, I hope you find someone."

He reached for my arm before I'd made it up the porch steps and spun me to face him. "I already did."

"Wow, that was easy." I tilted my head back to meet his determined gaze.

"It really wasn't. I had to put up with a lot. There were ghosts, near-drownings, irritation spells, poisonings..." His voice dropped to a whisper. "I hear she may have even started a plague."

My lips flattened on an emerging smile. "The horrors! She sounds like a ton of trouble. Maybe you should keep looking."

"Not a chance. There's no one else for me."

Were hearts supposed to stutter like that? This probably wasn't a good sign.

"I think you mean there's no one else for the case, Detective."

"No, I got it right the first time." Derrick took my hand and led me up the stairs. "Nice sign," he commented, pushing open the door.

Inside, he surveyed the shop, his gaze roaming

over the shelves of potions and display racks loaded with tonics and powder. In the corner, I'd set up a desk. Fresh notebooks were stacked on the surface, ordered and neat, not a speck of dust. He smiled and pulled out a folded piece of paper from his jacket pocket.

"What is that?" I asked.

"It's an agreement from the agency. We would like to hire Tessa Daniels of Daniels Curses, Cures, and Crimes to support current investigations on a contract basis." He lifted his shoulder in a sheepish shrug. "I stopped there first, I hope you don't mind. I didn't want to show up empty-handed, especially not when you're in such high demand." His gaze shifted toward the entrance, where the bell above the door remained silent.

I couldn't help it. I laughed.

"The mornings are slow. It picks up."

He cocked a brow. "Don't make me check your ledger."

"I missed you." The admission slipped from my lips, and I felt my cheeks heat. *So much for playing it low-key.* I'd figured I'd last a little longer than that, at least. "You were gone for so long, I was worried. How is your family?"

He placed the agreement on my desk and pulled me to him, fingers sifting through my hair. "They're good. Telling them about Abrams was a little like losing Sophie all over again, but now, everyone has a chance to heal and move forward. A lot of that is thanks to you."

My blush heightened. "A witch does what she can."

"So modest." He smiled. "You must have missed me a lot considering you're not even asking how much we're going to pay you."

"Oh." I tilted my head to peer around him and glance at the agreement.

Derrick chuckled as my eyes went wide. I untangled from him and rounded my desk, moving the document closer.

"What are you doing?" he asked.

"Reading the fine print. I need to know if this contract is worth signing." I reached for a pen and made a notation.

He read the amendment over my shoulder. "Lunch breaks?"

"They're mandatory, Detective."

"Will you be taking them alone?"

Ignoring his question, I kept reading, dipping the pen in ink and crossing out the figure at the bottom to add a little extra.

"Are you negotiating with me, Miss Daniels?"

I flashed him an innocent smile. "It's a fair amount. I'd never gouge you."

"Yes, you would. You have, in fact. Multiple times." He slipped the pen from my fingers and initialed my new terms, then tapped the signature line and handed it back. "Are you ready to sign?"

My name flowed across the page. I sprinkled a little powder on the parchment, drying the ink and sealing the deal.

Derrick refolded the agreement and tucked it back inside his pocket before pushing my notebooks and folders aside, a few of them landing on the floor. His hands circled my waist, lifting me up to sit on the desk.

I made a sound with my tongue. "How dare you? Those were ordered alphabetically."

"No, they weren't."

Wrapping my arms around his neck, I scooted closer. "You caught me, Detective."

"It's what I do." His head dipped, and his mouth captured mine, cutting off my sarcastic remark. Not that I minded. Much. I'd get the last word in later.

He deepened the kiss, holding my face in his hands. After three weeks without him, I couldn't get enough. The shop faded away. The bell could ring a hundred times, and I wouldn't even hear it. Taking a breath, Derrick smoothed his fingers across my cheekbones and locked our gazes.

"I missed my witch. I love you, Tessa."

Okay, he could have the last word after all.

I curled my fingers into his collar and pulled his lips back to mine. It was ages before I remembered he'd mentioned another case.

"Derrick," I murmured while he was dropping a kiss against my neck.

"Yeah?"

"About the new case…"

His soft laugh fanned my skin. "Took you long enough."

"Aren't you going to tell me the details?"

He groaned and braced his fists on the desk to keep me trapped. Not that I was going anywhere.

Derrick leaned in. "This one's a doozy. A body was found in the woods. At first glance, it appears to have been an animal attack. Then, they found a second body, inside a shop, doors locked, same claw markings."

"So, we're not dealing with an animal?"

"Not exactly. I hope one of your magical books has a section on werewolves. We're going to need it." His mouth lifted in a half-smile. "Ready to hunt killers with me again?"

I grinned. "Always."

# Books In This Series

*Ever Dark, Ever Deadly*

## Spellbound After Midnight

## Wolfish Charms - Coming July 2020

Printed in Great Britain
by Amazon

27485685R00223